HANNA WHO FELL
FROM THE SKY

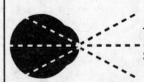

This Large Print Book carries the
Seal of Approval of N.A.V.H.

HANNA WHO FELL FROM THE SKY

CHRISTOPHER MEADES

THORNDIKE PRESS
A part of Gale, a Cengage Company

Farmington Hills, Mich • San Francisco • New York • Waterville, Maine
Meriden, Conn • Mason, Ohio • Chicago

LIBRARY OF CONGRESS CIP DATA ON FILE.
CATALOGUING IN PUBLICATION FOR THIS BOOK
IS AVAILABLE FROM THE LIBRARY OF CONGRESS.

ISBN-13: 978-1-4328-4400-4 (hardcover)
ISBN-10: 1-4328-4400-8 (hardcover)

Published in 2017 by arrangement with Harlequin Books S.A.

Printed in the United States of America
1 2 3 4 5 6 7 21 20 19 18 17

To Joan Witty and Anne Craig,
without whom I would be lost . . .

1

The wolves were lurking. Hanna could sense them in the brush just beyond her line of sight, and others closer, the most daring of the pack camouflaged by thickets of timber. When her father sent her out into the woods, Hanna didn't argue. It was forbidden to argue and this needed to be done. Hanna was to retrieve the moonshine. She was to bring it home. She was not supposed to be afraid.

With daylight fading, Hanna had expected to be watched. She'd anticipated the wolf pack might hunt her now that winter was ending and food was still scarce. What she didn't expect was the quiet. Out in the woods, over two hundred yards from Jotham's house, there was nothing but silence; no cawing crows or cooing doves. The crickets' chirp had long fallen prey to the cold. Even the trees — at this, the onset of spring — had yet to come alive as they awakened from their seasonal slumber.

Hanna adjusted the cap on the jug. Her father's associate, the man with the white whiskers and the wide scars lining his cheeks, hadn't been able to find a proper lid in the shack where he sold his hand-crafted spirits. He'd wedged an ill-fitting piece of cork in its place and told Hanna to carry it carefully. She pressed the cap down firmly now, and then she looked up. In the distance, a set of yellow eyes was watching, sharp and harrowing, like lemons crystallized in the sun. Hanna made out the fur along the bridge of the creature's nose, a toughened patch of skin along its jaw. Then finally a sound, this one from above, a raven swooshing its wings. Hanna looked into the sky, only for a moment. When her gaze returned to the wolf, it was gone.

"It's getting dark. We have to hurry," Hanna said.

Emily stepped forward, a single step where her foot landed on uneven ground. At the last moment, Hanna reached out and caught her, almost spilling the jug in the process. The girls watched it swish and swoosh but never lose a drop.

"Father would be upset," Emily said.

"He would be furious," Hanna said. She took her sister's hand and led her back through the woods.

Emily had insisted on coming with Hanna. Seven years her junior, Emily had been following Hanna around since she could crawl. Emily started life differently than the rest of the children. She'd emerged from the womb with a strong mind and a twisted back. Now eleven years old, Emily struggled to walk. As an infant, she had crawled for three years before the adult women insisted Jotham take her to a doctor in the city. Jotham balked. He stormed around the house in a rage before declaring that no member of his family would ever travel to a place where the minds are base and the souls corrupt. He brought a doctor home instead.

The diagnosis was an abnormal lateral curvature of the spine. Emily's back was shaped like a question mark that leaned too far to the right. Over the years, Hanna had assisted Emily in doing the exercises the doctor recommended. Her efforts had helped to a degree. Still, Emily's spine looked like a tree that — bereft of sunshine — had tried to reach around a boulder to find light. It was Hanna's responsibility to look after Emily. Hanna gave Emily her bath. She walked her to the classroom for their daylong lessons on faith. Hanna locked arms with her sister at church and helped her kneel. She helped Emily stand.

What would happen to Emily in ten days' time, when her big sister no longer lived in Jotham's house, Hanna still didn't know. That was a subject she had yet to broach and there was no time to think about it now. Dusk hung like vapor in the air. Darkness would soon fall.

A stream appeared up ahead, its frigid water tinted blue by the first glimmers of moonlight. Beyond the water, the ground was a foreboding maze of shadows burdened with steep, imperceptible cliffs and rabbit-sized holes that led to nowhere. Hanna took a hard step and her foot lodged in the swampy mire. She pulled her boot out, careful to balance the jug in her hand and Emily against her hip. In the distance, a light beckoned. Jotham's house. Still too far away. Hanna kept moving. In her haste, she pulled Emily along beside her. Emily didn't complain (the girl never complained), but Hanna could tell from her labored breaths, they were moving too fast. She looked into the sky again. The darkness hadn't fully set in. They still had time. There was no reason to panic just yet.

Three weeks ago, this ground was covered in snow. At the peak of winter, it was two yards deep. Now all that remained were occasional piles of slush. Hanna found she missed the snow. There was contentment in knowing everything was silver and white, that the world was asleep and that time had managed, as incredible as it seemed, to slow down. Hanna had spent the entire season willfully ignoring what was coming, pretending her body hadn't changed.

Hanna would turn eighteen in a little over a week's time, the age she'd always feared. She'd seen how others looked at her, how the men at church glared without shame, how their eyes grew wide as they tried to imagine what was underneath her floral dress. Hanna knew what they wanted, what men expected from women. She couldn't lie to herself any longer. Winter was gone and what she'd been afraid of her whole life was rapidly approaching.

"Did you hear that?" Emily said.

"Yes."

How could she not? The wolves were howling. Since the moment she spotted those yellow eyes, a warm worry had fluttered in Hanna's chest. In the minutes since, it became clear they were being followed. Hanna hoped it was just the one wolf. More likely, up to a dozen were tracking them, the leader of the pack sending silent signals to his brethren to surround the girls, to find the perfect moment to strike.

The sun was gone now. Moonlight had taken over the black-blue skies. They'd stayed out too long and now they had to move quickly. Hanna pressed forward with Emily clinging to her arm. The wolves would take Emily first. They would sense her deformity and, like adept hunters, prey upon her weakness. Hanna's mother had persuaded her to take a knife out into the wild. The weapon pressed against the seam of her dress, the metal cold against her skin. But what good would one knife do against an entire pack of wolves?

Back at the stream, Hanna had tried to lead them astray. She'd splashed through three consecutive piles of slush and then turned sharply, thinking that if they altered their course, what they would lose in time, they'd make up for by confusing their trackers. It had turned out to be a remarkably ineffective strategy. There is nothing more futile than evading destiny. Nothing more frightening than knowing you're powerless to stop what is coming.

Hanna heard a wolf panting, another slipping through a nearby patch of bushes. Three times she'd almost dropped the moonshine. She pictured her father's face, that vein above his eye, the one that throbbed and turned purple when Jotham was angry. The batch of whiskey he'd distilled in their woodshed was all but gone. If the children feared him when he was hard at the drink, they feared him doubly so when he was sober. Hanna adjusted the cap again. Despite her efforts, it wouldn't stay. Rather than drop it and spill what was inside, she set the jug down on a patch of solid ground and kept moving. Jotham could return tomorrow, in daylight, with his gun if he so chose.

Hanna leaned into Emily's ear. She whispered hard.

"We have to run."

"I can't."

"Yes. You can."

"I'm afraid."

"No. You're not."

Emily looked up and Hanna caught a glimpse of the girl's eyes in the moonlight, little circles of blue and gray surrounded by startled, shivering white. She grabbed Emily's arm and they ran as fast as they could. Hanna's chest throbbed. Her blood pulsed in her arms, her legs pumping, her feet crashing through the underbrush. The howls disappeared and the swift patter of footsteps took their place. Emily was running on one foot. Hanna hoisted her up and she pressed toward the edge of the forest, afraid that, at any moment, a predator would steal Emily's leg, that the girl would collapse into the darkness and Hanna would be powerless to save her. Still, she stormed into the night.

Suddenly, the girls stopped. Hanna's heart leapt into her throat. The lead wolf was standing in their path, its yellow eyes gleaming in the moonlight. Emily tripped and Hanna grabbed her. Her wrists weakened and Hanna almost lost her grip, but somehow she pulled Emily up before the girl dared touch the ground.

Slowly, the other wolves emerged from the darkness. Seven in total. The creatures led with their noses, baring their teeth, their spindly legs a disguise for their ferocity, lurkers whose time had finally come.

The woodlands' edge was only a few yards away. Jotham's house was fully visible. Hanna could see the window of the bedroom she shared with her brothers and sisters. She pictured herself reaching across the long patch of grass and touching the front door. Only, the house might as well have been an ocean away. Hanna wanted to call out. She wanted to scream for help. But who would hear her? Who would make it there in time?

The lead wolf gritted his teeth. He tilted his snout, arched his back and took a single step forward. Hanna clutched the knife in her hand. She pictured the next ten seconds in her mind. The wolf would lunge. He would leap at Emily, and Hanna would step between them and strike the wolf down. She would strike them all down. In a single moment, Hanna would transform. She would find her true self and be both Emily's heroine and her own. Hanna took a short breath. She waited for the wolf to pounce.

How long in my life have I been waiting for the wolves to pounce?

Just then, a shotgun blast rang out. The booming sound overtook the air, another following seconds later. Hanna looked toward the light. It was her father, Jotham, standing on his front porch, shooting his gun into the air. He stepped forward and shouted. Jotham fired a third blast and the wolves cowered in confusion.

This was Hanna's chance. She dropped the knife and picked Emily up in both arms. Then she ran. With all her strength, she carried the girl straight into the grass field. She felt nothing around her — not the cold air against her face or the ground beneath her feet. There was only her and the girl, the beckoning light, the darkness echoing in her

15

wake. Hanna pumped her legs as fast as they would go. She was almost at Jotham's doorstep when she finally realized the wolves had given up the chase. She set Emily down and together they collapsed to their knees. Hanna let out a long gasp filled with relief and agony and fear all at once. She fought back tears.

Jotham was standing on his porch, his face shrouded in shadows, a lone figure clutching his gun. Home was where the real danger was. Only ten days remained until Hanna's birthday. That was all she had left. Ten days. She had grown into a woman and very soon now, her time would come.

2

The next morning, the family assembled in the driveway. The young children's feet shuffled along the gravel, the oldest standing perfectly still, the toddlers clinging to their mothers' legs — all waiting for their father to speak. Hanna could see her breath in the brisk air, her footprints in the frosted ground. An hour earlier, when dawn's first light weaved through the stick-thin trees, the skies promised warmth. Only, it was still cold.

Hanna stood next to Emily and watched Jotham without ever meeting his gaze. Last night, when Hanna had arrived without the moonshine, Jotham's anger overtook him. His hands shook. His skin — ashen during the summer months, anemic now at winter's end — turned a bright, boiling red. It was Hanna's mother, Kara, who calmed him, who spoke quietly in his ear, who implored with her eyes. It was Kara who steered

17

Jotham toward the liquor cabinet, who poured the last drops of whiskey into a glass and placed it in Jotham's hand. It was Kara who helped Jotham's anger crawl back down into his belly.

Jotham paced the driveway now. He labored in his steps, dragging one foot behind the other. For as long as Hanna could remember, Jotham's back brace had limited his movements. In the past year, his impairment had progressed. The occasional spells of discomfort had morphed into bouts of unbroken anguish. Hanna could see it in the way her father clenched his jaw when he stood up from a chair, in the slight hesitation before he turned his head, in the darkened circles around his eyes.

Jotham took a long, wheezing breath and surveyed the group. His four wives stood amongst the fourteen children, aged seventeen through four months, all dressed in their best attire; the boys in white shirts and trousers held up by hand-woven suspenders, the girls in almost-matching floral dresses. From five yards away, Hanna's dress looked identical to her mother's. From a yard away, tears in the fabric were obvious. Below her jacket, the seam had frayed. Her dress looked ratty, as though she didn't take care of her things and, by extension, herself. In truth, Hanna owned only two dresses. The others she had outgrown and passed down to her sisters.

The thought was unavoidable, particularly when they attended church services: Jotham's family was poor. It was evident in the holes in the children's shoes. In the stains on their tattered clothes. In that a family of nineteen had eight winter jackets between them, the rest clasping ragged sweaters close to their chests, the youngest children wrapped in blankets. It was evident in how the lot of them looked as though they'd been freshly dredged from a lake.

Jotham ran his hand along his jaw. Hanna waited for him to say something about Emily's tangled hair or the slumped shoulders of one of the toddlers, for a reprimand that never came. Instead, he stepped toward Hanna and examined her closer. This was her day, after all. There would not be an ordinary church service. Today, the minister would conduct a ceremony to formally announce who Hanna's husband was going to be.

"The entire town is coming to see you this morning. Are you prepared?" Jotham said.

Hanna nodded.

"I'm going to need you to say it."

"I'm prepared, Father," Hanna said.

It seemed for a moment that Jotham would speak again. Words formed inside his mouth. Were they instructions for how Hanna should behave? What she should say when she set foot inside the church and all eyes turned toward her? Were words of encouragement — however unexpected — on the tip of his tongue? Hanna would never know. Jotham turned and stepped into the passenger's seat of his old open-back truck. He settled in alongside his first wife, Belinda, who had taken over driving duties as recently as three seasons ago. Emily was allowed to sit in the back. The others had to walk.

Belinda started up the truck. It struggled at first, buzzing and clanking before letting out a long, uncooperative wheeze. The truck's frame convulsed and a dripping sound filled the air. Behind the wheel, Belinda pursed her lips. The skin tightened on her face and she turned the key in the ignition again. This time the truck roared to life. It billowed out a hazy black cloud and then the wheels spun on the gravel driveway.

Hanna watched the vehicle pull away before setting off down the street with the others. She clutched her jacket close, her collar turned up to offset the breeze.

"Carry me?" a little voice said.

Hanna looked down to see three-year-old Ahmre with her arms outstretched. She picked the girl up. "What are you dreaming about today?" Hanna said. "Pixies? Unicorns?"

Ahmre leaned into Hanna's ear. "A squirrel that tricks her brothers and sisters."

Hanna laughed. "Would this squirrel trick me, as well?"

The little girl paused to think. "How could it trick you? You won't be here."

Hanna held Ahmre closer. The child was right. Soon, she wouldn't be around to ask Ahmre about her daydreams, to help navigate the child's intricate network of imaginary friends. Hanna surveyed the family now, walking together, the youngest children holding hands, their mothers steering them away from the woodlands' edge, the twins sharing — or were they fighting over? — a torn blanket. She pictured them a week from now, walking without her. It wouldn't be all that different than if a giant hand reached out of the sky and plucked Hanna away.

"Can I ride on your shoulders?" Ahmre said.

"You're getting too big."

"Just this once?"

Hanna lifted the little girl up and felt Ahmre's warm legs wrap around her collarbone. Together they made their way down the gravel path. The journey would take just over thirty minutes. Clearhaven was a small town, isolated by woodlands on its sides, with a dense, impossible-to-traverse marsh at its southern end. On the far side of Clearhaven was The Road — the single entrance point into town. Hanna had never set foot on The Road. Only once, many seasons ago, had she stood at its edge. Hanna knew The Road didn't go on forever. But, at sunset, the way it dipped into the horizon, its view unbroken by mankind's creations, The Road seemed to lead straight into the blistering yellow orb in the sky.

In between The Road and the marshlands, Clearhaven's homes were clustered on winding semi-paved avenues, a tangled labyrinth leading in circles; counterintuitive and largely unnavigable to outsiders but second nature to Hanna and the other townsfolk. The newest and largest houses had been built near the church and the marketplace, quite some distance from Jotham's home on a small street toward the edge of town. Farmland dominated the northeastern side of Clearhaven, offering abundant livestock as well as fields full of produce and grains that all contributed to the town's self-sufficient nature. It was a settlement sovereign by design. If ever there was a more autonomous township, Hanna had yet to learn of it.

What Hanna knew about Clearhaven's bureaucracy, its internal operations, she gathered mostly from conjecture. Her sister-mothers were masters of deflection on the subject. From what Hanna understood, the town was managed by a council of which Jotham had once been a part. Hanna remembered being seven years old, hiding behind the banister at the top of the stairwell and watching important men visit Jotham's house. They made a great commotion as they entered through the front door, each of them with raucous voices and cigar smoke hovering over their heads like buttermilk clouds.

The important men hadn't visited in years. What role Jotham now played — whether it was essential, occasional or tenuous at best — Hanna didn't know. What she did know was who was in charge. It was Brother Paul, the minister at church. It was Brother Paul who ran the police force, Brother Paul who negotiated Clearhaven's independence from the city beyond The Road. It was Brother Paul whom Hanna was walking to see that morning; Brother

Paul who spoke often of *understanding*. At least, that was the word he used. Faith, to Brother Paul, was equal parts obedience, conviction and understanding.

Hanna set little Ahmre down. She watched the girl run to catch up with her brothers and sisters, and then she shook her head. When that didn't work, she shook it again, anything to push today's church service from her thoughts. She hadn't arrived at the church yet. There was still time to masquerade in her mind, still time to imagine none of this was happening.

She gazed into the woodlands on either side of the street, at the tall trees covering the hills, the vastness just beyond her reach. What would happen, she wondered, if she simply slipped away? It wasn't impossible. A girl could disappear into the woods and no one could ever find her. Hanna had never been outside Clearhaven. The big city was somewhere beyond those hills. The place Jotham loathed was that way.

A break in the trees appeared, a patch of worn shrubbery signaling the traces of a pathway. Hanna pictured herself walking into the woods, her feet settling into the moss-covered ground, the first few steps toadstool-soft, then the sudden sinking sensation of quicksand. For a split second, white stars of terror would explode in her head. Hanna would stretch out her arm — grasping for anything: a boulder, a tree branch, her mother's hand — before strength gushed like waves inside her. Then Hanna's foot rising, the ground beneath her boots turning firm, Hanna striding deep into the woods, bold and unafraid, the wolves cowering as she marched past their den. The tension inside her stomach — balled up like a fist for weeks — would finally relent.

Inside Hanna, a second person pulled free from the first. Hanna stepped away from the pathway and kept walking with her family, wondering what would happen if she dared enter the wild, while the other — the Hanna she wished she could be — bounded bravely into the unknown.

A hand touched her elbow.

Hanna jumped. She turned to see Kara walking beside her. Her mother's cheeks were unusually pale, a glint of perspiration on her forehead despite the chill in the air. Earlier that morning, Hanna had noticed Kara scraping her fingernail against the edge of her thumb. She looked down to see Kara's skin frayed, the edges red and worn.

"It's okay to be afraid," Kara said.

"You look more afraid than me."

"I'm serious," Kara said.

They were passing houses now, the large homes that had been built close to the church. Hanna pictured the forest, green and blooming and alive as it had been before winter took root, those trees into which a girl could escape and never be seen again.

"I'm not afraid," she said.

Kara took her hand. She pulled her close.

"I know you are."

As the family rounded the final corner toward church, Hanna saw fully the house that Brother Paul had built. Two seasons ago, work had been completed on a massive edifice, a wide, dome-shaped structure, multitiered, with enough lights that its glow could be seen from almost every home in the township. The new church, with its white walls and abundant skylights, was the focal point of Clearhaven. Beside the new church stood the old tower cathedral, taller than the new building, with an abandoned congregation room at its base, decrepit and ramshackle in comparison. The lights inside the tower cathedral were turned down this morning. No one was inside. The stained glass Hanna knew so well growing up — replete with tear-shaped roses blooming in a golden orchard — had not been washed since Brother Paul ordered the construction of the new building. The sunlight still caught the stained glass in places, but a thick layer of dust obscured its brilliance.

Jotham's truck sat in the distance. Belinda had parked at the edge of the lot in order to better see the rest of the family approach. Other vehicles were arriving. Parishioners were greeting one another, exchanging pleasantries, talking about the ceremony about to take place. And Jotham was waiting, his arms crossed, jaw clenched, impatience in his stony eyes.

He called out. "We shall not be late!"

When they arrived at the truck, Emily locked arms with her big sister. As she'd done several times over the past few weeks, Hanna wondered if she'd done Emily a disservice, allowing her to become so dependent. Hanna slipped away from her sister's grasp and joined the family congregating around Jotham, to see if he had any final words to say before they stepped inside.

Jotham shifted his back brace. He placed his hand on the truck to steady himself and then coughed, a single whooping hack that spoke of a burgeoning cold. He didn't make eye contact with Hanna this time. He didn't have to. She already knew what he needed her to do.

"If I see a single act of disobedience today, it's the lash," he said.

Beside Hanna, her brothers cowered. Just four days ago, Jotham had caught Hanna's seven-year-old brother, Pratt, spilling a can of paint thinner on the back deck. Jotham's rage overtook him. Hanna could still remember Pratt's screams, Kara's frenzied, fruitless attempt to intervene, the sound of Jotham's belt striking the boy's legs, her sisters crowding behind her, the hawkish air in the house. When it was over, Hanna had watched Jotham storm down the hallway, belt in hand, panting and desperate for whiskey; his eyes curiously devoid of emotion; his hulking frame shuddering from the adrenaline surge it took to hold the boy down. Afterward, Pratt couldn't stand properly for twenty-four hours. It took two days before he could walk. He stood next to the truck now, coatless and shivering, a lopsided cowlick sticking out of his head, still wobbly on his two feet.

Jotham surveyed the family one last time and then turned and walked toward the new church doors. The others followed.

Hanna's rib cage suddenly felt tight. Her breath came out in rapid puffs. Every sound, from the pushing breeze to the hum of car engines pulling into the parking lot, resonated tenfold. Hanna's childhood was over and her life was about to change. There would be no cocooning, no holding on to the moment she was in and never letting go. With age came responsibility. There was purpose. There was womanhood to attend to. She followed Jotham toward the church doors, aware of every loose pebble on the pavement, of the movement of her legs, the mechanics of her arms brushing against her sides.

The moment Hanna's foot crossed the threshold, the wind sailed out of her. She felt as though she'd run into a brick wall. Her knees buckled and it was all she could do to stay on her feet. Six hundred sets of eyes turned toward her. They'd all been waiting for Hanna. They were staring, expecting, knowing.

And in the center, clad in white robes, was Brother Paul.

3

"Without obedience, there exists only chaos."

Brother Paul stood on a raised platform, his arms spread wide. The room was dim, save for one bright overhead light that clung to Brother Paul like a magnet, casting a reflective sheen over the pristine robes of Clearhaven's chief luminary. He looked otherworldly, a far cry from the Brother Paul Hanna had met in his office last week, the one in the collared shirt with the spot of mayonnaise clinging to the corner of his mouth. Hanna wondered what the darkened faces looked like to him, whether he saw their eyes at all. Brother Paul's mouth hung open. He was close to concluding his sermon and soon he would turn his attention to Hanna, to selecting her husband.

"Children, when your father brought you into this world, he did so with the knowledge that the Creator believed this was good. The Creator wanted you here. Take a moment to think about that. The Creator plucked your soul out of nothingness and instead of casting you into a place of eternal torment, he brought you to our little township. Now, why would he do that? Is it because he acts in random ways, dropping souls to the earth as though scattering pebbles in a lake? Or is it because he knew you'd be safe?"

Brother Paul paused to allow his words to sink in. Hanna looked past him to the faces on the other side of the room. She searched for their smiles, their nodding heads.

"The Creator knew you would be safe because he had someone in place to protect you, someone who had sworn allegiance to him. And that someone is your father. Look at your father now, all of you. Look at him and understand the Creator chose him for you. He chose your father to be your instructor in the ways of the world, your protector against all things duplicitous and corrupt."

Hanna looked at Jotham. All the men were standing, even the boys. The women were kneeling, their arms resting on the same glossy support board that circled the auditorium. Jotham gazed down at Hanna. Their eyes met and quickly she turned away.

31

"Without your steadfast obedience, how can your father protect you? Wives, I ask you, without your husband to watch over his flock, how could you ever truly know you're out of harm's way? The taking of multiple wives, our very way of life, is an extension of the Creator's wish to protect the ones he loves."

Brother Paul stepped over to the podium where he kept his notes. It was so quiet in the church that Hanna could have heard a leaf falling from a tree. Beside her, Emily was starting to slouch. She held the girl's elbow, helped her find her balance on the kneeling board. On Hanna's right was Jessamina, Jotham's fourth wife — his newest wife — who at nineteen had already given birth to a baby boy. Hanna had endured Jessamina's intermittent scowls during the service. She tried to ignore her and concentrate. At any moment, Brother Paul would invite Hanna up onto the stage.

"Before we get to the objective of this gathering," Brother Paul said, "and announce the two souls who will be joining together under the Creator's loving embrace, I want to first take a moment to acknowledge some young men who will be leaving our township. For as important as it is for our young women to be protected, treasured and loved, it is equally important for our young men to find their true purpose, to go out in the world and carve a niche of their own."

Brother Paul called seven people to the stage. It took a few moments and then a family slipped out of the darkness and approached the podium. It was the Rossiters: a man, his three wives and their two sons. Hanna recognized their faces, although she'd never spoken to them before. The Rossiter children had long been schooled at home, away from Jotham's clan, and they hadn't been to church services in quite a while. Hanna counted six family members, not seven. If she recalled correctly, there was a third son. However, if Brother Paul was surprised that one of the family members was absent, his face certainly didn't show it.

Brother Paul placed his arm around the father. "Finally, our beloved benefactor has returned from his excursion outside our borders," Brother Paul said, eliciting a smile on Francis Rossiter's lips. "From my sermons these past few weeks, you all know how excited I've been to have Francis come back to Clearhaven. I've said it many times, but it bears repeating. We owe him an enormous debt of gratitude. For it was

Francis who financed the hallowed hall in which we now stand. It was Francis who arranged its construction. It was Francis who transformed the Creator's vision into a reality."

Brother Paul lowered his head.

"In the name of the Creator . . ."

Hanna closed her eyes. She lowered her head and recited with the others. "In the name of the Creator, may he protect my eternal soul." The six hundred voices speaking in unison sounded different in this new church than they did in the old building, where the families who arrived late had to crowd into the balcony and stand by the door. This room, with its white walls and arched glass ceiling, made the voices sound dreamlike, their echo arriving at Hanna's ears before she spoke her next word, creating a sensation that the walls were talking to her.

Brother Paul looked up again. "Together, and with my guidance and counsel, Francis Rossiter and his wife Eileen took their three sons, James, Kenneth and Daniel, on a journey of discovery beyond The Road, to teach them about life outside our borders, to prepare these young men for their future."

He wrapped his arm around the benefactor's oldest son. "How old are you now, young man?"

"Nineteen," James said. "Kenneth is eighteen."

James was tall and plump, with thin lips that made him look like he'd just sucked on a lemon. Beside him, his brother Kenneth was a little shorter, with a youthful face and a faint mustache that grew fainter in the light. The third son was nowhere to be seen.

Brother Paul beamed, a wide, overcompensating smile. "Ah. The perfect age to stake your claim in the big world out there." He leaned into the young man's ear and whispered. The quiet words went on for some time and as they did, the young man's stone-faced expression wavered slightly but never cracked. Brother Paul shook the hand of the younger son who looked like he might burst into tears at any moment.

"As James and Kenneth will be leaving us shortly to seek a new life outside our borders, I would like to thank them for their contributions to our community," Brother Paul said. "Fear not for their well-being. These two strong young men were born to thrive. And rather than say goodbye, which has a certain finality to it, I say instead — Godspeed. James and Kenneth, remember us in your hearts and in your minds. Remember Clearhaven and the lessons you've learned as your journeys continue."

Hanna watched the family step offstage and slip back into the darkness. The father, Francis Rossiter, looked just like any other man in Clearhaven, with his plaid shirt tucked neatly into his pants, his black hair combed over to conceal a bald spot, wire-thin glasses resting above his nose and his face shaved clean. The brothers, though, had grown into young men in the time they were gone. For all their height and broad shoulders, their features were soft and unmarred by age. They were a strange sight to see, the older one especially, a boy not a child and not yet an adult.

"You know why Brother Paul pushes them out, don't you?" Jessamina whispered.

Hanna glanced at Jotham's newest wife. Jessamina had her baby positioned between her knees and was looking at Hanna from the corner of her eye.

"Shh," Hanna whispered, wary of drawing Brother Paul's attention.

"It's to rid themselves of their competition," Jessamina whispered back. "It's so a man like Jotham can marry a girl like me."

Hanna knew exactly what Jessamina was saying. She'd seen it time and time again. Clearhaven's patriarchs would select a single male heir (often their youngest child) to take their place as they grew old. The other boys were ushered out of town as soon as they reached adulthood. It was the only way for a polygynous society to survive. If the fathers let their sons stay, and allowed an equal number of men and women, there would be competition. A slew of younger, stronger and more physically attractive rivals would arrive with each generation. Men like Brother Paul would no longer be able to claim dozens of wives. Jotham could never claim a bride as young as Jessamina. Hanna would never be brought to church on a day like today.

Hanna bit her lip and turned away from Jessamina. Jessamina might have been correct, but that was no reason to encourage her. Hanna needed to focus. Her moment was fast approaching.

Brother Paul cleared his throat. He took a sip of water from a clear glass. "Today we have another member of our congregation eager to start the next phase of her life. Jotham, I understand your daughter Hanna is about to reach the age of eighteen."

Jotham stepped forward. "In nine days' time," he said.

Brother Paul spread his arms and curled his fingers upward. "Hanna, please rise."

Hanna almost stumbled as she stood up. Her forehead felt unusually warm, her insides fragile like they were coated in glass. Hundreds of eyes turned her way, pressing against her slender figure. She placed her hand on the glossy support board. Hanna steadied her feet and gazed straight ahead.

"Who amongst us," Brother Paul said, "has heard the word from above that he should take this woman into his family and give her purpose — to fulfill her destiny of wifeliness and womanhood?"

For a brief moment, it seemed as though no one was going to speak, that not a single soul would step forward and claim Hanna for his own. Then, from across the room, a figure emerged from the darkness. It was Edwin, Jotham's childhood friend, the man to whom Hanna had been promised. Edwin stood under the bright lights with his thick glasses and squat little legs, his belly that protruded as though his collared shirt concealed a glazed ham. Edwin's eyes were stoic. His mouth formed a straight line.

Emily reached up and Hanna grabbed her hand. Their fingers intertwined. Hanna pressed her thumb into the girl's palm and braced herself. This was what had been planned. This was what she'd known was coming all along.

Then the unbelievable happened. A second man stepped forward, then a third. One was a lantern-jawed farmer from the outskirts of town, the other the butcher from the marketplace. Hanna barely knew the farmer: she'd only seen him at church and they'd never spoken. But she knew the butcher well. When she was five years old, the butcher had allowed Hanna to throw a piece of meat to the stray dogs begging outside his tent. She still remembered the mongrels leaping, their teeth gnashing in the air, bodies crashing together in a desperate attempt to win the prize. She remembered the butcher's boisterous laugh, his bloodstained apron. The cleaver in his hand.

The butcher stood proudly before Brother Paul.

Hanna almost gasped. She turned to Jotham, who shifted uncomfortably in his back brace. He looked equally taken aback. Everyone in this room already knew to whom Hanna had been promised. Ceremonies like this were a formality in Clearhaven, marriages being arranged years in advance. That these men — each with several wives already — stepped forward at all was an act against reason.

Hanna's skin flushed. Her heart pulsed against her rib cage.

"You're hurting me," Emily whispered.

She looked down to see Emily's fingers turning purple in her grasp. Hanna loosened her grip, but she didn't let go. The succession wasn't complete. Another man stepped forward and then another, their shoulders colliding briefly, the one on the left knocked momentarily off balance in his haste. In total, seven men stepped forward, all middle-aged, all men with multiple wives. For weeks, months even, Hanna's mother had told her to prepare herself for each step in this process. Kara never mentioned this possibility.

Jessamina nudged Hanna with her elbow.

"Do not grow satisfied with yourself," she whispered. "This owes only to the way you look and not the person you are."

Hanna didn't move. She couldn't. It was as though an invisible hand was pushing against her throat.

"It appears there are many suitors," Brother Paul said. "Jotham, as father and guardian of this young woman, can you tell me — has the Creator spoken to you? Have you had a vision declaring the rightful suitor for your daughter's hand in marriage?"

Jotham moved farther toward the center. "I have. The Creator told me that Edwin will marry my oldest daughter."

All eyes turned to face Edwin. Jotham's oldest friend adjusted his glasses. "The Creator spoke to me, as well," he said.

Brother Paul lowered his head. In deep concentration? A private conversation with the Creator, perhaps? As Hanna watched him closely, Jessamina leaned in again and whispered. "This is all for show. You know what will become of you."

This time Hanna met Jessamina's gaze. She stared back at Jotham's young wife: pleading, imploring, desperately searching for some sign of compassion. Six hundred sets of eyes were upon her. The men who would decide Hanna's fate were standing only yards away. And still she searched in vain.

"The Creator has spoken," Brother Paul said.

Hanna turned to see Brother Paul with his eyes open, looking straight at Edwin.

"Edwin is to marry Hanna on the anniversary of her birth," Brother Paul said. "In the name of the Creator, may he protect my eternal soul."

The congregation lowered their heads and repeated.

"In the name of the Creator, may he protect my eternal soul."

4

After the ceremony, refreshments were served. Jotham often allowed the children to roam free at church, so long as they remained within the building. Today, however, he stayed within an arm's reach of Hanna at all times. As members of the congregation approached to offer their congratulations, Jotham listened to every word, hovering like a satiated bird of prey unwilling to let a field mouse out of its sight. Then Edwin came over and placed his hand against the small of Hanna's back. He received the well-wishers alongside his fiancée, a gap-toothed grin on his face.

Last week, Edwin had approached Hanna and attempted to make light of their arrangement. "What strange bedfellows we make," he said and then seemed to realize his mistake right away. He took Hanna's hand and told her not to worry. Life in his house would be "grand and fine, without worry or concern." Still, Hanna felt his eyes upon her. Edwin's mouth could speak all the kindnesses in the world. His eyes told a greater truth and what they said, what they hoped for — moreover, what they had planned — sent shivers rippling down Hanna's spine.

All week she'd felt like a bell that couldn't stop ringing. She felt it at rest and when she walked in the woods. She felt it as the family sat down to supper. Amidst the chaos of the older children eating and the toddlers competing for attention, with her sister-mother Katherine perpetually chatting about the evening's stew and Jessamina staring daggers at her from across the room, that look on Edwin's face echoed through Hanna's rib cage, into her limbs and all the way to her fingertips.

Today, with his hand on her back, Edwin had yet to look at her. He was too busy shaking hands with the other congregants, too busy holding court to glance at his soon-to-be bride. Before long, Hanna would no longer kneel with Jotham's family at church. A baby, perhaps the size of a pea, might soon be growing inside her belly. Hanna would be Edwin's for all eternity. And he knew it.

"What dress will you be wearing?"

A woman's voice pulled her from her thoughts. Only, whose voice was it? Hanna scanned left and right, searching the faces.

"I'm sorry?" she said.

"I was wondering about your wedding dress. Also, have you chosen the flowers for your headdress yet?"

The voice belonged to Paedyn, one of Edwin's wives, a woman with a pointed chin and pencil-thin eyebrows framed by a cluster of curly hair atop her head. She took Hanna's hand, and Hanna felt her smooth skin and manicured fingernails. Paedyn pulled her close. While Hanna's feet barely shifted on the hardwood floor, it felt like she couldn't move — like Hanna *wasn't allowed* to move — entangled in this woman's invisible, unbreakable web.

Paedyn watched her expectantly.

"The headdress?" Hanna said. "I haven't found the time, no."

"Oh dear, you can't leave these things until the last minute." Paedyn tightened her grip on Hanna's arm. She leaned in to where Hanna could feel the warmth from Paedyn's body, ensnaring Hanna completely.

"Perhaps Paedyn can assist you," Edwin said, smiling widely.

"Yes, perhaps . . ." Hanna said.

From across the room, Brother Paul approached. He didn't just walk. The man glided, as though under his robes he was drifting on ice. The parishioners reached out their hands and Brother Paul shook each and every one. He listened to their greetings and spoke to a select few. Brother Paul spread his arms wide and offered a gentle embrace to a young boy, all the while keeping his gaze locked on Hanna, pinning her feet to the floor.

Finally, he arrived. "How are you today?" he said.

Hanna went to take a step back, only to be held in place by Paedyn's grip on her arm, Edwin's hand on her back. "I'm quite well," she said.

"And you remember our talk from last week?"

"How could I forget?" Hanna said.

"Do you have any questions?"

Brother Paul loomed over top of her, so close she could feel his breath against her forehead. There was nothing informal in Brother Paul's speech. He orated more than he conversed — each sentence a continuation of a sermon he'd begun long ago — and Hanna didn't believe for a second that he was about to answer any of her questions with all these people listening. His query was only for show, and it was all Hanna could do to get her words out.

"No, thank you. You were quite clear."

Jotham lumbered up beside them. He shook Brother Paul's hand and the two men smiled. *Reptilian smiles,* Hanna thought.

"We have much to discuss," Jotham said.

"Can it not wait for another time?"

"I'm afraid it cannot."

Brother Paul's expression shifted, his peaceful look slipped away. His jaw tightened ever so slightly and his shoulders tensed. He placed a cold hand on Hanna's cheek. "Will you excuse us, child?" he said, and the two men walked away.

Paedyn released her grip on Hanna's arm and went to speak with one of Brother Paul's wives, leaving Hanna with Edwin. Hanna scanned the crowd for her sisters, who had yet to return from the restroom. As she waited, a familiar face approached, a woman Hanna had seen at the marketplace. The woman shook Hanna's hand and quickly launched into an absentminded monologue about gardening. And flowers. Something about the variant moisture of topsoil. Hanna tried to be polite, but she could barely listen. The longer she stood under these bright white lights, the more her eyesight wavered. Everything around her: the people, their faces, the paint on the walls, suddenly distorted. The room felt tilted on its side, the ground misshapen, the air fused with halos; long and orange and shimmering like schools of fish. This woman's voice, the sincerity in her brown eyes, the discreet way she whispered about her horticultural endeavors as though unearthing and replanting begonias was a mystery to be unraveled . . . all became too much for her.

Hanna stepped away from Edwin — if he noticed her leave, he didn't show it — and moved quickly toward the exit. She slipped into the front hall and made her way toward the open door. The air grew hotter and denser with each step. The exit was twenty paces away and then fifteen. A purple panic manifested in Hanna's chest. A great weight pressed against her temples, the oxygen fleeing her body. Now only ten steps away, Hanna didn't believe she was going to make it. Her legs grew weak, her very thoughts plastic and uncontrollable. The heat in her head intensified until it was five steps and then three and then one last step and finally Hanna was outside. She hurried around the side of the church and collapsed against the wall.

Alone in the crisp afternoon air, the

overwhelming fear slipped away like a ghost. When it was at its worst only moments ago, the alarm inside her head had felt as real as the ground beneath her feet. It was tangible, unrelenting and impossible to control. Now she suddenly wondered why she'd fled through the church doors at all. Hanna had long known what was expected of her. It wasn't like her engagement came as a surprise. Still, she'd pushed the truth out of her mind as though she could suppress it with her own strength of will. Like a child, she'd pretended none of this was happening. She'd lied to herself for so long.

The future had been ordained. There was no denying destiny.

Hanna leaned back against the wall. She fought her welling tears. Soon Jotham would notice she'd gone missing and come for her. Or worse, it would be Edwin, with his kind words and wanton eyes.

A voice came from over by the parked cars. "You're Hanna, aren't you?"

Hanna looked over to see a young man she didn't recognize. Her first instinct was to jump up and rush back inside, but she was so startled and still so out of breath that her legs refused to move.

"Are you okay?" he said. When she didn't answer, he said, "You don't remember me, do you? I'm Daniel."

Why hadn't Hanna seen it right away? This was the benefactor's son, Francis's third boy, the one Brother Paul had called out but who didn't go up on the stage. Hanna hadn't seen him at church in a long while. Daniel looked different now, unlike the other boys in Clearhaven. His hair dangled over his forehead in waves, unkempt and yet perfectly arranged, as though he woke up in the morning with each strand effortlessly in place. Daniel was wearing dark blue denim and a gray jacket, and his arms were gangly, as though he'd just grown into his body. He'd been standing two yards away. He'd watched her run out and collapse against the wall and Hanna had been completely oblivious.

"You snuck up on me," Hanna said.

"It's easy to sneak up on someone when they're not paying attention. Besides, I was standing right here. *You* snuck up on *me.*"

Hanna glanced back toward the church doors.

"Are you going to marry that man, Edwin?" he asked.

Hanna didn't know quite what to say. After the ceremony, not a single well-wisher had asked how Hanna felt, what *she* wanted, whether she truly intended to marry Edwin. Now, faced with this young man's question, she couldn't bring herself to answer out loud: *of course I'm going to marry Edwin. What other choice do I have?* Her mind raced, mulling over unsaid words, contorting them, rephrasing them in a futile attempt to change their meaning. Hanna was about to stand up and walk back inside when she stopped herself. She refused to run away from two conversations today.

"I thought you weren't in the church. Brother Paul called your name," she said.

"I was there. I just didn't feel like being paraded up onstage."

"Then why are you out here now?"

Daniel leaned against the wall and cocked his head to the side. "I wanted some fresh air."

"I see," Hanna said, wondering whether even Daniel believed his own excuse. "Were there too many people looking at you and your brothers?"

"Oh, I think they were all looking at *you.*"

There was an unfamiliar inflection in his tone, like he was engaging her in banter to which she was completely unaccustomed. In the distance, a starling was calling. Hanna looked into the sky but couldn't spot the tiny bird.

"So you're going to be Edwin's third

wife?" Daniel said.

"He has four wives. I will be the fifth."

"Doesn't that bother you, the thought of sharing your husband with four other women?"

Hanna didn't answer. She ran her fingers through her hair and looked back at the church doors again, knowing full well Jotham would not approve of this conversation. She started to stand up when Daniel reached out and touched her hand. Hanna recoiled, her eyes wide and afraid.

The young man backed away. "I was trying to help."

"I can stand just fine on my own, thank you."

Hanna climbed to her feet and dusted off her dress. It was colder outside than she'd remembered and in her haste, she'd left her jacket behind. Hanna felt compelled to run her hand along her sleeve, to remind herself that she was present, that this entire day hadn't all been part of some uncanny dream. There was no one else in the parking lot except her and the young man, whose eyes remained locked on her.

The sunlight caught a shiny black string dangling around Daniel's neck.

"What is that?" Hanna said.

Daniel pulled on the string. As he reached

into his jacket, Hanna stepped back. She was all too aware of how improper it was for her to speak with this boy alone. And she didn't really know him. Daniel could have pulled anything out of his jacket. A cigarette. A knife. A hangman's noose. Instead, he produced a small silver box. Attached to the box was the shiny black wire and fastened to that was what looked like the world's smallest, most ineffectual set of earmuffs.

"They're headphones."

Hanna's expression grew more confused.

He held up the small silver box. "You seriously don't know what this is?"

"I'm not stupid."

"I didn't say you were," he said, and his tone softened. "I got this on the trip with my parents. It plays music. You put these soft little things to your ears and you listen to it."

"And you're the only one who hears it?"

"Yes. You do listen to music, don't you?"

"Of course," Hanna said.

"What kind?"

"I don't understand."

"What kind of music do you listen to?"

Hanna's mind grew cloudy. No one had ever asked her to describe her taste in music before. It occurred to her that were she ever to be magically plucked from her bed like a heroine in a storybook, and wake up in an entirely different place, hundreds of miles away, she would know nothing of the world around her. Strangers would sense she was different. They'd know she didn't belong.

"We have a record player and six records," she said. "The music is soothing. There are violins. And a piano."

"But no singing?"

"No."

The young man held the headphones out to Hanna. Cautiously, she slipped them over her ears and, in a single moment, the world opened up. Hanna heard music like she'd never heard it before. It was similar to the records Katherine and Kara played at home, except this song featured a woman singing. Hanna would have imagined the banging of the drums, the clang of the strings and the singing would all battle for attention and a great convoluted noise would result. Instead, the woman's voice rose above the music. It pulsed and soared. It sailed inside Hanna and through her and deep down into a place in her stomach where she didn't know she could feel things. The woman uttered the word *redemption* softly, tenderly, like it was her own personal proverb. Hanna stood next to Daniel, transfixed by the melody, amazed by the power in the woman's voice, how something so fragile and haunting could also be so uplifting. She could imagine herself, in altogether different circumstances, wanting to sway her hips.

"Do you like it?" Daniel said.

"It's remarkable."

She glanced at the open doorway. Any minute now, someone would come for her. "Thank you," Hanna said and handed the headphones back to Daniel, who was watching her closely.

"What is it?"

"You look down at your feet a lot," Daniel said.

"Excuse me?"

"You're always looking down. Only guilty people look at their feet."

Hanna blinked twice. "You've known me for exactly three minutes. It's quite presumptuous of you to say I *always* do something."

"Okay. Then you *mostly* look down at your feet." He paused and then he said, "I bet your doppelganger would never do that."

The odd statement puzzled Hanna. She wasn't sure if he was teasing her now. "How do you mean?"

Daniel grinned. "There are people beneath us, far down through thousands of layers of mantle and crust on the opposite side of the planet. I like to think I have a doppelganger down there and maybe one day the two of us will meet and he'll look just like me, only opposite. Do you see this scar?" He pointed to a little divot above his eye. "He'll have one on his right side, not his left. And he'll write with the opposite hand and have sisters instead of brothers. He'll be free, instead of . . . instead of growing up in Clearhaven."

Hanna wanted to smile. "These are very involved thoughts for a young man to have."

"I took a lot of long car rides with my parents this year," Daniel said. "Maybe I had a little too much time to think."

Hanna did smile this time. Then, almost too quickly, she looked down at her feet. Hanna's cheeks flushed when she realized she was doing exactly what Daniel had accused her of doing.

"What's that word mean — *doppelganger*?" she asked.

"It means your double. A person's counterpart."

"Could you spell it for me?"

A smile curled in the corner of his mouth. "I don't think I can."

From over by the entrance, Hanna heard the church doors open and shut. "I have to go. It was nice talking to you," she said.

"Wait. My family just moved into the old Grierson place. Have you heard of it?"

Of course Hanna had. It was the second largest home in Clearhaven. Gregor Grierson, a successful livestock rancher, amateur blacksmith and father to six boys, had only recently uprooted the Grierson clan and left Clearhaven after a series of scandalous rumors and scurrilous allegations.

Hanna nodded.

"Then you've heard about what happened to Mrs. Grierson."

"It's terrible what happened to her," Hanna said. Only, she couldn't think about the Grierson woman just now. Voices by the door set her heart fluttering. At any moment, they might be discovered. She started walking backward, edging her way toward the church.

"Well, we live in the Griersons' old house now, the one between the mill and the lake that drains into the marsh."

Hanna stopped midstep. "I know of it."

"There's a pier on the lake. The view from there is the best in town. You can stop by sometime if you like."

"It's still winter. And cold."

The young man leaned against the church wall. "You only feel cold if you allow yourself to feel cold."

Hanna pictured herself approaching the pier on the lake. She pictured Daniel's father — Brother Paul's prized benefactor — discovering her and Daniel speaking alone. Francis Rossiter calling Brother Paul. Edwin learning she'd visited a young man only hours after their engagement. The furious faces of the powerful men. Hanna resumed walking. "I cannot accept your invitation."

"Well, I'll still be there in case you change your mind."

"I won't."

When Daniel moved to follow her back inside, Hanna flashed him a look. *We cannot walk in together.* Then she stepped back through the open doorway, out of the cold and into the warm air. Hanna shook her head. An invitation to the pier? That boy must not have been paying attention in church. The Creator had spoken. She was betrothed. In nine days, Hanna would be married.

5

An hour later, Hanna knelt down next to the cast-iron tub in the downstairs bathroom at Jotham's house. The cold floor tiles — some chipped, others unfastened from their plaster — comprised a mishmash of patterns. Orange and brown triangles lined the room, while, in the center, paisley-red tadpoles swam on a cluster of pale blue plates.

She reached into the tub, placed two fingers at the base of Emily's spine and ran them upward. The girl's first few vertebrae were perfectly aligned, normal by any stretch of the imagination. Then her spine pulled hard to the right, twisting her back and spreading her shoulders far apart. Hanna rode the little bumps and indents like waves. At the midway point, Emily's backbone transformed into a long, thick protrusion that looked sinewy, almost unnatural, as though this part of Emily's body belonged to someone, or something, else.

Hanna often imagined what it would be like to place her hands on Emily's back and twist with all her might. She imagined the sound it would make. The scream her sister would let out at first — *"What are you doing?!"* — and then the sharp-drawn breath of relief Emily would exhale the moment after Hanna had forced her spine back to where it was supposed to be; and Hanna with her arms wrapped around the girl, Emily's savior, the one who could take her away from all this.

Hanna placed a cloth into the soapy water and brought it up to Emily's shoulder blades. The left one sat lower than the right. It jutted out like the tip of an elbow forcing its way through her skin. Hanna handed the cloth to Emily — "You have to wash your lady parts yourself" — and leaned back against the tub.

"Are we done?" Emily said.

"We still have to wash your hair."

Hanna rubbed the bar of soap until the lather was full. She placed it on her sister's hair and worked it in as best she could. The family had no shampoo. They'd had some last summer, a blue bottle covered in numbers and unfamiliar words that Jotham had brought home from the marketplace and tossed onto the kitchen table like a prize for the women to fight over. But it was long gone now. There were only so many times the girls could drip water into the bottle and shake it, hoping remnants would transform into bubbles. Hanna used the same soap to wash Emily's hair as she did the girl's feet, the curve in her spine.

"Hanna?"

"Yes, love?"

"I wish my hair was like yours."

Hanna smiled. "You mean dry?"

"No. I mean yellow like the sun."

Hanna dipped a bowl into the water and poured it over her sister's head.

"It's not fair," Emily said, "that your hair is beautiful and golden while the rest of us all have muddy-brown hair that sprouts like weeds."

Hanna forced a second smile. She'd heard this lament from Emily before. "Perhaps I'll braid your hair after supper."

"Will you make it beautiful?"

"It's already beautiful," Hanna said, massaging Emily's scalp. Emily winced as Hanna ran her hand through her matted locks, taking care to gently slide her fingers all the way through.

The girl was right. Her hair, especially if left untended, could be likened to a patch of sunburnt weeds. Emily had the same hair color as Jotham. She had her father's nose. Her eyes and ears resembled those of her birth mother, Katherine. The other children looked like their parents, as well. Charliss was a small, more delicate-featured version of Belinda. Ahmre and Minnet were two years apart, and one was slightly taller than the other, but otherwise they could have been twins. They both walked like Jotham — with their arms half-raised and their palms up, resembling clay figurines perpetually set to catch a marble, were it to fall. Hanna, on the other hand, didn't look at all like Jotham or Emily. There was nothing in her face, in her frame, in the way she moved her hands, to remind her of Kara. And Emily was right, Hanna's hair was different and not just from the rest of her family's. Hanna's long, wavy blond locks were unlike anyone else's in the entire township of Clearhaven.

A knock came at the door: swift and rapid and unexpected. Hanna's heart skipped a beat. Was it Jotham? Was he angry? Had Hanna — or worse, Emily — done something to ignite his rage? Then a voice came from the other side. It was one of the toddlers pulling on the doorknob.

"I'm giving Emily her bath," Hanna said.

"Use the bathroom upstairs."

A pause followed in which Hanna pictured a little one staring at the door, waiting for it to open. Then the patter of little feet sounded and the child took off running upstairs.

"There's no peace in this house," Emily said.

Hanna ran a brush through Emily's hair. "You say that now. But wouldn't you miss the noise if you lived somewhere else?"

"Maybe," Emily said. "I'm not sure."

A patch of tangles finally gave way and Hanna slid her fingers from end to end. There was pleasure in this, the most modest of victories. "Sometimes I imagine what we'd be like if you and I had been born on the other side of the world."

"Would we be princesses?"

"Perhaps we'd be warriors."

"Like soldiers?" Emily said.

"Not exactly. More like brave souls, the kind who battle monsters and beasts, who stop evildoers from committing their wicked acts."

"It's too bad there aren't any monsters in Clearhaven," Emily said.

"Yes . . ." Hanna said. She glanced at the door. The hallway was quiet, not a soul within earshot. Hanna set the brush down and whispered, "What if we weren't in Clearhaven? What if we went beyond The Road, past the woods and past the big city?"

"Why?" Emily said, her voice rising, sounding even younger than her eleven years.

"To be adventurers. Or, better yet — to be heroes. To defend those who can't defend themselves."

Emily met Hanna's gaze. Up close, Hanna could see tiny specks of gold in Emily's blue-gray eyes, her own silhouette mirrored in the girl's pupils.

"That's impossible," Emily said.

"Nothing's impossible. We could leave, just you and me. All we need is the courage to do it."

"What about Kara? What about Father? Wouldn't they miss us?"

Hanna placed her hand on Emily's cold, damp shoulder. She spoke softly. "They would be proud of us. Don't you think?"

Emily bit the inside of her lip. A crinkle formed between her eyebrows. "But the Creator wants us here. He needs us to stay in Clearhaven. We have a duty."

"Those are Brother Paul's words," Hanna said. "Not yours."

Emily shifted upright in the tub. "They're *my* words," she said emphatically. "I *learned* them from the Creator. And he never lies."

Hanna placed a dry towel on Emily's hair. She ran it gently over her shoulders. "I know. I know," she said. This seemed to placate Emily and Hanna pressed her mouth to the girl's ear. "We could always come back and serve the will of the Creator after our journey's over. I think that would please him greatly. What do you say? Would you come with me on an adventure?"

A second knock sounded on the bathroom door, this one sharp and swift. Hanna sat up straight just in time to see a tall figure open the door. Belinda stood in the door frame, staring with her dark valleys for eyes.

"It's time for supper," Belinda said. She ran her fingers along the door frame, and for a moment, Hanna thought perhaps Belinda had heard her, that her whispers had seeped out under the bathroom door, navigated the empty air and drifted up into the woman's ears. She imagined Belinda yelling out Jotham's name, Jotham storming down the hallway and demanding to know what Hanna had said. Hanna gripped Emily's arm. Her stomach muscles tensed.

"Do hurry," Belinda said finally. Then she turned and walked down the hall.

Hanna helped Emily dry off and, together, with a towel covering Emily's head, they joined the family in the kitchen. Kara was there, as were Belinda and Katherine. The young ones were crowded inside, as well. In descending order, the children in the house were Hanna, Charliss (age fourteen), Emily (eleven), Anastasia (nine), the twins Pratt and Violet (seven), Dawn (six), Minnet (five), Zelda (four), Decken (four), Ahmre (three), Reed (three), Zagg (two) and the infant Sayler. Hanna's family tree looked like a weeping willow with four descending limbs, all from one central point — Jotham. He fathered the children, first with Belinda and Kara, then with Katherine and most recently with Jessamina.

The only empty seats at the table were directly across from Jessamina, and Hanna braced herself, expecting another hostile glare for being late. As Hanna and Emily sat down, Jessamina's baby started fussing. She picked up Sayler, secured him to her hip and walked out of the room.

Charliss handed them each a plateful of barley and string beans. At fourteen, Charliss was the oldest boy and closest in age to Hanna. Charliss had an impish spirit. For years, he was infamous for eating absolutely anything, provided another child dared him to. Two summers ago, Charliss had, in a single day, ingested three worms, a slug, two snails — whole, including the shell — and something blue that Emily had found on the side of the road. Only recently, as Hanna prepared to leave Jotham's house, had Charliss begun to exhibit subtle signs of maturity. Charliss had started tucking his brothers into bed and had recently asked to help Emily with her morning stretches. Hanna still wasn't sure how Charliss would turn out as a young man, but his mood lately, the way he carried himself, was encouraging.

"Barley again?" Emily said.

Hanna looked up to see if Belinda or — heaven forbid — Jotham had heard Emily complain. Fortunately, Jotham was in the hallway rummaging through a stack of papers and Belinda was too preoccupied with scrubbing a cooking pot to hear. Only Kara, sitting a few seats away, took note.

"Be grateful for the food in front of you," Kara said and bit into a string bean. "Things could be worse."

Hanna looked down at her plate. The barley formed a thin porridge, perhaps of some meager nutritional value but not appetizing in the least. Full meals in Jotham's house had been scarce since midwinter, and though Kara and Katherine did their best — mixing powdered milk and diluted chicken stock into the barley to give it some semblance of flavor — the family's suppers this past month had had the aroma and consistency of pale brown gruel. Hanna dug her spoon in anyway.

She ate her string beans and was just finishing her barley when the children started to giggle. Katherine had stood up from the table and was preparing something on the counter just out of Hanna's view. From the toddlers gathered at her feet and the smell of candle wax, Hanna knew what was coming. She'd been expecting some kind of celebration, but, since this year her birthday would also be her wedding day, she hadn't known when.

The children started singing "Happy Birthday," their youthful voices filling the room. Katherine set the cake on the table as the children handed Hanna a present wrapped in colored paper. It was — without a doubt — a dress, the one she'd seen her mother sewing last week. Hanna knew how it must look: long, covered in a subtle floral pattern, with sleeves that stretched all the way to her wrists and a collar adhering to Brother Paul's strict edict of modesty.

The cake wasn't really a cake. There was no butter or flour, no whole milk or eggs baked inside. The brownish-orange sides suggested thawed pumpkin bread or perhaps date loaf. Still, the multicolored frosting on top was an extravagance. Katherine had sketched a large, silver bird in icing sugar, its wings spread, beak tilted upward, dwarfing the sugar-glazed trees and frosted mountaintops as it soared through the air.

Emily, unable to contain her expression of pure glee, stuck her finger in the icing, only to have Belinda slap it away.

"Do you like it?" Katherine said.

The entire family waited for Hanna to respond. All day, Hanna had felt like people were waiting for her to speak, for her to punctuate the moment with deep and reflective words. She'd felt Jotham's expectations. Brother Paul's presumptions. Edwin's shameless aspirations. A great weight hung upon Hanna's shoulders and even a single shift of her feet, an erroneous word, something as simple as an inadvertent glance, could cause it to tumble down. Now, even the children's eyes were on her.

"I love it," Hanna said.

Katherine clasped her hands together and smiled wide. She handed Hanna a paper crown the toddlers had constructed. The A's were crooked and one of the N's was sideways, but Hanna's name was written on one side next to a pastel rainbow. Hanna could see fresh globs of paste where the crown had been repaired earlier that day, while one of the little ones had gotten creative and painted a purple frog on the back.

"Now, blow out your candles," Katherine said.

Twelve candles burned in front of her, the only candles the family owned. They'd become something of an heirloom, having been used over and over again for birthdays for almost a year now. At each party, Katherine would light the candles and then the birthday boy or girl would blow them out. Then Jotham would trudge over from the other side of the kitchen, pluck the candles from the cake, lick the moist crumbs from their bottoms and place them back in their box, to be used again soon.

Hanna's stomach churned each time Jotham slipped the candles between his chapped lips and sucked each waxy bit before rubbing them against his unwashed shirt. Hanna knew it was wrong to feel this way. Her father had given her life. And he provided for her. Brother Paul taught that a father is a sacred role in a family, one of respect and, in Brother Paul's words, "unequivocal authority." Hanna should never have allowed such terrible thoughts to run through her mind. Still, she couldn't help herself. After each birthday party, she would wait until night had fallen and the entire family had drifted off to sleep, before sneaking downstairs to wash the candles with soap and scalding hot water. It was the only way Hanna could eat a piece of pumpkin bread in Jotham's house again. It was the only defiance — however silent — she found herself capable of.

She placed the children's crown atop her head and took a deep breath. Hanna was about to make a wish she knew would absolutely never come true when she changed her mind at the last moment. She wished for her little brothers and sisters to be safe and content in this house once she was no longer able to watch over them, and then she blew out the candles to the children's cheers.

Katherine and Kara set about slicing the cake and distributing it to nineteen separate plates. The family — adults and children alike — all waited for Jotham to select the first piece. He reached over Belinda's shoulder and picked the slice with the most icing. Then the birthday girl selected a medium-sized piece for herself. The moment Hanna's plate left the table, chaos erupted. The older children ransacked the table, sticking their fingers into the icing of the cake meant for the children too small to reach on their own. Three-year-old Ahmre erupted in tears.

Hanna stuck her fork into her cake, took a bite and felt the sugar cover her tongue like tiny malleable crystals. She went to take a second bite when little Ahmre appeared at her side. The child's cheeks were red and puffy from crying, her eyes big and wide and pleading. Hanna handed Ahmre her plate and a clean fork. She removed the paper crown and placed it on the girl's head and then stood up.

Before she could leave the kitchen, Jotham grabbed her wrist. His touch was sudden, his hand dry with calluses.

A scream rose in Hanna's throat. For the first time, she wondered — what would happen if she let it out? If she screamed as loud and as long as she could? Hanna's eyes darted around the room. Kara had already left the kitchen and Katherine was helping a child who'd dropped her fork. The little ones looked so content. She glanced down at Jotham's hand. His grip wasn't tight enough to hurt, but it was secure. Hanna had grown into a woman and still Jotham dwarfed her. She could pull with all her might and never escape. In the end, Hanna did what she always did. She gave in to his brute strength without a fight.

"It's a special day for you," he said, his mouth full of icing sugar.

"I know."

"You have just a week left in this house."

"I know that, as well."

"You deserve some peace and quiet. Tonight, Jessamina will sleep with the children. And you will have her room alone," he said.

"It's not necessary."

"I insist."

Hanna searched Jotham's face for some type of subtext, his true intentions. She saw only two days' stubble. Sweat pooling at the base of his neck. The pain from his back echoing up into his eyes.

"Thank you, Father," she said.

"Jotham. Call me Jotham."

"Thank you . . . Jotham." The word slipped from her tongue with great reluctance.

Jotham released her arm and took another bite of cake, his eyes still locked on her.

It took all Hanna's strength to turn her head, to step away. She could still feel the imprint of his fingers, her veins throbbing where the blood had been constricted, the slight indent from his thumbnail.

Hanna took another step and suddenly she couldn't move. A feverish heat overtook her. Hanna's breath fell short and inside her ears rang a bombastic, serpentine laugh. Hanna hesitated, hoping the feeling might fade, when a terrible choking sensation encompassed her. It was like hundreds of hands were on her throat, on her chest, all over her body, wedging her in place like iron blocks.

Visions of the future beset her: Edwin gaping at her with those indecent eyes. His wives watching her every move. Edwin's adult desires. His cravings. Being forced to lie in his bed. Hanna shackled to her oppressor, a man she'd known since her earliest days. Months passing. Years. Decades until she was an empty shell, hollow to the touch, until she wasn't herself anymore.

"Hanna?" Jotham said.

She glanced upward. Hanna was standing perfectly still, one foot in the kitchen, the other in the hallway, half a yard from Jotham. For the life of her, Hanna couldn't tell how long she'd been stuck inside her head, whether she'd said anything, what was real. She'd been rubbing her wrist and it was red now. Was it from Jotham's grip? Or had Hanna rubbed it so hard in an effort to forget Jotham's touch that she'd injured herself?

A line formed between Jotham's eyes.

"I'm going to find my mother," Hanna said.

"Perhaps it's best you do."

Hanna ran her hand along her wrist one last time and set off down the hallway, the sensation of being outside herself dissipating, an urge pressing inside her to feel her mother's touch, to wrap herself in Kara's safe, warm arms.

When she was young, as the day slipped into evening, Hanna would find her mother sitting in the front alcove on the sofa cushion nearest to the fireplace, drinking tea and watching the embers in the hearth pulse orange and red, the sparks dancing like fireflies. Hanna would crawl onto Kara's lap and nestle in, her mother's skin warm and inviting. As she grew taller, Kara would place Hanna on her side and lean Hanna's head against her chest. She would stroke Hanna's long blond hair and whisper into Hanna's ear that she loved her.

Hanna found Kara in the same seat while the others were still eating their cake, and sat down beside her. Two logs were ablaze in the fireplace, strips of birch-tree bark smoldering in the corners. Along the far wall, Hanna saw the warped panel wood, the ever-widening cracks in the ceiling and patches of discoloration where water had seeped in from a leak in the roof. She and Charliss were supposed to climb on top of the house and plug the leak weeks ago, only the lingering frost and icy morning dew made the shingles too slippery, the rooftop too dangerous to scale.

She tucked her head into Kara's shoulder and breathed in the scent of tea leaves and oranges from her mother's sweater. For a moment, Hanna considered telling Kara what Jotham had said, where she would be sleeping that night. But the last thing Hanna wanted to do was dwell on Jotham and Edwin.

She wrapped her arm around Kara's waist.

"Tell me the story again."

"Again?"

"Please?" Hanna said. "I need to hear it."

Kara tucked a stray hair behind Hanna's ear. She glanced over her shoulder, to make sure the others couldn't hear, that they had enough time.

"Okay," Kara said and Hanna shifted to hear her mother better.

"Don't leave anything out."

"I won't," Kara said and set down her cup of tea.

Then she began.

6

"It was eighteen years ago, on the first real day of spring. Winter had finally passed and you could feel the warmth in the air. If I remember correctly, cherry blossoms had turned the trees pink and the grass was the color of emeralds and shamrocks."

"What about the ocean?" Hanna said.

"Shh," Kara said gently. "Of course there was the ocean. This happened far away from Clearhaven, in a hamlet by the bay — where the tides crashed in white foamy bursts against the shore, where instead of ravens soaring in the air, seagulls picked fish from the salt water. My mother and I lived in a small village, and I could see the water from my window.

"That day, as evening set and I turned in for bed, a noise struck. It was loud like thunder, but instead of rumbling, it came in one swift boom. I ran outside and saw the most incredible sight. Out of nowhere, the sky broke open. A white crack formed in the heavens above. At first I thought maybe it was a star speeding toward Earth or some massive fire. The longer I stared, the clearer it became. Somehow I just knew: I was looking up at God. If it wasn't God Himself, it was Heaven. Hanna, the heavens opened up in the nighttime sky.

"If I hadn't seen it with my own eyes, I never would have believed it. The villagers came out of their houses. Men, women and children — they all stared skyward, transfixed. We started walking toward the field where the light was the brightest, trying to get closer. The opening hovered for almost an hour and then, quickly, it started to grow. People became scared. Some fell to their knees and prayed. Others fled. Part of me wanted to run away. Only, I was mesmerized. I watched as the edges of the opening turned bright red and green. The colors were so clear, unlike anything I'd ever seen before, and in the center was a whiteness so magnificent, so stunningly pure.

"A tiny dot emerged from the white space. The villagers wondered out loud. *Do you see it? What is it? Is it real?* Within seconds, the dot left the light and started racing toward the ground. More people ran away in fear. Still others ran toward where they thought the object might land. I ran to it, Hanna. I ran as fast as I could. The thing, whatever it was, broke through the air at such a speed that it could never slow down before it reached the earth.

"Suddenly, the ground shook. For a second it felt like the world might split in two. I fell to my knees and then stood up with the others and pressed onward. No one said a word. The air was so quiet. The crickets weren't chirping; the waves weren't crashing against the rocks in the bay. There was just silence, like the rest of the world was frozen in place and we were the only ones moving. Then, in a single moment, the light vanished. As quickly as it appeared, it dissolved into a hazy afterglow and darkness overtook the sky. My eyes took a moment to adjust. Little yellow circles dotted my vision. I saw the men who'd reached the object first. One of them was holding a lantern and I ran toward the light and found a hole in the ground almost a yard deep."

Hanna sat up on the sofa. She hung on Kara's every word. Kara paused — a brief moment where her eyes lowered and she retreated inward, and Hanna wasn't sure Kara could go on — before taking Hanna by the hands.

"Wisps of smoke trickled from the soil

around the crater. Scorch marks blackened the earth. I pushed my way to the front where the ground felt hot under my feet and looked inside. It was like a dream, but a crystal clear dream where every little detail was magnified. Finally, I saw what had fallen. There, lying inside the crater, covered in fluid and crying out into the night, was a baby girl. Hanna, it was you. You fell from the sky and landed unscathed."

"How loud did I cry?"

"Very loud. Although all babies cry out when they're born," Kara said.

"But I wasn't like all babies, was I?"

"Of course not," Kara said.

She kissed Hanna on the forehead, and then she leaned back and tucked Hanna's head against her shoulder again. Hanna breathed in deeply, imagining the astonished looks on the villagers' faces, the white light shining brightly in the night sky. She gazed out the window to see the soft, diffused light of nightfall had fallen prey to utter darkness. A low moan emerged, distant and indecipherable at first. Hanna thought it might be the wind gusting through the trees, perhaps a gale rising out of the marshlands. Then a second sound succeeded the first and Hanna knew it was no wind. It was the howling of wolves in chorus: alternately high-pitched and muted, sustained and doleful. Hanna thought the creatures were in agony. She imagined a pair of yellow eyes appearing in the window. Ferocious, snarling teeth. The brethren lurking. Her skin crawled at the thought that she wasn't safe in Jotham's home. Hanna wasn't safe in the only place she'd ever known.

"Did you hear the wolves?" she said.

"They can't hurt you right now," Kara said, her voice cracking, the sound tinged with emotion. She took a deep breath to steady herself. Still, her shoulders trembled.

Hanna sat up. "What's wrong?"

"It's nothing."

"It's clearly something."

For a moment Hanna thought Kara wasn't going to speak. Then she brought her hand up to her cheek and said, "The days just passed. They passed by without me even realizing it. I've had eighteen years. There were so many things I could have done for you."

Hanna took Kara's hand, but it wilted in her fingertips. "Don't say that. You've been a great mother. You *are* a great mother."

Tears formed along Kara's lower lids. Where they came from — regret, a deep-seated unhappiness Kara had never shared or the emotion of seeing her only daughter get engaged to a man more than twice her age — Hanna could only imagine. In the next room, the children had finished their cake and Hanna could hear Emily asking where she was. It wouldn't be long before she found her big sister.

"You always think there's more time," Kara said, "that there will be another day, another tomorrow when life will finally start." Her gaze drifted to Hanna's forehead, to her mouth, to the warped panel wood in the far corner, anywhere except Hanna's eyes.

A warm pit of worry swirled in Hanna's stomach. Her mother never spoke in abstractions. She never avoided eye contact. Rarely, if ever, did she cry in front of Hanna.

"I don't understand," Hanna said.

"I should have done so much more."

"Tell me, what could you have done?"

Before Kara could answer, Emily rounded the corner with three little ones in tow. She leaned against the wall with her hand on her hip. "You promised you would braid my hair."

"Let us have two minutes alone first, please."

Emily looked from Hanna to Kara and back to Hanna again. Her eyebrows raised. "What are you two talking about?"

Hanna waited for Kara to offer an excuse and send the children away, but her mother's eyes were fixed on the fireplace, spellbound by the flames. Hanna stood and whispered in Emily's ear, promises that soon she would braid Emily's hair and help the little ones brush their teeth and change into their sleep clothes. Emily glanced at Kara and nodded. She took the young ones down the hall and Hanna sat next to her mother again.

Outside, the wolves' howl had waned as the wind whipped the skeleton-thin trees.

"Mother, that story about me falling from the sky — is it true?"

Kara finally met Hanna's gaze. The color had left her face and she looked exhausted, as though she was aching for a long rest. "What do you think?" Kara said.

"I wish it was."

More children scampered through the hallway and Hanna wondered if this was the last moment she and her mother would ever share in this house alone. Kara's breathing had steadied, the tremble in her shoulders diminished, and while Hanna had more questions, she didn't want to say anything to further upset her mother. Over the years, Kara had told Hanna the story of her falling from the sky dozens of times. It was a bedtime fable that Kara told only to Hanna and Hanna alone. There were no special tales for the others — none for the toddlers or even Emily — and it made Hanna feel special. It made her feel unique. Tonight, however, the story didn't just make Hanna happy. It didn't just distract her from the tribulations of the day. Tonight — the way Kara told it, the wistful timbre in her voice — the story made her wonder, wonder about what the future held. About her past. It made Hanna wonder what exactly was true.

7

The noise through the wall was loud but muffled, her sisters' voices indistinguishable behind the layers of wallpaper and plaster. Ten minutes earlier, Hanna finished helping the little ones wash their faces and made sure they used the toilet, before tucking Ahmre into bed and then retiring for the evening in Jessamina's room.

For as long as she could remember, Hanna had shared a bedroom with her brothers and sisters. As the family grew, Belinda and Kara had constructed bunk beds out of lumber salvaged from old milk crates. They erected six such structures in the children's room upstairs. Hanna slept on the bottom bunk across from the window. It was one of the better beds in that it didn't wobble and the siblings above her rarely woke up in the middle of the night.

For years, Emily had insisted on sleeping with her big sister. The two of them would curl up under a wool blanket, the young girl's back pressed firmly against Hanna's chest, and drift off to sleep. Hanna could distinctly remember the smell of Emily's hair when she was five years old, the way their heartbeats synced, Emily's soft breaths an echo of her big sister's. As Emily grew older, she became a restless sleeper and the two girls would shift during the night, a wooden plank on the side of the bed the only thing keeping them from falling to the floor. Each night they would end up with their blanket lost at their feet and their limbs entangled like a pair of newborn puppies.

When Emily turned eight, she declared she would be requiring her own bunk. Hanna knew it was selfish, but she felt wounded when her sister left her bed. It wasn't just the girl's warmth she missed. Hanna had been her sister's protector since her frightening emergence from the womb. She could still remember that day: Katherine screaming, the gore of the blood, the panic all around. Hanna had long believed that if she could only keep Emily close, her sister would be safe and the image of how she came into this world might somehow fade from her memory.

Hanna found herself sleeping alone. Despite the safety in numbers in Jotham's house, nighttime still brought out her most fearful thoughts. Brother Paul often spoke of an impending conflict with the cities beyond The Road, and some nights, she'd lie awake waiting for men from a faraway land to come storming through the woods, brandishing pitchforks and torches, crimson in their appetent eyes. It was only this past autumn, when three-year-old Ahmre climbed into Hanna's bunk and began sleeping next to her, that Hanna's nocturnal worries subsided.

The bed in Jessamina's room felt empty without Ahmre beside her. Slivers of moonlight slipped through the curtains, illuminating the sparse furnishings: a bureau, a wicker bassinet, a pot without a plant and an armless rocking chair. As the children fell silent through the wall, Jotham's house settled. Joints and floorboards creaked, the pipes clanked and the aged roof clicked and clattered with the wind. Hanna breathed in fully. She allowed the air to fill her chest and turned on her side in Jessamina's bed.

Hanna could hear Jotham lumbering up the stairs, his footsteps heavier than usual. In the past, Hanna had heard him pacing the hallway at night. She could tell by the metallic creak of the door hinges which wife he'd chosen to sleep with. Hanna could tell by the groan of the bedsprings when he lay with Jessamina. In a few short months, Hanna would be the same age Jessamina had been when Jotham planted a baby inside her belly. In their private conversation last week, Brother Paul had described the physical relations between a man and his wife as sacred, witnessed by the Creator. "The Creator's divine wish is for you to bring your husband closer to his light. It is your sacred duty," he said. Hanna didn't know what to think. She had often been confused by the intentions of grown men. And she'd long been wary of them looking at her.

Age thirteen was the year Hanna had sprouted — growing nearly three inches in a single month. That was the year her chest developed and her hips widened ever so slightly, the year she first noticed men staring at her, their flagrant gazes running up and down her body, piercing her, cutting into the fabric of who she was in a way she didn't yet understand. Thirteen-year-old Hanna still thought the moon followed her in the sky, that the blue wisps of early-evening light were fairies come to life. And now grown men wanted her. Hanna had never thought of herself as an object of desire. But when the rest of the town weighed in, when Hanna turned fifteen and then sixteen and caught women glaring at her the way Jessamina did, she knew there was something different about her. Hanna had never expected so many men to step forward to claim her hand in marriage. Too much beauty in a town bereft of it, was something Hanna had never wished for.

Outside the door, Jotham reached the top of the stairs. He paced back and forth. Jotham paused outside Katherine's room and then shuffled off-kilter to the children's bedroom, where Jessamina was sleeping with her baby. Jotham turned on his heel. A second passed and then another. Then his feet appeared at Hanna's door.

Hanna tensed up. She hadn't expected Jotham to come to her — never had he done such a thing before — and she held her breath until she could hold it no longer. Hanna exhaled as Jotham turned the door handle and stepped inside.

He closed the door behind him. His frame loomed large, a confluence of shadows hovering over the bed.

Hanna's heart throbbed in her chest and yet she didn't move. She feigned sleep, breathing slowly, her eyes closed. She heard her father drag the rocking chair over to the side of the bed. Gracelessly, Jotham sat back in the chair and started rocking. His gaze lingered on her for what felt like an eternity, until it dawned on Hanna that he wasn't going to leave.

"Father?" she said.

Jotham shifted in the chair. He tugged at a strap on his back brace.

"You're a young woman now," he said. "The time for formalities is gone. You may call me Jotham."

"I could never be so informal," she said. To punctuate her words, she added, "Father."

Jotham leaned in closely, and Hanna could feel the air from his nostrils. She smelled his dry sweat, the liquor on his breath. Hanna thought perhaps he might offer his thoughts on her impending nuptials, what life would be like in Edwin's house. Only, he didn't say a word. Jotham reached out and touched her arm through the blankets. First the coverlet compressed, then the sheet beneath it offered no resistance and finally Hanna's nightdress pressed against her skin. Jotham wrapped his fingers around her elbow.

"You're special to this family. Special in ways you don't even know," he said. "It's given me great pleasure to see you blossom into such a beautiful young woman. Does it please you that I am pleased?"

Hanna forced the words out of her mouth. "Yes, Father."

Slowly, deliberately, Jotham's fingers crept up and down her arm. "Many men in our community have made wives of their own daughters," he said. Jotham paused and when he did, his hand rested against her rib cage. He pressed the coverlet down against the edge of Hanna's breast. Hanna swallowed hard, unsure where Jotham's courage would take him.

Outside, a gust of wind swelled against the window. The trees trembled, their leaves crinkling like parchment paper. Inside, the curtains shifted, disrupting the moonlight's steady stream. Indigo and then silver and then indigo again. Jotham's silhouette emerged from the shadows. He loomed over top of her.

"Some daughters want their fathers to bring them into womanhood. Some relish it," Jotham said.

His grip on her arm tightened. The stench of whiskey echoed off him in waves. Inside Hanna's brain, a clash of cymbals sounded. Her thoughts raced, everything within her afraid. Jotham inched closer. His other hand slinked onto her mattress and Hanna pictured him crawling onto the bed, his weight crushing her, his stubble scraping her cheek, Hanna lying exposed, fragile, defenseless. A moment passed in haunting silence with nothing visible save Jotham's face, pale and feral in the moon glow. Jotham opened his mouth, a single drop of saliva stretching from lip to lip, like seeping molasses. Hanna clenched her fists. Every muscle in her body tightened. She felt him about to pounce.

Then Jotham coughed, a sudden, painful tremor that caught him by surprise. He pulled away. Jotham ran his hands over his face.

"I would never make you my wife," he said, leaning back in his seat. "You have a more important role to play in this community. Edwin will make you an honorable woman. He has money to provide for you. He has money to provide for your brothers and sisters, if need be."

"Thank you for everything, Father —"

"— Jotham."

"Jotham."

He lingered without moving. Hanna shuddered under her blankets, terrified that — despite his words — Jotham's hand might still reach out and grasp a treasure greater than just her arm. Instead, he stood up awkwardly out of the chair. Hanna caught him just as he opened the door to leave.

"Jotham?"

"Yes, child?"

"What will become of Emily when I leave?"

Jotham arched his back and grimaced. He heaved a grunt. "I'm not sure what you mean."

"Can I take her with me?" Hanna said.

The question seemed to catch him by surprise. Jotham tapped his fingers against his chin, demurring. "Katherine's her mother," he said.

"I know. But Katherine has so many little ones who need her already, and I'm the one who helps Emily with her exercises. I'm the only one who can take care of her."

"You'll have your own children to take care of soon enough," Jotham said.

The conceit in his voice — as though there was humor in the idea of Hanna bearing Edwin's offspring — sent a fury racing through her. It was all she could do to suppress it. "Just for a few years," Hanna said, "until Emily's of age. Until she gets married."

Jotham snickered. "No man in his right mind would marry a cripple."

Hanna glowered at him. Whether Jotham noticed, she couldn't tell; he'd turned to the side and the light from the hallway obscured his features. Above, the roof creaked. She heard the patter of animal feet and then scratching. Some creature — a raven or a squirrel — was trying to gain entry into this cold room inside Jotham's crumbling house.

Jotham dug his back brace out of his ribs and went to close the door. "You can take the crippled child with you, if you wish," he said.

"And you'll discuss this with Edwin?"

"I will."

Jotham paused with his hand on the door handle. He looked down at his oldest daughter lying alone in the dark and then scanned the room. Hanna wasn't sure what he was searching for: a reason to stay, an excuse to explain his presence in the first place, the Creator's image embedded in the wallpaper. He looked at her one last time. "Good night, Hanna."

"Good night, Father," she said. As he closed the door, Hanna caught her mistake. "Good night . . . Jotham," she said.

8

The next morning, Hanna was still fast asleep in her nightclothes when Jessamina barged through the bedroom door. She set her baby in its bassinet and then stood over the bed, arms folded, teeth clenched, her foot tapping on the hardwood floor. Hanna sat up, bleary-eyed.

"Get out!" Jessamina barked.

Hanna climbed out of bed and stepped into the hallway as Jessamina yanked the sheets off the mattress. The new mother held them at arm's length, as though afraid a single dead skin cell might touch her. She tossed the bedsheets at Hanna, who barely caught them in her foggy state. Hanna watched Jessamina place a new coverlet over the mattress and then shift the rocking chair back to the corner where it belonged.

"I heard you'll be visiting Edwin's household today," Jessamina said.

Her tone was probing, but Hanna simply

gave Jessamina a blank look.

"One wife is dry like sand," Jessamina mumbled, as much to herself as to Hanna.

"What do you mean?"

Jessamina didn't make eye contact. She grabbed the door handle and slammed it shut, leaving Hanna standing in the hallway alone. In the next room, the children were stirring. Soon there would be chaos. Hanna tapped her knuckles on the door frame, and when Jessamina didn't respond, she knocked loudly. A moment passed before the door flung open. Jessamina had a diaper in one hand, baby Sayler naked in the other.

"What do you mean — *dry like sand*?" Hanna said.

"One of Edwin's wives can't have babies. I haven't the faintest idea which one," she said. Jessamina's lips twisted into a self-satisfied smirk. "It bodes well for you, doesn't it? Knowing he'll probably keep you, even if you're barren too." Jessamina's mouth hung open, basking in her own callousness. "Barren like your mother proved after you." Before Hanna could say another word, Jessamina slammed the door and baby Sayler started to wail.

An hour later, Hanna stood on the front steps as Charliss led the children down the street for their first day of school since the winter break. It was strange to watch her siblings leave without her and to not have Emily by her side. Hanna would have liked nothing better than to accompany them. She'd become accustomed to the routine of attending classes, of interacting with their instructors and helping teach arithmetic to children from other families. There was safety inside the schoolhouse's doors, in knowing what each day would bring, in the structure of Hanna's life before.

Hanna leaned against the column that held an awning aloft. Its faded blue paint had chipped, revealing rotting wood underneath. There was some give to the column, as if a strong wind could dislodge it and cause the awning to come crashing down. Hanna picked off a sliver of wood. She felt its damp underside and was twirling it in her hand when Kara appeared at the doorway.

"Are you ready for your visit to Edwin's house?"

Hanna looked down at her new blue dress. She caught a glimpse of her reflection in the window. Thirty minutes ago, she'd taken a quick bath and ran a brush through her hair.

"I think so."

"Then come inside and help me in the kitchen," Kara said.

The kitchen in Jotham's house wasn't just for cooking. It doubled as a storage room, a laundry and a play area for the toddlers. As Hanna entered, her sister-mother Katherine was pulling a steaming wet pile of clothes from the washing machine and dangling them over a clotheshorse to dry. The whole while, she kept her head half out the window, gossiping with the neighbor's wife and unleashing a hearty laugh every few seconds. Kara stood by the sink, washing a bushel of spinach while the toddlers dashed in and out of the room.

"How can I help?" Hanna said.

Kara handed Hanna a knife and a half dozen strawberries. They stood side by side, Kara dicing almonds while Hanna chopped the strawberries into little cubes. Usually, when Hanna helped her mother in the kitchen, Kara would hum under her breath. It was an involuntary act, the melody always the same, a soft, gliding, wordless tune. Today, however, Kara was oddly silent, her chopping motion short and quick.

"Are you okay?" Hanna said.

Kara looked up, startled from her thoughts. "Why do you ask?"

"You're not humming."

98

"I never hum while I cook."

"You *always* hum while you cook," Hanna said and hummed the familiar tune.

"Oh," Kara said, slicing a cucumber. "My mother taught me that song."

"Was this when you lived by the bay?"

"Shh!" Kara said. She looked at Katherine, just three yards away, her head still halfway out the window. Beside her, little Ahmre had built a nest out of wet socks from the laundry machine. Neither appeared to have heard what Hanna said. "Keep your voice down," Kara whispered.

Hanna took the cucumber from her mother's hand and diced it, as well. "Yesterday you mentioned that you lived with your mother in the village. You'd never mentioned that before. It was never part of the story."

Kara's shoulders stiffened. She averted her eyes. "It's just a story. A story for you alone."

"I didn't say I thought it was the truth. I know babies are born at home, that the midwives assist in their birth," Hanna whispered. "But parts of the story are about you. You've never told me how you came to Clearhaven, about how you and Father met."

Just then, Belinda entered the kitchen. She marched straight past Katherine, past the kitchen table and over to the countertop beside the refrigerator where she began rifling through a drawer. She pulled out an old fountain pen, tested the ink and was about to leave when Hanna and Kara caught her eye.

Belinda scanned the ingredients on the countertop. "How much did all that cost?"

"It's for a spinach salad Hanna's taking to lunch at Edwin's today."

"But how much did it *cost*?"

Belinda clicked her fingernails against the wall, waiting impatiently. Kara, in turn, folded her arms and glared back at her sister-wife.

"We can't very well send Hanna there empty-handed, now, can we?" Kara said.

The room fell silent. Katherine ceased her chatter at the window and drew her head inside. The women stood in silence, eyeing each other, neither willing to concede defeat. Just when it felt like their silent quarrel might go on all morning, the toddlers spilled into the kitchen, crying about a broken toy. Katherine steered them into the other room. "Come along, little ones," she said.

Belinda gathered her eyebrows and churned her jaw, leaving Hanna to wonder whether she was really concerned about a few extra dollars spent at the marketplace. Perhaps Belinda was upset at not being consulted. Or maybe she was searching for an affront, something to legitimize her already-vexed mood.

Belinda pointed to the salad bowl Hanna was filling. It was the only bowl the family owned that was still in pristine condition, one Belinda had personally brought home from the marketplace. Their other serving plates, dishes and containers were all chipped or in some form of disrepair. Belinda glared at Hanna. "If you break that bowl, it'll be the end of you," she said. Then she turned and walked away.

Kara waited a moment to see whether Belinda would return to continue their silent standoff and then resumed dicing the almonds, furiously now. From the next room, Hanna could hear the toddlers singing along with Katherine, a joyful hymn from church, the sound in stark contrast to the mood in the kitchen. Kara's arms were rigid, the muscles in her neck tensed and she hadn't looked at Hanna since Belinda left. Hanna almost kept quiet. She almost held her tongue.

"Mother, about that story . . ." she said.

The moment the words left her mouth, Hanna knew she'd made a mistake. Kara took a deep breath, her shoulders tensed ever further. She brushed the almonds into the salad bowl and then looked around for something else to dice — some strawberries, a stray piece of spinach, anything. There was nothing left. All the ingredients were in the bowl.

"I'm sorry —" Hanna said.

"Don't apologize," Kara said. She turned, her face tight, the unexpected battle with Belinda having taxed her to her limit. "I'll tell you more about the story another time."

"Another time?"

"Another time."

Hanna wrapped a cloth over the bowl, kissed her mother goodbye and set forth down the street. She scanned the bottom-floor windows as she walked, the young children's silhouettes dashing by, the threadbare curtains sheer to the point of being transparent. Hanna searched the cloudy glass in the sash windows upstairs to see whether Belinda was watching, to see if her sister-mother was silently judging her from above, and found only shadows.

The house faded from view and Hanna came to a trail leading into the woods. Here she had a choice: to continue down the street or cut through the forest. Were Hanna to stay on her current course, her journey would last over an hour. Were she to traverse the woodlands, it would take closer to thirty minutes. She pictured the wolves in her mind's eye, their spindly legs and sharp yellow teeth. The wolves were nocturnal. They commenced hunting at dusk and Hanna's chances of crossing their path at this hour were slim. Moreover, Hanna had been through these woods hundreds of times. She knew them better than she knew Clearhaven's tangled tapestry of semi-paved streets. In the daylight, she could better sense danger. She could stay close to the riverbed and brave the freezing water, wade to the other side if the wolves appeared.

Hanna stepped into the forest. A mere ten yards in, where the trail splintered into several paths, a predator appeared. A white owl sat on a perch so close Hanna could almost reach out and touch it. The late-winter mist weaved through the trees, camouflaging the creature. It was still early and the sun had yet to reach its full zenith in the sky. The owl was awake, its wings pulled in tight, its front feathers forming a single white plume streaked brown on either side. Hanna passed by slowly. The owl's head didn't move. Its dark eyes darted within the wide discs on either side of its face.

Years ago, Kara had told Hanna that white owls were capable of sensing motion imperceptible to the naked eye, that they could *hear* a rodent crawling underneath three feet of snow, that their wings made not a sound and their talons were inescapable. Were Hanna small — perhaps the size of a beaver kit — she might have reason to be afraid. But she was ten times the owl's size. And it looked so calm and peaceful, like in a painting; the crowned king of the woodlands, its fierce talons dormant for the moment.

Hanna saw no other creatures, not a sparrow or a crow, during the rest of her walk. She steadied her feet across an arid creek bed and advanced along the river, past the small pool where at summer's end the trout came to their final resting place, their slick bodies beaten and bruised by the rocks. Hanna ran her boot along the icy rime underfoot. Just because the frost hid the ground from sight, it didn't mean the trees weren't busy. Underneath, their roots were growing, entwining, grasping hold of anything and everything within their reach. These woods were different than when Hanna last set foot in them. Hanna was different. Change, however gradual, had proven inescapable. It had proven real.

Above, the sun was rising. Hanna was due at Edwin's soon. She had little time to spend imagining tree roots interlinking and coronating birds of prey. Hanna secured the cloth over the salad bowl, buttoned up her jacket and pressed on.

It had been years since Hanna last crossed Edwin's doorstep. She could remember visiting often as a young girl. Back then both families breakfasted together, they gathered wild berries on the day of the Creator's birth and, in the warmest of months, played shuttlecock in Edwin's backyard. Eleven-year-old Hanna had joined Edwin's wives in making wine, squeezing the grapes with her hands, her arms elbow-deep in the cask. Hanna would leave Edwin's home with her skin stained red and Jotham wouldn't say a word. He even participated once, picking up a ladle and stirring the grapes until their form faded into mire and the purples and reds melded into one nebulous color. Together, Edwin and Jotham used an apparatus to test how much sugar was in the juice. The two old friends stood side by side, quite serious about their task, exchanging the kinds of whispers patriarchs don't share with their families.

Hanna distrusted those memories now. She wasn't sure when things changed. Perhaps it was as recently as this past autumn, perhaps earlier. But when she recalled those times, all she saw was her youthful naiveté, her inability to judge the intentions of grown men.

After that last trip to make wine, Jotham's family never visited again. No one, not even Kara, said a word on the subject. Hanna was left completely in the dark and she would have stayed that way had she not overheard one of Jotham's late-night drunken ramblings. It was two seasons ago, as summer wound down, the air still warm late into the day, the sun hanging in the sky long after the children's bedtime, when Hanna heard yelling downstairs. She crept out of bed and tiptoed to the top of the stairwell, where she heard Jotham's voice. Hanna couldn't tell if he was alone or if his wives were listening, and she dared not creep any farther down the stairs to find out. He was more intoxicated than usual, his speech slurred, monologuing in aimless, erratic sentences. Fragments rang out.

"He's a damn thief! We'd be rich now. *I'd* be rich now if Edwin would have acted with a little honor . . . I was a man of opportunity and now look at me . . . You can tell everything about a man by the way he conducts business."

The yelling stopped. Jotham's irate words still rang in Hanna's ears when she heard him collapse heavily into a chair. His voice softened. It was barely audible, almost pensive. "I'm going to make everything right . . . Paul will see. Edwin will see . . . I didn't do this all for nothing. The world is at the feet of he who holds the gold."

That was all Hanna could make out before Jotham stumbled toward the liquor cabinet, sending her dashing down the hallway and back to bed. What Jotham meant by *he who holds the gold,* Hanna didn't know. But one thing was clear: Jotham and Edwin had once been business associates, their affiliation having fallen apart years ago, resulting in Edwin thriving and Jotham's family living in squalor, their friendship growing sour, setting invisible barriers between their two families. For Hanna and her siblings, it was simply understood that they would no longer visit Edwin's home. That understanding lasted six long years, six years in which the two families saw each other only at church and the marketplace, the children meeting up only on the school yard. The families had once been so close that Hanna had considered Edwin's children to be her cousins, none of whom she regularly spoke to now, some whose names she couldn't recall. The older children would not be attending lunch at Edwin's home that afternoon. It would be Hanna, Edwin and his four wives.

Hanna finally arrived at Edwin's property. His residence was four times the size of Jotham's house, perhaps more, and it had a modern look, with a large, looming archway over the front door, brick pillars securing it to the ground and three chimneys that reached into the sky. Fresh caramel-colored paint coated its wooden exterior. Hanna counted eleven windows at the front of the house and, she imagined, dozens more on the other sides. Outside, hand-painted lanterns bookended the front veranda.

Perhaps it was the brightness of the lanterns or maybe it was the sheer size of Edwin's home, but there was a warmth to this house. Hanna imagined it had central heating and vents that pumped in warm air like those in Clearhaven's new church. Jotham's house had radiators in most of its rooms, some which routinely malfunctioned, others which had stopped working altogether. These radiators had long been the bane of the family's existence, shutting off inexplicably in the middle of the night or refusing to function at all, leaving Kara and Belinda to worry about the pipes freezing in the dead of winter. Hanna was often tasked with running the water every hour as Belinda hammered away at the base of the kitchen radiator with a mallet, while Jotham — hobbled by his bad back — stood over top of her and barked out counterintuitive instructions. Oddly, the radiator in the children's bedroom worked only when the one in the living room downstairs had been turned off completely. Hanna discovered this through trial and error and would often find herself enduring the lighthearted teasing of her siblings as she fiddled with the radiator upstairs while waiting for the downstairs one to grow cold.

Edwin's house looked like it experienced no such problems; even outdoors, where three cars were lined up along the gravel road, there was order and cleanliness, a lack of the ramshackle that was apparent with a passing glance. Past the vehicles was a pond with its edges frozen over and clear black water in its center. The veranda extended from the side of the house all the way to an enclosed gazebo where Hanna counted six claw-footed wicker chairs, each wrapped in heavy blankets to preserve them from the cold. She pictured this place in the summer, with the little ones splashing knee-deep in the pond as Edwin's wives kept a close eye from under the gazebo's shade. It was not an unpleasant thought: the life this family must lead.

Hanna walked up to the doorstep, her heart surprising her by pacing in her chest. She knocked three times and then stepped back. Edwin's first wife, Fiona, opened the door.

"Come in. You brought a salad? How thoughtful," Fiona said. She took the salad bowl and Hanna stepped inside, the heat enveloping her as she crossed the threshold. Her winter coat suddenly felt too warm. The lights inside too bright.

Fiona embraced Hanna, shoulder to shoulder. "You know everyone, don't you?"

Behind her, Edwin's three other wives were waiting, one holding a baby with a belly the size of a watermelon. First, a tall woman named Sage gave her a cold embrace. Then a short woman (whose name Hanna couldn't remember) introduced Hanna to her baby, a little boy with cookie crumbs on his cheeks and fingernail scratches across his forehead. Hanna wasn't sure whether to hold the child or take his little hand. All she wanted to do was take off her coat. She was just about to unbutton it when Paedyn, the woman who'd been so interested in her wedding dress, approached — arms outstretched — and enveloped Hanna in a tight embrace. She held on for quite some time before saying, "Welcome to our home," and assisting Hanna with her coat.

Hanna finally felt like she could breathe when four toddlers approached, three boys and a girl all too young to go to school. Each presented her with artwork they'd made that morning. Hanna took the pages covered in paint and pastels and oohed and aahed at each one. "A whole family of budding artists," she said. The little girl insisted on holding Hanna's hand and leading her to a playroom at the back of the house where children's toys were scattered about. The girl hopped on a rocking horse and beckoned Hanna to join her.

"I can't," Hanna said. "I weigh as much as a giant boulder. I might crush your toy."

Little Celeste looked at her, stone-faced, and said, "Cake makes you fat," to which Hanna was too stunned to reply. She placed her hand on her stomach. Hanna certainly wasn't fat. There was hardly an extra ounce on her body. But she could imagine how life in this place, with summers spent sitting by the pond, might make her so.

Hanna watched the little girl rock back and forth. Celeste reminded her so much of Ahmre that she couldn't help but think that many of the things she would miss from home might be almost identical in Edwin's house. The little girl hopped off her rocking horse and picked up a stuffed bear. "Do you like it here?" Hanna said. When Celeste didn't respond, Hanna said, "I remember your father from when I was a little girl. He used to do silly things to make me laugh, like pushing carrot sticks up into his nose."

Celeste smiled. "He still does that."

"What about your mothers? Are they nice?"

"I only have one mother."

"Your sister-mothers, then. What are they like?"

Celeste picked at her stuffed bear's ear. "Mostly they're nice."

Hanna glanced down the empty hallway. She sat cross-legged next to the girl. "But . . . ?" she said, leading her along. Celeste still didn't respond. "You can tell me. I'll keep it a secret," Hanna said, crossing her heart. "I promise."

"It's my sister-mother. Sometimes she —"

Fiona appeared in the door frame, startling Hanna and silencing the girl. Hanna wasn't sure how long she'd been standing

112

there, how much of their conversation she'd overhead. "Celeste, I have to steal your playmate away. There will be time to play with Hanna next week."

The little girl shook her head no. Her eyes quivered and her cheeks puffed up.

Hanna took her hand. "Did you know I'm going to live in this house?"

"Why?"

"I'm going to marry your father. I'm going to marry Edwin," Hanna said. As the words left her mouth for the first time, she realized the inescapable reality of her engagement. Hanna was surprised how readily it slipped off her tongue.

Celeste tilted her head to the side. "Why?"

Hanna paused, unsure of the answer herself. A truthful response would require a conversation about the birds and the bees, reproduction, the Creator and Brother Paul, whatever Edwin had promised Jotham. She ran her hand through the girl's hair, gently, maternally. "I like your bear," she said, changing the subject.

Celeste grinned and squeezed her stuffed bear tightly. "Let's have a tea party."

Hanna could feel Fiona's gaze in the back of her head. "Next week," she said.

"Do you promise?"

"I promise," Hanna said quickly, without

a thought as to what the promise meant. "Also, I'll make sure I say goodbye before I leave today."

The girl turned to play with a puzzle in the corner, and Fiona walked Hanna down the hall. "I must apologize for the state of that room," she said. "In every home there must be a single spot of disarray so order may reign over the rest. Now, let me take you to your bedroom."

Hanna followed Fiona through a sitting room and down a hallway. Along the way, it occurred to her how fresh the air smelled. Back at home, Jotham's house held a veritable motley of aromas: the living room smelled of campfire and tree bark, the upstairs bathroom of mildew, the pantry of dew and the stairwell of crushed charcoal. Edwin's house didn't have a discernible odor. *This is what cleanliness smells like,* she thought. *Perhaps this is what wealth smells like.*

As she walked, Hanna peered in three open doorways, briefly, so as not to have prying eyes. All three contained a bed and a night table. The beds were made, the hardwood floors swept. "Whose rooms are these?" Hanna asked. But while Fiona was a few steps away and could clearly hear her, she didn't respond. Fiona ran her finger along the hallway's crown moldings and examined them for dust.

"We try to keep the hallways uncluttered and encourage the children to limit noise to their playroom and the backyard," Fiona said. She paused to briefly make eye contact and then kept walking. "Keeping children well behaved isn't always practical, but in this house we aspire to a certain amount of structure."

Fiona led Hanna into the downstairs sitting room, which was tidy as well, its walls lined with mounted animal heads: a massive moose surrounded by four deer, the creatures stuffed, faces intact, their dim gray eyes equal parts knowing and naive. The moose's fur was surprisingly smooth, like brown silk, and the deer to its left had its head tilted, looking away, as though searching for something. Underneath the animals, a shotgun sat unfastened in its mount.

Hanna leaned against the sofa. The upholstery felt new, the fabric smooth to the touch, in stark contrast to the tattered couches in Jotham's house. Since the tour began, the only item she'd noticed out of place was a single teething ring lying next to the leather ottoman at her feet. Hanna took in the expansive room with its simple yet elegant decor. The size of Edwin's home was daunting, the thought that soon she'd be walking these halls each day overwhelming.

"There are six bathrooms in the household," Fiona said and opened a closet door to show Hanna where the toiletries were kept.

"Which bathroom will I use?"

Fiona gave Hanna an icy look. "Patience, child," she said, her expression thawing slightly. "We'll get to that soon enough."

She took Hanna on an extensive tour of the pantry, where she described the organization and arrangement of the family's dried goods before finally leading Hanna up a stairwell and down another hallway. Fiona opened a door to reveal a rectangular room with a bed and a lamp and a bookshelf. A wide window overlooked the backyard, with a neighbor's house nearby and, in the distance, the marsh; its lily pads looked like little green pebbles from this far away.

"This will be your room."

"My room alone?"

"Yes," Fiona said.

Hanna found herself speechless. She stepped inside and spread her arms. Hanna imagined waking up to the sunlight, lying in bed alone with her blankets to herself.

"This is your linen," Fiona said, pointing

to a stack of sheets and a sashed four-patch quilt folded neatly on a chair in the corner. "We wash the bedding on the first of every month and I do ask that you keep the room tidy in the interim." Fiona motioned toward an empty corner. "There's room in here for a bassinet, should you prove fertile."

Hanna's heart dropped into her stomach. In the events surrounding her engagement to Edwin, in the private meeting in Brother Paul's office, in Jotham's lectures on how she was to behave, in her mother's quiet, consoling words — not a single person had expressly told her it was her job to get pregnant. That she was expected to be fertile. To multiply. To push little Edwins out of her womb and into the world.

Hanna twitched in her skin. Since the moment she set foot in Edwin's house, Hanna had been tiptoeing around Fiona, daunted by the authority in her voice and her position in the house, when all along she should have been peppering Fiona with questions, probing this stiff, imperious woman for insight into what life was really like here. Hanna longed desperately to make herself heard, to stop following Fiona around like an obedient basset hound and force the woman to be honest with her. Only, Hanna couldn't find a break in the conversation, a

117

suitable opportunity to speak up. And now to hear Fiona casually state what everyone else had long implied — that she was to lie with Edwin as husband and wife, that Hanna was to make as many babies as Edwin saw fit — it was all too much.

Hanna searched the woman's heart-shaped face. She tried to get behind Fiona's eyes, to see whether Fiona wanted her here; whether she'd been dreading Hanna's visit or looking forward to it; what was to come when they inhabited the same walls, when they ate together, raised children together, became accustomed to each other's moods and mannerisms. Fiona might have felt just like Hanna did on the inside, biting her tongue, fighting the urge to speak her mind with every fiber of her being. Only, the woman's gaze was like a wall.

Fiona motioned to a door in the corner of the room. "That is your wash closet," she said and opened the door to reveal a small bathroom with a toilet, a sink and a tall brass bathtub. Bottles lined the shelf above the tub, five of them, each a different color: pink, green, purple, yellow and white. From a cursory glance, Hanna imagined they contained soaps and lotions similar to that blue bottle of shampoo Jotham had tossed onto the kitchen table months ago, only these were curved in ornamental shapes, with prominent labels and exotic designs. Hanna resisted the urge to pick each bottle up, to lift the cap and smell the fragrance within, to test the bottles' weights by shaking them.

An oval mirror hung over the sink and beside that was a painting of a faceless woman carrying a pot on top of her head. The rendering was strikingly realistic, down to the bales of hay bookending the village pathway and the long, sinewy crack in the pot atop the woman's head. Hanna stepped closer, enrapt by the woman's missing features. She wondered who had chosen this painting. Whether they'd done it with any foresight: placing the painting of a faceless woman in the wash closet of a child bride, a young woman unfinished, the lion's share of her journey still ahead.

"Do you like it?" Fiona asked.

"The painting?"

"The wash closet."

"It's mine?" Hanna said.

"Yes, dear. It's yours to use alone."

Had this been any other day, and Hanna had learned of a secret bathroom in Jotham's house, an offshoot only she knew about containing a bathroom in which one could sit for more than thirty seconds without a small child's inquisitive fingers appearing under the crack in the door, a smile would have spread over her face. Hanna would have danced with joy. Having her own bathroom was the extravagance of all extravagances. It was a dream come true. But a dream that came in the apex of a nightmare.

Hanna lifted a sandwich to her mouth and took a bite.

"It's been years, hasn't it?" Paedyn said.

The women were sitting at the dining room table, eating sandwiches and salad. There was orange juice in a carafe, fresh-baked rolls and a fruit plate in the center of the table. The toddlers were eating separately on a small table in the next room. Hanna had been doing everything in her power not to gorge like a savage on this wonderful feast, and now Paedyn was asking a question while she had her mouth full.

Hanna swallowed and endeavored a smile. "It's been six years since my last visit."

"If only Edwin and Jotham got along like they used to. For years, decades even, they were like brothers," Paedyn said. She was eating her sandwich with a knife and fork, careful not to spill a single crumb onto her dress. She was about to speak again when

120

Fiona cleared her throat. She met Paedyn's gaze and Paedyn turned her attention back to methodically carving her sandwich.

The tall woman across from Hanna took a sip from her glass. Sage was drinking wine, red wine — dark and crimson and aromatic — even though it was just past noon. "I have to admit," she said, "I was surprised when Jotham and Edwin agreed to your union. Maybe *surprised* is the wrong word. I mean, look at you."

At first Hanna blushed, thinking perhaps she was offering a compliment. But as the words hung in the air, as Edwin's wife swirled her wineglass and ran her tongue along her teeth one by one, the slow realization set in: Sage wasn't flattering Hanna. She was implying there was something tawdry about Hanna's appearance. This woman, with whom Edwin spent his days and nights, didn't want Hanna at her table any more than Hanna wanted to be there. Hanna picked at her fingernails. She focused on the mechanics of chewing her food, on not allowing herself to be baited, on what might come next.

Sage continued. "But after everything that happened, their business dealings, with Jotham coming away with — how do I say this delicately? — such a meager return, and

Edwin having all this —" she motioned around the room, at the house, the tall ceiling overhead "— it's a wonder they worked out an arrangement."

All four women looked at Hanna.

"I wouldn't know," she said. "My father doesn't speak about such things."

In truth, Hanna knew few specifics about Jotham and Edwin's past business dealings. She knew even less about the work Edwin did now. Hanna assumed it had something to do with construction. Whether that meant actually picking up a hammer and a nail or whether he was the person in charge, no one had ever said. She did know — from hearing her sister-mother Katherine gossiping out the window — that Edwin's work took him along The Road and outside Clearhaven's borders.

Sage finished her wine and poured herself another glass. "It must have been difficult for Jotham, with Edwin tossing him aside like . . . what do people toss aside? Trash. That's it."

Hanna's cheeks flushed redder. She attempted to come up with a rebuttal, something clever or affecting, an indisputable truth to refute the woman's wicked words. Nothing came to her. Hanna didn't know how her family had descended into poverty, and she couldn't defend Jotham if her life depended on it.

Sage swallowed another mouthful of wine. During the whole lunch, not a peep emerged from the short woman to Hanna's left. She drank her juice and took chipmunk-sized bites of her food, never looking up from her plate. If that young man, Daniel, thought Hanna had a habit of looking down at her feet, he should have spent five minutes with Edwin's third wife. Hanna thought of Daniel now, those stray strands of hair falling across his forehead, his lanky arms. She wondered if he really was sitting by the pier at the old Grierson place.

Paedyn motioned to the salad Hanna had brought. "Did you grow these vegetables yourself?" she asked.

Hanna looked up from her food, at the forkful of spinach in Paedyn's hand. "Our garden froze over with winter. These are from the marketplace."

"Really? From the marketplace?" Sage asked, reaching for the wine bottle again. "That's quite an expense at this time of year. Quite an expense."

Hanna glanced at Paedyn eating the last bite of her sandwich, at Fiona's impenetrable expression, at the short woman poking at her food like a mouse. She thought of a half-dozen responses: *I don't handle the finances; I wouldn't know; Who are you to say such things?* But the response that emerged was hasty, without restraint, her voice flush with more youthful naiveté than she intended.

"We're not poor," Hanna said.

"No one said you were, dear," Fiona said.

Hanna peered in the direction of the front door. "When is Edwin arriving?"

"He'll be home soon. He wanted us to get to know each other first."

"Yes, Hanna. Let's get to know each other." Sage set her glass down and leaned forward, grinning like a fox. The tall woman's words sniped the air. "Tell us about yourself. I bet you're . . . fascinating."

The room turned hot. Hanna's heartbeat hastened. Silence reigned. Then the short woman chortled, a short snicker that got caught in her throat. She looked at her fellow sister-wife across the table and they both howled with laughter.

Paedyn set down her knife and fork. "Come, Hanna, you can help me with the dishes."

Hanna joined Paedyn by the kitchen sink, scrubbing plates and then drying them, separating the leftovers that could be pre-

124

served and discarding the rest. Hanna found herself stealing glances at the woman's raindrop eyes and her pointed, elfin chin. She wasn't sure why — instinct, perhaps — but Hanna suspected Paedyn was the barren wife, the one Jessamina had called "dry like sand."

Paedyn bore down on a serving platter with a scrub brush. "Never mind those two. They're trying to get a rise out of you," she said.

"It felt like more than that."

Paedyn set the scrub brush aside and touched the ends of Hanna's hair. "I've never seen a color quite like this before. It's lovely."

That red glow returned to Hanna's cheeks. Paedyn spent the next few minutes trying to convince Hanna to cut her hair short in the front and leave it long at the back; an "easy style to maintain," she said. Hanna had seen this hairstyle on dozens of women at church. In fact, her sister-mother Katherine had recently cut her hair in this style. Hanna nodded and grinned, but she had no desire for her hair to look like a boy's up front, whether it was considered manageable or not.

"Do you like your room?" Paedyn said.

"Very much," Hanna said, drying Belinda's bowl with a dish towel. "It's more than I ever expected."

Paedyn leaned in close. "We don't always sleep in our rooms."

"Do you sleep with the children?"

Paedyn glanced back toward the dining room. One woman had the big-bellied baby in her hands and the wives were discussing whether he'd been getting enough milk.

"No. We sleep with Edwin," she said. "I doubt Fiona told you, and may the Creator bless her soul for keeping you in the dark. I just don't want you to be surprised." Paedyn drew close and Hanna could smell the soap from her morning bath. She whispered. "He doesn't lie with us separately, in the dark, like most men do. We all pleasure him together. We watch. We each . . . participate. With him. With each other."

Hanna dropped the salad bowl. It crashed to the floor with a terrible clatter and then rolled to the center of the room, where it spun in a circle. The women entered the kitchen and Hanna felt their eyes upon her. Finally, the bowl settled. Hanna meant to step forward, she meant to pick it up, but her legs turned to stone.

Fiona approached, a mixture of concern and consternation in her guarded eyes. "Is everything okay?"

"I'm so sorry," Hanna said. She picked up the bowl and then stood perfectly still.

Hanna wanted to storm out of Edwin's house right away, to march straight to the church, to barge uninvited into Brother Paul's office and demand to speak to him. This was not what he'd told her last week. What Paedyn described wasn't how men had relations with their wives. It was depraved. It was against nature.

"Don't be sorry. I'm quite clumsy myself sometimes," Paedyn said.

She placed her hand on Hanna's back and when she did, the woman's hair brushed delicately, almost tenderly, against Hanna's arm. Hanna shuddered. She became suddenly aware of her skin, her dress, the damp ceramic bowl in her hands, and the more aware she became, the more her eyesight grew murky. Specks of orange glistened in the air and, beyond them, skeletons: skeletons in the women's faces, in the outline of Paedyn's hair, in the papered walls. Hanna saw their long, emaciated cheekbones, the vertebrae jutting out of the tall woman's back like a patch of prickly metallic thorns; she saw Paedyn's hair as a thousand brown strands seeping like creeping vines. She struggled to catch her breath. Hanna needed to escape, to run to the bathroom and splash cold water on her face, to find some way to compose herself. She was about to step away when wheels sounded on the gravel outside.

The women turned to see Edwin's truck pull into the driveway.

The next twenty minutes passed quickly. Edwin entered. He kissed his wives and hugged his children. Sage hastily hid her wine as Edwin embraced Hanna, planting a single kiss on her wrist. He insisted on giving Hanna a second tour of the house and Hanna walked from room to room with him, listening to Edwin describe the stones he'd selected to refurbish the fireplace and his thoughts on hickory rather than oak for his hardwood floors. The adults reconvened at the front door again and Fiona was suddenly all smiles as Hanna buttoned up her jacket. She held Hanna gently by her arms and thanked her for coming. Hanna, feeling Edwin's eyes upon her, thanked Fiona "for a wonderful visit" and then slipped on her boots and stepped outside. As the wives waved goodbye, Paedyn called out how she'd love to help with the wedding preparations. Then the door closed and Hanna found herself standing across from Edwin, the two of them alone.

Hanna fidgeted nervously. She dragged her boots along the gravel underfoot. As the sound grew louder, Edwin looked down at her feet and she stopped. He was on his way back to work and Hanna was affording him a wary gaze. The musky smell of sawdust hovered about Edwin like a fog, threatening to overpower her. Hanna pushed her mind into his and saw him looking at her like a ripened plum; she could see his sharpened teeth impatiently anticipating that first bite. The longer they stood facing each other, the more Hanna's stomach twisted in knots.

"I know this is difficult for you," he said. "I hope to make your transition from daughter to wife as easy as possible. You know, when your father brought you home, you were the cutest, softest little baby I'd ever seen, with your little bald head and these tiny feet that never stopped moving. I like to think I had a hand in raising you in your early years and that Jotham and Kara have done a wonderful job. You've grown into a beautiful, intelligent young woman and I know I can provide a good home for you, if you'll let me."

A pang of remorse shot through Hanna's chest. Ever since Edwin arrived, she'd been finding fault in the way he looked, the way he carried himself — things Edwin couldn't control. Now here he was, saying he would take care of her, that he admired her. She felt she needed to apologize, and she almost did, only something Edwin said struck a chord inside her.

"What do you mean — my father brought me home? I thought I was born in my mother's bedroom. The midwife was there," Hanna said. "Was I born in a hospital? Was I born in the big city?"

Edwin stammered.

"Of course not. You were born at home, as all children in Clearhaven are born." His voice regained its strength. "What I meant to say was when your father brought you to *my* home." He touched Hanna's elbow. "It is a home, you know. And we'll be glad to have you as part of it."

Hanna's mind spun, unsure whether to be comforted or outraged by Edwin's sudden attempt at kindness. Edwin seemed to sense her unease. He didn't try to kiss her. He didn't lean in for another hug. All the same, Hanna positioned Belinda's salad bowl in front of her pelvis, to deflect him if need be. A yard away, a large dog was standing in the back of Edwin's pickup truck, the animal's brown hair freckled white. Above, gray clouds marbled the midday sky, the tall trees encircling her and Edwin, confining them, heightening how alone they were in that moment. Hanna imagined what they looked like from above, the two strange bedfellows, the middle-aged man and his teenage bride. She delved deeper into her imagination and pictured Daniel standing in Edwin's place, his dark blue jeans, the casual way he spoke as though they were long-lost friends, the music from his earphones, redemption. What would Jotham have said if he'd spotted the two of them together? What would Brother Paul say?

"Hanna?"

It was Edwin, standing closer now, his eyebrows busheled together.

"I'm sorry. I was lost in my head," Hanna said.

"Are you sure you don't want me to drive you home?"

Hanna envisioned a second goodbye, this one as she stepped out of Edwin's truck and onto Jotham's driveway, the entire family lined up at the window to see. She pictured Edwin spotting their audience and stepping out to take her hand. Wrapping his arm around her back and slow-dancing with her while Hanna's sister-mother Katherine cheered deliriously from the front porch. Hanna struggling to keep her revulsion at bay. She tried to imagine anything else.

Hanna thought about Emily and how her sister was attending school without her, whether Charliss was watching over his siblings. She thought about her mother back home, the emotion in her voice last night. For the third time today, that young man, Daniel, slipped to the forefront of Hanna's mind. She wondered what he would make of Edwin's wives, whether one of Daniel's sister-mothers also hid her wine the moment his father came home, whether Daniel would ever take her hand and dance with her cheek-to-cheek. Hanna looked down the street and not in the direction of Jotham's house.

"Thank you, but I could use the walk."

Edwin stepped into his truck. "Be safe."

"I will. And thank you for lunch, for everything," she said.

Edwin's truck pulled away and faded until it was a small blue speck in the distance. Then it disappeared entirely. Hanna fastened the last few buttons on her jacket. She took a final look at the big house she would soon call home and then stepped with purpose down the driveway.

9

As Hanna's foot touched the woodlands' edge, a gust of wind sailed through the trees, surging over the sound of the stream trickling nearby. Above, the treetops tilted toward her. Twice this winter Hanna had seen the same phenomenon. She'd noticed it in autumn, as far back as last spring, as well. Whichever way she looked — north, south, east or west — the breeze was pushing the trees toward the center of town. It was as though Clearhaven, a city alone, ardent in its disavowal of the outside world, inhabited the center of a vortex. What shocked Hanna wasn't how this was possible but rather how long she'd gone without noticing. She felt like a person living at the base of a mountain who, after years of blissful ignorance, had finally looked up to see the enormity standing beside her.

She thought back to just days ago. Who was that person who agreed to marry a grown man? And Hanna *did* agree — she realized that now — through her inaction, through her inability to muster the courage to defy Jotham and Brother Paul. She couldn't pinpoint the exact moment when she opened her eyes and saw the mountain standing beside her. But there it was, surrounding her on all sides — mammoth, insurmountable, and starting to cave in.

Hanna pictured herself a month from now, settling into Edwin's home, preparing supper along with his other wives. Their combative conversation. Paedyn's delicate hand touching her back. The tall woman's spiteful barbs. Only six sleeps remained until her wedding day. Time was now sprinting by. Even this moment, alone in the woods, listening to the starlings' coo and watching a chipmunk scamper behind a shrub, had become precious.

Her mother would be expecting her soon. Kara was probably watching through the window, anticipating her arrival. Perhaps Jotham was at her side, Jotham whose shadowy figure swayed back and forth in the rocking chair, his outstretched hand chasing its courage. Beyond the path and past the riverbed was the old Grierson place. Time was a clock in the sky, ticking away.

Hanna pictured Daniel leaning against the outer church wall, those wisps of hair dangling across his forehead. She recalled his conversation, the thoughts he'd shared. As much as she wanted to go to him today, she'd never been so bold before. Her hands became clammy and her chest nervous and warm at the thought, not just of defying Jotham's expectations by visiting a strange boy but of carrying the guilt with her, of sitting down at the supper table tonight with her family and knowing she'd been deceitful. Hanna imagined Emily finding out, her sister's eyes growing wide and then turning sharp, Emily accusing her of being false-hearted and untrustworthy. By calling upon Daniel, Hanna would be defying the Creator. She'd be confirming what she'd long believed: that she didn't *understand* the way Brother Paul expected her to. Hanna would be failing her family, her fiancé, what she'd been taught her entire life.

But by not visiting Daniel, she'd be failing herself.

Hanna quickened her step and set down the path to the old Grierson place.

She spotted the smoke from a mile away, puffing like melted sugar cakes piled one on top of another, until it faded and finally dissolved into the gray-blue sky. As Hanna ap-

135

proached, her heart beat faster. Her breathing quickened. Hanna's stomach started to churn, in disbelief that she was really going through with this.

She saw the fire pit at the edge of the pier, its flames standing almost two feet high. In the backyard was a small lake, too deep to stand in but narrow enough that a child could easily swim across. Hanna remembered this pool of water from when she was just a girl. When the rains came heavy in autumn, the lake would overflow and swallow the pier whole. It remained submerged until the water drained out into the marsh.

As she reached the driveway, Hanna passed a shiny blue truck. Compared to the rusted old jalopy Belinda drove, this vehicle looked state of the art. The back windows were tinted and Hanna could see her reflection in its glossy blue paint. It must have been only a few months old.

Past the truck, sitting close to the fire on a chair at the edge of the pier, was Daniel. Hanna saw the outline of his hair first, Daniel's profile against the ice-covered lake. He was playing a guitar, his fingers shifting smoothly along the strings. A nervous tremor shot through her as Hanna realized there was no turning back now.

At first Hanna could hardly make out the

sound of Daniel strumming his guitar. Her boots shuffled on the ground and in the distance, a loon was calling for a mate. As she drew closer, the melody became clear. He was playing on the higher strings, the pace alternating between fast and slow. The sound was beautiful like that of the viola one of Brother Paul's wives had played at the old tower cathedral, only less sad. Hanna found herself resisting the urge to hum along.

She stepped onto the deck and suddenly Daniel stopped playing.

He turned around, startled.

"I'm sorry. I didn't mean to surprise you."

"No. It's okay." He set the guitar down and stood up. "It's just, if I'd known you were here, I would have played better. I'm still learning."

"It sounded wonderful."

His gaze drifted to the salad bowl in her hands.

"I was at lunch," Hanna said. "It's my sister-mother's bowl. She might very well kill me if I lose it."

Daniel smiled and sat down on a blanket hanging over the edge of the pier. Hanna saw the empty space at his side. She understood the implicit invitation for her to sit next to him and wanted to think Daniel impudent for being so bold. But it was Hanna who had shown up at this boy's home unannounced, a week before her wedding. It was Hanna who'd been bold.

She set the salad bowl on the deck chair and sat down beside him. Hanna's feet dangled over the edge, an inch above the frozen lake. Up close the cracked ice reflected the light like slivers of stained glass, the water underneath black and, toward the center, almost purple. Hanna glanced over at Daniel, who hadn't said a word since he sat down. She had no idea what he was thinking, whether Daniel felt comfortable in the silence or whether his mind was racing, struggling to come up with something to say. All the same, she felt compelled to talk.

"You spend a lot of time outdoors."

Daniel motioned toward the old Grierson place. A patch of pine trees separated the house and the pier, yet they were close enough to see in through the windows. "It's weird inside my house these days," he said.

"How do you mean — weird?"

"It's hard to explain. My brothers have locked themselves in their rooms. They literally won't come out."

"Are they upset?"

"My dad's forcing them to move to the city. And they're furious about it."

"Are you leaving too?" Hanna said.

"My dad needs one of us to stay. It's really complicated." Daniel shook his head. "It's all Brother Paul's idea. I still don't know why he wants James and Kenneth to go."

"To eliminate the competition?"

"I'm sorry?"

Hanna stammered. Daniel was speaking so freely that she replied without thinking. Worse: these weren't her words. They were Jessamina's words coming out of Hanna's mouth. She composed herself as best she could. "My sister-mother Jessamina told me Brother Paul sends Clearhaven's young men out into the world to remove the competition for his middle-aged followers, so they can marry whomever they choose, as often as they wish. She says it's simple mathematics. If James and Kenneth were allowed to stay, then Brother Paul would have two more rivals to compete with. Your father would have two more rivals. *My father* would have two more. There wouldn't be enough young brides to go around."

"What do you believe?" Daniel said.

Hanna tapped the frosted lake with her boot. "It doesn't matter what I believe."

"Of course it matters what you believe. The only things that matter in life are what you do, what you say and what you believe,"

Daniel said, joining Hanna in pressing down on the ice underfoot.

Hanna watched him curiously. The boy she half remembered from a year ago was long gone. One moment Daniel's eyes would drift off into the distance and the next his gaze was fixed on her, hanging on Hanna's next word like the fate of the world hung in the balance. Hanna glanced over her shoulder to make sure no one was watching.

"Where are your parents?" she said.

"They're inside. My mom's taking a nap. She sleeps a lot. I think my dad's on the phone with Brother Paul again."

"What about your sister-mothers?" Hanna said.

"I'm not sure," Daniel said. "They're probably cleaning. They're always cleaning, even when the house isn't dirty."

"Don't you have any brothers or sisters for them to look after?" Hanna said. Her question wasn't really a question. She knew very well that Daniel had no younger siblings.

Daniel tousled his hair. He brushed the soft strands out of his eyes. "My parents had James, Kenneth and me, one, two, three, all a year apart. Then my dad had an accident. He was fixing his car in the garage and it slipped off the lift. He got hurt pretty badly."

"Oh no."

"Don't worry," Daniel said. "It was a long time ago. He's fine now. Well, mostly fine. After that, he couldn't have any more children."

"But he still decided to marry again?"

"Yes. I mean, he never really discussed it with me. It's not like we sit around the fireplace, smoking cigars and talking about his crushed pelvis and new wives. We don't have that kind of relationship."

"I didn't mean to pry. Or to be bold," Hanna said.

"That's okay," he said with a smile in the corner of his mouth. "I'll tell you if you're ever being a little too bold."

"Is that how people are in the big cities — bold?"

Daniel thought for a moment. "I don't know if I'd use that word. But there were definitely more people. In some places, the streets are teeming with them. And everything moves faster: the cars, the people, the conversation."

"What about the buildings?" Hanna said. "Are they really as tall as the sky?"

"Some of them. Some cities have buildings as far as the eye can see. The cities we

141

visited had skyscrapers taller than the old tower cathedral, buildings that reached all the way up into the clouds."

"That's impossible."

"Trust me," Daniel said, "it's possible. I saw it with my own two eyes."

"What else did you see?" she said and then immediately regretted posing yet another question. Daniel must have felt like she was interrogating him. "You don't have to tell me, if you don't want to."

Daniel rubbed his hands together to keep warm. "No. It's fine. I was really curious too." His eyes drifted upward into the hazy gray clouds and then back to Hanna again. "I did see something amazing a few months back. There was a street preacher at the corner of a busy intersection. He was standing on a wooden crate, calling out words from a book in his hand. It was like watching Brother Paul deliver a sermon, but people kept walking by not paying attention. As the preacher was talking, he saw a little old lady across the street in a wheelchair. I don't know how he knew her name, but he started calling to her. 'Angela! Angela!' he said. 'Rise and join me!' His voice was so loud that people stopped to watch. I stopped to watch. And then the most amazing thing happened. The old lady

— Angela — stood up out of her chair. She took a single shaky step and then another. Then she walked right into traffic. A car almost hit her. It screeched its tires and the driver honked its horn, but she didn't even look at it. She kept walking, her eyes glued to the street preacher.

"By now a crowd had formed. We all watched the lady shuffle toward the sidewalk. She almost stumbled as she stepped up to the curb, and then slowly, gradually, she reached the preacher. He stepped off his crate and took her in his arms and the entire crowd cheered."

"That really happened?" Hanna said.

Daniel nodded. "Right in front of me. My brother said it was probably a trick. You know, a way to get people to believe in something and give the street preacher money."

"I don't know. That sounds like a miracle to me."

Daniel raised his eyebrow. "There are no such things as miracles," he said. "Plus, the lady's name was Angela, which means angel. And as far as I've seen, there's no such thing as angels either."

"How can you know that for sure? It's a big world out there, and you only saw part of it."

"So you believe in angels and miracles?" Daniel said.

Hanna searched for the right words. "All I know is that if you don't believe in miracles, you'll never experience one."

Daniel looked at her curiously. The silence between them went on for quite some time until Hanna shied away from the young man's eyes. She reached back and plucked a single string on Daniel's guitar. A thin, metallic sound rang out across the frozen lake.

"Where did you learn to play guitar?" she said.

"A girl taught me during my family's trip."

"Oh."

"It wasn't like that," Daniel said. "She was old and hideous. She wore the same dirty, pink bathrobe every day and she had only one eyebrow." He ran his finger between his eyes. "And her breath smelled like onions. And you probably won't believe me, but her hair was gray, except on Sundays when it suddenly turned black."

Hanna smiled and then fought hard to turn her smile into a frown. "You're teasing me."

"I am."

"Why?"

"Because it makes you smile," he said. "At

least it makes you want to smile."

Hanna did smile this time. Above, a slight part appeared in the clouds, allowing the sunlight to glisten off the upstairs windows of the Griersons' old house. Hanna imagined Francis Rossiter peering through the glass, watching her, a telephone to his ear, reporting Hanna's whereabouts, her brazen behavior. All of a sudden, she felt an overwhelming urge to leave.

Hanna was about to stand up when Daniel picked up his guitar. For a brief moment, she thought he might serenade her, but then the young man brought the guitar to his lap and turned it over. He shook it until something inside fell against the strings. Daniel pulled out a single piece of folded paper.

"I wrote something for you," Daniel said.

"Like a letter?"

"More like a poem or a song," he said, unfolding the paper. "Do you want to read it?"

Hanna's stomach swirled. She strained to see the ink on the page. Somehow, she couldn't bring herself to take it from him. "You read it to me," she said.

He shifted one leg underneath the other. Daniel held up the paper and then read —

Champagne Girl
only you are sacred . . .
. . . the flickering aroma of your skin
leaps through
my naked voice
as I
whisper hard
a promise
to remember
your gentle
touch . . .

Daniel stopped and Hanna realized the poem was over. It went by so quickly that she barely had time to process it.

Daniel's eyes drifted to the plum-colored ice under their feet. "You don't like it," he said.

"No, of course I do."

"I was going to write some music to go with it, so it would be a song, not just words on paper . . ."

"When did you write this?" she said.

"Last night, after everyone went to bed."

"And I am?"

"The Champagne Girl." He looked down at the page. "*Champagne* is a French word for sparkling wine, the very best in the world."

Hanna's chest flushed. For the first time

this afternoon, the struggles of the day — Belinda's demands, Edwin's wives, the expectations of powerful men — slipped away. "Thank you," she said. "Truly, no one has ever done anything like that for me before."

Daniel smiled. He refolded the paper and held it between his hands.

Together they sat watching the water ripple under the ice. Slowly, inadvertently, Hanna's thoughts turned to Jotham, his bloodred eyes, that purple vein that throbbed in his forehead when he was hard at the drink, the screams of her brother Pratt as Jotham whipped him just days ago, the bruises Jotham had left on Charliss's back last month when Charliss accidentally broke a lighting fixture in the pantry. She pictured Daniel's parents bursting through the back door of their house, demanding to know why she was trespassing on their property. Hanna stood up quickly, without a word, and picked up Belinda's salad bowl from the deck chair.

"Leaving so soon?" Daniel said.

"I'm getting married."

"Not today, you're not," he said with a puckish grin.

Hanna gave him a look of disbelief. "You can't just throw around words like that in

147

this town."

The playful look slipped from his face. Daniel met Hanna eye to eye and his expression shifted further, becoming inquisitive and yet serious and unexpectedly empathic. He didn't say a word. He didn't have to. Hanna felt something inside her, like a voice had broken an unbearable silence. Everything — the air around her, the feel of the sun-warped boards under her feet, Hanna's awareness of her body, her flesh and blood and skin — intensified when Daniel was looking at her.

"We could both get in real trouble," Hanna said.

He folded his arms. Those strong, wiry hands wrapped around his elbows. "You're right," he said. "We could."

Hanna tore herself away. She stepped around the chair and walked quickly along the deck. Hanna didn't look back. But she wanted to. As her foot touched the dirt road, the words — *Champagne girl* — ran through her mind. She wanted to turn around, to see that look in Daniel's eyes, to speak to him one more time. Instead, she headed straight for home.

10

Hanna wrung her hands as she walked, twisting them, entwining them, grinding her knuckles from side to side. She had finally done something *she* wanted to do, not what Edwin wanted, not what Jotham or Brother Paul demanded, and she should have been elated, replaying the conversation with Daniel over again in her mind, reliving the feeling deep inside when he read the Champagne Girl poem. Instead, she couldn't stop thinking how close she'd probably come to getting caught. Mere minutes after departing Edwin's house, Hanna had gone to visit a young man she barely knew. And not just any young man; she'd visited the son of Brother Paul's benefactor. She'd sat beside him, spoken to him without a chaperone, shared confidences with him. All this with Daniel's parents inside their house, mere yards away. If Jotham found out, there was no telling what he would do.

For the life of her, Hanna couldn't imagine why Jotham had granted her this small freedom of traveling unaccompanied. At first she imagined it was part of some well-reasoned plan, perhaps a reward for her compliance in her engagement to Edwin. The longer Hanna walked, the more she thought it might simply have been a case of miscommunication. Perhaps Jotham believed that since Hanna was now betrothed, it was Edwin's responsibility to provide a chaperone. And perhaps Edwin was too busy with work and his own family to consider that Hanna was walking by herself.

She couldn't stop thinking that someone was testing her, that one of Brother Paul's cronies might be watching from the woods, reporting on her movements, making escape impossible. The very thought was irrational, paranoid even. Hanna was walking on a dirt road, forty minutes from Jotham's house. There wasn't a single person within earshot, not a wolf in sight. Hanna was alone. She was safe.

For as long as she could remember, there had always been someone at her side. In those early years, it was her mother. Later, it was Emily, the girl's breath and her young voice as much a part of the air as the sound of the pressing wind. Recently, it was little

Ahmre clinging to Hanna's hip. The solitude heightened her sensitivity. Without her sisters nearby, every crunch of frozen dirt under her boots, every swish of her arm against her warm winter jacket felt heightened, bordering on electric. Hanna found when life slowed down and she actually paid attention to the movement of her legs, her neck turning, her fingers curling into her palms, she felt slightly intoxicated. These were the moments in which Hanna most believed in an all-knowing power governing her life. It took being alone to sense a greater purpose.

She gazed at the ground beneath her feet and wondered what her brave other self might be doing on the other side of the world. Was she sitting next to a roaring fire, practicing her embroidery? Or was she in midflight, battling demons with a sword in her hand and vengeance in her eyes, protecting the meek and the weak alike? Hanna imagined a face identical to her own, wild and alive, a girl standing post-battle, chest heaving, legs strong, the blood of the vanquished flecked across her face, finally knowing and free.

She was fully in this fantastical dream world when a car approached her from behind. Hanna heard the vehicle from some distance and chose not to look back. If it was a neighbor or a friend from church, she could smile and wave as it approached, hope they didn't stop to ask where she'd been. If it was an out-of-towner on an unsanctioned visit to Clearhaven, she would turn her eyes away and pray they passed by without incident.

It turned out to be neither friend nor stranger. A blue-and-white police car pulled up alongside her. Hanna glanced over. Inside were Paul the Second and Paul the Third, Brother Paul's sons. Brother Paul had nine wives and twenty-one daughters. But he had only two sons and he'd named them both Paul, after himself. The way Hanna heard the story was that when they were young, a great confusion arose as to which Paul was being called to supper and which Paul was being admonished for sticking his fingers in the soup before anyone sat down to eat. Their father started calling them Paul the Second and Paul the Third, or quickly, Two and Three. They were seven and eight years older than Hanna respectively, two of the chosen ones: grown men who hadn't left Clearhaven to make their way in the world. The two Pauls still lived with their father and served as the only police force in town.

Hanna had disliked them since she was a little girl.

Paul the Second was the cruel one, the one who'd dipped Hanna's hair in ink when she was eight years old, the one who'd cut off a little girl's ponytail just to watch her cry. He'd grown up to look like a toughened, thick-chested version of his father, with deep-set lines on his forehead, patches of stubble on his chin and pomade comb lines forever adorning his hair. His brother, Paul the Third, was chubby and balding, like an off-kilter teapot always in danger of tipping over. Paul the Third wore a mustache that Charliss described as "four parts pubic hair and three parts bacon grease" and he perspired constantly. Paul the Third followed his older brother like a heavyset shadow and hardly said an unprompted word, which must have suited Paul the Second just fine because he couldn't stop talking.

The police car slowed to a crawl and Paul the Second stuck his head out the driver's side window. "Good afternoon, ma'am."

Hanna kept moving. His use of the word *ma'am* was clearly insincere. It was a ploy to trick her into bantering with him, a hopeless proposition.

"Whatcha doing out here all alone, girl?"

he said. "Does your father know where you are?"

Hanna rolled her tongue along the top of her mouth. The road underfoot was not a direct route between Edwin's and Jotham's homes, and Paul the Second was right to be suspicious. She couldn't explain being out here all alone in the middle of the day.

Paul the Third leaned past his brother. "What say we give you a ride, Hanna?"

"Thank you, but no," Hanna said. Her words came out quickly, forcefully, leaving no room for interpretation. Hanna made sure she stood upright and made eye contact when she spoke. Inside, however, that feeling of being slightly intoxicated with life dissolved into a tangle of anxious, stomach-turning knots.

She stepped away from the car and hastened her pace. Hanna only made it a few steps before the patrol car pulled up behind her, its front bumper dangerously close to the back of her legs. She stopped and glared at the brothers, who snickered under their breath. Hanna started again and the brothers followed, nearly bumping her with their headlight. Hanna looked around. The road was bordered by frozen woodlands. There would be no escaping the brothers Paul. They would follow her all the way to her doorstop if she let them, blaring their siren and flashing their lights, punctuating their gall with jeers and moronic laughter.

Hanna walked around to the open side window. "Do you promise to take me home?"

"We swear," they said in unison.

With no other option and against her better judgment, Hanna climbed into the back seat. The engine revved and the car started down the street.

Paul the Second was all smiles. "Do you know what I hate about winter?" he said. "The heavy jackets. It's impossible to see who's put on weight. Impossible to see who's . . . blossomed, if you get my meaning."

Hanna gazed out the window. "That must be very difficult for you. Your brain straining to use its imagination."

Paul ran his crooked teeth along his lower lip. He looked back at Hanna and his eyes narrowed into sharp, black slits. Immediately, Hanna regretted saying anything. She vowed not to speak unless spoken to for the rest of the trip.

They drove in silence until the police car reached a fork in the road. The semi-paved street to Jotham's house was to the left, clear of debris, stumps lining the road where

155

trees had been felled to let vehicles pass. The path on the right was swathed in tall, frost-tinged grass with leafless branches converging overhead, the ground still frozen, its texture unsullied by foot or car.

Paul the Second turned the wheel and headed down the remote path.

Hanna's eyebrows shot up. Her heart fluttered. "Where are we going?"

"Simmer down now." Paul the Second tilted the rearview mirror so Hanna could see his face. "It's not like we were out searching for lost little birds when we found you. We've got some official town business up here. Then we'll drive you home."

The car careened down a narrow slope. It lurched over a mound of stones.

"Drop me off here. I can walk," Hanna said. She pulled on her door handle, but it wouldn't open.

The car drove into a clearing and stopped next to a tree stump with a single hatchet jutting ominously from its frigid core, a throng of thorny, petrified saplings blocking out the sunlight. Paul the Second shut off the engine and leaned back in his seat. There wasn't another soul in sight.

A vision flooded Hanna's brain: of the brothers grabbing her from the back seat and throwing her to the ground, striking her, wrenching the hatchet from the stump and swinging it with abandon. Hanna fought the hysteria storming through her veins. Looking at the stark wilderness all around, she was convinced: Brother Paul *did* send them. Someone had witnessed Hanna's brazen visit to Daniel's pier and the brothers were here to administer the Creator's swift and merciless punishment. She took a quick breath and then another.

"You go this time," Paul the Second said to his brother. "I'll stay here with little Miss Tight Dress."

Paul the Third ran his fingers through his thick, moist mustache. He glanced back at Hanna before stepping out of the car. Without a word, the heavyset brother traipsed into the woods, toward a hazy plume of smoke over a hill in the distance. Now Hanna recognized where they were. The shack where she'd purchased Jotham's moonshine was nearby. Perhaps the brothers were telling the truth when they said they were here on town business, that they were going to shut down the old hermit's operation. Perhaps Brother Paul demanded a tax on all goods not sold at the marketplace. Or perhaps Paul the Third simply needed an excuse to wander off into the woods and leave her alone with his brother.

Paul the Second turned around and ran his fingers along the car seat. His musky odor filled the car, a pungent smell of dried sweat mixed with days-old cologne. He was so close; Hanna could see the little black dots along the bridge of his nose. She pressed her shoulder against the door, leaned as far away as possible. Hanna was as vulnerable as a calf and she knew it. Worse: Paul knew it.

"Let me go," she said.

He looked her up and down. "I don't think I'm gonna do that."

"I'll scream."

Paul the Second motioned out the window. "Scream all you want, little girl. Ain't nobody gonna hear you."

"What would Edwin say if he knew you had me out here? What would your father say?"

Paul the Second shoved a toothpick into the space between his front teeth. He pulled it out and examined it for debris. "Relax. I ain't gonna do nothing too bad. That is, unless you see fit to having me do it." He cast a glance in Hanna's direction and when she glared back, a smirk bent the corner of his mouth. "What we have here is a little one-on-one time. To get to know each other better."

"I know you perfectly well," Hanna said. "I've known you my whole life."

"Maybe that's true. Or maybe we're both different people now. People change all the time. Heck, sometimes I'm a different person than I was the day before. Maybe you and I'll be different people by the time we leave this car."

Hanna dug her fingernails into the car seat. The windows had covered in steam and she rubbed her shoulder against the glass to look outside. Paul the Third was nowhere in sight.

"You've got some big changes coming for you," Paul the Second said. "Becoming a woman, that's no small thing." He propped his elbows on his seat and leaned closer. "If I was less of a gentleman, I'd tell you about my first time. Let's just say it was a bad scene. Things got ugly, way uglier than anyone ever intended and nobody who entered that room left it unscathed. I've been thinking, though. About Edwin. About those wives of his. From what I hear — through the grapevine and whatnot — what I went through don't even compare to what you've got coming for you."

He bent his toothpick until the thin piece of wood snapped. Paul the Second leaned his seat back as far as it would go. In one swift motion, he slid to where he perched above her. Paul hovered. His pupils fixated on her.

Hanna's heart raced. Her hands trembled. She felt exposed, defenseless, wedged between the door and Paul's thick, muscular frame.

Calmly, deliberately, he rolled up his sleeves, baring his thick wrists and forearms. He reached forward and ran a finger along Hanna's collarbone, up along her neck, setting her hair on end.

"Don't," she said.

"Don't what? Don't stop?" he said. "You've got your mind in the wrong place. I'm only trying to help. It's that fiancé of yours you should be concerned about. Edwin might look like nothing, but what a man looks like on the outside don't tell you nothing about what's going on inside." Paul's thumb held her jaw in place. In a brief, swift motion, his finger parted Hanna's lips and felt the wet space in between. "Want to know what I'm thinking right now?"

A torrent of blood surged through Hanna's veins. It colored her face. Hanna pulled her shoulder off the door. If he was going to force himself upon her, if this entire abduction was leading to this moment, Hanna wouldn't shrink away. She wouldn't shudder in his presence.

She met his gaze. Hanna stared right through him. "Why don't you enlighten me?"

Paul the Second grinned, a sickening, duplicitous grin. A carnal glaze washed over his face. He leaned forward until he was almost on top of her. "I've been looking forward to enlightening you for years, little girl," he said.

Hanna balled her fingers into a fist. She tensed her arm and prepared to strike.

Just then, the passenger's side door flung open. A swoosh of cold air sailed in as Paul the Third sat his large backside in the passenger's seat, a bottle of moonshine in his hand. He looked from his brother to Hanna and then down at the driver's seat reclined all the way back. His brow crinkled. "Is everything okay?"

Paul the Second slid back toward the steering wheel, slippery like a snake. He pulled a lever and his seat shot upright again. "Never better," he said, cramming a new toothpick between his teeth.

"The windows are fogged up."

"It's called condensation, blockhead."

Paul the Second took the bottle from his brother's hands. He unplugged the cork and smelled the homemade hooch. "Woo-wee!" he hollered, his voice colliding off the windows. "Here, Hanna, take a whiff," he said. When she shook her head no, his eyes turned sharp. "We ain't leaving until you do."

Hanna looked to Paul the Third, who nodded with his jowls. Paul the Second pressed the bottle up to her face. She breathed in the pungent odor, like corn syrup mixed with gasoline. The bitter stench flooded her nose and Hanna coughed to the delight of both brothers. They howled and Paul the Second insisted she smell it a second time before replacing the cork. He fired up the engine and drove back the way they came, the brothers' sophomoric snickering filling the car.

Soon Jotham's house came into view. The car slowed down as it reached the driveway, the doors unlocked and Hanna climbed out the moment it came to a stop. She was only partially surprised when Paul the Second stepped out and leaned against the front headlight. Hanna was already three yards away.

"Ain't you gonna thank us for the ride?" he said.

Hanna stopped in her tracks. He was probably expecting her to flash him an angry glare or for her to break down in tears, to show he'd affected her in some way. Hanna wouldn't give him the satisfaction.

"Thank you. It was very considerate of you," she said.

Paul the Second ran his hand across his unshaven chin and Hanna could hear the sound of the stubble scratching under Paul's thumb. His brother stepped out of the car and they exchanged a look. Paul the Second hitched his thumbs in his belt.

"I can play this cat-and-mouse game all day."

"If you were a cat, you'd have a bell around your neck. And all the mice would hear you coming," Hanna said.

"Your wedding night's not for six days," he said. "A lot can happen in a week's time." Paul shifted his belt buckle and looked down at his pelvis. His voice slid to a sinister whisper. "I didn't have time to show you back in the woods, but I've got something here for you. The past couple years, it's been thinking about you at night."

Hanna stopped at her front door. She knew she should turn around and walk inside, that any reply would only encourage him. But she couldn't help herself. She looked Paul straight in the eye. Then down at his pants.

"I'm surprised."

"Is that so?"

"Yes. I'm surprised you can keep that thing out of your brother's loving embrace long enough for it to think about me," she said.

They locked eyes and Hanna saw the fire seething in Paul the Second's black gaze. Instantly, she regretted her words. This wasn't a game to him. And Hanna knew it wouldn't end well for her the next time they crossed paths. Quickly, she opened Jotham's front door. Hanna stepped inside, fastened the lock and pressed her back against the door frame, terrified that the next sound she'd hear would be the two Pauls stomping up her front steps and barging inside. Instead, they opened and shut their car doors. The engine revved, the wheels turned on the gravel road and the two brothers drove off the property.

It was only after they'd left that Hanna realized she'd forgotten Belinda's salad bowl in the back seat of the brothers' car.

11

The foyer was empty. Hanna could hear the children in the living room, Kara and Katherine in the kitchen, clanking spoons, husking and chopping as they prepared the family's supper. Hanna was surprised when none of them ran up to her, that no one had been watching through the window eager to ask about her visit to Edwin's house.

She stepped into the front alcove and took off her jacket. In the fireplace, orange embers smoldered under the metal grate, its misshapen frame thick with soot, the singed remains of kindling jutting from a mound of white-gray ashes. The cracks had widened in the ceiling above, the leak in the rooftop in dire need of repair. Hanna removed her boots and hurried down the hallway, desperate to see her sisters, to hug her mother, to do anything except think about her interaction with the two Pauls. She found the children in the living room writing in their journals from school. Charliss was sitting cross-legged on the floor, helping his brothers with their spelling, all of them too busy to notice Hanna leaning against the door frame. Jotham was nowhere to be seen.

Finally, Emily looked up. She hobbled over, her limp more pronounced than usual, and embraced her sister.

"How was school today?" Hanna said.

"Good."

"What did you learn?"

"A girl in my class taught me how to say the alphabet backward. Do you want to hear?" Emily asked.

"Maybe later. Did you learn anything else?"

"That the Creator loves us and watches over us."

Hanna held her tongue. She adjusted Emily's dress so it sat evenly on her shoulders and then straightened Emily's neckline before her sister gave her one last squeeze and hurried back to her space on the floor.

The soft tones of a piano were playing on the record player as Hanna watched the toddlers drawing in coloring books featuring the Creator atop a white steed, the word *understanding* — Brother Paul's personal proclamation — emblazoned on each cover in large, uppercase letters. Hanna had done the same thing hundreds of times. For years, she'd penned journal entries detailing how the Creator brought structure and joy to her life. She'd submitted her work to her teachers for evaluation. She'd helped the little ones write their stories.

For the children in Clearhaven, every aspect of their lives always came back to the Creator. When she was a little girl, Hanna had been terribly afraid of the Creator, especially when she swiped pieces of sweet bread from the kitchen. It was a small act of disobedience, taking more than her fair share, and Hanna remembered lying in bed afterward — bits of bread clinging to the spaces between her teeth, her tongue tingling from the doughy mixture of sugar and honey — and wondering whether the Creator was looking down at her at that very moment, his wisdom replaced by an ardent, uncharacteristic wrath. For hours before she fell asleep, she would lie motionless in bed waiting for the Creator to grab her by her hair and hurl her into a pit of outstretched flames — owing to her theft, yes, but more for the deception that came with it. The remorse beat in her chest so strongly that she swore she'd never steal another piece of sweet bread in her entire life, until of course the next time the warm smell of yeast and butter came drifting from the oven.

Hanna wasn't sure whether the Creator knew about her unauthorized visit to Daniel's pier, whether he kept that close a watch on her comings and goings. She only knew that ever since Brother Paul had called her name and Edwin stepped forward to claim her, Hanna had felt like a rubber band stretched to the point of breaking, pulled so tight that its color had all but disappeared. Hanna had spent so very long worried about what others thought, about the consequences for the slightest misbehavior, that she hadn't stopped to think about what *she* wanted, what was right for her.

Hanna thought back to the pier by the lake, to the sound of Daniel's fingers shifting along the guitar strings, the warmth of his words . . . *Champagne Girl, only you are sacred.*

"Hanna?"

Kara was calling her into the kitchen. She had to call twice, so lost was Hanna in her thoughts. Hanna joined Kara by the countertop where her mother was stirring a pot of stew.

"How was the visit to Edwin's?" she asked.

Hanna peeked at the muddy-brown broth that was for supper. She thought back to the emotion in Kara's voice moments after she'd told the story about Hanna falling from the sky, the way Kara had stared spellbound at the fire. *I should have done so much more.* As much as she wanted to tell her mother all about Edwin's wives, how they lived, the tall woman's wicked barbs, how Paedyn said they spent their nights, she held her tongue.

"It was wonderful," she said.

"Really?"

"Yes. His wives are all delightful."

Kara looked at Hanna out of the corner of her eye, studying her, trying to decipher whether Hanna was telling the truth. A moment passed before Kara returned to stirring her stew. Then a creaking door sounded and Jotham lumbered in from the bathroom. He passed by without so much as a hello. Hanna glanced from her mother to her father, amazed that neither of them knew about her unchaperoned visit to Daniel's pier, about the harrowing car ride into the woods. They didn't know what Hanna had been thinking. She wondered if anyone — Jotham, Edwin, the Creator — even knew who she *was*.

A secret burned inside her. Brother Paul's words, his edict of understanding — frozen in Hanna's mind for so long — melted away, replaced by her desire to hear more of Daniel's amber-tinted words, to live like her brave other self. Hanna stepped away from her mother and started setting the table for supper. She listened to Katherine's cheerful chatter as she adjusted the little ones' booster seats. Hanna kept her mouth closed, her eyes focused on her task. On the outside, everything was as it had always been. But, inside, a fire had been lit. Hanna resolved to see Daniel again. She would find a way.

Even if the flames engulfed her.

12

After supper, Hanna sat down on the sofa with Ahmre standing in front of her. She took the child's hair and divided it into three parts. Hanna crossed the right section over the middle and then repeated with the left. Halfway through, Ahmre brought her hand up and placed it in the braid. Gently, so as not to start again, Hanna steered the little girl's fingers out of the way. She kept braiding until she reached the end and was twisting an elastic in Ahmre's hair when Emily hobbled around the corner.

"I need a bath."

Hanna kissed Ahmre on the forehead and sent her running into the next room. "You had one yesterday."

"I smell like soup," Emily said.

"Excuse me?"

"I spilled soup on myself at supper. I smell like soup."

Hanna leaned in close and smelled her

sister. She almost laughed. Emily was right: she smelled like tomato broth and burnt lentils. She took Emily by the hand and led her to the upstairs bathroom where Hanna helped her sister remove her clothes and step inside the bathtub. She ran her fingers along Emily's back the way she always did. Hanna felt the juts in her spine. She washed the girl's hair.

Emily dipped her head underwater and poked it back up to reveal droplets dangling from her eyelashes. She pushed her wet hair from her face and placed her chin on the side of the tub.

"When I get married, I'm going to wear chrysanthemums in my hair," she said. "Orange ones with just a smattering of white. You don't want to wear yellow chrysanthemums. My mother told me yellow ones symbolize sadness. But white and orange are all about love."

Hanna nodded. "You seem to have your wedding all planned out."

"I do," Emily said, scooping a handful of water and dousing her face. She wiped the drops out of her eyes. "And nobody's going to stop it. Not even the evildoers."

"Evildoers?" Hanna said.

"You know — the ones from the other side

of the world. The ones that commit wicked acts."

Hanna ran through their last bath-time conversation in her head. "Ah yes, the evildoers. That story was more about being brave in the face of wicked acts."

Emily paused to think. "But what wicked acts do they do?"

Hanna sat down on the cold floor and leaned against the tub. "Terrible things. They hurt people. They threaten people, which is sometimes worse."

Emily shook her head. "Getting hit is worse than getting threatened."

"But what if you're always afraid? Isn't it better to get struck and know the pain than to always be terrified of what might come next?"

"I don't want to be hit," Emily said.

"Neither do I."

Emily dropped her bar of soap into the tub and searched for it under the water. She grasped it and it slipped out of her hand and the girl giggled. When Hanna smiled, Emily did it again, intentionally this time. The two sisters sat quietly, Emily playing with the soap, Hanna staring at the tattered wallpaper, until Emily said, "How would we get to the other side of the world?"

Hanna's ears perked. She cast a quick

173

glance at the door and kept her voice low. "We could walk through the woods."

"The wolves would find us."

"I'm done being afraid of wolves," Hanna said.

"But they have sharp teeth. And Kara says they turn on their own. They eat their friends when their friends get hurt."

"Forget the woods, then. We could drive a car far away from here," Hanna said. "My mother taught me how. It's hard to get it into second gear, but once I do, we can drive as fast as we want. We could be gone by midnight tonight if we really wanted to."

Emily gazed at the cracks in the ceiling, at the wide, discolored splotches where water had damaged the far wall, anywhere except her sister's eyes. She shifted back and forth in the bath as Hanna sat perfectly still on the crooked floor tiles; aware of the moisture in the air, the cold iron tub against her skin, the hair on her neck standing on end. Emily dunked her head underwater and re-emerged.

"I don't care what anyone thinks. I'm going to be a bride one day, just like you," Emily said.

"I know you are," Hanna said, perhaps a little too gently.

"I *am* going to be a bride. I'm going to

wear a white dress and orange chrysanthemums in my hair. Father's going to give me
away and the ceremony will be held in the
old tower cathedral, and all my brothers and
sisters will be there. Of course, you'll arrive
with Edwin's family, but you'll still watch
the ceremony, won't you, Hanna?"

"I wouldn't miss it for the world."

Emily leaned forward so her shoulders
were outside the tub. Water dripped off her
naked body onto the floor. "Then promise,"
she said.

"Emily . . ."

"Just promise."

Hanna's words failed her. That feeling of
falling inside herself returned. Emily's
bathwater trickled along the floor tiles,
dampening Hanna's dress and seeping into
the exposed flesh of Hanna's legs. Before
she could speak, a woman's voice came
through the door. It sounded shrill, almost
unnerved, and it took Hanna a moment to
realize it was her mother.

"This is a terrible mistake!" Kara said.

A second voice rang out, this one deep
and angry. "Then it's my mistake to make.
It's my decision," Jotham said.

Emily splashed in the tub. "Are they fighting?"

Hanna put her finger to her lips. "Shh!"

"You pretend it's your decision when others are making it for you," Kara said.

"I am the husband and the father in this house. And my decision is final," Jotham said.

"But what about Hanna?"

"What about her!?"

"You can't seriously tell me you want her to serve out her life as Edwin's fifth wife."

The hallway fell silent. Both Hanna and Emily held their breath. Jotham and Kara were shouting and whispering at the same time, clearly unaware that the girls were listening on the other side of the bathroom wall.

"What would you have me do?" Jotham said. "Take her into the city? Marry Hanna off to some liberal coward?"

"Of course not."

"Then what? What!?"

"I don't have all the answers," Kara said. "But can you honestly tell me a voice from above told you to give your daughter away while she's still a child? For her to live a life of servitude under Edwin? Did the Creator really speak to you in a vision?"

"You know perfectly well that he did not," Jotham said.

"Then why do this? Why give her away? For the money? We don't need the money."

"We *do* need the money."

Kara's voice rose. Her whisper disappeared. "I've stood by quietly for eighteen long years, never complaining when you come to me at night, never speaking out of turn or offering an opinion, because you told me our daughter was special. You told me you could protect her. All your talk about Heaven and the path of the righteous all these years was just that — talk. Now it seems your will is all that matters. Your will is not the will of God!"

A sudden, swift sound rang out — a violent collision of skin against skin — Jotham's hand striking Kara's cheek. The sound reverberated off the door, and then a terrible thud. Emily gasped. The bathroom grew very quiet, the only sound a trickle of water dripping from the tap. When Jotham finally spoke, his voice was so low Hanna could barely hear it through the door.

"When you married into this way of life, my will became your will. I am your husband, damn it! You forget your place, Kara. Be sure it doesn't happen again."

Jotham's heavy footsteps lurched along the floor, coming closer. Hanna's eyes darted to the bathroom door; she'd forgotten to lock it. A frenzy erupted inside her. She leapt up and grasped the handle. Hanna's hand was shaking so hard that she thought she might jar the door and Jotham would hear them. She looked back at Emily's naked, twisted body, soaking wet and vulnerable. Very carefully, she locked the door.

"Hanna . . ." Emily said.

"Quiet!" Hanna whispered hard.

She pressed her back against the door and felt how fragile it was, how someone Jotham's size could easily barge through. Jotham paused near the bathroom door and the blood in Hanna's veins turned to ice. Her heart beat so hard she thought he might hear it on the other side.

Jotham shifted his back brace. He let out a phlegmy, anguished cough and then lumbered to the stairs, the wood creaking under his feet. Hanna heard Kara stand up and slam her bedroom door. Then silence.

"Why, Hanna?" Emily said. "Why are we being quiet?"

Hanna looked into Emily's wide, innocent eyes. She saw not a future bride or a budding young woman, but a child too naive to know what was coming for her big sister. What would one day come for her.

13

It was midmorning five days before her wedding when Hanna helped Charliss prop an old wooden ladder up against the side of Jotham's house. They had delayed too long in fixing the roof. Last night, more rainwater had seeped into the walls of the front alcove, so much that, on the ceiling, wide drops of condensation were visible to the naked eye. When Hanna placed her hand against the wallpaper, it felt damp. Ten minutes ago, Jotham had yelled to Hanna from the other room, told her to plug the leak before nightfall.

"Are you okay to do this now?" Hanna said.

"I think so," Charliss said.

Hanna's brother had already spent hours chopping firewood and a pink fatigue had crept in behind his eyes. For over a year now, every time Hanna looked at Charliss, it was like watching a clock slowly tick down to zero. At some point, he would be made to leave. Jotham and Brother Paul would sit Charliss down and lecture him on responsibility and what it means to be a man, how the Creator chooses a different path for everyone. They wouldn't say a word about ridding themselves of their competition, not a word about how — were Charliss to stay — their crop of young, unsullied brides might diminish. Jotham would place him in the back seat of a car and drive Charliss down The Road and Hanna would never see her brother again. Charliss wasn't living on borrowed time. He was living on *finite* time, and Hanna wondered whether Charliss was savoring every moment, every small interaction with his family, or if he'd long grown detached, knowing he was powerless to stop what was coming.

In less than a week, Hanna wouldn't be around to assist him anymore. This might be the very last chore she and Charliss did together.

Charliss hoisted a satchel over his shoulder containing a trowel, rubber cement, a paintbrush and several pieces of asphalt he'd salvaged from the neighbor's trash, and then he scrambled up onto the roof. He climbed easily and fearlessly, and Hanna felt a little foolish for approaching the old

180

wooden ladder with such caution behind him. Hanna placed her foot on the first rung. The left side was shorter than the right by a couple of inches, enough to make it tilt off-center. Very carefully, Hanna ascended the ladder. As she reached the roof and placed her boot on the gutter, Hanna's dress snagged on a shingle, its jagged edge tearing the fabric. For a second, Hanna thought she might lose her balance and fall to the ground below. Then Charliss grabbed her hand. He pulled her onto the rooftop.

"Thank you," Hanna said.

Charliss freed Hanna's dress. He secured the satchel on his back and climbed on all fours toward the chimney while Hanna knelt down against the damp shingles and followed, still wary, still tentative. They advanced to the highest point on the rooftop, where the tall chimney stack met the edge of the house, three stories above ground. Hanna steadied herself and together she and Charliss pulled the tools out of the satchel.

Hanna had done this type of work before. Three seasons ago, she'd assisted Kara in replacing the roof on the shed out back. However, that was a large undertaking and Kara had had a detailed plan. She insisted they follow it to the letter, to ensure the shed's new ceiling would last for years to come. This was different. Hanna and Charliss were doing piecemeal work. The shingles on Jotham's house were too old and decrepit, too porous to repair them all. Hanna and Charliss were to plug the leak. It didn't matter how the repair looked so long as it functioned, so long as they wouldn't have to place buckets beside the fireplace the next time the storms came.

Hanna lifted three shingles by their edges and the wood came out of its nails like butter sliding through a warm knife. She set them atop the chimney and dug into the thin layer of asphalt with the trowel, clearing out the debris. Then Charliss unfastened the jar of rubber cement and poured it over the crack. Hanna braced her shoulder against the chimney stack. She flattened the rubber cement with the trowel. Once it seeped into the fissure, Charliss smoothed it with the paintbrush.

"How long does it take to dry?" Charliss said.

"A few minutes."

"Then we put the shingles back on?"

"First we hammer down the new strips of asphalt and then the shingles."

"Do you think it will hold?" Charliss said.

Hanna ran her finger over a loose shingle

and felt the indent from where she'd pressed her thumb down just a minute before. "I'm not sure," she said. Under her boots, moss had sprouted in tufts, creeping across the rooftop and down the walls. The gutters were clogged with soupy, green debris and the outer shell of the chimney stack crumbled when touched. From this vantage point, Jotham's house looked like it might be better off condemned.

"Will you still visit after you've gone to live with Edwin?" Charliss said.

At first, Hanna wasn't certain whether he was making casual conversation or if he really was concerned about seeing her again. One look was all it took to see where his heart lay. Charliss was leaning against the chimney, gazing up at Hanna, a nervous apprehension in his eyes. Hanna wanted to reach out to comfort him, only they were too high on the rooftop, the shingles too uneven under their feet. "I suppose Edwin will have a say in what I do, whom I visit."

Charliss ran his hand along his brow, an involuntary action Hanna had seen countless times in Jotham. "Will you come by yourself? Or will Edwin come to the house with you?"

Hanna shrugged, a simple lift and contraction of her shoulders, the slightest movement. Barely a fraction of Hanna's weight shifted from one foot to the other. But it was enough. Hanna slipped. Her foot slid on the mossy rooftop. She felt herself about to tumble back the way they came and, in an act of desperation, she turned hard to her left. Hanna overcompensated. She grabbed for the chimney but found only empty air. Hanna fell straight backward, off the side of the house. Three stories to the ground.

Hanna reached out, a wild, stabbing grasp for anything she could grab hold of: a tree branch, a stray shingle, Charliss's hand. But there was nothing. She clawed at the air, falling fast toward the ground. A burst of shock and fear shot through her and then a flash of disbelief. Just seconds ago, her footing had been secure, her equilibrium stable, her feet attached to the spongy roof shingles. Now she was descending so quickly that she could barely think. A wild, uncontrolled hysteria seized her in its grasp. Above, the sky refused to move. Its picturesque clouds offered no help, staring back: cold and detached, utterly unresponsive. Falling between the heavens above and the ground below, Hanna didn't see the side of Jotham's house sailing by. She saw not her brother's outstretched arm, nor the raised wings of the raven swooping nearby. She saw only endless, boundless space.

Suddenly, a gust of wind surged. Time — that crushing weight — evaporated and the sensation of falling disappeared. Even as she plummeted to the ground, Hanna felt suspended in midair, as though she were lying still and the world and all its enormity was speeding toward her. Hanna's dress fluttered around her and, for a split second, she thought she might float like a feather and the earth would envelop her in its gentle embrace. However, no squall would ever be enough. She continued to fall.

A scream started in the base of Hanna's throat. It roared to her mouth. Hanna was inches away from the ground and there was no last moment of peace. She unclenched her fists and then clasped them shut again. Hanna couldn't relish the final sensation of the wind passing through her outstretched fingers. She couldn't let go. Not yet.

Hanna screamed — a jarring, terrified cry into the oblivion above.

The world turned black.

14

"Hanna? Hanna?"

She opened her eyes to see Charliss stand-ing over her, his face red, his lips trembling. He pulled on her arm to help her stand, to make sure she was okay. Hanna held back a moment. She mumbled something — "One moment" or "I need to breathe" — she wasn't quite sure. The soil and the prickly weeds lay damp underneath her. To one side was the fresh firewood Charliss had stacked that morning; to the other, a boulder, its surface veined in lines.

Hanna lifted her neck. She felt her hair pull away from the earth and then her arms. Charliss offered his hand and Hanna stood to her feet. She looked up to the spot from where she'd fallen. The wild, white panic of moments ago was now a memory. Every-thing — the firewood, the sky, the concern etched in Charliss's face — was coated in a pristine, pink glow. Hanna couldn't believe what she was seeing. It was as though her entire life, her vision had been blurry, like she'd been squinting to see and now everything was crystal clear.

"Are you okay?" Charliss said.

Hanna pulled a piece of grass from her hair. "I think so."

Together they looked up at the chimney stack, at its height, the path from rooftop to ground Hanna's body had just taken. Before either of them could say another word, Emily rounded the side of the house with two toddlers in tow.

"Hanna, Father wants to see you," she said.

Hanna gaped openmouthed at her sister. Emily's skin was tinted raspberry red. The curls dangling over her eyes appeared coral rather than muddy-brown: lush and silken and streaked red toward her roots. A luminous aura surrounded her and when Emily gazed down at the toddler to her side, her profile looked like a watercolor portrait come to life.

Emily didn't seem to notice Hanna gaping at her. She stepped closer. "Father really does want to see you," she said. Then she turned back, the young ones toddling along after her.

Hanna dusted off her dress. She ran her

hands along her torso and down her thighs. There was no pain in her back. Nothing broken where she'd landed on her neck. Hanna didn't feel injured. Only her vision had changed. Hanna meant to follow Emily. She meant to go see what Jotham wanted, but she was still astonished and amazed: astonished she'd fallen, amazed she wasn't injured whatsoever.

"You're really not hurt?" Charliss asked, his voice tentative, shaky.

Hanna didn't know what to say, how to explain what had happened, what was real anymore. She was standing still, her mouth half-open, marveling at the radiant pink color all around when Charliss said, "Do you need me to come with you to see Father?"

"Yes. I mean — no. I think I'll be okay."

"I'll attach the asphalt," Charliss said. A long pause followed before Charliss put his hand on her arm. "Father's waiting."

"Yes, of course."

Hanna put one foot in front of the other and walked around the house. She stepped through the back door, expecting to find Jotham sitting in his chair in the living room, waiting for her alone. It came as a surprise to see him standing beside Kara in the kitchen. Belinda was there as well, leaning against the far counter. Hanna's gaze shifted to the deep bruise along Kara's cheek, the one her mother had refused to talk about that morning. Kara's and Jotham's jaws were clenched, their eyes like stones.

"What's wrong?" she said.

"Where were you yesterday?" Kara asked.

Hanna took a small step back. "Why do you ask?"

"Makala called from the police station. Were you in a police car yesterday?" Kara said.

Hanna looked from Kara to Belinda and then to Jotham. Her mind returned to the dirt road, the sour smell of Paul the Second alone in his car, her impromptu trip to Daniel's pier. Hanna swallowed hard. Every muscle in her chest contracted, unsure how much her parents knew. The rosy-pink glow weakened.

"You never should have gotten into that car," Jotham said.

"It's not that we don't trust you," Kara said. "It's those boys, those men, the deputies Paul."

Suddenly Hanna realized what was going on. They hadn't learned about her visit to Daniel's pier. They were upset with her for accepting a ride from the two most unscrupulous boors in town.

"You're angry at me because Brother Paul's sons drove me home?"

"We trust Brother Paul completely," Jotham said. "His sons, that older one especially, are another matter."

Hanna looked to Kara in the hope her mother might come to her defense. Only, Kara's arms were folded. There was nothing in her eyes, in the way she stood or held her shoulders to suggest Hanna could make her understand. Still, she tried. "How could I have said no?"

"You just say no," Kara said.

"They came upon me in the middle of a deserted road. What did you expect me to do?"

"Certainly not get in their car."

Hanna closed her eyes in frustration and again the pink glow diminished. Magenta dissolved into an ashen rouge.

"But —"

Jotham pointed a single finger and Hanna could see the veins pulse in his hand. "You find a way."

Deep in Hanna's belly, a fire raged. If Brother Paul truly was the Creator's conduit, as Jotham had insisted time and time again, then who were they to question his judgment? Clearly, it was flawed nepotism

190

at its worst, Brother Paul endorsing his two sons — the vulgar bully and his dutiful follower — as the law in town. The hypocrisy was astonishing. The entire system was corrupt and Brother Paul was wrong. Shouldn't the back seat of a police car be the safest place for her? The safest way for any young woman to travel?

An urge to yell billowed inside her. Hanna felt that same loss of control that came with the wind passing through her outstretched fingers, time evaporating, the unmovable sky. In front of her, Jotham lifted his chin, his face covered in a look of accomplishment. How dare he tell her what to do when he'd already sold her off to the highest bidder? How dare he give her that look of righteous indignation? And Jotham wasn't alone in this. Hanna wanted to yell at her mother. How could Kara stand there beside him — devout, obedient and worse . . . complicit — when last night he'd struck her across the face, the bruise now pushing its way deep from her cheekbone to her skin?

Hanna turned her gaze to Belinda and suddenly it was like she was falling all over again. Arms grasping. The gusting wind fluttering around her. Terror erupting, the feeling that it was too soon, that she wasn't ready, that she'd never be ready. Hanna fought hard to restrain herself, but with one look at that coldhearted woman, the pristine pink glow faded into nothingness. All she wanted to do was scream and keep screaming, scream at Belinda to stop staring at her with those dead, black eyes, to stop being so incredibly hard — in her speech, in the way she moved her hands — hard on her children, on everyone. What was Belinda doing here? What were any of them doing in this small room in this small town when there was an entire world outside of Clearhaven where they could live vibrant and free?

Just as her inner kettle reached full boil, Hanna stopped herself. For the first time, Hanna held her tongue not out of submission, but because there was a handsome young man waiting at the dock, dangling his feet over a sheet of purple ice, wondering when the Champagne Girl would come calling again. If she were to fly into a rage now, if her parents were to perceive Hanna as irrational or worse — disobedient — Jotham might lock her down in the house. He might insist Hanna go live with Edwin not in five days but tonight, her fiancé instituting a new, harsher set of rules. She had so little time left.

"I'm sorry," she said. "I'm very sorry."

Kara took Hanna by the wrists. "Don't be sorry, angel," she said. "Just be safe. That's all we want — for you to be safe."

Hanna leaned her head against Kara's shoulder and breathed in the smell of her mother's powdery skin. Instantly, she regretted wanting to yell at her. How would Kara feel, being berated by her daughter the day after her husband struck her? Kara was resilient, but she had her limits.

"What about the salad bowl?" Belinda said. "Makala told me you left it in the police car."

It was the first time Belinda had spoken during the entire conversation and it had nothing to do with Hanna's safety or bad decision making or the louts with guns who'd driven her home. Hanna looked deep into Belinda's eyes. Just moments ago, Hanna had fallen three stories to the ground. The fall could have killed her. It should have crippled her. And she'd walked away without a scratch. Yesterday, a young man had poured his soul into verse for Hanna, igniting inside her a feeling other than dread or dismay for the first time since she could remember. Hanna had finally awakened after what she could only describe as a stifling, uninvited slumber to realize she wasn't meant to be paraded about in a white dress. That she wasn't meant to be a Clearhaven bride, clinging to a middle-aged man's arm.

And now this woman wanted her bowl back.

Hanna gritted her teeth. She steadied her tongue and held back the emotion in her voice. "I'll retrieve it today," she said.

Belinda nodded curtly, her tongue pressed firmly against the side of her mouth. "Make sure you do," she said and stepped out of the kitchen.

15

Hanna passed the marketplace at a distance. Much of the town was crowded around the booths, wives from the same families shopping together, their young children clustered about their feet. A shipment must have arrived from outside Clearhaven, bringing fresh fruits and vegetables, spices and grains made scarce by the long winter's chill. Hanna held her jacket close to her chest and lowered her head, wary of making eye contact, lest some well-meaning woman approach and offer her congratulations on her upcoming nuptials, lest she draw attention from the butcher, the man who'd stepped forward with the others to claim her at church.

She saw him now, his mutton-chop whiskers protruding from his face, his apron smeared with blood, shoulder raised, cleaver suspended in midair. A woman was waiting for her purchase with a brown paper bag already in hand while her young daughter splashed in the puddles nearby. The butcher sliced down into a meat shank and then flashed the little girl a comical glare. The girl squealed and the butcher unleashed a raucous laugh. Before she could run away, he softened his tone. The butcher called the little girl over to his table and spoke gently in her ear, offered her a piece of taffy from the bowl on his shelf. Hanna noticed the mother covering her mouth, her cheeks reddened, clearly enthralled by the butcher's strong chin, his massive shoulders covered only by a T-shirt on this chilly late-winter day.

With tentative steps, Hanna approached the police station, a two-room trailer located behind the marketplace. The brothers' police car wasn't parked out front, but that didn't mean Paul the Second wasn't nearby, that he couldn't force her into another car ride. It didn't mean he couldn't trade his graceless innuendo for actions. In the back of her mind, there was always the butcher. He'd known Hanna since she was a child. Were Paul the Second to accost her, Hanna could scream his name, compel the big, strong man to come running, cleaver in hand.

Hanna opened the trailer door and was

relieved to see Makala sitting at a desk all by herself, the clickety-clack of a typewriter filling the room. Makala was one of Brother Paul's wives. Which number she was or where she stood in the pecking order, Hanna wasn't sure, but he must have thought a lot of her to assign Makala an office job at the police station.

Hanna stepped inside and was immediately struck by the curious aroma of fresh paint and perfume in the air. Above Makala, a faded tapestry depicted the town symbol: a collection of conjoined triangles converging into a central point. The lemon-green walls were illuminated by a single light bulb, partially shielded by a gold-pleated lampshade, while Makala's desk featured all manner of knickknacks: little ceramic owls, crochet cats and a row of cherubic gnomes resting against a handmade birdhouse. It was a wonder the typewriter fit on her desk.

The woman didn't look up when Hanna entered. Hanna waited in silence, fidgeting with a loose thread on her sleeve, until she noticed a bell on the counter with a sign that read Ring for Service. Hanna rang the bell once, catching it with her fingers before the shrill noise resonated too loudly.

Makala looked over. She held her reading glasses up to her face. "Yes?"

"You called to say you have Belinda's salad bowl."

Makala held her gaze. "Oh right," she said. "The girl who takes rides from boys."

"It wasn't like that."

Makala rolled her tongue along the inside of her mouth. "Mmm-hmm."

Hanna opened her mouth to defend herself but stopped short. The moment she engaged this woman in an argument, she would have already lost. She looked past Makala to the desk in the far corner. There, sitting on a plastic orange chair, was Belinda's salad bowl. Makala had already filled it with random scraps of paper. Though the bowl was only a few yards away, Hanna felt like she wasn't allowed to walk over and pick it up herself. This office — its clutter, the pale light — was Makala's domain. The place even smelled of her. Hanna would do herself more harm than good by defying her.

"May I please have Belinda's bowl?" she said. "She needs it. It's her only one."

Makala made a great showing of inconvenience. She stood up slowly. The woman brushed the creases from her dress and moved a pile of file folders out of her way. Leisurely, she lifted each scrap of paper out of the bowl and found a new place for it amidst the clutter, before finally walking over to her desk with the bowl in her hands. Makala didn't pass it to Hanna. Rather, she set it down in front of her, forcing Hanna to step forward and pick it up. The moment Hanna touched it, Makala grabbed the other end. They locked eyes and Makala's expression turned from feigned inconvenience into something darker, something Hanna hadn't expected.

"You were all Paul the Second could talk about last night," Makala said. "You must have done something to make him take such a shine to you."

"I didn't do anything," Hanna said.

"Is that so?" Makala's eyes ran up and down Hanna's body, the bowl still firmly in her grasp. "There's something to be said for modesty in this day and age, young lady."

Hanna followed Makala's gaze. Her jacket was open. Her breasts were pressing against her dress but otherwise the fabric dangled loosely from her shoulders. Her neckline was high, the garment's hemline all the way to Hanna's calves.

"We're wearing the same dress," she said.

The speed with which Hanna replied — the brief, combative disbelief in her voice — set something off inside Makala. The woman clenched her jaw. Makala's whole body trembled as though, at any moment, she might erupt. All the while, her eyes burned slow like blackened beehives.

"It's not *what* you wear. It's *how* you wear it," Makala hissed.

Hanna yanked the bowl out of Makala's grasp. She squinted and crinkled her brow. "Why are you doing this?" she said, her tone wounded on purpose, to let the woman know the damage she was causing. But Makala's glare never wavered. She stood up straight and adjusted her glasses, sovereign ruler over this small trailer and all the papers and flags and ceramic owls within. Her contempt surrounded her like a fog.

"Because you are the town whore, little girl. Because of the way you look at men and because of the way you make them look at you. You think you can flutter about, twirling your hair and bouncing your little body around town and the decent-minded amongst us won't have the courage to say anything? How dare you perform this lost-little-girl act? Everyone knows what's really going on."

Makala wasn't done. She was just warming her resolve. The words swelled inside her, like a dam about to burst. Hanna turned to leave.

"I'm not finished with you yet," Makala said.

Hanna pulled on the trailer door and bounded down the steps. She hadn't gotten very far when Makala opened the trailer door behind her. The woman was too large, too out of shape to give chase. Makala called after Hanna. She yelled at the top of her lungs, the billowing words engorging her.

"Your mother is barren now because she gave birth to such a dirty little whore!"

Hanna wasn't sure who else could hear. The marketplace was so close. She kept her eyes glued to the ground and put one foot in front of the other as Makala's malicious taunts rang out. A wave of dizziness overwhelmed her. Hanna took a step and almost tumbled onto the gravel road. She righted herself only to find the trees amassing overhead, their famished limbs clawing at the air. The ground shivered beneath her feet. Hanna gasped for breath, unable to fill her lungs. Above, a watery silver glow enveloped the windswept sky and all around were menacing streaks of color: barbaric blues and shocking scarlet reds. Storm clouds swirled in Hanna's mind. She was certain that, were she to turn around, Makala would be standing right behind her, howling, enraged, heaving her wicked words into the air.

It took every ounce of strength she had, but Hanna trekked down the pathway until the weight on her legs relented, until the clouds in her mind dispersed and her pace recovered. The silver glow dissipated from the sky. The marketplace was far behind her, Makala's voice a memory, the only sound a lone chipmunk chirping at the side of the roadway.

As Hanna walked, she couldn't stop her mind racing, wondering what others really must think of her. The other day at church, when the seven men stepped forward and Brother Paul made a faint showing of pretending to consider them, Hanna didn't think to look at the crowd. She was too focused on Brother Paul in his spotless white robes, on the faces of the men who'd stepped forward, on Edwin and Jotham. She'd never stopped to consider what the women were thinking.

Years ago, on the eve of her eleventh birthday, Kara had pulled Hanna aside to explain how relations work between men and women. She'd gone into great detail about reproduction, monthly cycles, the private areas between the legs (*snakes and flowers,* she'd called them). She'd spent fifteen minutes explaining how love differs in real life and storybooks. At the end of their talk, Kara ran her fingers through Hanna's hair. "You look different than the other women here," she said. "Don't be surprised if they hate you for it."

Hanna remembered thinking Kara was being too candid and that *hate* was too strong a word. Hate meant loathing and revulsion; it meant seething with anger and craving vengeance. It had to be rooted in some kind of truth. To think that others would hate her because her hair was blond and her features soft and symmetrical — it didn't make sense to her then and it didn't make sense to her now. Hanna struggled to recall what injustice she might have incurred on Makala over the years. Had she really twirled her hair and cast come-hither looks at the men? Had she been vulgar? Had she put her body on display? Perhaps. Perhaps Hanna had done shameless, sinful things without realizing it. But then, Daniel told her she always looked down at her feet. And Hanna almost always had a young child with her, a child she nurtured, a child she focused all her attention on. Hanna didn't know what to think.

She fought to stop herself from crying. Hanna wiped her eyes and kept trekking through the woodlands. With each step, another tear threatened to flow. Hanna gritted her teeth. After what Makala said, Hanna should have been furious. She should have been irate and exasperated and intent on attaining some manner of revenge. Instead, an aching melancholy enveloped her. Hanna thought about the way people saw her and she wanted to cry. She thought about how, days from now, she would be forced to live with Edwin and his overbearing wives, and she wanted to cry even more. Hanna thought about Emily and how in a short while she might be powerless to protect her, and she could barely keep the tears from flowing.

Hanna stopped in the middle of the forest. She looked up at the trees and at the stream in the distance. Hanna turned in a circle. She couldn't believe what she'd done. She'd been traveling in the opposite direction of Jotham's house. Without realizing it, she had walked east, toward the old Grierson place, toward Daniel. Rather than turn around, she kept going. She doubled her pace. Hanna lifted her knees and ran toward Daniel as fast as she could. She cut across a thicket of trees and ascended a rocky embankment at the river's edge to come to the grove of weeping willows adjacent to the old Grierson place.

She rounded the front of the house, hoping to find Daniel at the pier. Hanna was startled to see Daniel's brothers standing with him next to their father's shiny blue truck. Instantly, she regretted everything — her clumsy approach, the way she stumbled through the trees like a big blind bear, her hubris in expecting to find Daniel outside alone, waiting for her. She regretted having spent time brooding on Makala's cruel words and not constructing an elaborate excuse were she to be discovered trespassing on the Rossiters' property.

Quickly, Hanna slipped behind a tree. She kept low, her dress concealed by dangling leaves. Hanna could hear Daniel and his brothers talking. They were so quiet at first and their voices so similar that it was difficult to tell who was speaking, but it was clear they were in the middle of an argument. One of the brothers raised his voice. "You don't have to listen to him!" Another brother cursed and raised his voice right back. "Yes, I do. And so do you. Don't pretend we don't!" This went on until Hanna heard the sound of the truck doors slamming shut and the engine starting up. Hanna peered out from behind the tree trunk. Daniel was standing by himself, his brothers speeding away in the truck. He turned to walk back inside.

"Daniel," Hanna whispered. He kept walking, so Hanna called out. "Daniel!"

He glanced around and then stopped when he saw her. Daniel looked shaken, harried from his conversation. He stepped behind the tree, next to Hanna.

"Shh! What are you doing here?" he asked.

His tone was sharp; Hanna didn't know what to say. She'd clearly come at a bad time. Perhaps she shouldn't have come at all.

"I should go," she said.

"No, please. I'm sorry." He moved his hand toward Hanna's cheek. "Are you okay? Have you been crying?"

Hanna flushed with embarrassment. "No," she said as convincingly as possible. "I ran here. I slipped on an embankment. But I'm fine."

"Well, I'm glad you're here," Daniel said. "It's just — my brothers left a few seconds ago, and they're not coming back." He glanced at the street they'd driven down. "I thought James and Kenneth were going to live with us until summer, maybe even the fall. But they had a huge fight with my dad last night. James said he couldn't spend one more second in Clearhaven."

"Where did they go?" Hanna said.

"I'm not sure. They said they'd call and give me a phone number to reach them."

"Are they ever coming back?"

"I don't think so. Probably never."

"What about you?"

They were so close that Daniel's arm grazed her jacket. "I'm not sure," he said. "My dad's taking me to meet with Brother Paul later this week to talk about my future. He says he has plans for me. Big plans. He says —"

"Daniel?"

It was a woman's voice, coming from Daniel's front steps.

Daniel stepped out into the open. "They're gone, Mom," he said.

"But you're staying," his mother said, her inflection flat, her tone devoid of any emotion.

Daniel rubbed his neck and looked up at the gray sky. "For now," he said and then walked toward her.

Hanna couldn't hear what they were saying. All she could see was the back of Daniel's head. She imagined his mother openly sobbing, distraught that her sons had left, begging Daniel to talk to his father, to find some way to convince him that James and Kenneth should stay. Or perhaps she had her arms crossed, her posture rigid, her foot slowly tapping on the concrete steps, wondering why Daniel's brothers hadn't left sooner, furious that Daniel had argued with them instead of encouraging them to leave. Hanna couldn't tell.

Eventually, his mother went back inside and Daniel returned to the tree line. His skin was pale and his expression had grown serious. He placed his hands to his temples as though to block a stabbing pain inside his head. "My mother wants me to come inside, to talk some more."

"Oh," Hanna said, surprised their interaction was over so soon. "I'll leave."

"Wait." Daniel touched her arm. He glanced back at the house and then turned to face Hanna. Their eyes met. "I'll come see you later."

Hanna's brain flooded with an image of Daniel approaching Jotham's front door. She pictured her father reaching for his shotgun, Daniel fleeing into the woods, Belinda and Jotham giving chase. The wolves. Hanna put up her hands, as if to stop him from suggesting it again. "That's the worst idea I've ever heard," she said.

"It's probably not the *worst* idea ever. You live close to the marshlands, right? It's not so far away."

"Are you serious?" she said.

"I'm dead serious," he said. "I'll come by after nightfall."

"Don't you dare."

The door of the house opened again. Hanna wasn't sure if it was Daniel's mother or his father. She just knew she couldn't be discovered. She backed away toward the street.

"I'll see you tonight. I promise," Daniel said.

He walked toward the house, looking back only once to smile out of the corner of his mouth. As Daniel reached his front step, the trees obscured Hanna's view. She heard voices, but they were distant and indecipherable. Hanna hurried along the path into the woodlands, butterflies turning circles in her stomach. A brisk breeze swept through the trees and Hanna held her jacket up to shield her neck. She marched quickly, the frosted earth crunching under her feet. With each step, Hanna replayed Daniel's words in her head. She pictured his confident smile.

Hanna still couldn't believe what he'd said. She couldn't imagine what would compel him to propose such a thing. Daniel must have forgotten where they lived, who their fathers were, that Hanna was about to get married. He must have forgotten who ran Clearhaven, what the punishment was for insolence in this town.

What was that young man thinking . . . that he could walk straight up to her front door?

16

Hanna examined the assortment of dried flowers Katherine had arranged on the living room floor. There were pink roses, red roses, assorted carnations and daffodils. A month ago, Katherine had hauled a sack of oats over to a neighbor's greenhouse. She must have bartered well because she came home with handfuls of flowers and a bag of powdered crystals for drying them. The crystals had been used many times before and were massed in clumps. Katherine baked the crystals in the oven to separate them and spent days methodically drying batch after batch of flowers. Now Katherine's cheeks were glowing, her smile spread from ear to ear.

"You can't avoid this forever," she said.

"I trust you to do the task," Hanna said.

"Ah, but it's your task. I'd be doing you a disservice if I sent you to live at Edwin's home without teaching you a little personal responsibility first."

Hanna shuffled her feet. She glanced over her shoulder, hoping one of the children would rush in and create a distraction. Only, they were all outside, helping Kara search the deck for woodlice. Hanna couldn't avoid this any longer. Her wedding was only five days away and she still hadn't selected the flowers for the ceremonial wreath that would sit upon her head. It was a bride's responsibility. The flowers she chose were supposed to represent her character, to let her husband know the kind of woman he was marrying. A half dozen times this past winter, when the snow drifts had risen waist-high and the family was cooped up inside, Katherine had cornered Hanna and insisted they flip through a book on flowers together. Hanna knew most of their symbols by heart by now. Pink carnations represented gratitude, red roses embodied passionate love, red and white roses together signified unity. There were many choices.

Hanna picked up a dried daffodil. "What does this symbolize again?"

"Chivalry."

"Chivalry?" Hanna said.

"Yes. It means valor. Or being gallant."

"As in gallant in the face of adversity?"

"That's correct."

Hanna brought the white daffodil up to her nose. Any aroma it once possessed had been stripped during the drying process. The daffodil's center cup was pink like a strawberry, fading into a peachy-orange as its petals spread, while the white outer shell was so delicate that it felt like it was made of air. Valor and gallantry. Two qualities that did not exist in Jotham. Two qualities Hanna had yet to see in Edwin. Two qualities to symbolize who she was as a bride.

Hanna twirled the dried flower in her hand. "I choose daffodils."

Katherine clasped her hands together. "Excellent! But what color — yellow or white?"

"The white ones are perfect," she said.

Katherine started sorting the daffodils. "I'm so excited. Now let's get started."

Hanna and Katherine sat on the living room floor with the fireplace burning bright in the corner, attaching dried greenery to a wire Katherine had measured atop Hanna's head. It was hard to get anything done, what with the children constantly poking their heads in the room, offering to help, wanting to make their own ceremonial wreathes, feeding Hanna questions about what her dress would look like and what their roles would be in the event.

Hanna couldn't focus on anything: her task, Katherine's instructions, her sisters' queries. She kept peering out the window, wondering whether Daniel would appear on their front step. Every sound — every crackle of the fire, every chance melody from the neighbor's wind chimes — sent Hanna's mind racing. She pictured Daniel standing on her porch with a bouquet of wildflowers in his hands, and Kara — or, worse, Belinda — answering the door. Hanna envisioned the chaos that would ensue.

Edwin would learn of his visit. Brother Paul would too; and he'd make sure Hanna felt the Creator's wrath. She'd heard tales of Brother Paul taking the lash to his daughters for the slightest infractions: dereliction of household chores, speaking out of turn at the supper table, even for casting an impudent look. At school a few years ago, one of his daughters showed Hanna the welts on her back, her arms and legs. Her flesh was covered in purple bruises.

Still, Hanna couldn't help but think that, no matter the consequences, seeing Daniel would be worth it for the momentary escape of fate's tightening grip on her. So Hanna waited. And waited. And she waited some more. She and Katherine paused their wreath-making to eat supper with the family. Jotham emerged from his room at mealtime. His cheeks were ruddy, and the monster had yet to climb out of his belly. At times he was downright jovial, engaging Kara in conversation, even embracing Katherine before she sat down to eat.

The whole while, Hanna felt like she might burst with anticipation. As she returned to the living room after supper, as she finished her wreath and modeled it for Emily, as her sisters tried it on one after another, walking arm in arm through the hallway, playing the part of a blushing bride, her excitement faded. Night overtook the day. The sunset turned the sky amber and then pink and finally mulberry red before collapsing into darkness, and eventually Hanna stopped gazing out the window. She retired upstairs. She read the little ones a book from church, a story about a sheep who told a lie and the righteous man who taught the sheep the virtue of truth and *understanding*. Slowly the realization set in that perhaps Daniel wasn't going to show up after all.

As Hanna changed into her nightclothes, she thought perhaps Daniel's parents forced him to stay home. There was always a chance he'd followed his brothers out of town, never to return. Maybe he simply changed his mind. She couldn't be sure. Their conversation that afternoon had been so quick, the fear of getting caught so great, that Daniel's words escaped her. Did he really promise to visit? Hanna thought he did. Perhaps, she thought, this is what young men do: they promise in the moment, only the moment fades and the promise becomes a suggestion and then just a whim and finally an afterthought.

After Kara came into the children's bedroom and sang a good-night song, Ahmre climbed into Hanna's bunk and leaned in close. Hanna played with Ahmre's hair and watched the half-moon through the window as, one by one, the children slowed their breathing into a steady nocturnal rhythm. The room grew cold. Too cold.

Hanna stood up and stole quietly over to the radiator underneath the windowsill. She crouched down and placed a hand on its side, only to find the metal frigid to the touch.

"It's not working," a voice said.

Hanna looked around the darkened room. One of the twins was snoring. Emily was facing Hanna, but her eyes were closed, her mouth half-open. Hanna's other brothers and sisters were fast asleep. Only one was awake. In the bottom bunk by the doorway, Charliss's eyes were wide-open.

"Go back to sleep," Hanna whispered. "I'll go downstairs and fiddle with the radiator in the living room."

She tiptoed across the room and had just opened the door a crack when Charliss said, "You should be dead."

A chill shot through Hanna's body. Her skin tingled under her nightdress. Outside, the trees creaked, settling in the cold, and, for a fleeting second, Hanna felt outside herself. Strange in her skin. Afflicted. Haunted. *You should be dead.*

"What do you mean?"

"The fall from the rooftop. I watched you land. Your head hit first. Then your neck. Then your back. It was like it happened slow and fast at the same time," he said. "A fall from that height should have killed you. Or broken your neck or split your head open. It should have hurt you somehow."

"Shh," Hanna said. In the next bunk, Emily was shifting in her sleep. Down the hall, Jotham had turned in for the night with Belinda. "You have to whisper. You don't want to wake everyone."

Charliss was still gaping at Hanna, the moonlight swimming in his eyes.

"What is it?" Hanna said.

"How are you still alive?"

She took Charliss's hand and sat down on the floor next to him. So much had happened since her fall — the police station, Makala's cruel taunts, rushing off to see Daniel, Hanna's second unabashed rebellion in as many days. Life had inserted itself. She'd almost forgotten the pink afterglow that swept over her in the wake of her fall.

Hanna wanted to offer Charliss some comforting words, to explain why the fall from the rooftop didn't injure her, to assuage him. Nothing came to her. Hanna could hardly make sense of it herself. She refused to believe it was sheer luck or a twist of fate. These past few days, Hanna had finally asserted herself. She was finally controlling her own choices.

"I'm glad you survived," Charliss said.

Hanna leaned her head against Charliss's arm and ran her hand across his back. In a few short years, after Charliss had been forced to leave Clearhaven, his brothers and sisters would exist only in his memory and Hanna would be a ghost to him. The trouble with leaving people behind is that they're as good as dead, and the days that would follow for Charliss would be a tangible afterlife, wandering through the future without ever knowing whether the past really existed.

She kissed Charliss on the forehead and stood up. Hanna pulled the door open, held it tightly to stop it from creaking and then slipped into the hallway.

The heat was still on downstairs. The radiator's side valve had loosened as the base cooled, causing it to stay lukewarm and interfere with the pipes leading upstairs. Hanna climbed to her knees and turned the valve with all her might. She wedged it shut with a hardcover book and then waited to make sure it held in place before standing up.

Out of nowhere, a figure appeared in her window.

Hanna gasped. A scream rose in her throat.

At first she saw only eyes and a mouth, ghostly and pale in the moonlight. Her heart pounded in her chest. Her mind erupted with thoughts of men from a faraway land storming through the front door and murdering everyone inside. She took a single terrified step back and prepared to run upstairs.

Then the face came into full view. It was Daniel, standing by himself outside. He waved to her and Hanna looked over her shoulder to make sure they were alone. Her gaze drifted to her nightdress, to her exposed neckline, her bare arms and legs. She grabbed a blanket and wrapped it over her shoulders. Carefully, so as not to make a sound, she opened the window a crack. Hanna expected Daniel to say something, but he just tilted an eyebrow at her.

"You scared the life out of me," she said. A gust of cold air seeped inside and Hanna shivered. "It's freezing outside."

Daniel didn't say a word about the cold. He looked past Hanna to the stairwell where up above the family lay sleeping. In the distance was a car, his car. "Want to go for a ride?" he asked.

Daniel drove slowly, without his headlights on to avoid detection. In the passenger's seat beside him, Hanna had her jacket over her nightdress. Twice she'd turned around to look back at Jotham's house but couldn't see it in the dark. They were two streets away when Daniel asked Hanna where she wanted to go. Before she had a chance to think, the words "the tower cathedral" popped out of her mouth. Daniel nodded and turned onto a main road.

The car's headlights lit up, casting a sheen on the weathered aspen trees lining the way. With their broad leaves still absent for winter, the frosted tree branches looked like crooked white chalk lines drawn by a child on the darkness. In any other instance, Hanna would have found these foreboding, the blackness surrounding the car overwhelming, reason to turn back and return to the relative sanctuary of Jotham's house. But Daniel's quiet presence, the way he shifted his strong hands along the steering wheel, the tenderness in his voice as he asked her if she was comfortable, whether she knew how to drive, quelled Hanna's nerves.

They turned down another street and then another before entering the beating heart of Clearhaven. At night, the tower cathedral was steeped in shadows. It stood taller than any other structure in Clearhaven and yet was so dark. Daniel and Hanna might have missed it if not for the new church, Brother Paul's pulsing white orb, lighting up the sky. The new church's glow reflected off the tower cathedral's stained glass, the accumulation of dust concealing the deep reds and cobalt blues. Hanna asked Daniel to pull his car up to the tower's unlit side, where the white light split and nighttime loomed. The vehicle came to a stop and Daniel climbed out. He hurried around and opened Hanna's door.

They'd parked directly across from a small cemetery atop a grassy knoll. The scattered tombstones glistened with frost, their inscriptions crumbling, unreadable after so many years. When she was younger, Hanna had been fearful of this small graveyard. It wasn't just that bodies were buried underneath the ground. It was that they were corpses of people who'd lived before her time. Hanna didn't know them. She'd never known them. The unknown dead were far less trustworthy, far more restless, far more likely to haunt her dreams.

"Do you see that?" Daniel said.

Hanna turned around to see a handful of fireflies skittering and gliding in short, swift bounds at the woodlands' edge, peppering the tree line for the briefest of moments and then vanishing into the dark, only to reappear again. Last summer, hundreds of glow bugs had swarmed the forest near Jotham's house, but Hanna had never seen them so early in the year. Watching them now, she wondered whether there was purpose in their flight, what they were searching for, what secret drove them to dance. The fireflies plunged deep into the tall grass and Hanna shifted her gaze upward. She pointed to the top of the cathedral. "That's where we're going."

Daniel looked up. "It's awfully high."

"It's *very* high," she said. When Daniel gave her a skeptical look, she said, "From up there, you can see The Road. I bet we can see the big city, the tip of the horizon and everything beyond."

"And you don't think we'll get caught?" Daniel said.

"I'm positive," Hanna said. And she *was* positive. Hanna knew how the township was managed. The brothers Paul didn't patrol the innermost regions of Clearhaven at night. They lurked on the outskirts, more concerned with who was trying to get in or out than with what was happening at the church. It was *because* they were being brazen that Hanna had no fear of being discovered. If Jotham were to find her missing, the last place they would look would be the old tower cathedral.

Together they walked to the front of the cathedral where two large doors were bathed in light. Daniel pulled on the handles as hard as he could. When that didn't work, he pulled again.

"Maybe we should drive past the market-place, see what's happening there," he said.

Hanna ran her hand along the thin divide where the doors met. She looked up, to the left and the right. Just minutes ago, she'd left Jotham's house in the dead of night and driven off in a young man's car for the very first time. The tower cathedral was her idea. She couldn't imagine turning back now.

"Never give up until you exhaust all options," Hanna said.

She walked around to the back entrance that led to the bridal preparation room, the one where husbands came to claim their young brides in the minutes prior to their weddings. Hanna peered in through a closed window. Just days from now, she and Edwin would be praying together in this very room, alone, with Hanna in her white wedding gown and Edwin in his grandest attire. Somehow the night and the hazy white light made it all feel unreal, like Hanna's visit to Edwin's house, her upcoming wedding, this life she was expected to live without complaint was all part of a bizarre fiction she'd conjured up in her head.

Hanna pulled on the side door and found it locked as well, but up above, just beyond her reach, a window was cracked open.

"Lift me up," she said.

Daniel glanced upward. "You're insane."

"Perhaps," she said. "Lift me up all the same."

Hanna stepped toward Daniel, surprised

at how forward she was being. Underneath her jacket, Hanna was wearing only her nightdress. Daniel had seen her bare skin when he came to her window. She exposed herself further when she stepped out onto the porch, when she discarded the blanket, placed her jacket over her shoulders and the two of them slipped away like ghosts in the night.

Hanna braced herself against his shoulders and lifted her foot to his stomach. Daniel steadied himself and then cupped his hands and hoisted her up to the window. She pried it open and lifted herself through. This was where the difficulty arose. Hanna had no real plan for how to climb down. The cathedral was dark inside, far too dark to see and Hanna wasn't sure what was on the other side.

"Is everything okay up there?" Daniel said.

Hanna dangled on the other side, her feet swaying in the air, her fingers struggling to maintain their grip on the windowsill. The fall from Jotham's roof returned to her memory — that stiff twinge of terror, time evaporating, the immovable sky, the scream erupting out of her mouth; the powerless feeling the instant before she hit the ground. Below Hanna the darkness waited to swallow her whole. It was the darkness she feared, the unknown. Hanna's fingers started to slip.

"It's better to leap than it is to fall!" Daniel called from the other side.

Hanna steadied her resolve. She bent her knees and let go, fully expecting to plummet into a vacuous pit of some kind. Instead, her feet touched the floor less than two feet below. Hanna groped through the dark. She fumbled aimlessly about a nearby desk and discovered a single candlestick. Hanna felt her way through the desk drawer for a pack of matches and lit the candle, and then she unfastened the dead bolt and opened the door.

Daniel stepped inside. He rubbed his eyes until they adjusted to the candlelight.

"Where are we going?" he asked.

Hanna pointed to a set of stairs. "Up."

The candle cast an eerie sheen over the cathedral. The pews, the stairs and the stage, the carpets turned red in the flickering light. Hanna's breath hung like mist in the cold air and through it she saw the Creator's face etched in the stained glass hanging high in the rafters, his eyes all but concealed by dust, his somber countenance shrouded in black.

Hanna stepped on the stage. Last autumn,

she'd watched a child bride burst into tears on this very spot. The girl's father ran to her, not to console her but to stop her wailing. He grabbed her by the wrists and held her in place. Her father shouted in his daughter's ear, while the groom — a hunchbacked poultry farmer with one bloodshot eye — stood absolutely still, a haze of disinterest surrounding him. It took almost an hour for the girl to stop crying long enough to complete the ceremony. That was the greatest defiance Hanna had ever witnessed and still it achieved nothing. The girl was married and whisked away. Months later, Hanna saw her in the new church, her belly plump and round.

"Is this where you're getting married?" Daniel said.

Hanna nodded. "Brother Paul still insists on performing all marriage ceremonies here. I don't know why he and your father built that new church if they don't intend on using it for everything." Hanna really did wonder why. As her wedding day approached and she'd started to picture the ceremony in her mind, she could only imagine Brother Paul still used the tower cathedral because it was a link to the past, to his past, to the time of the first settlers. "Did you witness any marriage ceremonies while you were outside Clearhaven?" she said.

Daniel stepped onto the stage with her. "No. I didn't have a chance. We were moving around from place to place a lot. I did meet a lot of people, though, mostly families. They were really different."

"Different how?"

"To begin with, men only have one wife. The families are smaller," Daniel said.

"Aren't they concerned about The Rapture?"

"The Rapture?"

Hanna held the candle up to her face. "The Creator teaches that a man must have at least three wives to be allowed into Heaven. Those without three wives must bear the burden of the forsaken. They wait in purgatory for a hundred years before the Creator looks at them again, and still, there's no assurance they'll be chosen. They might never live in paradise. Plural wives are a necessity. Surely you remember your teachings from school."

"I was homeschooled, remember? We had a slightly different curriculum," Daniel said.

"You must have heard Brother Paul speak of this before."

"Yes. Of course. I mean, I suppose," Daniel said, staring off into the stained glass.

228

"My mind tends to drift."

"I think it's drifting right now."

Daniel let out a short, soft laugh. "Perhaps you're right."

He stepped off the stage and felt his way toward the pews where he sat down. Up above, the rafters shifted. A low whistle, uncannily similar to a wolf's howl, originated high in the belfry and bled through the structure, fading as it reached the uneven floorboards. Hanna took a step and a half dozen boards shifted under her feet. She sat down beside Daniel, the wood cold against her legs.

"Are you okay?" Daniel said.

"Why do you ask?"

"You're trembling."

Hanna touched her cheek. She flushed with embarrassment. Now that Daniel mentioned it, she felt like her whole body couldn't stop trembling.

Daniel set his hand on her arm to steady her. "It's okay to be afraid," he said.

"You're the second person to tell me that."

He took his hand back and shifted one leg under the other. Daniel met Hanna's gaze. His eyes burnt bright in the candlelight.

"Someone once told me that fear only subsides when joy is so powerful that you refuse to be afraid."

"Who told you this?"

Daniel smiled. His gaze lingered. "Okay, you caught me. I said it. But just because I said it, doesn't make it any less true."

"That's profound," Hanna said.

"I'm far from profound. I promise you I don't sit around waxing philosophical all day."

"But you have these thoughts, *involved* thoughts, like about people on the other side of the world. It's a wonder you can get through your day what with everything running through your head."

Daniel opened his mouth and then closed it again. He shifted in his seat.

"What is it?" Hanna said. "You can tell me."

"It's . . . it's just — there's a huge world out there, all these amazing things I've never seen. Sometimes I look around Clearhaven and I wonder if there isn't something else I should be doing." Daniel placed his hand on Hanna's arm and then pulled it away. "I don't mean right now. Trust me, there's no place I'd rather be at this very moment . . ."

"But?" Hanna said.

"But everyone wants me to stay in this little town. It's not just Brother Paul. My parents are planning on me being their successor. You know, their heir. Only, for some reason, whenever I'm sitting in my family's living room or splitting firewood or cleaning out the back shed, I . . ."

"You wonder."

"That's it," Daniel said. "I wonder and then my mind . . . wanders."

A warm stream of wax dribbled down Hanna's fingers and she turned the candle on its side, allowing it to drip onto the floor.

"What about you?" Daniel said.

"I'm not sure my thoughts are as involved as yours."

"Come on," Daniel said. "There must be some hidden desire, something you want to do with your life that you've never told anyone about."

Hanna handed Daniel the candle and pulled her jacket in close. She tucked her nightdress under her legs. All week, her mind had been preoccupied with secrets, visions of what it would be like to walk off into the wild and never be seen again. And now here she was, in the midst of her secret life and when Daniel asked, when she finally had a chance to speak her mind — she couldn't. Not yet.

"It's okay," Daniel said and then nudged her with his shoulder. "Maybe just tell me one thing?"

Hanna thought for a moment. "I've always

wanted to wear a red dress."

"Really? A red dress?"

"The Creator forbids women from wearing red. Any other color is fine, so long as your neckline's covered and your hemline is modest." She paused. "Haven't you noticed that women around here never wear red?"

"I suppose."

Hanna rolled her eyes. "Boys know nothing of fashion," she said. "It's something they teach us girls when we're young. They pull us aside and tell us never to wear red. Brother Paul says it's the color harlots wear in the big city."

"You don't sound convinced."

Hanna ran her fingers along the floral pattern on her nightdress. "It's not that I don't believe him. And it's not that I was born desperately wanting to wear a red dress. But it's strange — when something's taken away from you, you just want it so badly. I love red. Late at night in the summer, those few minutes when the sun sinks into the horizon and the sky turns this brilliant bright red color, like a matchstick that just burst into flames. I've always wanted to wear red."

"You should."

"Are you suggesting I come sauntering into church in a strapless red frock?"

"Why not?"

"I would be tarred and feathered in the town square," Hanna said.

Daniel laughed out loud as though he never expected those words to come out of her mouth.

"I don't think they'd actually cover you in feathers," he said.

"Still, all the same . . ."

The candlelight flickered. A breeze from above pushed on the flame and when it settled, a silence enveloped the room. A bold notion popped into Hanna's head. She thought about reaching over and holding Daniel's hand, entwining their fingers, pressing their palms together and feeling the touch of his skin. Her hand was resting on her knee, palm up, fingers open. It had been there for a minute, maybe more, and still Daniel hadn't moved to take it. Hanna made up her mind. She would hold his hand. Her skin felt warm. Her stomach swirled. She closed her eyes. Hanna breathed in softly and reached over.

"Are we still going upstairs?" Daniel said.

Hanna's hand hung in the blank space between them. Quickly, she brought it back, and Daniel glanced down. Hanna wasn't sure whether he saw her reaching for him. The candlelight was faint and she'd already tucked her hand under her leg. Hanna longed to reach out again, to break free from of any worry, to be audacious and unashamed. But she couldn't bring herself to do it.

Suddenly, unexpectedly, a light tinted the stained glass. It came from outside, a vehicle's headlights illuminating the cathedral, and Hanna's heart jumped, thinking it could be the two Pauls patrolling the church grounds. It might have been Brother Paul himself returning to the old tower cathedral to reclaim a long-forgotten item, one of his files perhaps. The bright light lingered, alarming Hanna, shattering any sense of security that she and Daniel were alone.

Hanna and Daniel sat perfectly still as the light flashed across the walls and then faded before disappearing as the car pulled away. Together they breathed a sigh of relief. Hanna looked up into the rafters, at the winding stairwell that led to the belfry.

"Yes. Let's go," she said.

They were halfway up when Daniel lost his footing on the rickety old boards. Hanna was leading the way and though their eyes had grown somewhat accustomed to the darkness, it was still difficult to see. Daniel stepped on a loose board and slipped. Instinctively, Hanna grasped hold of his hand. She pulled him close and their fingers entwined. Daniel's cheek brushed up against hers and rather than retreat from her touch, Daniel lingered, his warm skin inviting. "Thank you," he said and pulled back slightly.

An ocean of emotions flowed inside Hanna: excitement, trepidation, anticipation, and for a moment, she thought their lips might touch. That Daniel might kiss her right there in the middle of the stairwell. Instead, he placed his hand against the wall, steadying himself. They walked up the stairs together, ten stories in total, though the spiral staircase lacked partitions.

Hanna stepped into the belfry first. Up top was a large black bell and four pillars. She wrapped her arm around a pillar and looked out at the open expanse. There was Clearhaven in all its glory. Beyond the white church's glow, Hanna could see the marketplace. She saw the tip of her father's rooftop in the distance, the sprawling woodlands, the marsh and the lights in the houses like little cubes of sunlight dropped into the darkness. The Road lay directly west. From the ground, The Road seemed to go on forever. But from this great height, a hazy orange glow hovered in the distance, faint like a painting with too many layers of gloss, but still — an end point, a resolution, proof that Clearhaven was not alone.

Careful with his footing, Daniel stepped out beside her and pointed toward the glow. "I'm going there two nights from now," he said.

Hanna almost lost her balance. "You're leaving?"

"Just for one night. Do you remember that singer you heard on my headphones? Well, she's coming to town. I saw an ad for the show the night before we returned home, so my brothers and I walked to the venue and I bought tickets."

Daniel took in the view fully now. He breathed in deep and looked at Hanna. A bundle of nerves thundered inside her each time he glanced her way. She looked down, to her side, in the distance, anywhere except his eyes. But he kept looking at her. Daniel's eyes drew hers upward. They were soft and speckled with silver and they made Hanna want to get behind them and see Clearhaven, see The Road, see Hanna the way Daniel saw her.

"You can come with me to the show, if you like," he said.

Hanna shook her head. "I couldn't."

"Of course you can. You can do anything."

"I've never left Clearhaven."

"Don't worry. It's only one night and I'll

have you back before dawn."

Hanna turned away. "I'm getting married in five days."

Daniel's tone changed. His smile faded. "You don't have to do that, you know. You don't have to do what they say."

Hanna's stomach felt hollow, her arms as light as feathers. She looked at Daniel again, his delicate cheekbones, those penetrating eyes. With his one arm around the pillar, he edged toward her and put the other arm around her shoulder. Hanna's first instinct was to step back inside and hurry down the stairwell. Only, she didn't want to leave. The cool wind washed against her face. It seeped under her jacket and against her skin. But Hanna could barely feel it. Everything inside her felt on fire.

She leaned forward, brought her face close to his.

Hanna closed her eyes and Daniel's lips brushed against hers, much softer than she expected. He pulled back and gazed at her, maybe to see if she was certain. Of course she was certain.

Hanna's lips quivered. She brought her tongue to her teeth. Hanna closed her eyes and kissed him lushly, passionately. Daniel put his free arm around her back and in Hanna's mind, colors spun in dizzying circles, greens and reds and the brightest blues penetrated the grayest of shadows. Her heart raced. Daniel's lips tasted sweet like honey and as he reached his hand up to her cheek, Hanna felt safe. She felt free. She felt like she could do anything.

The world drifted away and all that came before and all that was to come after were forgotten. She leaned in farther, blissful and jubilant in the apex of her secret life.

17

The next morning, Hanna walked into the kitchen to find Kara sitting at the table, staring out the window with an empty cup in her hands. When Hanna said "good morning," Kara glanced her way. She offered a smile that looked painful to wear and then returned to gazing off into the woods, the bruise on her cheek now yellow like butter, a slight greenish color forming along her jaw. The young ones dashed through the kitchen, chasing each other in a game of tag, and Hanna waited until they passed before checking the kettle on the stove. It was still warm.

"Would you like some more tea?" she said.

Kara shook her head. She pressed her fingertips to her cheek, right where it had swelled, and continued staring out the window.

Hanna sat down next to her mother. Outside, frost glistened on the grass, an

early-morning mist obscuring the woodlands' enormity, in contrast to the crisp,
clear sky of last night. Hanna had seen these
trees, these pockets of leaves and the pathway into the woodlands hundreds of times
before. But she'd never focused on them.
The woodlands' stillness was soothing, re-
assuring in that the world would still be here
tomorrow and the next day and the day
after that. Hanna exhaled. Her mind returned to her candlelit conversation with
Daniel, the thoughtful way he opened her
door for her, the taste of his lips. Hanna
brought her legs up. She cradled her knees
in her arms and allowed herself to savor the
memory, to replay it, to relive the burst of
excitement she'd felt the moment their
hands touched on the stairwell.

Her mother's voice pulled Hanna from
her thoughts.

"Let's go for ice cream today," Kara said.

She was looking directly at Hanna; for
how long, Hanna didn't know. Kara's fingers were spread across her breastbone,
curling slowly inward, as though she was
holding herself upright. Her eyes were puffy,
and yet her jaw was clenched, the lines
around her mouth rigid.

"All of us?" Hanna said, thinking how
Jotham would balk at the cost.

"No," Kara said. "Just you and me. Let's go to the marketplace after lunch. Do something together for a change."

Hanna thought it strange that her mother wanted to go for ice cream when it was still so cold outside. And she almost said something, but Kara's expression told her not to question anything she said today.

From the hallway, Emily approached. She braced her hand against the wall for support. "I need help with my jacket," she said.

Hanna reached inside Emily's jacket and righted an inside-out sleeve. As she watched Emily struggle to slip it over her shoulders, a wave of regret washed over her. Hanna still didn't know what was to become of Emily after her wedding. She hadn't found the courage to ask Jotham if he'd arranged for Emily to live with her and Edwin. Jotham was out on the back porch now, reclined on a deck chair, smoking a cigarette, something he rarely did and usually only when he was hard at the drink. Early morning was not the time to approach him with requests. In the late afternoon, his disposition might improve. The midway point between his first and his sixth whiskies was still a long way off.

She helped Emily with her zipper and walked the children to the door for their

241

day at school. "Try to be good today," she said as they stepped outside.

Before he left, Charliss surprised Hanna by embracing her. Hanna braced herself for Charliss to tickle her or tell a silly joke. However, the punch line never came and only when she was sure he was serious, did she hug him back.

Charliss whispered in her ear. "You never came home last night."

Hanna pulled away. Her hand clasped Charliss's shoulder, to brace herself for what he said next.

"I heard you leave," he said. "I heard the front door shut and a car drive away. I waited for you until I couldn't stay awake any longer. When I woke up this morning, you were downstairs." He locked eyes with his big sister. "Where did you go?"

Katherine called out from the other room. "You're going to be late!"

Hanna ran her hand across Charliss's cheek, gently, tenderly, the way his mother, Belinda, never would. How could she explain what she'd done, the way she felt last night? Even now, hours later, each time Hanna took a breath, a warmth beat like a second heart inside her. Her skin still tingled. And Charliss was just a boy. He would never understand. He couldn't. "It's

242

best not to keep your teachers waiting," she said.

Charliss's eyes narrowed. They lingered, clearly suspicious of Hanna's obvious deflection. Katherine called again, and this time Charliss joined his siblings.

Hanna watched him walk out the door. Seconds later, little Ahmre reached her hands in the air and Hanna hoisted the child onto her hip. They'd just stepped back inside when Jotham appeared in the hallway. His tall figure blocked their way. Jotham scratched a patch of ingrown hair on his neck and held out a jug. "It's empty," he said.

Hanna didn't ask what he meant. She knew he wanted her to fetch more whiskey and not from the marketplace. The liquor there was too expensive, too watered-down. Hanna would have to visit the old hermit again. She would have to cross the woodlands, and she would have to hurry to complete her journey in the daylight while the wolves still slept. Hanna took the jug.

"How will I pay?" she asked.

Jotham undid a buckle on his back brace. He loosened it and secured it again, almost stumbling into the wall as he found his balance. His skin looked clammy this morning, his movements sluggish, as though he hadn't slept. "Tell the man I'll pay him soon. He knows my credit's good."

"Will that work?"

Jotham clamped his jaw shut and stepped forward. His massive figure towered over the girls, hot air billowing from his nose, but he didn't raise his voice. "Of course it'll work," he said and lumbered past Hanna, down the hallway and into the front alcove, where he collapsed onto the couch.

Hanna set Ahmre down. She thought of Emily and Charliss, already walking to school, and her mother staring off in the kitchen. Hanna didn't want to make the trip alone. Briefly, she toyed with the idea of asking Daniel to go with her. Then she remembered Paul the Third traipsing off into the woods to fetch the bottle of moonshine. This town was too small, the old hermit too likely to tell Brother Paul's sons of her comings and goings to be wandering about with a strange boy accompanying her.

Ahmre had uncorked the jug and was blowing on it, creating a low, hoarse drone. Hanna leaned so they were face-to-face. "What do you say, angel? Do you want to go for a walk through the woods?"

"What about the wolves?"

Hanna shook her head. "The wolves only come out at night. And besides, we can't spend our entire lives being afraid of wolves, now can we?"

Minutes later, they were out the door. For all her brave words, it would have been foolish not to protect Ahmre as they traveled deep into the woodlands. Hanna didn't ask Jotham's permission. She opened the storage bench on the deck and pulled out his shotgun. She felt its weight in her hand, ran her fingers along the scuffed wooden stock and the cold metal of the trigger guard. Hanna checked to make sure it was loaded, engaged the safety and slung its strap over her shoulder before taking Ahmre's hand and setting down the gravel road.

Together they kept to the footpaths. Hanna steered clear of the mossy underbrush and the steep rocky patches, lest the three-year-old have difficulty navigating the terrain. Only twice was Hanna forced to pick Ahmre up, once to cross a shallow stream and a second time to climb a crumbling tree stump. Ahmre never complained once. She chatted the whole way, toddler talk, asking Hanna if she was married yet and detailing incidents in the past week in which her brothers had "swiped" her toys.

As they passed the river, a small beaver dam came into view. Ahmre squealed with delight when three yearlings poked their heads out of the water. The creatures submerged and resurfaced, and Ahmre cheered as they poked their noses into the misty morning air.

Eventually they came to the old hermit's dilapidated cabin in the woods. The cabin existed in two parts. The left side had long collapsed inward and now housed all sorts of unkempt foliage and uninvited woodland creatures (last time Hanna visited, she spotted the masklike stripes of two raccoons peering through a hole in the rotten wood). The cabin's right portion was a teetering shack held aloft by several precariously perched wooden beams and a rusted-out car bumper wedged on its side. Hanna could see the old recluse's moonshine distillery through the open door.

She led Ahmre over to a tree and told her to stand still, to wait where Hanna could see her and, most important, to scream if danger reared its head.

"What do you do if you see a wolf?"

"I scream," Ahmre said.

"If you see a person?"

"I scream."

"If you see a police officer?"

Ahmre hesitated.

"You scream. Do you understand?"

Ahmre nodded and Hanna kissed her atop her head. She untied the empty jug from a string over her shoulder and hitched Jotham's shotgun against her hip. As Hanna approached, a great clank sounded within the cabin. Then a jangle, followed by three more clanks. Hanna poked her head in the door. The old hermit was surrounded by wires and copper tubes, pots and condensers, two large stoves and a set of diamond-shaped metallic frustums. Despite the chill in the air, he was shirtless, on his knees, hammering away at a misshapen boiling chamber with a wooden mallet.

"Hello?" Hanna said.

The hermit looked up. His face twisted into a knot at the sight of Hanna's shotgun. "You'd best leave that outside," he said.

Hanna steered the barrel of the shotgun toward the ground. She leaned it against the front door, within reach, just in case.

The hermit rolled to his feet. He pulled a dirty brown shirt off a hook and slipped it over his shoulders, and then he ran his hand across his eyebrows, where he struggled to tame his wild white hairs. He gritted his teeth. Hanna counted two at the top and a throng of incisors at the bottom, by turns black and yellow, like a decomposing ear of corn.

She held out the empty jug. "Jotham sent me to get whiskey."

"Do you have any money?"

"Well, no. I can return later, with money, if you'd like," she said.

The hermit picked up his mallet and for a moment Hanna thought he might come at her. Her heart rate soared and Hanna lifted her hands to deflect the blow. Then he clanked the boiling chamber. The hermit aimed for a warped protrusion jutting out of the metal and clanked it again. This time the protrusion bent inward. He flashed his crooked teeth, undoubtedly pleased with his results. The hermit set the mallet down and took the jug from Hanna.

"Tell Jotham he can pay me within a fortnight. Less time is better. More would be ill-advised," he said and walked over to a large decanter in the corner. He uncorked it, took in its fumes and then poured the brown liquid into Hanna's jug, with surprising care not to spill a drop.

Hanna glanced out the open door at her little sister. Ahmre was sitting in front of the tree where she'd left her, pulling frosted blades of grass out of the earth and laying them flat on her palm. These past few days, Hanna had been so preoccupied with her engagement, with Daniel, with her mind working itself into a frenzy over what the future might bring, that she'd almost forgotten how young Ahmre was. How much she still needed her oldest sister. Ahmre looked up and showed Hanna the grass she'd collected. Hanna waved and then turned back to find the hermit standing an arm's length away, his back hunched, his pupils glistening in the dim light.

Hanna's breath caught in her throat. She tried to step back but bumped into a damp metal cauldron.

The hermit inched closer. "You're Hanna, aren't you?"

She eyed the old recluse warily. Hanna had entered this cabin a dozen times, twice with Emily, the rest with Charliss at her side, always to purchase Jotham's liquor. Not once did she tell the hermit her name, never before did he ask.

"That's correct," she said.

He handed Hanna the jug. "From what I hear, you're fighting a losing battle."

Hanna secured the cork. She tied a string to the jug and slung it over her shoulder. "What battle?"

"You're getting married soon, aren't you?"

"In four days."

"But you don't want to marry that old man, do you?"

Hanna edged toward the door. "How do you know all this?"

In the corner, a gush of steam shot forth from a pipe. The hermit grimaced. He climbed onto a countertop and hammered away with his mallet. When that didn't work, he grabbed a wide roll of industrial tape and wrapped it around the leak until the copper pipe disappeared from view. He sat on the counter, his eyes bulging.

"I hear things," he said. "Everyone who walks through that door tells me a little something. Words out of people's mouths are like puzzle pieces. It only takes a bit of patience to fit them together."

Hanna pushed her hair away from her eyes. She twirled the strands, puzzled by this strange man, whatever he was implying. "I should be going," she said.

She was halfway out the door, weapon and whiskey in hand, when the hermit called. "You'd be better off protecting yourself."

Hanna stopped. She searched the woods with her eyes — the pathway Paul the Third traipsed down, the rounded hilltops to the west, the endless trees in all directions — to make sure no one else was nearby. Stillness surrounded her, every danger, every threat secreted away, lurking behind the hazy mist. Hanna brought the shotgun closer, her thumb on the safety, prepared to dislodge it if need be. She met the old hermit's gaze. "Are you speaking in riddles?"

"A riddle is a mystery. Mysteries are meant to be solved, and your solution is right under your nose, child." He pointed at Ahmre, now building a tiny fort out of sticks.

Hanna still wasn't sure what the old hermit meant. He was confusing her, most likely on purpose. Hanna regretted not inviting Daniel along on this excursion after all. Last night, he'd listened to her as though Hanna was someone with something to say. The more she thought about it, Daniel was the only one who hadn't placed any expectations on her.

The old hermit was still staring her down. Hanna turned to walk away when the hermit followed.

"Why did you bring that little girl with you today?" he said.

"I wanted company."

"Ah, but I bet you have company all day long. I bet you come from a large family. There probably isn't time for you to sit on the toilet without some child climbing on your legs." He cracked his neck and five vertebrae popped in succession, a nauseating sound. "You think you need someone to

251

protect."

Hanna looked back at Ahmre and then at the hermit again. "Speak plainly with me."

"I've seen you with that girl, the one with the twisted back. Now I see you with this little tot, out here in the woods, calling upon a madman." He tugged at a blackened tooth, wiggled it loose, as though to punctuate his madness. "I'll tell you the truth, Hanna with the golden hair: you can't protect everyone else, at least not when you should be protecting yourself."

This time Hanna heard the old hermit clearly. That feeling of falling inside herself returned. Only, it was different. *Hanna* was different now. She wasn't the same person she'd been just days before. She couldn't pinpoint exactly when the change occurred. If it was when she kissed Daniel in the belfry or when she stole away in the dead of the night with him. If it was when she refused to cower in Paul the Second's presence or when she rose to her feet after the fall from the rooftop. But something had changed. And now this old hermit — this stranger, as odd and outlandish a soul as she'd ever met — saw that she was trying to protect Emily. Trying to protect Ahmre. That Hanna wished with all her being that she was able to protect Kara from Jotham, when, in truth, Hanna couldn't even protect herself. She couldn't protect herself from Edwin, from Brother Paul and his uncouth underlings. She couldn't protect herself from becoming like everyone else. In four days' time, Hanna would be married and she would be no different than her sister-mothers, no different than Edwin's wives: commonplace and ordinary and subservient, trapped like an animal in a cage. If she ever came face-to-face with her brave other self on the other side of the world, what would Hanna tell her? That she didn't have the courage to protect her family? That she wasn't brave enough to protect herself?

Ahmre tugged at her sleeve. She was hiding behind Hanna's hip, out of view from the old recluse. "Hanna? Can we go home?"

Hanna picked up the girl and turned to the hermit. "Thank you."

"For what?"

"For your sage advice."

"Ain't no sage advice," he said. "Only the truth."

Hanna delayed a second. She eyed the hermit one last time. Underneath the white whiskers and the wide scars lining his cheeks, there was a man who, like Hanna, had faced divergent paths in his life, whose choices led to him living in the woods. A man who'd elected to walk away from the expectations of others.

"Then thank you for the truth," Hanna said.

She turned and walked back the way they came. Ahmre placed her head on Hanna's shoulder and closed her eyes. Hanna didn't look back, even when she heard the hermit's clanking mallet resonate through the woods.

18

Two hours later, Hanna approached the marketplace on Kara's arm. She was slightly taller than Kara now, the days of reaching up to hold her mother's hand long gone. The marketplace was full of activity, with vendors calling out their wares and customers looking to barter. A hodgepodge of aromas filled the air: fresh-baked bread and confectioner's sugar, basil and sage, the sharp, acidic odor of leather-tanning compounds. A blend of lavender and sandalwood wafted from the salves and ointments on the apothecary's table. Over by the police station, a toddler was feeding bread crumbs to the pigeons when a cluster of crows swept down from the trees and thieved the scant morsels. The child ran sobbing, looking for his mother, only Hanna didn't see whether he found her.

Hanna kept her gaze locked on the trailer where Makala worked. The very sight of it filled Hanna with unease. She couldn't help but wonder what Makala might say if she saw Hanna today, the harsh words she might offer Kara, what the vendors who'd heard their previous exchange must have thought.

Hanna tried her best to push these thoughts from her head. She was here on a special outing with her mother, a rare occurrence and perhaps the last time they might get to spend a few hours alone.

She took her mother's hand and Kara walked Hanna to the dairy vendor. Kara chose vanilla ice cream with little flakes of toffee in a cup. Hanna chose strawberry, in a cup, as well. Together they carried their cups to the picnic tables set up by the roadway. Kara sat down in an isolated spot, loud enough to hear sounds from the marketplace — women scolding their offspring, stray dogs yelping, the occasional truck churning up gravel as it passed by — but quiet enough to keep their conversation private.

Hanna dipped her spoon into her cup. The strawberries and milk had mixed into a frozen lather and the ice cream felt smooth against her tongue. Over the years, Hanna had only eaten ice cream from the marketplace a handful of times, her experience

with desserts limited to homemade pud-
dings and yogurts, each diligent preparation
resulting in varying degrees of success.
Perhaps the most enjoyable aspect was not
having a young child standing within arm's
reach, watching her with wide, pleading
eyes, hoping Hanna might share. She ig-
nored the cold air and dug into her ice
cream. Hanna had finished half her cup
when she noticed her mother hadn't taken
a bite.

Kara ran her hands over her face and
when she took them away, her eyes welled
up. Wrinkles flourished on her forehead,
where just hours ago there'd been none.
Kara brought her hands to her chest, wrung
them together and then dropped them to
the table. Hanna had seen her mother upset
before. She'd even seen her cry. But this
was different. Kara looked drained, as
though all the blood had left her body.

Deep down, Hanna wondered if this
wasn't somehow her fault. Had she said
something inappropriate at Edwin's house
the other day? Something to jeopardize their
union? Had her mother found out about
her time with Daniel? Hanna had thought
she'd been so careful. But, truthfully, she
hadn't. There were prying eyes all over
Clearhaven and they could have spotted her

inside Daniel's car, outside his parents' home, climbing in through the window of the old tower cathedral.

"What is it?" she said.

Kara wiped her cheeks with her sleeve. She reached inside her jacket and pulled out a plain white envelope, and then she passed it across the table.

Hanna opened the envelope and peered inside. Her eyes grew wide.

"Now, don't hold it up for the world to see," Kara said.

"How much is it?" Hanna said.

"It's two hundred and eighty-six dollars. I want you to have it."

Hanna pulled out the money and felt it against her hand. The bills were soft and worn as though they'd passed through hundreds of hands. Quickly, she tucked them back inside. "Where did you get this?"

Kara stammered. "The past few years, I've been trimming from the household expenses. I wish it were more, only Belinda watches our costs like a hawk. I should have been saving your whole life, ever since you were born."

Hanna peered inside the envelope again. Most of the bills were singles with a smattering of fives. No bill was larger than ten dollars. Still, it was an impressive amount, more money than Hanna had ever seen in one place.

"But I won't need this," Hanna said. "Edwin has more than enough to take care of me." She flipped the envelope facedown and looked away from it. "You should take it. You could buy a roast or a turkey. Or buy yourself something nice, like a new scarf."

Kara sobbed, a soft, anguished cry. She dug her fingernails into the table.

"What's wrong? Is it Father? Did he hit you?" Hanna asked, knowing full well what Jotham had done.

Kara shook her head. "You don't understand."

"Then help me. Help me understand."

Kara leaned in close. "You have to go," she whispered.

Hanna glanced over her shoulder, at the marketplace, at Makala's trailer in the distance, at the gravel road curving into the woodlands.

"Where?"

"Anywhere!" Kara yelled, surprising them both. "Now listen to me carefully," she said. "I want you to take this money and run away, away from Jotham, away from Edwin, away from this terrible place. You can take your father's truck. Do you still remember when I taught you how to drive?"

Hanna nodded.

"You can take The Road and drive to the city. Once you get there, I want you to leave the truck at the train station and buy a ticket to another city. And not a city nearby. If you stay too close, Edwin and Jotham will find you." Her voice sharpened. *"Brother Paul* will find you. They'll hunt you down and bring you back. You have to choose a city far away and you can't tell anyone where it is. And this is the most important part — once you leave, you can never come back."

Hanna heard her mother's brittle voice. She watched the tears flow freely down Kara's cheeks, her shaking hands. Hanna couldn't believe this was really happening. All week, she'd dreamed of running off into the woods, of living a different life, of waking up one morning in another place; and now that Kara was telling her to go, to leave Clearhaven forever, all she could think about was the people she'd leave behind.

"No," she said.

"Hanna . . ."

"You want me to leave without you?"

"I have to stay to watch over the children."

"Can't Katherine do that?"

Kara shook her head. "I might not be their mother, but I've known those children since the day they were born. I nursed them when they were sick. I raised them. After you leave, Jotham will be furious. Someone has to stay to convince him to act reasonably. I won't allow the little ones to suffer." She steadied her voice. "You have to trust me. This is for the best."

"You want me to leave Emily? To leave you behind so Father can hit you again?" Hanna pushed the envelope back along the table. "I won't do it. I won't take your money. I won't leave."

"Please," Kara said.

A fury rose in Hanna's chest. Where her anger came from — from Jotham or Edwin, from Brother Paul and his lecherous son, or her mother's simple, unfathomable plan — Hanna wasn't sure. She just knew she couldn't sit here any longer. She couldn't watch her mother cry anymore. Hanna stood up from the table. She walked past the deserted picnic tables, as fast as her legs would take her.

Kara chased after her. "Wait!"

Hanna was twenty paces away, headed toward the gravel road, with no plan for what she was going to do when she got there.

"Wait!" Kara stopped chasing her. Hanna was almost out of earshot when Kara called out one last time. "Hanna, you fell from the sky!"

Her words came out of nowhere, startling Hanna, shaking something deep inside her. Hanna turned around. How could Kara say this, of all things? On the street, no less, where anyone could hear.

Hanna stormed back, the rage boiling in her veins.

"This is no time for fairy tales, Mother."

Kara's tears flowed in waves, her brave veneer washed away. "It's true," she said.

"Did Charliss tell you about the rooftop?"

"Yes," Kara said quickly, and as Hanna turned away again, Kara grabbed her arm. "But that's not what I'm talking about. I mean that's not *all* I'm talking about. Hanna, eighteen years ago, almost to the day, the sky opened up. A baby fell from the heavens and landed unscathed. Hanna — that was you."

"That's just a story."

"It's not just a story!" Kara raised her voice and then quieted it right away. "I saw it with my own two eyes."

Hanna searched Kara's face. She studied the lines around her eyes, the way Kara held her jaw, to find where her intentions lay.

"You only know part of what happened," Kara said. "I need to tell you the truth. The *whole* truth. And I need you to listen to me. I never wanted to tell you like this, but just remember that I love you and I will always love you . . ." Kara said, her voice trailing off.

"Please just tell me."

Kara swallowed hard. She pressed her hands against her temples, breathed out a long breath and then began.

19

"I grew up far away from here, in a city where the buildings towered in the sky and there were lights so bright you could barely believe they were real. My mother and I lived in a one-bedroom apartment on a busy street. It was so different from Clearhaven. Throngs of people bustled by at all hours of the day; men in suits, women wearing T-shirts and pants, people of all shapes, sizes and colors. We got along well, my mother and I. She worked as a receptionist at an attorney's office and I helped out there sometimes. When I was your age, I graduated from school and then I started college, the school you go to when you're no longer a child, with the intent of learning to take care of animals.

"The year I turned twenty, my mother fell ill. It was bad. I hate to use the word *grave*, but that's what it was. My mother's sickness was in her lungs. It was in her stomach and her bones. For weeks on end, we were in and out of the hospital, the doctors giving her worse and worse news each time we visited.

"Eventually my mother had enough. She told me she didn't want to spend her last days dying in a strange bed inside a hospital room. She wanted to go back to the place where she was born, a small village one hundred miles west of Clearhaven. I drove my ailing mother to a place by the bay, a town too small to be called a town, called Baker's Hamlet, the quietest community on Earth.

"Baker's Hamlet was much smaller than Clearhaven. There were just a few dozen families living by the water and a handful of boats docked nearby. My mother and I moved into a small cabin and I did everything I could to take care of her. Only, hope was fleeting. My mother was dying. Her skin turned gray almost overnight and eventually she could no longer climb out of bed. A doctor came to visit and he told me it wasn't going to be long until she passed.

"That very night, consumed with grief, I stepped outside and saw the most glorious sight. The sky broke open and a white crack formed in the heavens above. Hanna, everything I told you in your story is true. The crack took over the sky. The villagers fell to their knees, some in fear, others in prayer. And then this little dot appeared high above. I ran to it. Hanna, I saw you fall and watched you crash into the ground. The noise that rang out was louder than anything I'd ever heard. When I finally reached the spot where you'd landed, there you were: a baby with the widest eyes I've ever seen — a gift from Heaven — staring back at me."

"No," Hanna said. She closed her eyes tight and opened them again, as though that might change what Kara had just said, as though somehow she could go back to how things were just minutes ago. All her life, she'd wanted the story of falling from the sky to be true, for it to be more than just a family fable. But to hear her mother tell it now, to hear that Kara truly believed she fell from the heavens, was overwhelming. Hanna felt light-headed. Her hands — from her fingertips to her palms — felt numb. She felt like Kara had just taken a brush and painted over everything Hanna had ever known, everything she'd ever believed.

Kara took Hanna's hand and held it close. "This really happened. You have to believe me."

"But —" Hanna said.

"Wait. There's more, so much more I've

wanted to tell you for so long," Kara said. "One of the men wrapped you in his jacket. He brought you back to Baker's Hamlet, where the entire village celebrated your arrival. Not a single soul slept that night. Even my mother — who was barely able to speak — insisted on seeing you from her deathbed. We were all so amazed. A few of the villagers debated what to do, whom to tell, whether to call the authorities. Everyone else was enthralled. This nice woman carried you into the village square and we all sat around looking at the miracle baby who'd fallen out of the sky.

"Then, as the sun rose in the morning, you began to wail. And you didn't stop. You cried like no baby had ever cried before. We tried everything we could think of to soothe you. Two women who'd been nursing their own babies tried their milk on you, only you refused their breasts. My neighbor tried rocking you and feeding you from a bottle and still nothing worked. You cried for two days straight. The sound was piercing. It was agony. Suddenly, this baby — this gift from above — didn't seem like a gift anymore.

"A meeting was held. People were angry. They felt deceived. No baby could wail as much as you did. No child of this world could cry so many tears. As a group, we decided to wait until morning and then take you into the city, to drive you to the nearest hospital and tell them what happened.

"Later that evening, my mother passed away. It happened rather quickly. She had no last words, no dying declaration. One moment she was breathing and the next . . . she just stopped. My neighbor, a childhood friend of my mother, stood over her, rubbing my mother's hair, singing a lullaby. That soft song pushed me past my breaking point. The tears I'd been holding back for weeks poured out of me like rain the moment I stepped out of that room.

"I wandered the bay — weeping — unsure what I was going to do. I had no family to speak of, no place to go. I didn't know whether to return to the city or stay in Baker's Hamlet. I was struggling with all this when I passed the house where you were being kept. I could hear your heart-wrenching screams from outside. Through the window, I saw the woman who lived there. She looked exhausted from lack of sleep, and when she stepped out into the backyard for some fresh air, I slipped into the parlor and picked you up from your crib. I held you close and, I swear, in that instant you fell fast asleep in my arms. Oh,

Hanna, I was so happy. We both stopped crying together and all I wanted to do was hold this little gift from Heaven.

"The peace didn't last long. Jotham — a man I barely knew, a man visiting on a stopover in Baker's Hamlet — was the first to discover me holding you. He couldn't believe how quietly you lay in my arms. Jotham steered me into a corner and stood over top of me. He pushed his finger against my chest and told me he was taking you away, that the villagers were a threat to you and that he knew of the only safe place to raise a child who fell from the sky. Looking back, I wonder why I didn't run, why I didn't stall until the villagers came to see that you'd stopped crying. I should have screamed and screamed until I couldn't scream anymore. But Jotham was a large man, an intimidating one. He had a presence, even more so when he was young.

"Jotham gave me a choice — go with him or stay behind and never see you again. Hanna, my mother had just died. I was overwhelmed with grief, with uncertainty. And yet, feeling your little body against mine, I knew I could never let you go. I'd discovered you, and I felt like you'd discovered me too. I couldn't let Jotham steal you away. That evening, he and his wife Belinda ushered us out of town.

"Before dawn's first light, we arrived in Clearhaven. Ten days later, I joined Jotham's family. Brother Paul arranged a quick marriage ceremony and before I knew it, I was living in this strange place with all these different rules. It was so odd being here at first, with talk about the Creator and men with three, four, often five or six wives. I didn't think I could live here. But I made Clearhaven my home so I could always look after you. I left my mother behind without giving her a proper funeral. I left my friends in the city behind forever. I left everything behind just as I'm asking you to do now. I'm not asking — I'm begging you to run far away from here."

Kara stopped and looked to Hanna to say something. Only, Hanna couldn't find the right words.

"What is it?" Kara asked.

"Why are you telling me all this now? I mean — why didn't you tell me about your mother years ago? About what happened in the village, with you and Father?"

"I couldn't," Kara said. "You were a child and it was my job to take care of you. How could I tell a little girl that I never gave birth to her? That she fell from the heavens while my mother lay dying? That Jotham forced

270

me to come to Clearhaven or else lose you forever?"

Hanna stood up straight. "But I'm not a little girl anymore."

"No. You're not. You're a young woman now and that's why I'm telling you the truth — the whole truth — now."

Hanna's thoughts stormed inside her head: images of a young Kara kneeling next to her dying mother's bed, of Kara discovering Hanna — the crying baby who'd fallen from the sky — and holding her close, soothing her tears, the fear that must have been etched in her face when Jotham threatened to steal the baby away. She thought about Edwin and Jotham, their proud expressions as they decided Hanna's fate in the white church; Emily hobbling through the hallway at home, unable to zip up her own jacket, let alone take care of herself; Daniel and his clay-colored eyes; those soft, crumpled dollar bills in the white envelope. Hanna imagined herself standing at a train station, without her brothers and sisters, without her mother, all alone, waiting for a locomotive to take her far away.

It was all too much to think about, too much to consider at once.

"Even if all this is true," she said, "I still

don't understand why you want me to go away."

Kara's voice grew calm. When she spoke, it sounded like she'd rehearsed these words in her head a hundred times. "Because you were meant for so much more than just being Edwin's fifth wife. You were meant for great things. I'm sorry I haven't been able to give you a chance to succeed at life. I thought I was being strong by staying here with you." Kara struggled to keep her hands from shaking. "I know what everyone thinks about me. I see their looks of pity at church. The women here think I'm incapable of having another child. But the truth is that, all these years, I refused to let Jotham put a baby in my belly. I thought, in that way, I was empowered. But somehow, my power slipped away without me even realizing it.

"If you stay here and marry Edwin, you will be pregnant within the year and any hope of doing something special with your life will be gone forever. You must know you were meant for more than this."

"Mother . . ." Hanna said.

"That fall from the rooftop would have killed anyone else. Don't you see? You weren't conceived by a man and a woman. The heavens gave birth to you. You fell from the sky." When Hanna didn't respond, Kara

272

held out the envelope. "Please, take this money. I know it isn't much, but it's all I have."

Hanna's fingertips touched the envelope. "I can't leave without you," she said.

"You can. You must."

A few scattered leaves sailed down from the trees, slow and haltingly, like snowflakes. Above, clouds had gathered. A storm was brewing. Kara was standing close, her shoulders hunched, her eyes red and swollen from crying. In the distance, Hanna saw a woman exiting the police station. Was it Makala? Another one of Brother Paul's wives? She couldn't tell. She only knew she didn't want to be seen out in the open, holding an envelope full of dollar bills.

"I don't know what to think," she said.

Kara pushed the money into Hanna's hand. She bowed her head against Hanna's chest and then met her gaze. "You have to ask yourself, deep in your heart — what do you believe?"

20

At dusk, the overcast sky was dim as though someone had thrown a blanket over a lampshade. Hanna walked down the roadway with her sisters on either arm, trying her best not to think about the ceremony about to take place. Tonight, a special pre-wedding ritual would precede the regular church service, one in which she would be forced to kiss Brother Paul's palm, to give herself over fully and completely to the Creator, ensuring she was virtuous and chaste before her wedding night.

She tried to take comfort in her sisters' voices, their conversation about their school day. But Hanna felt inordinately aware of her family's eyes. She couldn't stop thinking that one of them knew she'd kissed Daniel in the belfry, that they'd overheard her mother's astonishing story.

I fell from the sky. I am meant for more than this.

They rounded the bend past the tower cathedral and Jotham stepped out of his truck to survey the family. The white church's glow hung about him like an aura, transforming him — momentarily, at least — into a looming apparition. His face dissolved into shadows and Hanna could see why she'd been so afraid of him all these years. It wasn't just his imposing size. It was the way his boots rattled the floor when he walked. It was the haste with which his rage surged to the surface. It was the wild, uncontrolled look in his eyes as he stormed down the hallway, belt in hand, intent on whipping one of the boys.

He straightened his back and stared at Emily and Charliss. His eyes shifted toward Hanna and her heart sank, fearing that her father had learned about Daniel. She gripped Emily's hand tightly.

Then Jotham coughed, a hacking cough that started out as a single surge. It seemed to finish quickly, and then Jotham convulsed again and all of a sudden he couldn't control it. Jotham doubled over. His back brace clasped him in place and he cried out like a wild dog. The women ran to him. Belinda struggled to lift him up, only he cried out again, hacking and coughing on his knees. Some of the children backed away, but others, including Emily, rushed over to help.

Hanna observed them all with a peculiar detachment, like she was watching a beehive fall from a tree and turn on its side, the bees buzzing with what looked like purpose but really just zipping around, colliding into one another in a frenzy.

If Kara were to be believed, then this man wasn't her father. He'd had no part in creating her. He was a stranger, as alien to Hanna as any big-city interloper, as foreign as any random man on the other side of the world. Jotham was a thief who'd stolen her in the dead of night and forced Kara to come along. This life Hanna had led — the one Jotham dictated, the one Brother Paul ordained — wasn't hers. If Kara was telling the truth, none of these people were her flesh and blood. And Hanna was meant for more than this.

Hanna knelt with the other women and placed her arms on the long, circular board surrounding the white church's stage. As a child, Hanna had grown accustomed to kneeling on the padded boards in the tower cathedral's pews. She was used to the stiffness, to the mild ache in her kneecaps, to aligning her posture in order to distribute her weight evenly. This new floorboard cut like a knife. The longer Hanna knelt, the more it felt like her legs were being split in half. For almost a year now, Hanna had had bruises on her knees, deep, round discolorations the shade of burnt leather.

Hanna had seen women collapse in church before. She'd seen the pain become too much and the women fall to the side and drop backward. But she'd never seen one of them stand up and be forced back down. Hanna had never seen a woman in Clearhaven rise to her feet and yell "no!" at the top of her lungs.

Emily leaned into her big sister's ear. "They're calling you," she said.

Hanna looked up. The entire congregation was watching. Brother Paul was standing on his raised platform, his robes glimmering in the white light. A dull heat wafted in waves from the vents overhead and those eyes were still on her, devouring her piece by piece. Did any of them think Hanna would be the first girl in Clearhaven to refuse to kiss Brother Paul's palm? She doubted it. When obedience is ingrained, defiance is beyond consideration. Insubordination isn't just sacrilege; it's contrary to reason. These women kneeling, the boys behind them who — save a chosen few — would soon be pushed out into the world, had no reason to suspect what she was thinking, no reason to know she led a secret life.

She stood up and steadied herself. Now was not the time for histrionics. This was a formality. Hanna approached the stage and got down on one knee. It was so quiet; Hanna could hear her sleeve brush against her dress, the sound of her knee touching the ground. She took Brother Paul's outstretched hand. Hanna felt his dry skin and saw how, up close, it was cracked like shattered marble. She turned his hand over and pressed her lips together. Brother Paul's flesh smelled like medicine, the sleeves of his robes like soap. Hanna felt his finely manicured fingernails, the contours of his knuckles and the slight tremble in his hand. She closed her eyes. Hanna placed her lips to his palm and kissed his dry, callused hand. No sound came from the masses, just unnerving silence as Brother Paul helped Hanna to her feet, his smile wide like a crocodile's.

Hanna faced the crowd. She didn't feel any more pure or chaste than she had a moment ago. She didn't feel absolved of her sins. If anything, her resolve hardened: that this place — this town, this church, this very room — was in direct opposition to everything she wanted, everything she held true in her heart. Yet still she walked back to her family as she was told, still her lips held the taste of Brother Paul's salty palm.

As she reached her kneeling place, Hanna spotted Daniel's mother and his father's two other wives. It was dark in their corner and Hanna could barely make out their faces. She scanned quickly, her heart fluttering. Hanna couldn't see Daniel anywhere.

Then one of the men shifted. His head pulled out of view and there was that disheveled mop of hair, those gentle eyes. Daniel was standing beside his father, a dark denim jacket covering his shoulders. Hanna caught his eye. They shared a glance and before she could find some way to signal him, to implore Daniel to stay after the service, Emily grabbed her hand. She knelt down and Daniel slipped out of view.

After the service, juice and tea were served in the auditorium. On a separate table, stacks of homemade cookies overflowed from one tray to the next. Emily stood with her sisters, gaping in astonishment at the assorted delicacies: chocolate chip, peanut butter with white sugar, caramel-striped biscuits. Children from other families were openly devouring the treats in front of them and all Emily could do was watch. Months ago, Jotham had forbidden the children from eating after church. Hanna understood his motivation. He didn't want others to think his children needed food. That argument might have swayed her, if not for the fact that the family had dined on nothing but shallow bowls of soup and dried bread crusts last night. This morning, the twins had to share a bowl of porridge. Ahmre had eaten soup again for breakfast. The children *did* need these cookies.

Jotham had taken refuge in a large leather chair in the far corner of the church. His skin still looked sallow and Belinda and Katherine were tending to him with hot tea and a facecloth. His eyes were closed and even if he could see, he was in no shape to intervene. Hanna picked up a cookie and handed it to Emily.

"Really?" Emily said.

"Go ahead. You deserve it," she said. Hanna picked up six more and handed them to her sisters. The boys didn't wait. They ran past Hanna and stuffed themselves full of snacks.

Hanna stepped away from the table, a sense of accomplishment rushing through her veins. Before she could bask in the moment, her mother walked by, carrying lemon slices for Jotham's tea. She mouthed a single word. "Go." Kara held Hanna's gaze for a moment and then kept walking.

Hanna turned away. All afternoon, Hanna had felt an enormous weight on her shoulders. Just yesterday, she'd thought the pressure of marrying Edwin, of living in a house with his wives — that wretched woman who challenged her at every turn and the other one who never uttered a single word — was too much to bear. Now Kara wanted Hanna to believe she never came from her body, that Kara hadn't carried Hanna for nine full months, that they never shared the same blood, the same air — that Hanna's heart had never beat inside her.

Kara was across the room, speaking with one of their neighbor's wives. Hanna watched her reach up and touch her hair, the delicate movement of her hands, the gentle way Kara listened to the woman's story. She found it hard to believe that an accident of happenstance had brought them together, that Kara not only wasn't her mother but not a mother at all.

Hanna wanted to find Daniel and tell him everything her mother had said, to gauge his response, to see whether Daniel thought Hanna was foolish to question Kara's story, whether she'd have to be a hopeless dreamer

— perhaps even a little mad — to believe it was true. But she couldn't see him anywhere.

Hanna resolved to walk through the crowd, to try to meet Daniel in passing. Before she could take a step, she felt a hand press against her back, fingers caressing. Hanna shuddered. Her arms rippled with gooseflesh. Edwin was beside her, his hand playing with her dress, brazenly sliding along the strap of her undergarment. He was emitting a shrill sound like a broken whistle, his breath pushing in and out through his nose. She didn't need to look at him to picture the wiry gray hairs swaying under his nostrils.

It was all Hanna could do not to glare at him. This man beside her had no idea who she was. He cared even less about who she wanted to be. Edwin could never imagine the joy that erupted like cannon fire inside Hanna's chest when Daniel kissed her. No . . . when *she* kissed him; Daniel's lips brushing against hers, the soft touch of his hand against her cheek, that feeling deep inside, like she was glowing. Edwin might have wanted to be her husband. But he didn't want *her*. He didn't know *her* at all.

"Isn't that right?" Edwin said.

Hanna snapped out of her inner musings.

Edwin's mouth was open, his teeth jumbled like a pile of misshapen stones. Four sets of eyes were upon her. Three parishioners, none of whom Hanna knew by name, had been listening to Edwin tell a story. Only, Hanna didn't have the foggiest idea what he'd been saying.

Edwin was still staring at her, waiting.

"Yes. Of course," she said.

The men laughed boisterously, as though Hanna had put an exclamation point on some uproarious joke. One of them pointed to his young wife at the other end of the hall. "She'd probably say the same thing!" he said, and they broke out into a second raucous laugh. Edwin, in particular, convulsed with laughter.

Hanna leaned into Edwin's ear. She moved closer to him than ever before. "Is this how it's going to be?" she said.

Edwin stopped laughing. He dropped his hand from her back. "What do you mean?"

Hanna looked into his dull, gray eyes. If he didn't know, she wasn't about to explain it to him. In the distance, Daniel's father, Francis, and his three wives were getting ready to leave. Daniel was still nowhere to be seen.

"Excuse me, please," Hanna said, and stepped quickly toward the exit. Hanna reached the Rossiters just as they were gathering their things.

"Good evening," she said.

Francis Rossiter already had one arm in his jacket. "Good evening."

An awkward silence ensued. Hanna reached out to shake the man's hand, which, rather than rectifying matters, only served to punctuate the unease.

"I'm Hanna," she said.

Francis Rossiter took her hand. "I know who you are, young lady. It's nice to finally meet you."

His three wives shook her hand, as well. The older woman — Daniel's mother — grazed Hanna's palm with her dainty fingers.

"I saw you before with your sons," Hanna said. She paused, hoping Francis might feel compelled to speak. Instead, he folded his arms and smiled, revealing nothing, waiting for her. "I spoke to one of them. What was his name?" she said. "Daniel, is it?"

Francis kept smiling. This time, however, Hanna refused to fill the void in the conversation. She smiled back, with her teeth, not her eyes, like so many others had taught her to do. A second passed and then another — tiny eternities soaring through the air — until eventually, Francis conceded defeat.

"Daniel's using the facilities. He'll be along in a moment."

Hanna glanced back toward the restrooms. It was an unconscious act, an involuntary swivel of her head, but far too eager, far too conspicuous. When she turned back to Daniel's father, the benefactor's tightly controlled features slackened. His lips formed a straight line. "We have to be going. My son's meeting us outside," he said. One of Francis's wives, a woman half his age, turned to leave. The others edged toward the door. "Congratulations on your upcoming wedding," Francis said.

"Thank you," Hanna said.

"You're a very lucky young woman."

"I consider myself very lucky. Thank you." Hanna shook his hand again and watched them walk out the doors and into the night.

She started moving toward the hallway leading to the restrooms. A throng of people stood in between her and Daniel, and Hanna walked as quickly as she could without drawing attention. There were women queued to enter the restroom, children running about, men chatting in circles. They all looked Hanna's way. She should have known this would happen. Just minutes ago, she'd knelt down and kissed Brother Paul's hand. It would've been absurd to think she could walk freely without eyes upon her. She'd only traveled a few feet before Paedyn caught her eye and waved. Hanna waved back, but she didn't stop. She passed Emily and Charliss, the two of them feasting on strawberry wafers. Emily reached out and Hanna gave her a quick kiss on the forehead and then kept moving.

As Hanna slipped through the crowd, the parishioners' faces blurred together. The white walls began to pulse. The voices beat like a drum, thumping, thumping. A woman bumped into Hanna's shoulder and she saw the woman's pastel eyelids, her chalklike skin, blemishes glistening like gemstones. She smelled the butcher's cologne. Hanna felt his gaze upon her and still she marched straight ahead. Her legs glided on their own volition. In her mind, she was still atop the old church cathedral. Hanna was still falling from Jotham's roof, three stories to the ground, still standing on the dirt road with Kara, still looking up from a crater with an infant's eyes moments after descending from the white light, the villagers dumbstruck, confounded and amazed.

Finally, Hanna reached the hallway. She stood in the restroom lineup and said hello to the woman beside her. One minute passed and then two and still Daniel didn't appear.

Hanna was almost ready to give up hope when he emerged from the crowd. She saw his shoulder first, then the profile of his face, and then Daniel smiled, a bright, genuine smile. He moved toward her, fidgeting as though he didn't know how to greet her in front of all these people.

The woman beside Hanna — one of Brother Paul's many wives — turned her head and immediately Daniel's smile disappeared. He stepped forward and slipped past Hanna, resting his fingers on her forearm and his thumb on her elbow.

"Excuse me," he said.

He was so close that Hanna could see her reflection in his eyes. Her cheeks turned red. Hanna wanted to clasp hold of his hand, to feel his fingertips grace the soft flesh of her palm. Only, people were watching. He let go of her arm and when he did, Daniel slipped a small piece of paper into her hand. Then he turned and walked back the way he came. Hanna resisted the urge to watch him leave. Hanna tucked the paper into her sleeve and waited in the restroom queue for a minute, maybe more, before turning around and heading back toward her family.

All she wanted to do was open the paper and read what was inside. Was it another poem, perhaps? Was it a drawing? Hanna was dying to find out. Before she could find a quiet spot to unfold it, Paedyn waved to her again. Hanna saw Edwin's wife from twenty paces away and this time, there was no way to avoid her. Paedyn had a gleeful look on her face, as though she was delighted to be at church today, delighted to see Hanna, delighted to be alive. Hanna couldn't tell if this was all for show — a flawless performance by a seasoned actress playing the part of Edwin's jovial wife — or if Paedyn was really excited to see her. For all Hanna knew, Paedyn's cheerful disposition could have been a mask, her façade concealing countless secrets underneath.

She wouldn't have long to speculate. Paedyn hurried over, a spring in her step.

"I'm dying to see your dress," Paedyn said.

Hanna looked down at the new blue dress she was wearing, the one she'd received for her birthday. She stepped back and held out her arms.

Paedyn laughed. She wrapped her arm around Hanna and her hair brushed against Hanna's neck, soft like velvet. "No, dear. I mean your wedding dress."

"Oh. I'll be wearing Jessamina's wedding dress."

"Have you tried it on?"

"Yes. In autumn, just before winter. It's in a closet upstairs at home."

Paedyn furrowed her brow. She whispered in Hanna's ear. "Edwin wants to know you'll be dressed appropriately for the big day."

The word *appropriately* rattled in Hanna's brain. She knew what Paedyn was really saying: that Edwin wanted a presentable bride. It wasn't enough that he'd made some kind of arrangement with Jotham, that the two old friends had bartered an exchange the way they'd trade a bag of potatoes for a fistful of dollar bills. Edwin also wanted her to look a certain way. He wanted Hanna to be on display when he claimed her. Paedyn ran her hand up and down Hanna's arm. Her words still burned — *We all pleasure him together. We watch. We each . . . participate. With him. With each other.*

Just then, Edwin approached and gave Paedyn a chaste kiss on the cheek. Edwin put his arm around Hanna and half embraced her. Instantly, Hanna regretted her earlier boldness. Edwin might have been furious with her and he'd have every right to be. Only, if he was, she couldn't tell.

"So, is Paedyn going to see your dress tonight?" he said.

"I'm not sure . . ." Hanna said, her voice fading.

"I'll go ask Belinda. I'm sure it will be fine." Paedyn turned to find Hanna's sister-mother.

Hanna found herself alone with Edwin. The noise from the other parishioners surrounded them and Hanna could make out every voice, every idle bit of chatter. She glanced at Edwin, who had a glass of sparkling water in his hand. The urge to apologize twisted in her rib cage. It wrapped around Hanna's lungs until she felt like she couldn't breathe unless she blurted it out.

"I'm sorry."

Edwin shifted his glasses along the bridge of his nose. "Whatever for?"

In the distance, Jotham had risen from his seat and was lumbering toward the children. Charliss and the boys saw him coming and quickly concealed the biscuits in their hands. Emily, however, was facing the other way, licking the frosting off a cookie. Jotham approached her from behind and Hanna watched him snatch the cookie out of her hand and point his finger at her, berating her. Emily trembled. She kept her eyes locked on the floor, unsteady on her feet, cowering in Jotham's presence.

A sudden fury exploded inside Hanna. She didn't pause to think. She stepped forward to intervene, to tell Jotham to leave the girl alone, to stay away from Emily, that a real father would never put such fear into his child, when Kara took Jotham's arm. She distracted him with words in his ear and steered him away from the terrified girl.

Hanna clenched and unclenched her fingers, struggling to regain her calm. She returned her attention to Edwin, who hadn't seemed to notice the scene unfolding on the other side of the room. "Edwin, I was wondering if you've set aside a bed for where Emily will sleep?"

Edwin's gaze clouded. "Do you mean for when she visits?"

"No. I mean for when she comes to live with us."

Edwin scratched his head. His gaze drifted across the room to where Kara was offering Jotham a cup of tea. "I'm afraid I'm the one who's sorry," he said. "But your father hasn't made any such arrangement with me."

"I look after her," Hanna said. "She needs me."

"And Emily is the one —"

"— with the twisted back."

"Ah yes. Is she twelve now?"

"Not yet. Not for a few months."

From far away, Jotham raised his voice, his tone fierce, his anger ignited. The crowd turned to look and Brother Paul moved toward the commotion, his white figure towering above the others, his two sons following behind like obedient basset hounds.

Edwin cupped his hand on Hanna's shoulder. He made that familiar whistling sound through his nose. "I'll discuss Emily's living situation with your father."

Hanna remained stone-faced.

I should hope you would.

"Thank you, Edwin," she said.

A fellow parishioner called him over and Edwin stepped away, leaving Hanna alone, or as alone as she could be in a room packed with hundreds of people. Hanna made her way to an empty bench by the window. She pulled Daniel's piece of paper out from her sleeve just as Emily and Charliss approached. She would have to read quickly.

Hanna unfolded the paper in her lap. She scanned the blue ink, the shapes that made up the letters, the sentences Daniel had composed, and a lump formed in her throat. This time, it wasn't from fear or frustration. Hanna's flesh buzzed. Her thoughts raced inside her head and she felt like she might burst in anticipation. Quickly, before she could be discovered, Hanna folded the paper and tucked it back into her sleeve.

It was, of all things, an invitation.

21

An hour later, upstairs in the master bed-room, Belinda cinched the wedding dress around Hanna's waist. She stepped back, took a second look and cinched it tighter.

It was strange spending time with this woman. Hanna had lived her whole life in the same house with Belinda and yet she felt like she knew absolutely nothing about her. She recalled when she was just four years old watching Belinda's mohair stockings rush past her, too busy to help Hanna dress her only doll in its sweater, her hair pulled so tight in a ponytail, her forehead appeared stretched to the point of discomfort. Belinda was always undertaking several chores at once, rarely speaking unless spoken to, never with a moment to spare. She and Hanna had been alone together many times, but only for fleeting moments: the passing of one another in the hallway, those brief seconds when they were the last two to fasten their boots and put on their jackets before leaving the house. They had done housework together and, before Charliss was old enough to help, Hanna had split firewood with Belinda in the backyard, the two of them always too focused on their task for idle chatter.

Kara made a point of hugging Hanna every day. Her sister-mother Katherine was also prone to outbursts of affection, surprising Hanna with wet kisses on the cheek when she least expected it. But Hanna couldn't remember Belinda ever laying a tender hand on her.

Now they were alone together and, for the first time since she could remember, Hanna felt a kindness from Belinda. When Paedyn arrived with the family after church, she attempted to usher Hanna upstairs to try on her wedding dress right away. Belinda had stepped in and assured Paedyn that Hanna needed to rest and take off her boots before she did anything else. She'd actually advocated on Hanna's behalf. Perhaps something else was going on. Perhaps Belinda and Paedyn weren't fond of one another. Maybe they'd had some sort of contentious interaction in the past that Hanna knew nothing about. More likely, Belinda was letting Paedyn know that Hanna was still a child under her care. Hanna still lived in *her* house.

Hanna watched Belinda in the mirror, fastening the buttons at the back of the dress. "Will we ever see each other again?" she said.

Belinda looked at Hanna like she didn't understand the question.

"I mean, after I leave this house. Will I ever see you?"

Belinda spoke with a sewing needle between her lips. "Of course. At church and the marketplace."

"But the families won't visit."

Belinda took the pin out of her mouth. "Jotham and Edwin have a complicated relationship."

"Like ours?" Hanna asked.

Belinda hesitated. She pressed her hands on Hanna's hips where the dress was still a little loose and met Hanna's gaze. "You've been a good daughter," she said. "You assist Emily without complaint and you listen to your mother. You will make a good wife."

Hanna didn't know what to say. Those were the kindest words Belinda had ever spoken.

Belinda inserted a pin near Hanna's hip. It broke through the dress and grazed her skin, forcing Hanna to stand upright in front of the mirror. For days now, ever since her engagement became official, Hanna had avoided her reflection. Aside from those first few minutes when she got ready in the morning, she would hurry past the mirrors in the house, afraid of seeing her image staring back at her. It was one thing for Hanna to rationalize her engagement to Edwin, to justify why she had submitted to Brother Paul's will — *everyone else had submitted, how could she not?* It was another thing altogether to face herself and wonder what she could have done differently, how her life would have changed if she'd had the courage to trek off into the woods and never look back, whether there really was a brave version of herself inside Hanna, waiting to break free.

Her reflection stared back at her now. Hanna saw her hourglass figure, the dress clinging to her hips, her shoulders framed by lace, smooth and subtle, intricate in arrangement only along the neckline. Hanna was a woman now — a young woman but a woman all the same. Long gone were her days of imagining the moon followed her in the sky. Long gone were the days when she could pretend.

Belinda pressed her thumbs against Hanna's shoulder blades. "Now, how does this feel?"

Hanna ran her fingers along the sparkling blossoms and understated embroidery. Marriage ceremonies in Clearhaven were held at night and Hanna's dress would surely shimmer in the candlelight. She turned her head. Along her back, fifteen buttons were locked in place, then a drooping bow, then another five more buttons before the dress cascaded to the floor. She thought of Edwin and his tortoiseshell glasses, his stubby fingers. Hanna imagined the difficulty he would have unfastening all these buttons on their wedding night. A slight chuckle slipped from her lips.

"What is it?" Belinda said.

"I was just thinking — these buttons are quite old," Hanna said. "Is there any way we can make them tighter? As tight as possible would be best."

Only Kara had seen Hanna in her wedding dress the first time she tried it on and that was months ago. The children came running when they heard Hanna at the top of the stairs, their eyes wide and amazed. She descended the stairs to the eager squeals of the little ones. Charliss took her arm and led Hanna into the living room, where the adults were waiting.

Paedyn approached first. She took Hanna

by the arms and examined her as though she were inspecting a horse at auction, or, rather, one assigned for breeding. Paedyn felt the tiny rhinestones bejeweled across Hanna's torso. She turned Hanna in a circle and studied the interlocking buttons across her back. It took a moment, but eventually the barren wife nodded her approval. "It's gorgeous. Edwin will be pleased." She looked at Kara, standing with Emily by the doorway. "What does the mother think?" she said.

Kara, who'd done nothing these past few hours except gaze at Hanna with wet eyes, forced a smile. She put her arms around Emily and held the girl close. "You're beautiful," she said, her voice all but cracking.

In a spontaneous burst of exuberance, Charliss took Hanna by the hands and twirled her around the room. The children cheered and the moment absorbed her. Hanna picked up Ahmre and Charliss spun the two of them in delirious circles. It was the first joy Hanna had felt in this house since winter's end and she would not deny it. Hanna locked hands with the little ones. She spun them one by one, each child laughing dizzily, until Hanna herself wobbled and another pair of hands grabbed hold.

At one point, Hanna almost tripped, but she righted herself and kept moving, her bare feet sinking into the old woolly carpet. The room filled with energy. Hanna's heart pounded. Ahmre ran into her arms again and together they danced without care. Hanna cast a quick look at Jotham, who happened to be on his fourth whiskey. He nodded his approval and the children twirled and skipped without music. Their mother Katherine stood in the center of the room and sang a boisterous church hymn to the children's delight.

Hanna took Emily's hand. She couldn't lift Emily without knocking over the little ones, so she wrapped her arms around her and sang along with Katherine. They swayed together, Emily's feet following Hanna's for the first few steps before coming to a halt. The girl's shoulders started to tremble. Emily buried her head in her big sister's shoulder and sniffled.

"Don't cry," Hanna whispered. "There's no reason to be upset."

"There is, though," Emily said. She stepped back and took in Hanna's white dress fully. "I want this to be me."

Hanna pressed her lips to Emily's cheek.

Still, the children danced. "It will be one day."

"No one will want me," Emily whispered back.

"Of course someone will."

"But I can barely walk . . ."

Emily pulled away. Their eyes met and Hanna saw for the first time what her wedding was doing to her sister. Hanna had been so caught up in her own desires, in battling dragons in her head, that she hadn't stopped to notice Emily. The girl looked brittle. Her chin quivered. Emily ached for the one thing Hanna didn't want: to be chosen as a bride. To be like everyone else.

Before Hanna could say another word, Charliss picked Emily up from behind and spun her around in a circle. All the while, Katherine's bright voice filled the room. Hanna danced until she felt winded. She flopped onto the couch in the corner where Jessamina was feeding her baby. The young mother glared at her. There was something different in her expression, something new that Hanna couldn't quite place. Hanna sat up straight and met Jessamina's gaze. She couldn't spend another moment enduring Jessamina's cruel looks, her abject, arbitrary hatred. Under the sound of the children's laughter, Hanna mouthed the words, *Don't hate me.*

Jessamina dropped the baby from her breast. She mouthed back, *I don't hate you. I pity you.*

The blood fled Hanna's face. "Why?"

Jessamina whispered so no one else could hear. "Because, soon you will be like me."

A long reptilian smile spread across Jessamina's face. She placed her hand on the back of Sayler's neck and forced the already-satiated baby onto her breast.

Hanna's mouth hung open in disbelief. The room grew heavy around her, the children's dancing, their rhythmic swaying, suddenly at a snail's pace. Each syllable of Katherine's lively hymn resonated as though it were a song itself. Hanna's thoughts slowed to a crawl.

She would have stayed in this suspended state, had the children not rushed over and offered their hands, had they not pulled her up off the couch and pleaded with Hanna to rejoin the dance. The revelry lasted ten more minutes: ten minutes in which Katherine continued singing her lively hymns, in which the children threw their bodies joyfully around the room, ten minutes in which a girl in a white wedding dress moved from one child to the next, taking their hands and holding them close, staring not at her young sister-mother but at her reflection in the window. Hanna couldn't help but think how she looked like every other young bride in Clearhaven to don a wedding dress. How, in four days' time, she would become exactly like everyone else.

22

The next morning, Hanna awoke to the sound of Katherine and Belinda arguing. Ahmre was lying beside Hanna in her bunk, still fast asleep, when Hanna slipped out of bed and opened the door. Katherine and Belinda were standing in the hallway, quarreling over whether the brown vest Katherine was holding could be altered to fit around Jotham's back brace.

"Of course it can," Katherine said.

"You take a pair of scissors to that fabric and he'll never be able to wear it again!"

Kara emerged from her room and chimed in, all three women talking at once. The quarrel went on for another minute before Jotham barked, "Enough!" from the bottom of the stairs. Hanna stepped out of her bedroom and was nearly bowled over by Katherine, red-faced and fuming, storming down the hallway, crochet hook in hand, mumbling something to the effect that her "prowess in needlework has long been overlooked in this house." Moments later, Belinda followed to resume their dispute.

It wasn't just the women. The whole house had tensed up, like it was a living thing sucking on the inside of its mouth in order to avoid screaming. Hanna shut the door and slipped back into bed as Jotham paced the hallways in halting, tentative steps rather than his usual formidable stride. An hour later, Jotham — wearing his suit but no vest — was waiting on the deck outside. The children all clambered to the window, eager to see who would pick him up. They watched Jotham rub his cold hands and gaze off into the distance in anticipation. He checked his watch, looked up and then checked it again.

Soon a pickup truck pulled up to the house and Edwin's face peered out the window. He saw Hanna, Emily and the others crowded behind the glass, and he gave a quick wave. Then Jotham stepped into the truck and they drove off down the street.

Almost immediately, the tension in the house abated. Katherine fed the little ones their breakfast and Kara assisted the older children with their boots and jackets before ushering them out the door for school. Belinda, in particular, seemed pleased. She sat down at the kitchen table and took out a folder containing cards and envelopes and proceeded to write several letters with a big smile on her face. Hanna leaned against the doorway, watching Belinda, thinking this was all very peculiar. Belinda's smile was peculiar. Jotham wearing a suit was peculiar. Edwin showing up in their driveway for the first time in years was particularly peculiar.

"The money's coming in," Katherine said.

"Pardon me?"

"The arrangement your father made with Edwin. They're going to excavate the marshlands and Jotham is going to manage the project."

"Who's going to excavate it?" Hanna said.

"Workers from the city. They're going to build a whole new division in Clearhaven. And Jotham will be in charge."

Katherine's words took a moment to register, and still it was difficult to fully comprehend. Hanna looked out the window where just moments ago her father had been fidgeting restlessly as he waited on the deck. Hanna had long known of a business arrangement contingent on her hand in marriage. It was strange, though, to see plans coming to fruition, the details revealing themselves. Clearhaven would grow. Brother Paul's flock would multiply. Change had manifested out of conjecture. And Hanna had been too wrapped up — in her thoughts of Daniel, in her mother's fantastical story — to notice.

Later that afternoon, Jotham and Edwin returned to the home with Brother Paul and Francis Rossiter. The men took over the living room, their voices resonating through the floorboards. Hanna was upstairs with the toddlers and Jessamina. The adult women were in the kitchen, preparing the men's coffee. It was a big day in the household. To the best of Hanna's recollection, Brother Paul had never visited before. His voice was the loudest, his tone embellished with authority, and she could make out some of what he said from the room upstairs.

Francis Rossiter had the quietest voice. But when he spoke, the others listened. When Hanna first saw him step out of Brother Paul's long white car and up onto the deck, she could hardly watch. The other day when Daniel visited, Hanna was too startled by his appearance in her window to be embarrassed by where she lived. Afterward, she'd been grateful he only saw the house from the outside. Now, in the light of day, with these influential men drinking cof-

307

fee in the living room, Hanna cringed at the thought of Francis going home and reporting the house's state of disrepair to Daniel. Jotham's place was a shack in the woods compared to Edwin's luxurious home. It was an outhouse compared to the palatial estate Daniel's family had just moved into. Hanna pictured the men sitting on the sofa's frayed fabric, looking out the living room window held together by masking tape and a little bit of hope, drinking coffee from chipped, mismatched cups. It was easy to ignore the family's poverty when it was just Hanna and her siblings. It was impossible to ignore when their house was put on full display.

"They probably think the roof's going to collapse over their heads," Jessamina said.

Hanna watched her out of the corner of her eye. She wasn't sure what — if anything — Jessamina knew about her and Charliss's attempt to fix the leaks in the roof. She only knew that Jessamina had become oddly chatty since the men arrived. It was as though, in all the excitement, she'd momentarily forgotten to hate Hanna.

"I'll be right back," Hanna said and slipped out of the room. She stole quietly down the hallway and sat at the top of the stairs just as Edwin and Jotham split from the group and entered the front alcove. Hanna kept her head low, her curiosity outweighing her fear of getting caught.

"What do you think?" Edwin said.

Jotham peered down the hallway toward the living room, forcing Hanna to hide behind the wall at the top of the stairs. "I think you'd better keep your part of the agreement," Jotham said. "That's what I think."

"There's no reason to be like that, old friend."

"We're *not* friends," Jotham said crossly.

"All this resentment. It's been years, and if you remember, it was you who broke your word the last time."

"Broke my word?"

"About the girl with the golden hair," Edwin said.

Jotham paused and Hanna found she was holding her breath. She exhaled as quietly as she could. "We don't call her that anymore. We call her Hanna."

"She was supposed to be mine," Edwin said. "You were supposed to hand her over years ago."

Jotham spat his words. "If *you* remember, it was you who changed the terms at the last minute."

"It's always about the past with you, isn't it?"

The room fell quiet. Hanna's heart beat heavy in her chest as she waited for Jotham to speak again.

"So now Hanna is going to be your wife instead of your daughter," Jotham said. "You should be pleased, not bitter. Just imagine the babies she'll deliver."

Edwin's tone turned reflective. "Golden children. That's worth the price."

"Just remember what the price is. Not just the dollars. The position. The standing you promised me."

Edwin's voice softened further. "Of course, old friend. Of course." He turned to face Jotham. Edwin's profile came into view and Hanna dug her fingernails into the wall, terrified of being discovered. "Now," Edwin said, "tell me — are you sure we can trust Francis?"

Jotham didn't say a word. Hanna could only imagine the look he gave Edwin — a nod of the head, an evasive shrug — because moments later, the subject changed.

"Now, about Emily," Edwin said.

"What about her?"

"Hanna mentioned something about her coming to live with me?"

Upstairs, the bedroom door creaked open

310

and Jessamina poked her head out. Edwin and Jotham fell silent in the alcove and Hanna motioned for Jessamina to close the door. Only, Jessamina edged closer. She mouthed silently, *What's going on?*

Jotham poked his head into the hallway. He yelled up the stairwell and Jessamina disappeared, the door slamming behind her.

"You know, that Emily has a pretty enough face, I suppose," Edwin said.

Jotham chortled. "The girl can hardly walk."

"Some men wouldn't care."

"Emily will live here," Jotham said.

"What about Hanna? Won't she be upset?"

A long pause followed — with whispers likely exchanged — and then Jotham and Edwin shared a laugh, a short, blustery snicker that was far too juvenile for their years. They stepped into the hallway and walked back into the living room to join Brother Paul and Francis.

Hanna stole quickly back to the children's bedroom, shocked by the men's exchange. She hadn't known that Jotham planned to give her away when she was a child. To Edwin, no less. Hanna's first thought was that Kara would never have allowed it. But perhaps she hadn't known. Perhaps no one — save Jotham and Edwin — knew the details of their failed agreement.

Hanna turned the doorknob to the children's bedroom as quietly as possible, her mind reeling. *She* was the reason Edwin and Jotham's relationship went sour. Hanna thought back to Jotham's late-night drunken monologue. Jotham's words were slurred, at times barely above a whisper, but Hanna still heard them. She still remembered them: *the world is at the feet of he who holds the gold.* Was that what Edwin meant when he called Hanna his girl with the golden hair?

Hanna struggled to process what Edwin and Jotham had said, not just about herself but about Emily. Jotham's voice was firm when he told Edwin that Emily would still reside in his house. It was resolute. Hanna couldn't tell whether Jotham was protecting Emily or if he was merely guarding his property, refusing to let Edwin take another piece of his family away without paying full value for his crippled child. The intentions of grown men — their true ambitions, desires, the subtext behind their words — still bewildered Hanna. She had little time to dwell on them. Hanna shut the door behind her and joined her siblings.

The goodbyes took almost as long as the

meeting itself. The four men stood on the driveway outside while Hanna and the others watched from the window upstairs. The older children had come home from school only to be quickly ushered upstairs by Belinda, who wasn't keen on suffering a moment's disobedience. They entered the bedroom a curious and energetic lot, taking turns hopping on the bunk beds and asking what was going on outside. The children crowded beside Hanna at a window too small for all their faces, and watched the men, her sisters volleying questions into the air.

What are they talking about?

Why are they pointing into the woods?

How much money do you think that Rossiter man has?

After exchanging handshakes and a few parting remarks, Edwin climbed into his truck. Brother Paul and Francis stepped into Brother Paul's shiny white car and the vehicles churned gravel on their way off the property.

When Jotham came back inside, he was grinning like a moose who'd found a maple tree and had been licking its sugary sap for hours. Belinda approached him first. She and Jotham shared a look and then he nodded and Belinda couldn't contain herself any longer. She ran to him and Jotham took her in his arms. He lifted her as far off the ground as he could and they shared an embrace, the relief clear on their faces. Katherine ran to him next. Jotham kissed her flush on the lips and then he lumbered past the women toward the liquor cabinet. He fumbled with his key until the latch clicked open and Jotham poured five glasses of whiskey. At first Hanna thought he was going to drink them all in succession. Then Jotham handed a glass to Belinda. He handed one to Katherine and one to Kara, who surprised Hanna by taking it. Jessamina set her baby down and pushed past the little ones in the front hall. She took her glass and the four wives held them in the air, waiting for Jotham to take the first sip.

"Hanna?" he said.

"Yes, Father?"

"Come here."

She stepped delicately down the stairs, all eyes upon her. Hanna approached Jotham, fully aware that his mood could change at any moment. He surprised her by setting down his drink and wrapping his arms around her. His neck stubble scratched her forehead and the strap from his back brace pressed into her chest, the musty smell of his suit sailing straight up her nose. Jotham squeezed her tight and then poured a sixth glass of whiskey.

"Our entire family owes you a debt of gratitude," he said, handing Hanna the whiskey. "This is because of you. Don't ever forget that." Jotham lifted his glass. "To a future full of prosperity."

He shot the murky brown liquid down his throat and poured himself another. Jessamina also gulped her whiskey down as quickly as she could. The other wives were more restrained. Belinda raised her glass to her lips and took a short sip. Katherine did the same and instantly began coughing, then laughing, then coughing some more. Kara took a taste and then stuck out her tongue and scrunched her nose. It was only Hanna who hadn't touched her drink.

The entire family watched Hanna swirl the whiskey and breathe in its vapors, like burnt toast and molasses. She placed her tongue inside the glass and felt the sensation of burning ice. Jotham was still watching. For years he'd been watching Hanna, isolating her, biding his time until she grew into a young woman, until he could work out a better arrangement with Edwin. This liquid in Hanna's glass was Jotham's lifeblood, his crutch, the one thing he couldn't live without. Hanna wondered what would happen if she set the glass down and refused to drink it. Or better yet, if she dared to pour it out on the floor, wasting valuable drops. She almost did. Then she looked at her brothers and sisters lining the stairs, at her mother's bruised face and thought: *Is this the one rebellion I should afford myself? Is it worth the bedlam that would ensue?*

Hanna tilted her glass. She poured the whiskey into her mouth, felt it like a bee sting against her cheeks. Hanna gulped the whole mouthful down and immediately regretted it. The whiskey singed its way down her chest and into her stomach where it bubbled and boiled, threatening to lurch back up. Hanna braced her arm against the wall. She sneezed inexplicably and shook her head. One second passed and then another before the desire to throw up was replaced by a rousing surge resonating through her body. It started in her stomach and then quickly soared to her rib cage, where it spread like wildfire, filling her arms and legs and fingers and everything in between with an unparalleled zeal, a feeling of being invincible, unhampered by burdensome thoughts, brilliant and gleaming like a bright red sun. She pushed her glass toward Jotham.

"More."

The entire room burst out laughing. Only, Hanna wasn't joking. She stared straight at Jotham, imploring with her eyes, and while he took his time, he eventually poured her a second, smaller glass. She drank it straight down.

The celebration was still in full swing thirty minutes later. The children were sucking on ice pops and Charliss was chasing them between the kitchen and the living room, growling like a monster and swinging his arms. Rather than tell them to keep quiet, Belinda made repeated, hushed calls on the telephone, all while holding her free hand over her ear to block out the sound of Katherine gossiping excitedly out the window to the neighbor's wife. A curious, unfamiliar energy raced through the air. Every word, every movement of the children running by, every clink of a glass and trickle of water from the kitchen tap was amplified, accelerated by a fraction of a second. Hanna's feet felt light, the alcohol fresh in her belly, its effects stronger than she'd expected.

She had just joined Kara at the counter to help prepare supper when Jotham called the women over to the kitchen table. He unfolded a detailed geographic map of Clearhaven.

"Here's what we're going to do," Jotham said. "The river that leads to the marshlands drains in the wrong direction." He dragged his finger to the eastern portion of the woodlands. "This inlet is only half as full as it should be. If we redirect it here, the water will flow back to the inlet and from there into the lake. The engineer we met with today is convinced that once the water flow changes, the marshlands will dry right up. Not right away, of course. But within three months we'll be able to bulldoze all the way from here to here." He dragged his fingernail again.

Jotham arched his back. He undid his tie and rubbed his neck until Belinda reached up to help him. Since the men left, Jotham had slowly been removing his suit. First his jacket and then his belt. Now his tie flew through the air. Jotham laughed boisterously and there was a swagger to his step Hanna had never seen before. She'd never seen him so happy.

"Francis is providing the money. Edwin secured the contracts and I'm going to supervise the construction. I'll be running the show," he said proudly.

"Why?" Hanna said.

The women all looked at Hanna. Jotham shifted his gaze, as well.

"I mean — what are you going to build? Another church?"

"Houses," Belinda said.

"Not just houses. Estates," Jotham said. "Huge homes you'd be proud to live in."

He beamed when the word *estates* came out of his mouth. Hanna gazed down at the map and back up at Jotham's smiling face. So this was his plan. Jotham wasn't just planning on supervising the construction of these great houses. He was intending on *living in* one of them. Jotham was going to leave the squalor of his meager home behind to live in luxury and all he had to trade for the opportunity was his first child. So these were the intentions of grown men: power and wealth, comfort, extravagance.

Belinda hung off Jotham's shoulder. "Show them, show them," she said.

Jotham waffled, like he couldn't decide whether it was worth the effort to explain. However, this was his victory day. It didn't take much to convince him. He pulled out a second map and laid it over top of the first. "Here to the south is where the mansions will go, right along this ridge. This spot right here, in the corner, has already been claimed," he said, patting himself on the chest and smiling even wider. "And over here will be a concourse and a playground with all-new equipment. To the north will be the Rossiter estate —"

"But the Rossiters live in the old Grierson house," Hanna said.

"It's too small."

"It's huge," Hanna said.

Jotham shook his head. He slurped his whiskey. "Not for the boy who would be king."

"I don't understand," she said.

"Francis is financing the construction so his male heir, that boy Daniel, will have a place to live."

"By himself?" Hanna said.

Both Jotham and Belinda laughed.

"Of course not," Jotham said. "Once he's of age, Francis will find the boy a suitable wife. Several wives, actually."

Hanna suddenly felt flushed. She couldn't believe what Jotham said, his casual, flippant tone, how he thought nothing wrong with Francis deciding how Daniel should live, nothing wrong with him deciding whom Hanna must marry, nothing wrong with planning to sell her off when she was just a child only to back out when the terms of the deal didn't meet his liking. A hot, red swell gushed inside her. Hanna's hands began to shake. She looked from Belinda to Katherine and back to Jotham again. They all looked like strangers, like this was the first time Hanna had ever seen them.

Jotham pointed to another spot on the map and began explaining technical terms like *directional drilling* and *trench excavation*. The other wives looked on with interest while Kara sat in a chair in the far corner and picked at her fingernails.

"Who's Daniel going to marry?" Hanna said.

Jotham scratched his bristly cheek. "Whomever his father decides. That's who he'll marry."

Hanna stepped back to the counter. Daniel hadn't mentioned anything about his father clearing the marshlands, nothing about Francis building him the grandest estate Clearhaven had ever seen. This must have been those mysterious plans Brother Paul had for him. Her legs wobbled. Hanna's head ached, a stabbing in her temples so painful that she had to grab the counter for support. Meanwhile, Jotham was leaning over the kitchen table, firing his proud words into the air, his gleeful wives eating them up like candy. The liquor still swam through Hanna's veins. From her vantage, Jotham looked small and weak, like a sniveling brown toad. Jotham's considerable frame shriveled before her and suddenly

Hanna felt like a giant.

She laughed out loud. The adults turned her way and Hanna stared back defiantly.

A crinkle formed in Jotham's forehead. "Do you have something to say?"

"You think you're such a big, strong man, don't you?" Hanna said.

Jotham's eyes sharpened. "What did you say?"

Kara rushed over. She stepped between Hanna and Jotham and held up her hands. "It's the whiskey. She doesn't know what she's saying," Kara said.

Jotham's face grew redder, the vein pulsing in his forehead. He glared at Hanna furiously but also with a hint of bewilderment, like it had never occurred to him that Hanna could be angry, that she could communicate anything other than submission or servitude. He looked as though he was on the verge of bursting when Belinda whispered in his ear, something to pacify the man. He squinted and sneered, and then he turned back to his victory party.

But it was too late. A cannon had gone off inside Hanna's brain. Her blood had been replaced by fire.

"No!" Hanna yelled. "No. No. No! No! NO! NO! NOOOO!!!"

What she was saying no to — her wedding, Daniel being forced to marry half the women in town, Jotham's very presence in this room — Hanna wasn't sure. She tried to push past Kara, to lunge at Jotham, except Kara's grip was strong. Hanna lunged again, unsure what she would do if she reached him, whether she had it in herself to actually strike the man, what she would do if he struck her back.

Jotham slammed his fist on the table, powerfully, violently, sending the other wives scattering. His shoulders tensed, his face large and wide and so close that Hanna could almost reach out and touch it. Jotham's teeth gnashed the air. "You don't speak to your father that way!" he shouted.

"Father?" Hanna said. "Father?!"

She was so caught up in the moment, with years of suppressed rage billowing to the surface, that she couldn't get her words out. Hanna wanted to tell Jotham that he'd never been a father to her, that a father was a protector and a provider and a giver of unconditional love. That if Kara were to be believed, Jotham hadn't had a thing to do with creating her, that he was a thief who'd stolen her away in the middle of night. That Daniel would never be like him. That he wouldn't be like Francis or Brother Paul. That she'd finally known kindness. She'd finally known passion — however brief, however fleeting — and that nothing Jotham ever did could take that memory away from her. What emerged instead was a deafening scream. Hanna shrieked as loud and as long as she could until all the breath left her body.

It was only when she fell quiet that Kara whispered, "Angel, be reasonable."

Only Hanna was beyond all reason. She took another wild swipe at Jotham, but she didn't come close this time as Kara wrapped her arms around Hanna's waist and heaved her toward the hallway. At the last moment, Hanna gripped the door frame. She locked eyes with Jotham, who looked ready to strike anyone who came near him. Jotham glanced down at the maps on the table and back at Hanna. A smirk twisted the corner of his mouth.

"Not the happiest bride I've ever seen," he said.

Belinda laughed. Jessamina joined her from the next room, cackling at the top of her lungs. Jotham looked from his one wife to the other, a maddening, self-satisfied pride beaming on his face. He glanced down at his map again and then met Hanna's eye. Jotham chuckled — a cruel, heartless snicker that dug into Hanna's flesh from across the room. Then he averted his gaze without a second look, as though Hanna were an insect he couldn't be bothered to swat away, her outburst unimportant, the passion that triggered it inconsequential.

All the while, Belinda and Jessamina kept laughing.

Hanna went to leap forward. To scream once more. To finally strike Jotham down. Before she could move or say another word, Kara pulled her down the hallway, away from their taunts and jeers.

23

When Hanna was six years old, a baby fell out of a woman's belly at the marketplace. At least it looked like a baby. It was small and red and covered in pink ooze, and Hanna saw it the moment it escaped from the womb.

It was a bright summer's day and a stubborn heat had made the air dense. Hanna could still remember the bright blue, cloudless sky, the flowers along the roadway wilting under the sun's rays, the perspiration evaporating before it could drip down her forehead. Charliss was only three that summer and Hanna was holding his hand as they waited on Belinda and Kara, who were bartering (or, rather, Belinda was arguing) with the man who ran the vegetable stand.

The woman in the green dress appeared right before their eyes. Hanna knew her well. Almost a year ago, she'd come to live with Jotham, the sound of her constant

326

chatter reverberating off the walls in his house. The pregnant woman's face was covered in lines, her blood throbbing under her skin. She was carrying a loaf of bread in one hand and a bag of milk in the other. Without warning, she started to tremble. The woman shrieked, her voice awash with terror. She spread her legs and pulled up her dress, grasping at her undergarment to find it soaked through, red like crushed grapes. Then the baby dropped. It fell as though she'd been holding it in her hands and the baby hit the ground with a thump.

Hanna covered Charliss's eyes.

"My baby!" the woman screamed. But she didn't pick it up. She stood there as though her feet were locked in place, tremors rattling her body. The milk burst when it hit the ground and now the baby lay motionless, dangling from between her mother's legs like a puppet with one string, the pasty white umbilical cord. Hanna remembered its head looking three times smaller than that of any baby she'd ever seen, the milk turning the dirt a muddy pink color, the frenzied looping of insects between the woman's legs.

As Hanna gazed in disbelief, the man Belinda had been quarreling with over the price of cabbage leapt out from behind his stand. He scooped the child up in his apron, cut the umbilical cord with his pocketknife and ran for help.

The child lived. She was now eleven years old.

Her name was Emily and her back was twisted. The woman in the green dress was Hanna's sister-mother Katherine.

Hanna might have just been six years old, but not a day had gone by in which Hanna didn't regret her inaction. She could have picked the baby up, could have looked into its eyes for a sign of life, could have patted it on the bottom the way midwives pat newborns to encourage them to cry and fill their lungs with air for the first time. But she did nothing. True, she was only a child and Kara had told her over and over again that there wasn't anything Hanna could have done, that Emily's back would have been misshapen no matter how she emerged from the womb. But Hanna could never shake the feeling that if she'd just gotten to Emily a few seconds quicker, if she'd somehow managed to catch her sister before she hit the ground, Emily's back never would have been twisted. She'd be able to run and play in the school yard like the other children. Emily could one day find a husband. She could live a normal life, if only Hanna had acted.

That same feeling of regret lingered in Hanna's belly hours after her confrontation with Jotham. She had come so close to hitting him. Hanna lay in bed picturing her fist striking his jaw, the cruel, lopsided grin fleeing his face and Jotham reeling. He was big, but he was awkward on his feet and the element of surprise would have been on her side. Hanna had never lashed out before. He would never expect her to strike him now. Instead, Hanna had done nothing. She allowed Jotham to stand unopposed, stuffed with pride, basking in not one but two victories today.

What would the other Hanna say?

Through the floorboards, past the living room and the ground underneath, through the layers of molten rock and all the way on the other side of the world, Hanna's brave other self was battling serpents. She was leaping and bounding and striking down anyone who dared oppress her. If they were ever to meet face-to-face, could Hanna look her in the eye?

I fell from the sky. I am meant for more than this.

Hanna made a promise to herself. She would never falter again. She would never be kept down or stand idly by. She would soar or she would crash. There was no in between anymore.

24

The family was asleep when Hanna sat up in bed and slipped a handful of dollar bills into her undergarment. Earlier, the clouds had pressed the sun into the horizon until the purpling sky splintered into slender traces of orange. Then night fell. Hanna could hear Jotham's whiskey-induced snores from down the hall. She pulled out the note Daniel had passed her and read it in the moonlight. In the top corner, written in black ink, were the words *Dear Champagne Girl.* Hanna read it one more time. There it was, the question that stopped her breath — *Would you care to join me for a night of music in the city?*

Since she was a little girl, whenever the house became too chaotic — infants crying, children toddling about, the adult women corralling them, Jotham storming the hallways and yelling from one room to another — Hanna would close her eyes and imagine the big city from a bird's-eye view at dusk. Buildings as tall as the sky. People of all shapes and sizes bustling along paved footpaths and the sounds of car horns, of voices, of buzzing machinery, music emanating from every window. Lights everywhere like a moving painting, the landscape fluid and ever-changing. The fantasy would engulf her and suddenly Hanna wasn't sitting on a threadbare couch in Jotham's living room. She was inside a dream.

Now Daniel was waiting to take her to that very place, and instead of bursting with anticipation, Hanna found herself replaying a new scene in her mind, one in which the city dwellers spotted her from a distance, some gaping openmouthed, others pointing, each realizing with a single look that Hanna thought and spoke and acted differently, that she came from the backwoods. The vision worsened each time she replayed it, with more staring faces, more outstretched fingers. It was reason enough not to go, reason enough to stay in bed and close her eyes and drift off to sleep.

But Hanna had spent enough time worrying about what could possibly go wrong. She'd spent enough time sleeping. It was time to wake up.

She climbed out of bed and tiptoed across

the room. Hanna opened the door and peered down the hallway. As she pulled the door shut behind her — whether in haste or a moment's carelessness — it closed far louder than she intended. The wooden frame shook, followed by a quick, noisy click of the latch. Hanna held still, not sure what to do, whether anyone had heard her. She took a step and the floor creaked. Hanna lifted her other foot and set it on the floorboards only to have them release a slow, audible groan. From Jotham's room down the hall, Hanna heard the bedsprings squeak and then what sounded like knees cracking, someone standing up. She stole quickly down the stairs.

The downstairs was steeped in darkness and Hanna hid in the shadows. From above, a set of footsteps sounded in the hallway, and Hanna wasn't sure whom they belonged to. She cursed her luck. The other night when she went downstairs to turn off the radiator, she'd made all sorts of noise and didn't rouse a single soul. Now, with Daniel's invitation in hand and only three days remaining until her wedding, she'd been discovered.

The footsteps halted at the top of the stairs. Then Belinda's face appeared: white like a specter, peering, scanning the dark.

Hanna curled up in a ball and stayed perfectly still. She tucked her head between her
knees and tried not to make a sound.
Upstairs, Belinda's lungs filled with air. The
railing shifted as she leaned her weight on
it. A tickle formed in Hanna's throat, growing itchier by the moment. It took all her
power not to cough. She placed her hands
over her mouth to stifle anything that came
out, and waited. One second passed and
then two and then Belinda turned around
and walked back the way she came. Hanna
heard her enter Jotham's room and shut the
door.

She rose to her feet. Hanna slipped on her
boots and her jacket and stepped outside.

Daniel was waiting for her exactly where
his note said he would be. It had been three
days since they kissed at the top of the tower
cathedral; an eternity. So much had transpired since then, and Hanna didn't know
how she would be received. In the back of
her mind, she wondered how Daniel felt
about her, whether her feelings were re-
quited. Right away, Daniel put all her fears
to rest. He wrapped his arms around her
and they embraced in the shadows. Hanna
felt his strong shoulders. She smelled his
jacket and her cheek brushed against the
soft skin of his neck.

The way he held her, the way Daniel ran his hand through her hair, Hanna couldn't imagine him ever becoming like their fathers, making brides out of young girls he barely knew. She wanted to say something, to ask him about Brother Paul's plans, the impending excavation and construction of the marshlands, why Francis Rossiter had selected Daniel to continue his legacy and not his two brothers. But she didn't want to ruin this moment.

"Are you ready?" he asked.

"I have to be back before sunrise."

"Of course."

"I'm serious." Hanna glanced at the darkened house behind her. "Emily needs me. Ahmre needs me."

Daniel took her hand. "You can trust me."

They drove with the headlights off until they reached The Road. The clouds overhead blanketed the night sky, blocking out the moonlight and darkening the gravel roadways. Daniel used the lights from the scattered households to guide their way. He drove carefully as they passed the abandoned mill. In the distance, the white church gleamed and in its light, Hanna made out Daniel's features: his lips, pink like watermelon; those strong cheekbones; eyelashes that fell sharp and then floated

335

upward each time he blinked.

Daniel caught her looking and smiled warmly. *Smiles aren't always smiles,* Hanna thought. *Sometimes they're a forceful hand twisting your arm. Sometimes they're a plea for a moment to stop. Sometimes they're accompanied by the unhappiest of eyes.* What Hanna liked about Daniel was that when he smiled, he meant it.

They pulled onto The Road. Hanna had pictured this moment in her mind countless times. Ever since she first read Daniel's note, she'd known she'd be leaving Clearhaven for the first time. It never really sank in until the glowing white church faded from view and the darkness took over. Daniel still hadn't turned on his headlights, and Hanna gazed out into the night. It was pitch-black behind them, pitch-black on their sides and in front of them. Then the headlights switched on, illuminating The Road. One of the car's headlights burned brighter than the other and Hanna felt strangely safe in the faint, uneven light. Daniel turned on the radio and Hanna heard that music again, the kind he'd played on his little metal box: drums and guitars and a piano, the singer's soothing voice. Hanna heard the word *redemption*. She cracked open her window and the cold air washed against her face. Hanna stretched out her arms, the adrenaline from her confrontation with Jotham still bubbling in her veins.

They passed the township sign with Clear-haven's name spelled in big bold letters and underneath that, the slogan written in lush, calligraphic strokes.

CLEARHAVEN
The Creator's Orchard

Hanna could hardly believe it. They were really leaving. She suddenly felt as light as a feather, like a wild thing that had been caught in a trap and had only now shaken free. Hanna pushed her seat belt aside, leaned over and kissed Daniel on the cheek. He seemed surprised at first, then he took his foot off the gas pedal and the car slowed down. Hanna kissed him flush on his mouth. She felt his wet bottom lip, tasted the mint he'd placed on his tongue before he'd picked her up, ran her hand through his hair. Hanna sat back in her seat as Daniel accelerated again. She watched his hands. They were strong like a grown man's, only hairless and smooth. She imagined him touching her over top of her dress. She longed to know what his lips would feel like on her neck, the intoxicating shiver she'd receive as they slid over her goose bump–ridden flesh.

Far in the distance was the big city. Music. People. Freedom.

"Are you ready?" Daniel said.

Hanna clenched his hand, willing and unafraid. "I've never been more ready," she said.

"Then let's go."

25

The train tracks came first, crisscrossing and interwoven, their rails accompanied by caution signs and a series of flashing lights. A deserted railcar sat next to a building made entirely of metal. Then acres and acres of farmland. Next, a highway with concrete dividers separating vehicles on either side. Cars traveling north and south. Hanna caught brief glimpses of the faces inside and Daniel watched her, fascinated by her fascination.

Then, water. The edge of a great lake. Minutes passed and an orange glow appeared. It grew brighter and clearer until the city emerged: the buildings and street lamps and lights like a cluster of stars. Hanna had pictured the city a thousand times in her mind's eye. What she didn't expect was the beauty: the yellow lights peppering the windows, their pale, hypnotic reflection in the water, structures that dwarfed the tower cathedral and picturesque homes along a hill with white mailboxes and — when she looked closely — welcome mats across their front steps.

Daniel turned onto a main road and the first pedestrians appeared: an older gentleman with a woman in a green skirt and then a young couple holding hands, the man carrying their infant child in a pouch strapped to his chest. Hanna wondered where they were going, what they would do when they got there. It was exhilarating and terrifying at the same time, the thought that a person could get lost in the city — and not like a girl traipsing off into the woodlands alone — lost to the freedom, to the choices one might make when an infinite number presented themselves.

Daniel drove like he'd been here before. They turned down another road and the car slowed with traffic. Hanna saw traffic lights for the first time and her eyes opened wide as they turned red, yellow and green, almost as if a conductor was hidden in the sky, watching the cars, aware of when they were backed up, when they needed to go, how to stop vehicles traveling in both directions when a pedestrian wanted to cross the road. Daniel navigated the streets capably. Together, vehicles of all sorts plotted their courses in unison as though each knew when to stop, when to accelerate, which street to turn down.

As Daniel pulled up to a line of cars waiting for a light to turn green, a group of young men walked by. They were dressed in black clothes, bearded, with their hat brims slanted forward to obscure their eyes. One of the men turned his head and, for a split second, Hanna thought he was looking directly at her. His dark eyes pierced the space between them. Hanna pictured the man approaching the car and gazing in through the window, studying her, trying to place what was different about this girl from the backwoods. Then one of the young man's friends said something to make him laugh. His light chuckle brightened his eyes. It softened his features and he looked down the street, past Daniel's car. That young man wasn't going to judge Hanna's appearance or the way she was dressed. He hadn't even noticed her sitting in the car.

A traffic light turned green and Daniel drove another block before parking next to a building tinted green by a shell of emerald-colored glass. Hanna gazed up at the building's cascading stories. Personalized items lined the balconies: potted plants and patio furniture, colorful pillows and house pets pressing their faces against the windows. Hanna was wondering what kind of people might live there, when a woman exited through a grand door at the building's front entrance. She was tall with rouge-colored cheekbones, dangling earrings and flaxen hair. Hanna immediately gave the woman a name: Clarissa. And a job: writer of books. She imagined the woman torn between two lovers, the decision all hers — not her father's — and a difficult decision it was, what with both men showering her with affection. But Clarissa wasn't ready to be loved. She wanted to travel the oceans. To see marine life in all its forms. To dance free along island reefs, touch coral with her bare hands and swim with dolphins. Hanna imagined the woman stealing away to a giant ship to sail the seas, to travel to lands she'd only seen on a map. The exhilaration of the unknown.

The woman walked by Daniel's car and Hanna gazed at her through the window. Their eyes met briefly and the woman threw a scarf over her neck and continued down the sidewalk.

"Are you okay?" Daniel said.

It took Hanna a moment. "Yes. I mean, it's a lot to take in."

He placed his hand on her elbow. "I felt

that way my first time too. Don't worry. I'm here. We'll be safe together."

Hanna looked out the window again. "Is this where the concert is?" she said.

"It's close. I thought we'd walk first, maybe get something to eat at the restaurant next door."

Daniel stepped out and hurried around to help Hanna with her door. Together they walked along the pavement. It was late in the evening hours and Hanna expected the streets to be empty. While they weren't exactly teeming, dozens of people walked by. Hanna saw a man in a three-piece suit holding the hand of a beautiful woman with full, lush lips. She heard their voices, the man joking, the woman stifling her laughter.

"They're in love," Hanna said.

Daniel glanced back at the couple, who were turning around a corner. "How do you know?"

"I can just tell."

Daniel extended his arm and Hanna took it. She leaned her head against his shoulder and ran her hand along his wrist. Hanna touched the muscles on his forearm through his jacket as they turned at the next corner and came to a street where cars weren't allowed to travel. For the first time, Hanna stepped on cobblestones, hundreds of them fused together like pebbles on a beach. She bent down and ran her fingers along their outlines, felt the contours with the palm of her hand and gently pried at a loose stone before setting it back in place. Daniel helped her stand and together their feet glided across the uneven surface. They passed a bakery still open at this hour, one with beautifully decorated pastries and cakes in the window. Hanna smelled the sugary bread and touched the intricately carved placard on the confectionery's outer wall. Dangling white lights adorned the trees as Hanna and Daniel passed bistros and cafés.

Several clothing shops were surprisingly still open at this hour and Hanna gaped at the mannequins dressed in a variety of colors: blues, purples, pinks and reds. *Reds.* Hanna stopped in front of a store with a tall, thin mannequin wearing a silky red dress adorned with a simple black stripe. She pictured herself strolling into church, the red dress clinging to her body and the women covering their eyes, Brother Paul stammering in disbelief, his vile wife Makala fainting at the sight of her. They very well might tar and feather Hanna were she to be so bold.

"Do you want to try it on?" Daniel said.

"I could never."

"Of course you can."

Hanna shook her head. "The very idea is . . . preposterous."

A short laugh slipped from Daniel's lips. "That's a pretty big word when what you really want to do is say yes." He opened the store's front door. "Come on. They probably won't be open much longer."

Daniel pulled gently on her arm and at first Hanna resisted, uncertain whether she could do it. Then Daniel kissed her. He placed his soft lips to her cheek and put his hand on her back. "You don't have to, if you don't want to. But I know you'd look beautiful," he said.

Hanna wrung her hands. The restaurant they were heading to was just a few doors down. She pictured the scene when they sat at their table and Hanna took off her jacket, exposing her modest dress with sleeves that covered her entire arms, her constricting neckline in contrast to the stylish ensembles and tasteful tops of the women Hanna could see through the window. Hanna wouldn't just feel different, she would look different, she would *be* different, and not because she'd chosen a singular style to express herself, but because the men of Clearhaven had forced her to dress this way.

"Okay," she said. "But quickly."

Minutes later, Hanna poked her head out from the fitting room door. Daniel was sitting in a chair nearby, his one leg over the other, waiting patiently as Hanna imagined many men had done in that very same seat.

"I can't," she said.

Daniel glanced back at the saleswoman who was starting to close the shop. "Does it not fit? Do you want me to get another size?"

Hanna shook her head and stepped back inside the fitting room. There was a mirror against the far wall and in it the crimson fabric clung to her torso, revealing the contours of her stomach and her legs. The red dress's shoulder straps paralleled her undergarment, leaving the hollow between her breasts exposed and very little to the imagination. Daniel was silent on the other side of the door. She imagined the look of disappointment on his face were she to emerge wearing her flowery dress — Brother Paul's tiresome uniform — with the red dress in her hand.

She put her hand on the door handle and twisted. Hanna opened the fitting room door and Daniel stood up. His eyes widened. His mouth hung open but nothing came out.

Hanna rocked on her heels. "What do you think?"

"I don't think I've ever seen anything more beautiful."

Hanna looked at her feet and felt her cheeks flush. "My shoes don't match at all."

"That's okay. It's stunning. It really is."

"All right, playtime's over. I'll change back."

Daniel caught the door before she could close it. "Wait," he said. "Let me buy it for you."

Hanna lifted the price tag attached to the garment's hip. "It's too much."

"I have the money," he said. "Don't forget — I'm the benefactor's son, after all."

Hanna thought of the dollar bills still tucked against her waistband. There were so many other uses for it. Hanna could buy food for the family, she could purchase new coats for her brothers and sisters. But, then, Jotham would be able to do that soon, once her marriage to Edwin was finalized and his business dealings with Edwin were under way. Kara had given Hanna this money to start a new life, one outside Clearhaven. Wasn't this what her mother intended? For Hanna to spend the money in the city, for her to blend in, to leave Jotham and Brother Paul and all their tyrannical rules behind?

"No," Hanna insisted. "I'll pay."

Hanna scanned the menu for the umpteenth time. She counted twenty-three items on the right side and more on the left. "How does one choose?"

"It's never easy," Daniel said. "You know, some of the restaurants my parents took me to had pictures of the food next to each menu item."

"That's remarkable."

He chuckled. "I thought it was too when I first saw it. But it's not, really."

They were sitting in a restaurant attached to a small concert hall and the room was nearly overflowing with people. Hanna and Daniel were lucky to get seats, luckier still to be seated at a table near the window. A circular wicker lantern dangled from the ceiling, giving off a faint orange glow, casting the room in an auburn hue.

The waitress approached, a pretty woman with short black hair and small tattoos of birds on her wrists. She asked Hanna what she would like to eat.

"What are you having?" Hanna said to Daniel.

He pointed at the menu. "The third one on the left," he said and leaned in to whisper, "I recognize all the ingredients."

"Then that's what I'll have too," she said.

The waitress left and Hanna focused her gaze on the couple at the next table. The man was spooning noodles into his mouth, the woman telling him a story, parts of which Hanna could overhear. The woman's sister was thinking of taking a hot air balloon ride and the woman said she would never go on one of those things unless she had a parachute attached to her back. The man laughed. His pasta got caught in his throat and he took a sip of water to wash it down. These big-city people were definitely not the sinful villains Brother Paul had led Hanna to believe. In fact, they didn't seem all that different from Daniel or herself.

Just then, an announcement sounded and the concert hall doors opened up at the restaurant's far end. Most of the patrons started paying their bills and filing toward where the band would be playing, leaving a scattered few couples still finishing their meals. As the room cleared, Hanna could hear the music playing on the speakers overhead. She leaned back in her seat, and for the first time since she could remember, her shoulders relaxed. She breathed in deep without reminding herself to do so. Hanna looked directly at Daniel.

"What is it?" he said.

Hanna took a sip from her glass of water. "When I left the house tonight, I thought it might be strange being here with you. I mean, I barely know you."

"I don't know," he said. "I think you know me pretty well by now."

She thought for a second. "I suppose I do. But when I first met you, for all I knew, you might have been a murderer."

"A murderer?" he said, chuckling.

"I don't know. You surprised me that day. You could have been a killer or a criminal sent to do me harm."

"I assure you, I'm not secretly here to do you any harm."

Hanna laughed. "Are you sure you're not just saying that to lull me into submission, only to find the perfect time to strike?"

"I promise," Daniel said.

Overhead, the sound of cellos played on the restaurant's speakers. Soon the concert would start in the hall next door. But for now it was quiet, the cellos singing softly, the white lights twinkling on the trees outside.

"Is it as strange as you thought it would be, being here with me?" Daniel said.

A smile curled at the corner of his mouth, and Daniel's eyebrow raised slightly. He was teasing her. Hanna wanted to say that it was strange that it didn't feel strange, that there was no one else she'd rather be with at this moment. Instead, she reached her hand across the table. Their fingers meshed.

"I think you're definitely not a vicious criminal sent to do me harm," she said, to which Daniel laughed.

Hanna gazed at their fingers joined together. In a few short days, she would take Edwin's doughy hand in hers. Hanna would stand before the congregation at the old tower cathedral and pledge her undying love to him. She pictured Daniel standing in the same spot, linking hands with a girl he'd just met, marrying one after another until he'd amassed his own personal harem.

"You want to say something, don't you?" Daniel said. "Please, say it. Life is too short to not say what you feel."

Hanna pulled her hand away. She sat up straight. "My father told me something tonight about Brother Paul's plans for you."

"What did he tell you?"

"Are you really planning to marry half the town?"

Daniel laughed. "Is that what he said?"

Before she could answer, the waitress approached. Wisps of steam sailed off the food as she placed their plates down, each featuring a chicken breast covered in a thick, mouthwatering sauce and green vegetables; some Hanna recognized, others were completely new to her. There were potatoes, as well: crisp triangular slices sprinkled with herbs. The aroma was intoxicating. It was, without a doubt, the most luxurious plate of food she'd ever seen.

Daniel's voice lifted Hanna's eyes up.

"I can't follow in my father's footsteps. I'm not going to marry whomever he chooses. I still wonder too much about the rest of the world. My mind still wanders too much."

"Are you going to leave?" Hanna said.

"We're already gone. Look around. Your father's not here. Brother Paul isn't here. We can take a train to another city if we want, find my brothers. James and Kenneth could lend us money. They could help us get away, just you and me."

Daniel's tone was serious and Hanna could tell that he really meant what he said. Hanna's dreams of escape could come true. She could travel to the other side of the world. And she could do it *tonight.*

Except her sisters were still at home. Emily was there.

"I can't. My sister needs me," she said.

"That leaves me in a bit of a predicament, then."

"How so?"

"Well, I can't stay in Clearhaven and do what my father tells me. But I can't leave you."

"Be serious," Hanna said.

"Oh, I've never been more serious in my life," Daniel said. He shifted in his seat and placed his hands on the table. He seemed fidgety all of a sudden, as if he was nervous. "There's something about you. I don't know exactly how to describe it. I mean, there are things I love, like the way you smile and the way you get excited before you're about to say something. But I don't think that's it. There's something about you that makes me never — ever — want to let you down.

"I don't care if we're young. I don't care if we've only known each other for a week . . . you're the one for me. The last thing I want to do is pressure you. I'm not sitting here asking you to love me for all time or anything. There's a long life in front of you, Hanna. And I would never think of getting in the way of you having great love affairs and following your dreams. But I want you to know — you could go off and travel the entire world. You could sail the oceans and see the seven wonders, but I will always be there, waiting for you. Because you're the one." He picked up his glass and tinkled the ice inside. "Whether you decide I'm the one for you still remains to be seen."

Hanna put her hand over her eyes. She looked down at the table. "You shouldn't say such things."

"Because they're embarrassing?"

"Because I'm marrying Edwin in three days."

Daniel paused. He averted his eyes briefly, delving inward, contemplating, before turning back to face Hanna.

"Well, clearly I don't have everything figured out just yet," he said.

A moment passed, then another, and then music resonated from the other room. The band was playing. The drums and guitars sounded first, and then Hanna heard the woman's voice, muffled through the wall. The food still sat in front of them.

"Shall we eat?" Hanna said.

"First we eat," Daniel said. "Then we dance."

The music filled the theater. Blue lights illuminated the drummer, a mountain of a man with a neatly clipped beard. A tall guitarist played with his head down in deep concentration, while a second guitar player bopped to the music. Her hair dangled just

354

past her ears and her bright pink skirt was shorter than any dress Hanna had ever seen. At center stage, cast in orange and white lights, a woman with flowing brown curls sang into a microphone.

Concertgoers hovered around the edge of the hall, nodding their heads to the beat, their eyes glued to the singer, engrossed in the music, while toward the center, the crowd pulsed. Young men and women danced to the music. They joined hands and swayed their hips to the rhythm. They reveled without care.

Hanna and Daniel stood on the outskirts, Daniel watching the crowd while Hanna stared transfixed at the singer. The woman's voice rang out and yet she never shouted. She cradled the microphone in her hands, the music throbbing around her, encompassing her, the singer's shoulders rising and falling, her words flowing just behind the beat, never rushing. The singer gazed at the crowd and then stepped back, bringing the throng of people with her, her voice like a violin, uplifting and melodic even as the drums crashed behind her. The female guitarist leaned against her back and a brief smile pursed the singer's lips, the two of them immersed, engrossed, pulsing like a heartbeat, the audience hanging on the singer's every word, Hanna hanging on her words. Orange lights haunted the theater. The singer's face contorted like an anguished thing and she cried passionately into the microphone.

Hanna didn't just hear her words. She felt them. She felt the woman's sadness, her joy, how one was incapable of existing without the other.

The band launched into the song Daniel had first played for Hanna outside church, the woman singing "Redemption" in sweeping swells. When it came from her mouth, *redemption* wasn't just a word. It felt like an undeniable truth, an attainable thing. Daniel took Hanna's hand and together they walked into the center of the hall. Young bodies twirled all around them. Hanna felt the music in her bones. Daniel joined the dancers, swinging his arms and kicking his feet, his quiet confidence translating into fearless abandon.

Back home, Hanna had danced with her sisters many times. But she'd never danced in front of strangers before. Hanna had never danced in such a revealing dress. She felt like everyone in the concert hall could see her chest, that they could see the contours of her body.

Then Hanna saw Daniel's arms waving in

the air. The joyous look on his face. Clearly, he didn't care what everyone else thought.

How could she restrain herself in the face of such joy?

Hanna grabbed Daniel's hands and together they spun in a circle. The crowd pulsated around them and Daniel lifted her in the air. Hanna wrapped her arms around his broad shoulders and held on tight as the lights turned blue and then white and then orange. The chorus repeated and Hanna sang along. The red dress clung to her, accentuating every curve, and Hanna didn't care. She felt free. She felt liberated. She felt invincible.

They stayed at the concert hall for over an hour, but time was getting late and Hanna knew she needed to get home before someone discovered that she was gone. They left the revelers behind and walked the cobblestone path beneath the streetlights, back toward Daniel's car.

Hanna wrapped her arm around Daniel's. She took in the big-city lights one last time, committing images to memory: the emerald-tinted building, the tufts of steam puffing from the manhole covers, the placid lake water. Hanna filed them away like snapshots in her mind, to be revisited days, months and years from now. Before Hanna stepped into the car, she spread her arms wide and took in the freedom. Hanna basked in it.

All the while knowing that soon she would return home.

26

On the ride home, Hanna rested her head against the window in Daniel's car. They passed the railroad tracks, having long since left the city's orange glow behind. Every passing moment brought them closer to Clearhaven. It was an odd sensation, traveling back the way they came. Hanna tried to compare herself to the girl who'd left Clearhaven hours ago, to discern whether she was a different person now, whether this one experience had changed her. But the moment was still so fresh.

Hanna had long been told — by her mother, in church sermons and from books at school — that the journey is what matters, much more so than the destination. *A maxim like that is easy to proclaim while a journey is in full swing,* she thought. Once it's over, there's no greater longing than for the start.

Daniel looked over from the driver's seat.

They hadn't spoken much on the drive home. Hanna was still in her red dress, her jacket tucked in the back seat as Daniel's car passed the Clearhaven town sign. She was trying to think of a way to thank Daniel, not just for taking her to the city tonight, but for his kind words, for the promises he'd made at the restaurant, when a set of bright red and blue lights colored the night. A shrill sound rang out.

Hanna turned around in her seat and saw the police car gaining ground. Her heart leapt into her throat. "Don't stop," she said.

Daniel looked in his rearview mirror. He swallowed hard. "You're kidding, right? They're the police."

"You know who that is."

"They have guns," Daniel said. "I have to stop."

He slowed the car down and pulled over to the side of The Road.

Hanna grabbed his arm. "I can't be seen with you." She looked down at her red dress. Hanna wrapped her bare arms over her chest in a futile attempt to cover up. "I can't be seen like this."

She couldn't tell if Daniel had heard a word she said. He turned off the radio and put the car in Park as the police cruiser pulled up behind them. A silhouette emerged from the dark, and instantly Hanna knew who it was. The policeman walked toward the vehicle. He shined his flashlight in through the driver's side window so brightly it hurt their eyes.

"Would you shut off your automobile, sir?"

Daniel shut the engine off and then Paul the Second's hairy forearm reached inside and yanked the keys from the ignition. He scanned Hanna up and down with his flashlight. Paul pulled the toothpick out of his mouth. His brow contracted and he nodded his head slowly, eyeing Hanna and Daniel before walking back to the police cruiser where two voices sounded on the deserted strip of road. When Paul came back, his brother was with him.

"Step out of the vehicle," he said.

Daniel opened his door and stepped out right away. Hanna hesitated, her mind racing, searching for some other option, some way to stop the brothers, to go back to a minute ago when she was wrapped up in reflection. There was none.

Slowly, with great reluctance, she stepped outside. Paul the Second was holding his nightstick in one hand. Beside him, Paul the Third's face was camouflaged by the night. The red and blue lights flashed in strobe-like bursts, backlighting the brother's massive figure.

Paul the Second shifted his belt against his hip. He pointed his nightstick at Hanna's dress. "It looks like Aunt Makala was right. Red. Like a whore."

"Hey!" Daniel said.

"Daniel, don't," Hanna said.

"Listen to the streetwalker," Paul the Second said.

Daniel looked him in the eye. "I'm sorry I was speeding."

"That ain't the half of it, son."

Daniel stepped forward. "Paul, let me call my father. I'm sure he can help us figure this out."

With a sudden vicious strike, Paul the Second slashed Daniel across the face with his nightstick, sending a horrific sound into the night. Daniel's head flung back, blood dripping from his mouth. Hanna screamed. She ran to Daniel and caught him as he fell to his knees.

Paul the Second strutted back and forth along The Road. He threw his arms over his head and let out a single "Woo!" at the top of his lungs. His nightstick twirled in fast, furious circles. "Boy, you don't know what kind of trouble you're in."

The other Paul dragged Daniel to his feet

only to push him to the ground again. "Now, get up!"

"Leave him alone," Hanna pleaded. She tried to step in between them, but Paul the Second shoved her aside.

"You stay out of this, little girl!" he said.

Paul the Third threw Daniel against the car and fished out a pair of handcuffs. "What were you thinking, kid?" he said. "Driving out of town with another man's fiancée? A fiancée who was reported missing hours ago? I don't know what they taught you when your daddy took you to the big city, but around here we appreciate something called manners."

Paul the Third opened the door and pushed Daniel into the back seat. The other Paul approached Hanna.

"You had no right to hit him," she said. "He didn't do anything to you."

"Hands on the hood of the car, ma'am."

"You can't be serious, Paul."

"Oh, I'm dead serious, girl." He grabbed Hanna by the arm. When she refused to budge, he shoved her hard against the car. "Now put your hands on the hood."

Hanna looked past him, into the darkness. In the back of her mind, a voice told her to run. She pictured herself taking off as fast as she could, sprinting into the night. Hanna could run away and never look back. But could she? Hanna could easily outpace Paul the Third, but Paul the Second was in excellent shape. He would likely catch her. Hanna didn't want to think about what he would do to her all alone in the dark if his brother and Daniel weren't there to see.

She took a deep breath and put her hands on the hood of the car. Hanna let Paul the Second place his nightstick against the small of her back. Almost on cue, his brother shut off the cruiser lights and suddenly the blue and red evaporated and all that was left was the glow of the moon. Hanna's vision fell prey to the faint light. She squeezed her eyes shut and opened them again, struggling to see.

"Now spread your legs."

Hanna shot Paul a look of contempt and spread her feet a few inches. Paul muttered under his breath — an angry, guttural sound that didn't include any words — and with a single swift kick, forced her legs apart. He ran his nightstick along her hip, down her legs to her calves, pushed it hard up and down her arms, and then around to her stomach, where he let his hand take over.

Hanna suddenly felt terribly cold. Her entire body seized up as Paul reached under her dress and cupped her breast. His fingers moved slowly from one side to the other, his palm coarse and sweaty, grabbing her, fondling.

A scream rose in Hanna's throat.

"What's this?" Paul pulled the wad of cash from Hanna's undergarment. He meshed the money between his fingers and then dropped it on the hood. "What did you do to get all that cash, girl?" he said. "Did the rich boy over there give it to you for favors? Because that's illegal in these parts, you know."

Overhead, a crackle reverberated in the sky. The air smelled of rain.

Let him do this, Hanna thought. *It can't get any worse.*

Paul slid his hand under her dress and along her thigh. Hanna cringed as his hand moved farther up her leg. He blew a whiff of tangy hot air into her ear.

"Damn, Hanna," he said. "If I'd known you'd been giving it up to little milksops like that kid, I would have gotten inside this a long time ago."

"Do not touch me there," Hanna said through clenched teeth. She tried to stand up straight, but Paul pushed her against the hood. He knocked her hard on the back with his nightstick. His fingers curled under her dress.

Hanna started to shake. Inside her, something ignited. She didn't know what it was. Earlier that evening, orange flames had burst inside her chest when she confronted Jotham. But this was different. Hanna filled with rage. Her muscles clenched. She could barely breathe. Above, the night was swirling, swelling, transforming. And then it happened — a crack appeared in the sky. A white light emerged from the darkness and turned brighter with each passing second.

Paul laughed, his cackle wicked and ignorant and dumb. He placed the end of his nightstick squarely between her legs. "Oh, Hanna, don't pretend you don't like it."

Inside Hanna's mind, a storm erupted. She thought not only of Paul but of Edwin — cheerful, silly Edwin who used to carry Hanna on his shoulders and pretend to steal her nose — and how within three days' time, he would put his hands where Paul's hands were now, he would take her into his wedding bed along with the barren wife and those horrible women. Hanna's chest pulsed. Her arms burned. A strength grew inside her. The voice in her throat beat like it had its own heart, fast and unwavering and desperate to get out. She opened her mouth and screamed as loud as she could.

"I said — don't touch me there!"

She turned around quickly and hit Paul the Second in the chest. Hanna caught him by surprise and he reeled backward.

Up above, the clouds crackled. The ground started to shake. Paul looked up and saw the white glow in the sky for the first time. He stumbled back toward the car as a bolt of lightning raced down from the opening. It hit the ground with the force of a mountain collapsing. Quickly two more followed, one in front of the cars, another behind. The second collided within a yard of where Paul stood, knocking him off his feet, shaking the police car.

Paul the Second landed on his backside and gaped at Hanna. He looked up to the sky. "What's happening?" he cried.

Hanna saw the terror in his eyes, his meek, quivering expression and she glared at him, unabashed, knowing and fearless.

"Let Daniel go," she commanded.

The other Paul poked his head up from behind the police car. He scurried around the side of the car and opened the door. Hastily, he unclasped Daniel's wrists. Daniel stepped into the open road as the two brothers quickly jumped into their vehicle and sped off. As they departed, the white light evaporated in the sky. All of a sudden, Hanna's knees weakened.

She looked at Daniel, whose face had gone ghostly white. She wanted to tell him it would all be okay, that the brothers wouldn't hurt them anymore, but it was like she had forgotten how to speak. The rage had burst out of her and she couldn't feel it anymore. Hanna couldn't feel anything, not the cold air around her, not her hands, not the ground beneath her feet. She faltered. Hanna stepped back woozily and caught herself. She thought she might stay upright, that the dizziness was temporary, only she couldn't control her legs anymore. Hanna's eyes closed. The world turned black and the last thing she saw was darkness as she collapsed to the ground.

When she awoke in Daniel's arms, Hanna's first thought was that it had all been a dream. She was still light-headed but aware now, awake. The moon hung like a broken coin in the sky and in its light she saw the bruise forming along Daniel's jaw. Beyond him, a star pattern was etched in the soil. Twenty paces away, there was another outline and behind their car, though she couldn't see it, Hanna knew a third mark streaked the ground.

Daniel seemed surprised that she'd come to. "You scared me," he said.

"How long was I out?"

"I'm not sure. A few minutes, maybe more," he said, holding his injured jaw. "I thought I'd lost you." Daniel looked around. It was just the two of them. The brothers were gone. Above, black clouds hovered in the space where the opening had formed. Daniel's eyes were wide, his mouth open, his voice unsteady.

"What happened back there?" Daniel said. "What happened with the sky?"

Hanna opened her mouth to speak, but nothing came out. She didn't know what to say. Hanna herself barely knew what had transpired. She couldn't put into words the feeling when the scream burst out of her body, and she was still dazed, still struggling to stand up. Hanna climbed to her knees and then her feet. She pushed her hair out of her face and almost lost her balance.

"Careful there," Daniel said.

"I'm okay. I'll be okay," Hanna said.

She stared at the moonlit star pattern on the ground. For over twenty-four hours, Hanna had been telling herself that Kara had made up a story to get her to run away. *You fell from the sky!* she'd said. *The heavens opened and you landed unscathed.* Hanna had convinced herself it was nothing more than a fairy tale. She recalled the tumble from Jotham's roof, the wind passing through her outstretched fingers moments before she struck the ground, how a fall from that height should have killed her. Hanna pictured the lightning flashing in the sky.

And she wondered — how had there ever been any doubt in her mind?

27

Daniel didn't say a word on the rest of the drive home. The radio was silent, the only sound raindrops ricocheting off the roof of the car. The headlights cut through the darkness, illuminating the trees lining The Road; they were gray and barren, some sloped to the side, others with their trunks splintered and branches winding like misshapen arms. The dismantled frame of an abandoned car appeared in a quick flash of the headlights and then it was gone.

Daniel's careful lips now formed a thin line across his face and Hanna couldn't tell if he was angry, disappointed or in pain after being struck by the nightstick. She sat on her hands, unable to shake the feeling that the confrontation with the brothers might be the final breaking point for Daniel, the one that would cause him to leave Clearhaven forever.

Earlier, when Hanna stepped out of the

store in the red dress she'd paid for with her very own money and danced to the woman's hypnotic voice, the thought of leaving Clearhaven was real. She felt it as strong as any emotion, as distinct as any earthly sensation. Escape was truly in her grasp. Now, as they reached the end of The Road and Daniel started navigating Clearhaven's intricate series of intertwined avenues, that short burst of freedom felt like a fantasy, something she'd conjured up in her head.

Hanna had seen Daniel's face light up when the city came into view. She'd noted the ease with which he slipped into city life. And Hanna's wedding was only three days away. Soon she would be trapped inside Edwin's home. Hanna would be pregnant before the end of summer and have Edwin's baby in her arms by this time next year. How could she possibly convince Daniel to stay when the best she could offer him were occasional visits a few times a week at church?

Daniel pulled into Jotham's driveway and parked beside the old battered pickup truck. He turned to Hanna.

"Is there anything I can do?" he asked tentatively, but Hanna knew there was nothing. He couldn't turn back time. He couldn't change what had happened on The Road.

"No," Hanna said. And then she whispered, "I'm sorry," without knowing exactly why she was apologizing. She undid her seat belt and stepped out of the car as the light drizzle transformed into a full-fledged storm, spilling rivers of black rain onto the ground. Hanna's hair quickly turned wet and her red dress soaked through. She watched Daniel's car pull away and then turned to see a single light glowing in the downstairs window, outlining Jotham's tall, heavy figure.

Her siblings were watching from above. Hanna could see their small faces, their wide eyes crowded against the bedroom window. She climbed the front steps and before she reached the door, Jotham turned on the porch light and stepped out to meet her. His face came slowly into view, the veins in his neck bulging, his teeth clenched and his eyes narrowed to where any trace of white was completely obscured.

Earlier Hanna had felt emboldened in her new red dress. Now, in Jotham's presence, her dress heavy with rain and clinging to her skin, she suddenly felt ashamed. Slowly, Jotham undid his buckle and pulled off his belt until it dangled in his trembling hand.

"You disappoint me," he said.

At any moment Hanna expected Jotham to lift the belt over his head and take a savage swing. As with Paul in the deserted road, she tried to decide whether it was better to run. With his bad back, Jotham could never catch her. Hanna could leap from the porch. She could run to the neighbor's house and plead with them to take her in. She could sprint into the woods and find a safe place to hide until daybreak. In the morning she could return while Jotham was asleep and hope for the best.

Hanna had one foot off the deck when she glanced up at the faces in the window again. Were she to run, at least one of them — perhaps several — would endure Jotham's wrath. She pictured Jotham storming upstairs, flinging the children's door open and lashing his belt indiscriminately in the air. She envisioned Charliss rushing to protect the others; the metal buckle colliding violently against his arms, his chest and his face; Charliss falling to the ground, helpless; the children cowering in their beds. Hanna met Jotham's gaze. No brother of hers would suffer in her place tonight. Hanna braced herself. She stood in place.

Seconds passed like hours. The punishment, the belt, Jotham's unbridled fury never came. Jotham tossed his belt onto a deck chair. Without taking his eyes off Hanna, he opened the front door.

"Belinda!" he hollered. "Bring the girl."

Hanna's stomach turned to ice. "What did you do?" she said.

Belinda came thundering to the door, half carrying, half pushing Emily down the hall. Tears streamed down Emily's face, a trickle of blood seeping from her mouth. Jotham grabbed Emily by the arm and pulled her outside. He pushed her against the wall and yanked Emily's nightdress up to reveal three long welts swelling across her back.

An orange pulse gushed from Hanna's stomach to her throat. She felt like she might throw up. Hanna wanted to scream. She wanted to take Jotham's belt and strike him over and over again until he couldn't stand anymore. Hanna moved toward the girl. She went to put her arms around Emily when Jotham held up his hand.

"She says she knew nothing about you and the boy."

"So you beat her?" Hanna exclaimed.

Jotham's eyes were hard like steel. "I sought the truth."

"Emily didn't know anything," Hanna said. "She's just a little girl."

A crease formed in Jotham's brow. Moments passed in agonizing stillness, the only sound Emily's weak, anguished sobs. Finally, Jotham opened the door and threw Emily inside, and then he slammed it shut with a thud, leaving Hanna and Jotham alone again.

"What were you doing with Francis's boy?"

"We drove to the city."

"To run away?"

"No, Father."

"Then why?"

Hanna swallowed hard. "We went to see a music concert."

Jotham wheezed. He took a step back and held his hand to his chest. "Where'd you get the money?"

"What money?"

"Don't play dumb with me, young lady. You know what money. The money the deputy found on you. Have you been stealing from me?"

"No, Father."

Jotham threw his hands in the air. He pointed at the house. "You see the way we live around here. How can you steal from me when I have so little? When I do everything in my power to provide for you children?"

Hanna turned her eyes down. She would

never admit that Kara gave her the money. Jotham could beat her until she breathed her last breath and Hanna would never expose her mother.

"Paul the Second called," he said. "They told me what happened."

Hanna pictured the rupture in the sky. The lightning bolts. What had Paul told him?

"They said you were disrespectful and uncooperative. That the Rossiter boy took a swing at Paul and he had to strike him down."

Hanna's eyes widened. "Is that all?"

"Is that all!" Jotham bellowed. "Do not stand there and disrespect me the way you disrespected Paul's sons tonight. When you disrespect the deputies, you disrespect our community. You disrespect our faith. You disrespect me." His voice swelled. "I am your father! You are honor bound to obey me!"

Jotham stepped face-to-face with her, the liquor clinging to him like a fog. He was sweating profusely, and, though his red face trembled with anger, Hanna saw something brittle in the lines about his eyes, something she'd never seen before.

Fear.

Hanna couldn't believe it. Jotham was

afraid. He was afraid of her running away, afraid of losing his business dealings and living in poverty for the rest of his life, afraid of always being poor.

Jotham lowered his voice. "We will forget this ever happened. I've already spoken to Brother Paul. His sons won't tell anyone about tonight, especially Edwin. And neither will you. The Creator has spoken and his word is true. Three days from now, you will marry Edwin. You will join his family. You will have his babies and you will be a good wife." Jotham fixed his eyes on Hanna's chest where her new red dress had soaked through. "And take off that garish frock. You look like a whore."

He turned to step back inside.

"No," Hanna said.

Jotham turned back quickly. "What did you say?"

"I said no. I won't marry Edwin. I wasn't meant for this."

"You were meant for this!" His voice boomed.

"I am not!" Hanna cried, the volume of her own voice surprising her. She cast a quick glance upward, hoping for a crack to form in the rain clouds, for the lightning to return, but nothing emerged and Hanna returned her gaze to Jotham. "It's not your place to sell me off to the highest bidder. It's not your place to tell me to go make babies when just last year I was a child myself. You didn't bring me into this world. And you would never dare take me out of it. I fell from the sky!"

Jotham grabbed her shoulders. He shook her hard. "Who told you that? Who said that to you?"

Hanna fell limp in his arms. Jotham was gripping her tighter than ever before. His pores burst with perspiration and he looked like he wanted to shake the very life out of her. Only, he didn't. He *wouldn't.* Hanna saw it in his eyes. Jotham was never going to beat Hanna the way he'd beaten Emily. She was Jotham's one true asset, the only tradable commodity he had in this world. That's why, for all his threats over the years, for all his menacing words, he'd never hurt her. While the other children received beatings for the slightest perceived offense, Hanna had been untouchable. Jotham wasn't about to hit her any more than he was about to hit himself.

"Let me go," she said.

Jotham dug his nails into her arms. He glanced backward for a moment, as though waiting for someone to intervene, so he wouldn't have to follow through. When no one came, Jotham wheezed. He buckled over, panting. Jotham's breath caught in his throat. The air rattled his chest. Jotham stumbled and coughed into a rag.

"Are you dying?" Hanna said.

He flashed her a wicked glare.

"You sound like you're dying."

"I may very well be. But I'm not dead yet, little girl," Jotham said.

"If you're terribly ill, then does any of this really matter?" she said. "Why beat Emily like a dog? Why force me to marry someone three times my age? Couldn't you use this time to bring something to this family? Love, happiness . . . anything other than what we have now? We could be happy. There's no reason for us to live this way."

As Jotham grasped the door frame for support, Hanna realized how much she meant her words. If he would take Emily into his arms and tend to her wounds, if he'd beg her forgiveness and be a father to her, all would be forgiven. Hanna would look past what she'd discovered earlier in the day, that Jotham had planned to give her away when she was just a child. She would forgive him for pressuring her to marry Edwin. She would care for him and nurse him back to health and be a daughter to him, if only Jotham would let the past and the future go, and show compassion now. But the look he gave her, the scorn in his ailing eyes, the grimace stuck to his face like a painting warped by years of dry heat — it told her everything she needed to know. There would be no forgiveness. No joining of hearts tonight.

"I'm leaving this house tomorrow," Hanna said. "I'm going to travel to the city and I'm going to live far away from here. I will not marry Edwin."

Jotham reached back and grabbed the ledge for support. The sounds of the night became crystal clear: the raindrops colliding against the roof, the wind shaking the trees, Jotham swallowing his breath, Hanna's beating heart.

"You may leave," he said.

"Really? And you won't stop me?"

"How could I?" he said and turned to walk back inside.

Hanna couldn't believe what he'd said. A warm, wild elation swirled in her chest. She pictured herself leaving Clearhaven behind, The Road stretched out before her like an opportunity, the reflection of the city lights in the bright, glistening water. She would travel to the other side of the world, meet her brave other self face-to-face, join the people who lived free in a hamlet by the bay.

"Thank you," she said. "Truly, Father, thank you."

He flashed a callous smile. "You do realize, of course, that Emily will have to take your place."

Hanna froze. "What do you mean?"

"In three days, Edwin expects to marry one of my daughters and I won't disappoint him. If you won't obey your father and serve the will of the Creator, then it's my responsibility to choose someone to take your place. I choose Emily."

Hanna scanned the window upstairs but couldn't find Emily's face anywhere. She imagined her sister lying on the hallway floor, ice on her bruises, her tears flowing like a river.

"But she's just a little girl. You can't do that."

"I can and I will," Jotham said. "Three days from now, Edwin will take Emily as his bride. He will lie with her in his bed the way a man lies with his wife. And he will break her. And it will be your fault."

In the distance, a clap of thunder roared. Rain pummeled the ground.

"Only a monster would do something like that," Hanna said.

Jotham wiped a spot of saliva from his mouth. "You're the one forcing my hand. *You* are the monster," he said. "You think you're special, that the laws of our faith don't apply to you because you fell from the sky. Well, I say — you were brought into this world the same as any other child. You've been fed lies. Where is your proof? The storm outside? A freak occurrence of lightning almost hitting Paul's son?"

He knew about the lightning.

"You are no more special than any child in this family," Jotham said. "You're just a teenage girl, and a rebellious one at that, disrespecting your father. Your only currency is your blond hair and your pretty face. For that, Edwin was prepared to pay a hefty price. But now Emily's youth will have to suffice."

Hanna stepped back. She was standing upright, her feet planted firmly beneath her, and yet she felt like she'd tumbled into the center of a whirlwind. Doubt flooded Hanna's mind. Perhaps Jotham was right. Maybe the lightning was a freak occurrence. Maybe it had just been the storm breaking.

Hanna's shoulders wilted. She bowed her head. "You win, Father."

He arched his back and shifted his brace. Jotham tilted his chin upward. "I'm sorry?"

"You heard me."

"I'm afraid I didn't."

Hanna swallowed hard. Somewhere on the other side of the world, the girl Hanna dreamed she could be fell to her knees. The air split behind her, the sword slicing toward her neck. The brave Hanna, the courageous one, the one who'd escaped, braced herself for the end.

"I will marry Edwin," she said.

28

Hanna woke up to the morning light seeping through a crack in the bathroom window. Emily was lying on the cold tiles beside her, fast asleep; her bare back was exposed, her skin stained purple and red from the welts Jotham had inflicted, deep and swollen and connected by long abrasions. Hanna watched Emily's chest rise and fall. The girl's eyelashes flickered and for a moment Hanna thought Emily might be feigning sleep. Then Emily breathed out through her nose. She shifted and wrapped her arms around the pillow Hanna had placed at her side.

Last night, Hanna had been unable to calm the girl. She found Emily cowering in the bathroom upstairs. Katherine was applying a cold compress to her wounds and singing a song from church when Hanna knelt down to whisper in Emily's ear. She reached out to console her. Only, Emily screamed furiously. She swatted at Hanna and kicked her away. Hanna had sat outside the door, leaning against the banister, until Emily's sobs abated, until finally the girl fell asleep in Katherine's arms. Hanna brought in pillows and a blanket and took Katherine's place next to her sister.

She sat up on the tiles now. Hanna placed her hand on Emily's upper back, the twisted portion where no damage had been inflicted, and suddenly Emily awoke. She sat up quickly, startled by the morning light. Emily skittered back against the wall, trembling, clutching her arms to her chest.

"Emily —" Hanna said.

"No."

"But, Emily —"

"Don't!"

Emily slipped her dress over her head and pulled herself to her feet. She grasped for the door handle. Her left foot landed on its side and she stumbled. She grabbed hold of the sink, pulled the door open and hobbled down the hall.

Hanna stood up groggily and looked at herself in the mirror. Her hair was a shambles. Hanna had her nightdress on, and inside the sink the red dress lay in a sopping pile, like a soiled kitchen cloth. She lifted the drenched garment and rung it out, the faint, pink water dripping down the drain. She held the dress up to her chest one more time. Hanna pictured Daniel taking her hand, his body pressed up against hers on the dance floor. Then she rolled the dress into a tiny ball and tossed it into the wastebasket.

Hanna made her way downstairs where the quiet was unsettling. Usually the house was teeming with chaos — children scurrying every which way, an endless commotion. Now, when the women spoke, it was in whispers, even when Jotham wasn't in the room. Hanna had expected Charliss to ask questions. She'd expected the little ones to flock to her, as they always did. Instead, they barely said a word.

Dark clouds had gathered in the sky and Kara ushered the children outside to help search the outer walls of their property for woodlice before the rains resumed. Hanna opened the door to see a bucket containing a dozen writhing bugs, each struggling to climb the sides of their metallic prison.

Then the rains commenced. A single drop fell and thousands more accompanied it to the ground. In the distance, thunder struck in waves, as though an enormous anvil was being rolled onto its side, a fresh clap igniting before any echo could repeat. The children dashed inside. They knocked over the bucket of woodlice on their way through the door and Hanna helped Kara scoop them up. Her mother didn't say a word. She avoided eye contact and Hanna felt that if she were to hear Hanna's voice, Kara might cry enough tears to rival the storm.

Hanna went out onto the front porch to sit in the cold and watch the rain from under the awning. She fell back in a rickety old deck chair and wrapped herself in a blanket. Clearhaven had not seen a downpour like this in months. The winter had been dry, the snowflakes wide and languid, the white mounds they fashioned often unsuitable for packing. Now moisture hung heavy in the air. A labyrinth of puddles gathered in the driveway, the gravel and dirt giving way to tiny streams and lagoons, patches of moss and random weeds sprouting through the gravel.

A short while later, Jotham stepped onto the deck. Hanna wasn't sure if he noticed her under the blanket to his side. Jotham held up an umbrella and then plodded out into the rain toward his truck. Along the way, his heavy feet demolished the driveway's canals. Tiny dams breached. Little lakes overflowed. Creek beds crumbled. Jotham's truck pulled away and the rain persisted. It was as though the town had been thirsty for ages and had now drunk too much to compensate.

For over an hour, Hanna watched the rains. Then the winds began to settle and the clouds drifted apart, the darkest floating northward, taking their deluge with them and leaving soft white wisps behind. The raindrops dwindled and then stopped altogether. Hanna shifted in her blanket. She pulled her feet under her legs and closed her eyes to rest, only her mind was racing, her nerves jumbled. Sleep refused to come. The bright blue sky gleamed in the distance and soon sunlight reflected off the pools the rain had left behind.

The little ones came out to play in the front yard and Charliss sat down on the porch beside her. He looked at his big sister, but he didn't say a word. Charliss had a pair of Jotham's shoes in one hand and an old toothbrush in the other. He wet the toothbrush and scraped it against a bar of soap and then scrubbed the eyelets of Jotham's shoes as though cleaning were a war to be won. Hanna wanted to say something about last night, to tell Charliss she never imagined Father would hurt Emily so badly, but Charliss's eyes were combative and the words evaporated before they ever reached

Hanna's mouth.

Hanna wrapped her jacket over her shoulders. "I'm going for a walk."

"But you haven't asked permission," Charliss said.

Hanna looked back at the front door. The last thing she needed was Belinda interrogating her over where she was going and when she'd be back. Or, worse, insisting she come along as Hanna's chaperone.

"It will be okay."

"Do you need me to come with you?"

Hanna looked at her feet, up at the bright blue sky, anywhere but in her brother's eyes. "No," she said. "You're the big brother. It will be your responsibility to look after the little ones once I'm gone."

"Gone where?"

"To live with Edwin."

Hanna stepped off the porch and marched down the driveway without looking back.

Daniel wasn't sitting on the pier. Hanna could tell from a distance there was something there, perhaps his guitar, but as she made her way toward the lake, it became clear she was alone. She glanced through the pines at Daniel's father's house. Hanna considered knocking on his front door, only to think better of it, and then sat down on the wet wood. The lake had risen to where it touched the tips of her shoes. The purple ice had melted, and now only black water remained. Absently, Hanna picked up Daniel's guitar and placed it on her knee. It had been left outside all this time and the wood was warped, the strings a rusty orange color. She thumbed the lowest note and listened to it reverberate across the water. Before the soft tone faded away, Hanna heard footsteps on the dock behind her. At first she hoped it was Daniel, but then a woman's voice filled the air.

"Hanna, is it?"

Hanna turned to see Daniel's mother approaching behind her. Hanna climbed to her feet, and, in her haste, she almost dropped Daniel's guitar into the water. "Yes," she said.

"What are you doing here?"

"I came . . . I came to see Daniel."

Eileen Rossiter glanced back toward the house, at the sunlight reflecting off the windows. Hanna set the guitar down and her heel met the end point of the dock, dangerously close to slipping in.

"Did Daniel say anything to you?" Eileen Rossiter said.

"What do you mean?"

Eileen Rossiter took a step forward so she

was just an arm's length away. Hanna saw the long-healed pox scars on her cheeks, the slight tremble to the woman's hand.

"I know about last night," she said.

Hanna braced herself for Daniel's mother to unleash a furious verbal assault, worse than Makala's abuse at the police station. "I'm sorry," she said quickly, before the woman could get her words out. And she *was* sorry. Hanna was sorry for Emily suffering in her place. She was sorry for disappointing Kara by not running away. She was sorry for Daniel getting struck across the jaw. Hanna was sorry for interfering with this woman's son, for thinking she could lead a secret life in a place like this. Hanna's boot slipped. She almost lost her footing.

"You don't have to explain," Daniel's mother said. "Just tell me where my son is."

"You mean you don't know?" Hanna asked, tilting her head at the woman. Then it became clear. Hanna saw it in the star-shaped markings around Eileen Rossiter's eyes, in the pale, woeful look on her face. Daniel had left Clearhaven. He'd left and he was never coming back. "Is he really gone?"

Daniel's mother nodded weakly. It seemed all she could do to hold back her tears. "All my sons are gone."

"Did Daniel leave a phone number, some way to reach him?" Hanna asked. But before the words left her mouth, she realized the futility of her question. If Eileen Rossiter knew how to contact Daniel, she surely wouldn't tell Hanna. "I'm so sorry. I have to go," Hanna said and stepped past the woman. She walked to the end of the pier as quickly as she could.

"Wait," Eileen Rossiter said before Hanna reached the tree line. "If you hear from him, if he contacts you, will you please . . ." Her voice cracked and faded, and Hanna couldn't help but think of the Grierson woman and the terrible thing that happened to her, how fragile existence was for the women of Clearhaven, what Eileen Rossiter's life would be like without her boys.

"I'll tell him you love him."

Then she turned and walked away.

Hanna's feet sank into the mud on the way home. Her legs grew heavy and the longer she walked, the more she felt like someone had died. That's how it would be — like Daniel had died, like someone had placed his body in a wooden box and lowered it into the ground. She couldn't believe he'd left without telling her. Hanna knew the lightning had frightened him. It frightened her, as well. She knew the difficulties their relationship presented, how she wasn't in a position to promise him anything. But to leave without a parting word? It was cruel and Hanna was alone. There would be no grieving, no casket to throw herself upon, no ceremony or goodbyes. She would simply never see him again.

Hanna knew it was unreasonable to feel this way. She'd known Daniel for mere days — a small fraction of her life. If she confided to her mother how much Daniel meant to her, Kara would use logic to turn Hanna's feelings aside. She'd say Daniel just happened to come along at a stressful, uncertain period in Hanna's life, that she couldn't *love* him after such a short time, that Hanna was scared and in love with the idea of being in love.

Nothing could have been further from the truth. Hanna knew how she felt, like every part of her body ached, like a bell had clanged inside her chest and now the ringing would never stop for as long as she walked this Earth.

She paused in the middle of the muddy road. Hanna closed her eyes and tried to feel her other self, the courageous girl, the huntress on the other side of the world, and for the first time couldn't conjure up a single image to soothe her aching heart.

The only thing worse than being asleep on the inside is being awake and alone.

A desire to flee ignited in Hanna's chest. She started moving faster. Hanna sprinted through the mud, Eileen Rossiter's mournful expression burning in her thoughts. Hanna repeated Jessamina's derisive words, how the young mother pitied her, how Hanna was destined to become her. She thought of Edwin, how two nights from now he would pin her down. Who else would be in the room when he took her for the first time? Would Fiona be there? Would Paedyn? Would they whisper sweet kindnesses in her ear? Or would they hold her to the bed, squealing and cackling, robbing Hanna of all she had left?

Hanna lifted her knees. The mud splattered all over her dress and she didn't care. Hanna could no longer live in this town. She couldn't marry Edwin, no matter what she'd promised Jotham. Hanna pumped her arms. The cool air swept against her face. She ran all the way to Jotham's doorstep. She'd already decided.

She would leave Clearhaven tonight. And she would bring Emily with her.

29

Hanna waited until the family fell asleep. It was past midnight and her brothers and sisters had long drifted off into their rhythmic slumber. Three of them were snoring. Charliss had kicked off his blanket and his long legs dangled off the edge of his mattress. Hanna sat up in bed. She ran her hand through Ahmre's hair. For a moment, she thought about picking the girl up in her arms. Then she looked over at Emily. Hanna steadied her trembling hands. She could only take one.

She slipped out of her nightdress. Hanna threw her old yellow dress over her shoulders and reached under her mattress. A quick panic raced through her mind when she couldn't find the money. Then her fingers felt the paper's edge. She pulled it out and tucked the envelope containing the rest of her mother's money against the waistband of her undergarment. Hanna stole quietly over to Emily's bed. She ran her hand along the girl's arm.

"Angel," she whispered. "It's time to go."

Emily stirred briefly and then fell back asleep. Hanna didn't risk waking her again. With all the strength she could muster, Hanna lifted Emily, blanket and all, up off the bed. She carried the child into the hallway and down the stairs, each step creaking as though at any moment it might give way. Hanna left the half-asleep girl in a chair by the front door and retrieved Belinda's keys from the ceramic dish on the kitchen counter. Before she left the kitchen, Hanna unplugged the telephone receiver and hid its cord under a stack of papers to delay Jotham from calling Brother Paul once he realized they were gone. She hurried back into the foyer, where she picked Emily up again and carried her to Jotham's truck.

It was pitch-black outside, the moonlight obscured by clouds. Hanna waited until her eyes adjusted to the night and then she set Emily's feet in the mud and unlocked the passenger's side door. Emily stretched and almost slipped. Hanna caught her just before she fell and placed Emily in the passenger's seat.

"Where are we going?" Emily mumbled.

"Shh," Hanna said. She shut the door as

quietly as she could and hurried around to the driver's side. Hanna unlocked her door only to find the key wouldn't come out of the lock. She pulled fiercely. Hanna had seen Belinda struggle with the driver's side door before, had even covered her mouth to keep her laughter at bay as Belinda pulled a stone from the truck bed and hammered the key sideways until it loosened. Hanna looked over her shoulder for that stone now. She pulled on the key again, but it wouldn't move.

A gentle tapping came from the window where Emily had her face against the glass.

"Pull it down and then to the left."

Hanna looked her sister in the eye. She glanced back at Jotham's front door. The lights were still off. The family was still asleep. Hanna pulled down as hard as she could and pushed the key to the left.

"Softer," Emily said.

Hanna tried again, gently this time. The key slipped right out as though it hadn't gotten stuck at all. Emily moved over to the passenger's seat and Hanna opened the door and stepped inside. She placed the key in the ignition and then hesitated. Jotham's truck was older than Hanna and it rumbled like a wood chipper. The moment she turned the key and the truck's engine roared, the family would wake up. Jotham would realize something was wrong. The trick with the telephone would buy them time. But would it be enough?

Hanna had only driven three times in her life, but she understood the mechanics of what her feet were supposed to do. The difficulty would come from shifting the truck out of first gear. After that, she would have to drive as fast as she could if they were going to make it out of town without getting caught.

Emily touched Hanna's arm. The girl was fully awake now, confused but curious, completely unaware of what Hanna had planned. "What's happening?" she asked.

The key was still in the ignition. All Hanna had to do was turn it.

"We're leaving Clearhaven. We're going to the big city."

"For how long?"

"Forever."

"Why?"

Hanna ran her hand through her sister's hair. "We're going to start a new life, away from all this."

Tears formed in Emily's eyes, magnifying them, intensifying her confusion, Emily's bewilderment. "But I don't want to leave. I don't want to go away."

"We talked about this," Hanna said.

"No, *you* talked about this. I never said I'd go with you."

"You have to trust me. This is for the best."

"No," Emily said, more defiantly now. Perhaps more defiantly than she'd ever been with Hanna before.

"Yes." Hanna reached for the ignition just as Emily grasped for the car door. Hanna had to lean over and hold it shut so her sister couldn't get out. "Emily, please."

"But I can't leave my mother. I can't leave Ahmre and Zagg and Minnet. You told me I'm the big sister, that it's my job to look after them. Who will take care of them if I leave?"

"Emily, please stop struggling and listen to me for a moment."

The girl let go of the door and looked into Hanna's eyes.

"I cannot marry Edwin!" Hanna said. The words burst out of her, louder and with more emotion than she'd intended. She expected Emily to soften, perhaps utter some sympathetic words. Instead, Emily shook her head forcefully.

"You're ungrateful. Father said so. You don't *understand.* You don't understand love and you don't understand the Creator.

You're lucky to have a husband. No man will ever want to marry me."

"That's not true. Besides, you don't want a husband. Not like this."

"It *is* true. And you don't know what I want," Emily said.

Hanna touched Emily's shoulder. "Just think of what Father did to your back. Do you want that to happen again?"

Emily clenched her teeth. "Father loves me. It's your fault he hurt me. You ran off with that boy. He had to do it."

"That's just not true."

"It is."

Hanna glanced up at the house again. It was only a matter of time before someone heard them. "Never mind what Father said. Listen to what I'm saying now. I'm going to tell you a story. It's going to be really difficult to believe. I had trouble believing it at first too. But please — you have to try, okay?"

Emily gave a faint, skeptical nod of her head.

"I wasn't born from my mother the way most girls are born," Hanna said. "I fell from the sky, from some place above us. I fell from Heaven and Jotham and Kara found me in the ground and they took me home. They aren't my real parents."

"You're lying."

"I swear to you, I'm not."

"Well, if you're telling the truth, then you're saying I'm not your real sister."

Hanna's words hung empty in her mouth. She clearly hadn't thought this through. "Not by blood. But we are sisters."

"No, we're not," Emily said. "Brother Paul says that brothers and sisters have to come from the same father."

"You can't believe everything Brother Paul tells you."

"Yes, you can. He's the one who speaks to the Creator. He speaks to him every day."

Hanna ran her fingernails through her hair. She wanted to scream. "Don't you understand? I cannot grow old here. I cannot live in Edwin's house with those horrible women. I'm trying to tell you that I was meant for something more than this," Hanna said. "We have to get away from this place."

A light flashed inside the kitchen. Then a second one ignited in the foyer. Hanna leaned past Emily and locked her door. She turned the key and the truck roared to life. Hanna grabbed Emily's arm, but she squirmed free and threw open the passenger's side door before Hanna could put the vehicle in Drive. She pushed Hanna away and fell awkwardly onto the driveway. Hanna gasped. She jumped out and ran around to the side of the truck, where Emily was picking herself up from the mud. Hanna tried to help, but Emily swatted her away.

"Father!" Emily cried. "Father! I don't want to leave!"

The porch lit up and Jotham rushed out the door in his nightshirt with Belinda at his side. His face was red, his breathing short and Hanna feared he would lose control, that her father would finally strike Hanna for this — the betrayal of all betrayals.

Belinda grabbed his arm before he could do anything. She whispered in Jotham's ear. Belinda pointed to Emily, still reaching toward him, and Jotham's gaze shifted from Emily to Hanna. He caught his breath and steadied himself, the redness slowly fading from his cheeks. Hanna had expected him to shake with rage, to be overcome and infuriated. Instead, he stood as tall as his back brace would allow. His voice was surprisingly restrained and self-assured.

"Emily," he said, "if you don't want to leave, then no one will force you to go."

Hanna stepped back and Emily lurched up the front steps, past Jotham and into the house, crying hysterically the whole way. Above, faces hovered in the window again. Tears welled behind Hanna's eyes and this time, instead of holding them in, she let them flow. Hanna fell to her knees. The hard gravel cracked her bruised knees.

Jotham whispered in Belinda's ear and she went back inside. Once more, it was just the two of them.

"She'll never leave," Jotham said. "Your sisters won't leave. Your mother won't leave."

Hanna wiped away her tears. "That's because you won't let them."

"No. It's because I *protect* them. It's because I'm their one safeguard against the rest of the world and, as much of a monster as you might think I am, I am the father. I am *their* father. And I am the only father you will ever know."

Jotham crossed his arms and lifted his proud chin, the conceit coating him like a glaze. There was nothing Hanna could say to contradict him, nothing Jotham would listen to, no words he was willing to hear. She would have better luck reasoning with a yellow-eyed wolf than this hulking beast of a man.

From inside, Emily's cries rang out in the night. She was still sobbing, wailing unintelligible words. Jotham looked back. Of all things, a smile parted his lips. He rubbed his arms. "It's a chilly night," he said. "Make sure you cover up. The journey to the city is a long one. You wouldn't want to catch a cold."

Jotham shut the door behind him, leaving Hanna alone on her knees, the truck rumbling behind her. She put her face in her hands. Hanna thought of Daniel and how he'd left without her. She still couldn't believe she'd never gotten to say goodbye, that she would never see his face again, that he didn't care enough to see hers. Deep inside, though she didn't want to admit it, Hanna was furious at Daniel for leaving. But she was doubly angry at herself; angry for believing she'd found someone decent and genuine in a world filled with deceit; angry for trusting her emotions to a boy she'd just met, for opening up her heart to be hurt.

She pictured herself arriving in the city all alone and not knowing where to go or whom to talk to. Where would she live? How would she survive all alone? What if life in the city was just like Clearhaven, an identical play with different actors performing the parts? Hanna envisioned Emily wearing the white wedding gown in her place, Paedyn and Fiona carrying her sister's crippled body into that small room in the back of Edwin's house, Edwin's wanton eyes wide and willing, and Emily too confused, her brain too awash with Brother Paul's falsehoods to know to fight back.

Hanna climbed to her feet. She brushed herself off and walked around to the front of the truck. As she sat down in the driver's seat, she looked off into the woodlands. The night was still, the wolves satiated. Tears still streamed down her face. Her blood pulsed in her wrists. She felt a sharp ache in her knees where she'd just scraped them. At that very moment in the city, thousands of yellow lights peppered the lake's soft waves. Young people swayed, spellbound by the melodies of a woman standing onstage, singing of redemption as though this was her last night on Earth. Somewhere lovers embraced. Tender, devoted fathers tucked their daughters into bed. Somewhere, Daniel was starting a new life. Without her.

Hanna closed her eyes. She steadied her resolve. Then she wrapped her fingers around the keys and turned the engine off.

30

The walls were white. The desk was too. Even Brother Paul's chair was made of white leather. Each time he shifted to the side, the chair groaned and creaked, as though it was bearing his weight for the first time. Behind him the afternoon sun was blazing through the wide bay window, yesterday's rain clouds having abandoned the sky, the sunlight reflecting off the pomade lines in Brother Paul's hair with a silvery glow. Brother Paul pushed a pair of reading glasses along the bridge of his nose. He leaned forward, an earnest look in his eyes.

Hanna had been here just over a week ago for an awkward and particularly in-depth discussion on her impending wifely duties. That was supposed to be their only one-on-one conversation. What Hanna was doing in Brother Paul's office today, she didn't know. All she knew was that Brother Paul's eyes were burrowing into her, waiting for Hanna to talk.

Hanna fidgeted in her seat. "Why am I here?"

"Well, for spiritual guidance, of course." Brother Paul clasped his hands in a steeple. In this light, he looked very much like Paul the Second, only grayer, the circles under his eyes wider, more adept at concealing his emotions. "I understand you're having doubts about your upcoming union," he said.

"I never said that."

"Regardless, it's clear. The decisions you've made this past week aren't those of a young woman at peace with the Creator's plan. Just days before your wedding, you were found traveling to the city with the Rossiter boy. You do not strike me as . . ." He paused, searching for the right words. "Particularly grateful. It's a good match, you and Edwin. He's a good man, a kind man, a leader in our community. I know firsthand how happy his home is. You will be happy there." Brother Paul leaned back and his chair gasped for air. "You don't look convinced."

"It's not that I'm ungrateful."

"Then what is it? It must be something."

Hanna ran her hands along her arms,

unsure whether she should speak her mind. "My mother told me you lived somewhere else before you came to Clearhaven."

"That's correct."

"And you were called here by the Creator."

Brother Paul nodded. "That is also correct."

"What if I'm just like you? What if I belong somewhere else, some place other than Clearhaven? What if *I'm* being called away?"

"Has the Creator spoken to you? Did he call on you to leave?"

Hanna hesitated. Her eyes shifted upward.

"In times like these, we must put our faith in the one who made us," he said. "You must trust that the Creator's spoken to your father. You must believe in his plan."

Hanna glanced at the telephone on the white desk. She kept hoping for someone to knock at the door or the telephone to ring, only no interruption was coming. No savior was coming to intervene. Brother Paul stood up from his leather throne. He walked around the desk and sat down beside Hanna, dwarfing the second guest chair. He lifted one lanky leg on top of the other and put his hand on his ankle for support. Brother Paul was wearing black trousers and a white shirt with a small blue insignia on the breast pocket. Away from the window's silky glow, he looked nothing like the otherworldly figure who stood before the congregation in church.

"No one ever leaves," he said.

Hanna sat up in her seat. "I'm sorry?"

"The boys leave. At least, we choose which boys leave. The girls stay. That's the way it is and the way it's always going to be. Your father won't allow you to leave. I won't allow you."

"I'm not leaving. I promised Jotham that I would marry Edwin."

Brother Paul's earnest expression vanished. His steely gaze locked Hanna in place. "Whatever promises you made your father, I want you to understand something. And it's best you listen to me because I'm only going to say it today and then never again. No. One. Leaves. Ask Jessamina if you don't believe me."

"Did Jessamina try to leave?"

Brother Paul shook his head. "She's smarter than that."

"Was it her mother, then?"

Brother Paul's gaze drifted along the wall, away from Hanna. Very slowly, he dragged a single finger across his throat.

"You're trying to frighten me," Hanna said.

"You should be afraid," Brother Paul said. "Have you wondered why I haven't mentioned Daniel by name today? Did it occur to you why he wasn't beaten within an inch of his life? Why he wasn't locked away for the damage he inflicted on your family's honor the other night? It's because he's Francis's son and that's the only reason why. I can only thank the Creator that Francis has agreed to keep the news of your misadventures from Edwin." Brother Paul looked her in the eye. "I've known you since your father could hold you in a single hand, young lady. I know you better than you know yourself."

Brother Paul leaned in so closely Hanna could see the pores in his skin. His breath enveloped her. Chills rippled down her spine.

Brother Paul's eyes sharpened.

"No one ever leaves."

31

On the day of her wedding, Hanna awoke with Ahmre in her arms. Emily had refused to stay in the children's bedroom, sleeping instead with her mother, Katherine, down the hall. Despite Hanna's best efforts, Emily still hadn't spoken to her.

Hanna was waiting in line outside the upstairs bathroom when Jessamina walked past her with baby Sayler in one arm and a clean diaper in the other. Hanna grabbed her elbow. "I need to talk to you."

Jessamina wrenched her elbow away, startled. "We have nothing to talk about."

"I have money. I can give it to you," Hanna whispered.

Jessamina looked over her shoulder. Her eyes drew close. "How much money?"

Jessamina sat down on her bed, her baby in the bassinet, twenty of Hanna's dollar bills clasped tightly in her hand. "What?" she asked.

"No," Hanna said. "That's not part of the deal. You have to be nice to me. Or at least pretend to be nice to me."

Jessamina softened her expression. "What?"

"I spoke to Brother Paul yesterday," Hanna said.

"Did he tell you all about your wedding night duties? Because, believe me, he can describe the tubes inside your body all he wants, but at the end of the day, it doesn't help when you're on your back."

"No. I mean, yes, he told me about that last week. This time he mentioned something about your mother."

Jessamina sat up straight. "You can have your money back," she said flatly.

"I don't want the money. It's yours. You can keep it."

Jessamina crossed her legs. She rubbed her hands together. "I don't want to talk about my mother."

"Please," Hanna said. As the word left her mouth, she couldn't believe her tone. She was almost begging, and begging Jessamina, the one person least likely to be moved by such a performance.

In the corner, baby Sayler kicked his

chubby legs. He giggled and spit up a bit and Jessamina reached over to wipe his mouth. "You don't want to know," she said.

"I do," Hanna said and sat on the opposite side of the bed. "After today, you'll never have to speak to me again."

"It's not that," Jessamina said.

"Then what is it?"

"They killed her."

Hanna's breath stuck in her throat. "I'm sorry?"

"You heard me. They killed her."

"But I thought she got sick from bacteria in the well water."

Jessamina shook her head slowly. Her baby started to fuss and she sang a quiet, wordless tune in his ear until he stopped.

"It wasn't a stroke and there was no contaminated well water," she said. "I mean, there was. The Sopertons' daughter died after drinking it. So did that boy from school. But my mother never drank from the well. Here's what happened, and I swear — if you tell another living soul, it will be the end of you. Do you understand?"

"Yes. Of course."

Jessamina's features softened further and suddenly she looked so young, not a mother's age like Belinda or Katherine or Kara but a girl much like Hanna, just a few years removed from childhood.

"My mother's name was Maran. You might have known her from church. She was beautiful and smart and she was the only person in my whole house who was ever kind to me. One of my sister-mothers slapped me across the face on a daily basis. My brothers were equally cruel. The oldest, Derius, forced me to sleep next to him. When night came, he made me do things no young girl should ever do. It would have been a complete house of horrors if not for my mother. When she found out what Derius was doing, she never let me out of her sight. She held me at night and she sang to me and she cared for me.

"About a year and a half ago, my mother met a man at the marketplace. I only know this secondhand, so I don't know his name or which family he came from. But my sisters told me my mother fell in love with this man who wasn't her husband. My father discovered their affair and he beat my mother senseless. He blackened her eyes and broke her nose and then locked her in the cowshed for three full days. When I tried to sneak her water, he beat me too.

"After my father let her out, my mother tried to run away. She and the man even made it all the way to the city. Until Brother

Paul organized a half dozen Clearhaven brutes and hunted them down. They let the man stay in the city, but they brought my mother back. I saw them pull up in Brother Paul's shiny white car with her in the back seat. My mother's bruises still hadn't healed and the look on her face was . . ."

A pang caught in Jessamina's throat. She clenched her shoulders. Jessamina sucked her breath in through her teeth, anything to keep from tearing up. Hanna didn't know whether to offer her hand, how the gesture would be received, whether it would calm Jessamina or silence her.

"Afterward, my mother looked like a defeated thing," Jessamina said. "She refused to talk about what happened. Then, three days later, I found her lying on the floor of the downstairs bathroom, her eyes rolled to the back of her head. She'd ingested some kind of poison."

Hanna covered her mouth. "Did she kill herself?"

Jessamina locked eyes with her. "Don't you understand? She *never* would have done that. My mother might have been terrified. She might have been depressed, but she hadn't given up hope. My father did this. Brother Paul did this."

"How can you be sure?"

"I'm sure!" she yelled and baby Sayler started to cry. Jessamina rubbed his hair and rocked him in her arms. She whispered in his ear before standing up.

Hanna stood up, as well. A warmth pressed under her skin where a minute ago there'd been none. All this time, she'd thought Jessamina's cruel stares and nasty remarks were because Jessamina was inherently spiteful, unfeeling to the point of callousness, whereas, deep down, Jessamina had been grief-stricken from the moment she walked through Jotham's door. Hanna took a step to leave and then she turned back. Jessamina was holding the baby as close as possible, clinging to the one thing she had left in this world.

"I'm sorry about your mother," Hanna said. She thought for a moment. "It could have been like this all along — the two of us talking."

Jessamina shook her head. "No, it couldn't."

"Why not?"

"You think you're better than me."

"That's not true."

"It is. You think because you're beautiful and I'm not that the world owes you something, that you're worth more than the rest of us put together."

"You are beautiful," Hanna said.

"Don't insult me. We both know that isn't true."

Hanna grasped for words. She tried to bring Jessamina's eyes to hers, to find some way to tell her how truly sorry she was, how she loved her own mother more than anything and how she'd be devastated if anything ever happened to Kara. But Jessamina wouldn't look her way. She might never look at Hanna again without disdain in her eyes and Hanna had precious little time left — only hours — before her wedding. She stepped toward the door and was halfway out when Jessamina spoke again.

"Edwin has a lot of money invested in this. Brother Paul, that father of the boy you took off with — they all have a lot invested. After the other night when you tried to leave with Emily, I'm surprised you're not dead already. You heard what happened to that Grierson woman."

"I thought that was only a rumor," Hanna said.

"She didn't do it to herself."

"But —"

"It's true. Be careful or don't be careful. Just know, if you're not — you'll be the one dead on the bathroom floor. You'll be the one dangling from the rafters with a noose around your neck."

32

It was midafternoon when she found her mother sitting in the front alcove, drinking tea. The room was cold and three dry logs sat in the fireplace. Hanna knelt down at the hearth and placed strips of kindling and crumpled paper around the sides. She struck a match and squeezed the bellows, the oxygen feeding the flame. Along the wall, the panel wood had warped further, the cracks had widened and the discoloration spread. Rain had seeped through the roof, Hanna and Charliss's handiwork proving unsuccessful.

Hanna sat down on the sofa and rested her head against Kara's shoulder. Her mother smelled like soap and her sweater was soft as though it had just been washed. Kara lifted her cup to her mouth and Hanna saw the frayed edges of her fingers where her mother had scraped her thumbnails until she'd drawn blood. She wrapped her arm around Kara's stomach.

"Tell me the story again," Hanna said. "I need to hear it."

Kara set her tea down on the side table. Her hand settled on the dulling bruise across her cheek. "I can't."

From the other room, Katherine's voice sounded. She called to Hanna and then they heard the patter of little feet.

"I never told you a story. I told you the truth," Kara said. "What you choose to do with the truth is up to you."

Katherine rounded the corner with two little ones. "There you are! It's time to get ready," she said cheerfully. "We wouldn't want to keep your fiancé waiting."

Hanna sat up and met her mother's gaze. She'd expected Kara to be distraught, but the lines on Kara's face revealed not a hint of emotion. Her mother looked hollow somehow, like she wasn't the person she used to be. Days ago, Hanna had witnessed Emily's longing and frustration firsthand. She'd heard Emily's voice tremble inconsolably when she saw Hanna in her wedding gown, how desperately the girl wanted to be a blushing bride. Her wedding's effect on Kara had proven far worse. For years, Kara had known what was coming and yet nothing had prepared her for the realization that the time was upon them and that she was powerless to stop it.

Hanna looked down the hall. "Is Emily going to help?"

Katherine shook her head. "She doesn't feel comfortable, dear. She's next door, getting dressed at the neighbor's."

Hanna nodded like she understood, but deep down she didn't understand. She didn't just want Emily to be with her today; Hanna *needed* her to be there. She hadn't realized it until now, but Emily had made Hanna's life in Jotham's house bearable. Hanna had found purpose in protecting Emily. In helping Emily stand. In helping the girl get dressed each morning. And Hanna loved everything about her sister. She loved Emily's soft laugh; the way Emily's hair dangled in curls over her eyes; how she'd clung to Hanna's arm when she was little; the way they used to hold each other close at night, their blanket a shield, their bunk bed a fortress so secure even the wickedest of evildoers could never reach them. It wasn't the same world for Hanna without her sister. It wouldn't be the same world going forward.

One of the little ones took Hanna's hand. Kara held onto her other side. For so long, all Hanna's worries — however tangible, however terrifying — could be assuaged because she still had time. There was still a week until her wedding. Then there were days. Now only hours remained. Time had turned out to be a shadow and Hanna had no light left to shine on it.

"Let's get ready," she said.

"It doesn't fit."

"I assure you, it *does* fit."

Katherine and Belinda were attempting to adjust the buttons at the back of Hanna's dress. Nothing in the garment's design had changed since the last time Hanna had tried it on. She hadn't suddenly gained ten pounds. And yet, the dress wouldn't rise over Hanna's hips. Hanna slipped her legs out and sat on a stool in the master bedroom, where her mother added fresh blue starlets to her hair. Kara had spent the last hour braiding Hanna's long blond locks and tucking the braids inside a delicate twist at the back of her head.

Katherine held the dress up to Belinda. "Perhaps you made the buttons too tight."

Belinda, in turn, ran her thumb along the stitches. "That's how Hanna wanted them."

"It seems like you tightened them again after she took it off."

"I *secured* them. I did not tighten them,"

Belinda said.

Eventually, after much discussion, Belinda allowed Katherine to adjust the dress. She brought out her sewing kit and made several minor alterations. Hanna slipped into the white gown and this time it matched her frame. She stood on a footstool in front of the full-length mirror as Katherine inspected the buttons across her back one by one.

"Do you remember what's going to happen tonight, what happens first?" Katherine asked.

Hanna nodded. It had been explained to her many times. Tradition dictated her wedding night would follow a set course of events. At sunset, Hanna and her parents would travel to Brother Paul's house, where Brother Paul would offer Hanna a sip of wine from a bridal cup blessed by the Creator. Once it was fully dark, a procession of cars would caravan to the old tower cathedral. There, Hanna would meet and pray with Edwin alone in the same bridal room where she'd climbed through the window just days ago, the bridal room where she'd stolen a private moment with Daniel. Guests would light candles and file in to observe the service. There would be no reception as the newlyweds were expected to go straight home and consummate the marriage as soon as the ceremony was over.

"Are the alterations complete?" Belinda said.

Katherine had her favorite crochet hook in hand and was pulling at a loose string at Hanna's back. Seconds later, Hanna's sister-mother stood up with a look of accomplishment on her face. "There," she said.

Hanna stood before the mirror, a bride at last. The girl staring back at her looked different from the one who'd modeled her wedding dress for Paedyn the other day. It had still felt like she was playing dress up then, like Hanna was trying on a borrowed disguise. Hanna turned her neck and saw the wonderful job Kara had done with her hair. Not a single stray strand had escaped the braids and the twist at the back was subdued, not gaudy in the least. The tiny flowers looked like blue stars afloat in a yellow sky. Hanna ran her hand across the rhinestones along her hip. She felt the delicate fabric against her arms. What she was wearing was no longer a disguise. Hanna was a bride about to be married. It was impossible to deny it any longer.

Through the window, the sunlight grew

faint in the sky. Hanna was due at Brother Paul's house soon.

"Are you ready?" Kara asked.

Hanna glanced around the room, at her mother, at her sister-mothers, at the wreckage of stray threads and orphaned buttons abandoned on the bed.

"I'm ready," she said.

The family assembled in the foyer to watch Hanna walk down the stairs. The children were wearing their best clothes, the boys sporting suspenders and the girls in dresses, some of the younger ones with hand-me-down cardigans wrapped over their shoulders.

Emily had returned from the neighbor's house and her hair was pulled up in a bun, a single pink gerbera daisy over her ear. Hanna had never seen her sister look so pretty. Hanna tried to make eye contact with her, but Emily shied away. She had her hands clasped together and was standing as straight as she could. Every few seconds, Emily would cast a timid glance upward and Hanna longed to ask her what she could do to change things, if there were any words she could say. But the others were there, surrounding them, staring at Hanna in her dress. She stepped downstairs and embraced the little ones carefully, so as to keep her hair from falling out of its pins. Charliss approached with his dark hair combed to one side. He was wearing a bow tie and Hanna could have sworn he'd grown two inches in the past month. A hint of perspiration glinted off his forehead.

"You look more nervous than me," Hanna said.

Charliss smiled bashfully and Hanna thought how greatly she would miss him, not just when she went to live in Edwin's house but after Jotham pushed him out into the world. A brother so close in age could have been so many things — an antagonist, a tormentor, a blight on the other children's happiness if he so chose. Charliss was none of these. He didn't yell like Jotham. He wasn't hard — in his speech, in his manner — like Belinda. Months from now, when Hanna found herself at Edwin's house scrubbing a kitchen pan or toiling in the laundry room or performing some other mundane task, she would think back to Charliss, the way his wide, innocent eyes peeked out from under his covers at night, how she wanted nothing more than to hold him close and keep him safe. She put her lips to his cheek and kissed him softly just as Katherine ushered everyone into the living room for a family photograph.

The fireplace was unlit, but the air was warm with so many bodies crowded into one room. Hanna's sister-mothers spent several minutes debating whether there was enough light to catch everyone's faces in a single photo. "I'll go get another lamp," Katherine said, and bustled into the other room before returning with two lamps and an oil lantern ("just in case").

One of the neighbor's wives had been waiting patiently in the kitchen with a camera slung around her neck and she steered the family into a line. Hanna stood near the center, rocking uneasily on her heels, with Kara by her side and little Ahmre at her feet.

"Where's Jotham?" the photographer said.

In all the upheaval, in the children's excitement and her own nervous state, Hanna hadn't noticed Jotham was absent. He entered the living room now wearing his brown suit. By some minor miracle, he'd managed to fasten his vest in place. A folded blue handkerchief jutted out of Jotham's pocket and he'd recently shaved his face. It was the first time in years Hanna was seeing him sober after five o'clock. He approached Hanna and extended his elbow.

Hanna hesitated. She looked at his arm like it was a poisonous thing: a stiff, violent appendage she had no interest in touching. Hanna glanced at the photographer, at her sisters' smiling faces, at Kara and Emily both with their hair up, and realized this wasn't the time to start a battle. The war had already been fought. Victors had been chosen and Hanna — despite every conceivable effort — had lost. She slipped her hand around Jotham's arm, took a deep breath and steadied herself.

The family, all nineteen of them, faced the camera.

"Smile!" the photographer shouted.

Jotham drove Hanna and Kara in his truck. The three of them sat together in the front seat with Kara in the middle and the ruffles of Hanna's dress pressing against the passenger's side door. Kara had Hanna's headdress in her lap and hadn't spoken since they left the house. Jotham drove without saying a word. He shifted his back brace in the driver's seat and grunted as he changed gears. Otherwise, he remained silent.

The farther Jotham's truck bounded down the roadway, the more Hanna found it difficult to breathe. Twice she'd almost unrolled her window to allow some fresh air inside but couldn't raise her shaking hand to complete the task. Her pulse beat like a drum. Goose bumps riddled her flesh. She glanced over at Kara to see whether her mother sensed her tension, only Jotham made eye contact with her instead. He flashed a quick grin — a surprising, uncharacteristic upturn of his lips — and Hanna wondered what could possibly be going through his head, whether he could sense the nerves blazing like a bonfire inside her or whether he'd managed (in some inexplicable yet completely intentional way) to push the past few days out of his mind. Had he really forgotten Hanna's rebellion, how he had beaten his crippled daughter, the girls' desperate, unsuccessful attempt to flee?

Outside, the sun had fully set and Hanna gazed at the first few stars in the night sky, at their brightness, their distance. Jotham's profile still loomed on the periphery of her vision and each time she glimpsed it, a sharp twinge resonated inside her: repulsion mixed with loathing and a measure of distrust. Hanna watched her mother's face instead. She focused on Kara's long, slender eyelashes and her fine cheekbones. Slowly, gradually, everything in Hanna's line of vision turned pink and pristine. Her mother's flesh, the vehicle's dashboard, the darkened woods outside glowed with auras — like in the moments following Hanna's fall from the rooftop, only amplified a hundredfold. Hanna felt outside herself and inside herself at the same time, her mounting sense of dread abated momentarily by the spectral hues: corals and currants, gleaming lilacs and deep magentas. She imagined a silver-white raven swooping and diving in the air, following the truck as it plodded down the semi-paved roads. Hanna watched from the bird's-eye view. She floated high above.

Kara took Hanna's hand and all Hanna wanted to do was apologize: apologize for ever doubting her, for not listening when Kara needed her to, for taking so long to admit the truth. The brave version of Hanna might have abandoned her. The world might have been closing in, and, within hours, a baby would likely be planted like a seed inside her, but Hanna still had her mother. She still had Kara's words. Her story. Hanna ran her hands along her white dress. She whispered under her breath, "I fell from the sky."

Kara looked over. "What was that?"

"Nothing." Hanna paused, then said, "I love you."

Kara gripped Hanna's hand tighter.

"I love you too."

■ ■ ■ ■

Brother Paul's enormous estate made Edwin's magnificent home look ordinary in comparison. Hanna had only seen the front of his house from the end of its long, winding driveway, and it was another thing entirely to enter through the front door. A massive stuffed tiger, like a fantastical drawing in a picture book, guarded the lobby with wide, cream-colored fangs; its eyes glassy and gray as Kara led Hanna through the hallway and into the atrium, where Brother Paul's wives had gathered. Dozens of eyes fell on Hanna. Whispers abounded. Thankfully, Makala — Brother Paul's cruelest consort — was nowhere to be seen.

The women greeted Hanna one after another. One of Brother Paul's older wives examined the wreath atop Hanna's head. She placed her hands on Hanna's temples and squeezed the dried daffodil petals. The woman complimented the stitching on Hanna's dress and asked who had done Hanna's hair. "Where did she learn to braid with such finesse?" she said. Hanna didn't respond. She stared blankly into the woman's eyes, wondering how she could make small talk at a time like this.

Moments later, Brother Paul handed Hanna a chalice made of copper. The cup's edges were adorned with green and red gemstones and inside was a small amount of red wine. Hanna put it to her mouth and the sour red liquid touched her tongue. She handed the chalice back to Brother Paul and then he asked Hanna to pray with him. As Hanna bowed her head, she saw Paul the Second standing toward the back of the atrium, where a tangle of vines obscured the wall. Paul the Second rubbed his abdomen. He shivered as though he had a chill. Hanna locked onto him. The prayer ended and Brother Paul spoke to the assembled mass, but Hanna didn't listen to a word he said. She kept staring, her stomach tightening.

Finally, Paul the Second looked her way. His brother was conspicuously absent, but Hanna didn't care. Paul's skin had gone white and she could tell he was afraid — of the lightning on that deserted road, of the chance of it striking again, flashing down from the heavens and hitting him this time. It was in his eyes. It was in his timorous gaze. It was in his soul.

Brother Paul completed a second prayer, this one an appeal to the Creator, and the women raised their heads and applauded.

Jotham approached and handed Brother Paul an envelope and then, strangely, the women began milling about, engaging Kara in conversation and asking Hanna the history of her dress. Hanna was surprised how informal they all were. True, they'd seen many brides come through the atrium doors and listened to countless prayers by Brother Paul. But this was *her* wedding night. This was *her* life that hung in the balance. A woman she'd seen at the marketplace touched Hanna's hair and spoke in jest of paying "top dollar for a hairpiece made from such wonderful locks." All the while, Hanna watched the clock on the wall. The real ceremony was fast approaching. In less than thirty minutes, they would pile into their vehicles and the wedding procession would begin.

Hanna stepped toward the window. Brother Paul's home was closer to the white church than it was to the marshlands. Other homes sat off in the distance, their porch lights turned on, beacons in an ocean of blackened waves. Hanna watched her reflection in the glass and adjusted the crown of daffodils atop her head. It had been ten minutes since she'd seen her mother. She was about to turn around and find Kara when the shadows shifted outside.

Hanna's heart skipped a beat. Then she narrowed her eyes. Hanna looked closer. Outside, a lone figure stood amongst the trees, the distant church light silhouetting the figure's shoulders and long, gangly arms. He took a single step out of the darkness and Hanna's cold heart ignited. Was it really him? It couldn't be. Hanna put her hand up to the window. Her fingers pressed against the cold glass. She could have screamed. Daniel was standing in the dark outside.

She glanced over her shoulder to see whether anyone else had noticed, whether Brother Paul had seen him. If Brother Paul's sons discovered Daniel outside their home, they would thrash him with their batons, benefactor's son or not. They might beat him to the point of death. She shook her head and motioned for Daniel to leave.

He motioned back — *come outside.*

Hanna looked down at her feet. The boy standing in the dark had already left her. Two days ago, Daniel had driven The Road out of town without so much as a goodbye. She had no idea what lay in his heart at that moment, whether he'd agonized over the decision — pangs of guilt stabbing his belly — or whether Hanna had been an afterthought to him. For days now, she'd felt as though he'd forgotten their brief time together. But here he was, standing on the other side of the glass, motioning for her to come outside, imploring her with his eyes.

Hanna held up a single finger. *Wait,* she mouthed. Then she turned from the glass and walked toward the other side of the atrium. Hanna hadn't made it ten paces before a woman touched her arm. It was an elderly lady, drinking wine from a tall glass.

"How are you tonight, dear?" she said.

Hanna shook the woman's hand. "Could you please show me to the restroom?"

The woman put her frail fingers up to her ear. "Excuse me, dear?"

"I said — can you show me to the restroom?" Hanna said loudly, causing Brother Paul and Jotham to turn her way.

"Of course. Let me help you," she said.

The elderly lady took Hanna's arm and led her through the crowd. Together they exited the atrium and walked down a hallway. Hanna glanced back. No one had followed them. "Thank you. I'll find my way from here," she said. Then Hanna moved as quickly as she could without looking back. She passed a closet and a stairwell leading to the second floor before a doorway appeared. Hanna pulled on the door handle and the spring air enveloped her. She stepped out onto the grass and made her way to the side of the house.

"Hello?" she called. Hanna looked over her shoulder. She looked from side to side, thinking maybe Daniel had already left. Maybe, just maybe, she'd dreamed the whole thing.

"Hello," Daniel said.

Hanna turned to see him leaning against the side of the house.

"This is how we first met," he said.

Hanna glanced back at the atrium. She had precious little time. "What do you want?"

Daniel reached out and took her in his arms. He held her close. Only, Hanna shied away. She stood absolutely still, her hands at her sides.

"I'm so glad to see you," Daniel said.

"I thought you'd already left. Your mother didn't know where you were. *I* didn't know where you were."

Daniel looked back at the house. He put his hand on Hanna's shoulder. "I'm so sorry," he said. "My father was furious when he found out we went to the city. He yelled at me for hours after I got home. He kept telling me that I was the lucky one, that he'd chosen me instead of my brothers and that I should be grateful. He said things were going to change. That if I ever thought of leaving Clearhaven again, he'd lock me up in the house, that he'd hire someone to watch over me twenty-four hours a day."

"So you just left?"

"I had to leave when I did. I didn't have any other choice," he said. "The moment my father went to bed, I climbed into my car and left. I knew you wouldn't be able to leave your father's house, but I came back for you tonight. I can't let you marry that old man."

"You can't *let* me?" Hanna stepped back. "I don't need saving. I'm not some kitten stuck up in a tree."

"I didn't say that. I've never thought of you that way. I know I shouldn't have left without you. But I'm here now." He pointed to Brother Paul's driveway. "I have a car. If we hurry, they'll never catch us this time. Come with me. We'll leave right now and never return."

Hanna looked over Daniel's shoulder, at the outline of his vehicle at the far end of the driveway. "So you're not afraid of me? You weren't scared by what you saw the other night?"

"Scared by the lightning? Of course I was scared. It almost hit us. But I'm not scared of you."

"Don't you see?" Hanna said fiercely. "I caused the lightning storm. The sky opened and the lightning shot down because of me."

Daniel's features slackened. "What do you mean?"

Hanna thought back to Emily's confused expression when Hanna hastily tried to tell her Kara's story in Jotham's truck. She took his hand in hers. "I'm going to tell you something and it's going to be hard to believe. But you're going to have to try your best, okay?" Hanna said. She paused to gather her courage. "When I was a baby, I fell from the sky."

Daniel tilted his head to the side. "What?"

The subtle timbre of disbelief in his voice sent a tremor rushing through Hanna's body. She racked her brain for words that would make sense, a way to explain what happened so Daniel would believe she was telling the truth. But her thoughts were a jumbled, feverish mess from the shock of seeing him again, from the betrayal she still felt over him leaving without her, from the terror swelling inside her as the seconds until her wedding ticked away; Hanna couldn't organize them well enough to speak.

A line formed between Daniel's eyes. "Do you mean you fell out of a window?"

"No," Hanna stammered before finding her voice. "I mean I wasn't born like a regular girl. As a baby, I fell from the heavens and I landed unscathed."

He ran his hands together. Daniel squinted as though struggling to understand.

"My mother and Jotham found me on the ground. They brought me here to Clearhaven," Hanna said, her tone growing more desperate. "I know it's hard to believe. I didn't believe it at first. But I swear it's true."

Daniel spoke in slow, measured words. "I want to be with you. I really do. But what you're talking about is a miracle. And there are no such things as miracles."

"But there are miracles. You saw me that night on The Road. You saw the lightning come down to protect me."

"Hanna, I don't know what I saw."

She ran her hands through her hair in frustration, sending flower petals scattering to the ground. "What do I have to do to make you believe me?" she said, frantic now, her emotion rising. "Find me a mountain and I will jump from its peak. Find the tallest building and I'll leap off it. I'll land unharmed and you'll see I'm telling the truth."

From outside the atrium, a woman's voice called. "Hanna, are you out here?"

Daniel took her hand. "You have to decide right now. Are you coming with me?"

Hanna pulled her hand away. She shook her head slowly. "I can't go with you if you don't believe me."

"Hanna?" the woman called again.

Hanna's eyes welled. She couldn't feel her legs, her arms, her hands. A storm swirled inside her: panic mixed with fear mixed with a sadness so intense she thought she might be sick. When Daniel had left without saying goodbye, it was a torment beyond all reason. Now, standing here before him for what was likely the last time, she realized that this was far worse.

Daniel held out his hand and pleaded with his eyes. "Come with me," he said, his voice cracking. "Please, Hanna. Don't stay here. Don't do this . . ."

Hanna imagined how she looked to him now: a girl in a white wedding gown, tears in her eyes, flowers in her hair, unable and unwilling to leave. "Goodbye, Daniel."

Her words stunned Daniel. He stepped back, a look of disbelief on his face. A desperate silence filled the air. One moment passed and then another before Daniel said, "Goodbye, Hanna."

And then he walked away.

She turned around and moved quickly. Hanna met one of Brother Paul's wives at the doorway around the corner. Jotham and Kara were there, as was Brother Paul.

Brother Paul followed Hanna's eyes into the darkened woods. "What are you looking at?"

"Nothing," she said. "I was looking at nothing."

She stepped over the threshold and Jotham helped her inside.

"Take me to the chapel," Hanna said.

33

Earlier that evening, as Kara braided Hanna's hair, the sun had clung bravely to the sky, turned it purple and red and pink, melding a series of spectacular spectral hues before finally succumbing to the night. That dreamlike horizon was but a memory as Jotham walked Hanna to Brother Paul's car. Dark shadows loomed. Hanna found it difficult to see anything farther than a few yards away. Still, she looked over Jotham's shoulder in search of her mother. Hanna scanned the streets for a sign Daniel had been there.

Jotham blocked her view, his large frame hovering in front of her.

"This is for the best," Jotham said. "You'll be happy. You'll see."

Hanna flashed him a contemptible look. How could Jotham pretend now, in front of Brother Paul and his wives? Just moments ago, Daniel had walked into the woods and stepped into his car and driven away. Hanna would never see his soft eyes again. She would never touch him or kiss him or hear his laugh for as long as she lived. And now Jotham dared to utter hollow kindnesses as he latched her to shackles, the very shackles he'd chosen?

Hanna arched her neck to the side. Her lower back cracked and a noise like popcorn sounded underneath the taut buttons that lay in wait for Edwin's fumbling fingers. She locked eyes with Jotham.

"I know," she said.

Jotham's forehead crinkled. "What?"

"I know you were going to give me to Edwin years ago when I was still a child. You and Edwin were estranged not because he betrayed you but because you couldn't work out a deal for the girl with the golden hair." Hanna searched his face. She scanned his suddenly flustered expression. "You're not my father. You never were my father, were you?"

Jotham quickly grew anxious. He glanced over his shoulder at Brother Paul, into the distance where Paul's wives were gathered. Jotham tried to steer Hanna aside, away from eavesdropping ears. But she stood her ground. Hanna refused to move a single step for this man.

Above, the stars glittered in the sky. All around, the night surged restlessly, ravenously.

Hanna locked her eyes on Jotham one last time. "Don't ever speak to me again," she said.

Before he could respond, Brother Paul took Hanna's hand and helped her and her flowing dress into the back seat. Hanna was startled to see Paul the Second already sitting in the seat beside her. Hanna assumed he would be traveling ahead in the lead car with his brother. If someone had told her a week ago that she would be trapped in the back seat of a car with Paul the Second, in the dark, with his father driving, Hanna would have been paralyzed with fear. But the look of apprehension in his eyes eased Hanna's nerves. He was clearly anxious for this to be over, to be away from the girl who knew the truth about his roaming hands, the girl who'd summoned white fury from the sky.

Brother Paul climbed into the front seat. He fired up the engine and, without ceremony, they pulled away.

The procession took less than fifteen minutes, in which Hanna listened to Brother Paul humming to himself in the front seat. Brother Paul drove cautiously and Hanna watched his hands shift along the steering wheel. For the first time, she noticed a slight thinning of the hair at the back of his head, the difficulty he had turning his neck to the left.

He was human after all.

The glow of the white church came first. Next, the parishioners holding candles. Half the town was gathered outside the tower cathedral. The wedding procession slowed as they reached the crowd and Hanna felt the eyes of the townspeople on her. Their candles glimmered, some distant and hazy, others burning so close Hanna could see thick droplets of accruing wax. Hanna recognized the faces holding them: her neighbors, the bullnecked butcher, girls younger than Emily.

Brother Paul's car broke off from the pack. He steered around back of the cathedral, toward the room where Hanna would pray with Edwin before the ceremony. Brother Paul turned off the engine and stepped out of the car. He opened Hanna's door and Paul the Second ushered her quickly past the crowd and in through the back. To her surprise, the room was aglow with flickering light, an entire row of candelabras leading to a small circle containing two cups, one for Edwin, the other for

Hanna. Paul the Second took one last look and then shut the door. Suddenly Hanna was alone.

Amidst the smell of wax and burnt paper, Hanna brought her tongue to her lips and found them dry. Her hands felt like they belonged to someone else. She breathed in deep and the air entered her lungs like she'd never taken a breath before. Had Hanna really been walking and talking and breathing all this time? Had this been her life? Of course it had. This was not a dream. There would be no sudden awakening, no guardian angel swooping in to save her at the last moment.

The door opened at the top of the stairs and Edwin appeared, wearing a black robe that dissolved into the spectral light. All Hanna could see was his face and glasses, the light surrounding him. She forced a smile and knelt down in the circle of flickering light. Edwin paused to look at her. Then he descended the stairwell, little stripes of gold revealing themselves on his robes as he drew closer. The stairs creaked with his steps and Hanna could hear the dim murmur from the crowd outside.

As Edwin approached, Hanna wasn't fully afraid. Not yet. Edwin would never take her here, before the ceremony. She still had time. Hanna closed her eyes as Edwin walked around the candles and stood over top of her. She pictured him kissing her flush on the lips, the smell of his flesh up close, the stale taste of his saliva. Hanna held her breath. She relaxed her shoulders as best she could. Then Edwin placed his hand on the back of her neck. Slowly, almost tenderly, his fingers slid around the front.

His fingers gripped more firmly, closing around her throat. Suddenly, viciously, he yanked her off the ground by her neck.

The air escaped from Hanna's lungs. Edwin held Hanna aloft, her legs dangling above the candles' flames. Instinctively, she kicked at him, but her feet found nothing except soft, yielding air. Hanna couldn't believe his strength. Her breath slipped away, her chest heaving in desperate gasps. She struggled frantically to pull at Edwin's outstretched hand, only she could barely raise her arms. Hanna's vision clouded. Her eyes rolled into the back of her head and she lost the strength to gasp for air. Outside, the skies rumbled. Hanna clenched her teeth. She reached for the nearby window, hoping, praying for the heavens to open again. This time, however, no breach appeared in the sky. No lightning stormed the ground.

In one savage throw, Edwin tossed Hanna to the floor. Her lungs filled with air and Hanna coughed violently. She struggled to stand up but fell back down, toppling the candelabras.

"You must have known I would find out," he said.

Hanna wheezed, trying to catch her breath. She gave Edwin a confused look.

"Don't play dumb with me, little girl!" he yelled. "You know what I'm talking about. Makala just told me that Paul's sons found you on the outskirts of town with Francis's boy. And if Makala told me, just imagine who else knows."

Edwin kicked a candlestick in a swift, violent strike. It collided against the wall and then clattered back to his feet. He picked up a second candelabra and raised it like he was about to strike. Hanna held her hands in the air. She ducked her head. Only, Edwin heaved the candelabra against the window, cracking the glass.

He paced back and forth, swinging his arms, seething. "I treated you with respect! I was kind to you when I didn't need to be. And this is how you repay me? By humiliating me in public? You are betrothed to me!

Don't you understand what that means? Do you have the foggiest idea the opportunities I've given up?"

Hanna was still panting, still struggling to stand. Underneath Edwin's feet, the wreath had fallen from Hanna's hair and landed against the candles and now several flowers were smoldering in the flames. Edwin looked around at the damage he'd caused, his bottom lip twitching. He picked up the headdress and brushed off the burnt flowers. Edwin reached out his hand and Hanna flinched, unsure whether he was about to strike her or try to help her stand up.

"No!" Hanna yelled.

"Keep your voice down. They'll hear you in the other room," Edwin said. "Let's call your mother. See if we can fix your dress."

Hanna looked down at her wedding gown. The buttons in the back had ripped open when he threw her to the ground and now half lay strewn across the floor. Hanna picked up a handful and was staring at them — momentarily mesmerized — when Edwin moved to help her up.

"Don't you dare!" Hanna screamed, wildly this time. She threw the buttons across the room and climbed to her feet. "Don't you come near me. Don't you ever touch me again! I'm not going to live in your house,

Edwin. I'm never going to sleep in your bed."

Just then, the stairwell door opened and Brother Paul stepped into the room. He saw the overturned candelabras, the smoldering flowers, Hanna's torn dress, and his eyes bulged. He raised a shaky finger to his lips and hissed "Shh!" before clumping down the stairs. "You are in the Creator's house. This is not the place for unseemly talk. A little decorum, please! Now, what's going on here?" he said.

Hanna edged away from him. In the flickering light, Brother Paul's tall, awkward frame no longer looked like a blessed luminary in white. He was just a desperate man clinging to his authority.

Edwin stepped toward him and pointed an angry finger at Brother Paul's chest. "Makala just told me about Hanna and Francis's boy," he said. "Why didn't you tell me what happened?"

Brother Paul gaped at Edwin, speechless.

"I knew it!" Edwin yelled. "It's true, isn't it?"

"It's all an exaggeration," Brother Paul said. "I can explain everything."

As the men quarreled, Hanna stepped back against the far wall. A feverish desire swelled in her to flee, only their bulky

451

frames were blocking the back door and Hanna could never slip outside.

Brother Paul was whispering something in Edwin's ear, something to calm him perhaps, when, suddenly, without warning, Hanna darted past the two men. She rushed up the stairs and through the doorway into the cathedral. Hanna ran out onto the stage where the altar stood waiting. She stopped dead in her tracks. A sea of candles lay before her. The women were kneeling in the pews, the men standing, all eyes upon her. A collective gasp echoed when she appeared, running, half-mad, her wedding dress a shambles and clumps of hair fallen from her braids.

Jotham stepped forward from the front row, a wolfish look in his eyes. The crowd murmured as Kara and Emily stood up and stared in disbelief. Behind Hanna, Edwin thumped up the stairs. He entered the stage with Brother Paul following close behind.

Hanna held out her arms. "No!" she yelled.

She backed up perilously close to the edge of the stage and the crowd let out another gasp as Hanna nearly fell into the pews. On one side, Edwin drew nearer. On the other, Jotham lumbered up the stairs, trapping Hanna between them. The crowd stood to their feet.

"Stop!" Hanna screamed. "Don't come any closer." She held her arms up in both directions. Hanna looked at the townspeople, at her family. "I fell from the sky. Why does no one believe me?"

From the front row, Kara shouted, "I believe you, Hanna!"

Others yelled horrible things. Makala screamed out, "Whore!"

Hanna scanned the crowd frantically. She was met by a sea of faces with piercing, judging eyes. Then, Hanna saw him, like an oasis in a boundless desert. Daniel was in the far back of the cathedral, standing alone. He had come after all.

"Run, Hanna!" Kara shouted.

Jotham clomped down the stairs. He tried to cup his hand over Kara's mouth to silence her and Charliss defied his father for the first time, striking him closed-fisted and hard, square in the jaw. Charliss drew back his fist again and struck Jotham forcefully, sending him reeling. Jotham released a rattling, involuntary bark that brought him to his knees.

This was all the distraction Hanna needed. She took off running, past Edwin and Brother Paul, past the altar and up the spiral staircase that led to the belfry. Quickly, furiously, she raced up the steps, tripping and standing up again when her wedding dress caught beneath her feet. She felt the blood on her knees where she scraped them and Hanna kept running. Below, the men chased her up the stairs, gaining ground with each step.

Hanna leapt over the spot where Daniel had almost fallen, where it wasn't safe. Below, the screams of a hundred voices pulsed and still she ran. Hanna pushed up the stairs with all her might.

Finally, she reached the belfry. Ten stories above ground, she could see all of Clearhaven. Hanna edged out onto the ledge. She perched her heels at the farthest point and felt the breeze. It wasn't cold up here. It was almost warm. Spring had sprung. The world was renewing again and Hanna raised her arms into the night air.

This was where she'd stood when Daniel first kissed her, when her shackles fell off, when the brave Hanna on the other side of the world smiled and everything was good and pure and nothing and nobody could stop her. Hanna took in a deep, liberating breath. She thought not of Edwin or Jotham, not of Brother Paul or his cowardly sons.

Down below, a scattering of candles assembled. The townspeople had come outside to see her. Hanna paid them no heed. She stood with her arms raised in a V. Everything — her body, her mind, her soul — dilated.

"Hanna." It was Brother Paul's voice, calling to her from the other side of the bell. "Give me your hand," he said.

Hanna turned to face him. "Why, so that I might kiss your palm? Perhaps you might kiss my palm instead?"

"Yes. Yes, anything. Just please come down from there."

Others were standing behind Brother Paul in the stairwell now; as many men as could fit were clamoring for a better view. Hanna spotted Edwin. She saw the men who'd stepped forward to claim her last week. But Emily wasn't there. And neither was Daniel or Kara. There was just a sea of blank faces, men who had tried to control her.

Brother Paul edged around the bell and reached out his hand.

"You will see," Hanna said. "I wasn't meant for this. I can feel it in my blood. I feel it in my soul. I fell from the sky."

Brother Paul lunged at her, a desperate stabbing swipe that didn't find its mark.

Hanna let go. She pushed with her legs and leapt backward off the building. Hanna sailed through the air, her wedding gown fluttering in the wind. Up above, the men cried out. "No!" Below, the women screamed. The children gaped in awe. Hanna herself never made a sound.

As she fell, all sense of time slipped away. She closed her eyes and saw her other self again, the brave Hanna battling the evil, faceless men. The Hanna on the other side of the world beamed with pride, because the Hanna on this side was finally truly awake. This Hanna believed.

Floating through the air, between the life she had left and the ground beckoning below, she opened her eyes and kept them transfixed on the sky. Hanna smiled when she first saw it appear. There it was — a whiteness so magnificent, so stunningly pure, it called to her. Rapidly, with purpose, the fissure overtook the night. Around its edges were bright reds and gleaming greens, colors so vivid they'd only been seen twice before by the naked eye.

Hanna's smile grew wider as she fell. For the first time in her life, she had found her place. And why wouldn't she smile? She had seen the light. And in her heart, she knew how it would feel to land.

34

The girl leaned against her mother's chest as the early-morning sun colored the sky, the soft clouds brightening, their outlines accentuated by daybreak. The girl — ten years old, her sandy-brown hair cut short — gazed out at the seashore. She and her mother were perched upon a wicker bench in front of the beach house they'd inhabited for the past three weeks. A month before that, the family had slept in a cabin. Last summer, a ranch. Over the past seven years, they'd spent their summers traveling and had already visited three continents. The two of them were still keen on visiting the other four.

Soon the family would travel home in time for school to resume. The girl had classes to attend. The mother did, as well. But for now there was the sunrise. There was the amethyst sky.

"Tell me the story," the girl said.

The mother ran her fingers through the girl's hair. She'd just told her the story last night. Two days earlier, she'd repeated the tale while swimming in a nearby lagoon.

"Please?" the girl said.

"I suppose . . ."

"And promise not to leave anything out this time."

"I promise," the mother said. The girl sat up excitedly and the mother began. "Once there was a beautiful girl, a kind girl, a brave girl who wasn't born like everyone else. Instead, she swam out of the ocean —"

At that moment, a young woman walked into the room. She hobbled, her one leg touching the ground before the other, her back shaped like a question mark that leaned too far to the right. She was carrying a letter and gazing at it with delight. "He wrote me again," she said.

Hanna eyed the letter in her sister's hand. That boy had written Emily three times this week, covering multiple sheets of lined paper with words Emily refused to share. She almost told Emily to put the letter away and watch the sunrise, only to catch herself before she opened her mouth. Emily wasn't her *little* sister anymore. Soon she would be nineteen years old and Emily had gotten delightfully headstrong as she grew more independent. Plus, there was that boy back home, the one with the sweet nothings always at the tip of his tongue. Emily had taken to swooning at the sound of his sugary voice over the telephone and rushing to the post office each morning to see whether a new letter had arrived. Hanna wanted to make sure she didn't fall too deep too fast.

"Let me see it," Hanna said.

Playfully, with a wide grin on her face, Emily hid the letter behind her back. She went to step away when she slipped. Her foot landed on its side and her heel caught on a rut in the wood.

Hanna leapt from her seat to grab her. She saved Emily before she fell to the ground, and when she did, the purpling sky caught her eye. The sun had ascended and in that moment, Hanna saw melting lavenders, auras gleaming off the rising red orb. It captivated her. It enchanted her. The colors tore Hanna away from the present. Everything turned pink and pristine.

Hanna's knees buckled. In one instant, it all came back. The fall from the tower. The impact when she hit the ground. Lifting her arms in the air, pulling herself to her feet and realizing she'd landed unscathed. Like it was yesterday, she recalled the onlookers' gaping faces. Jotham's enraged scream, his guttural shriek piercing the silence, then her father collapsing to the ground in a fit, turning purple, then blue.

She remembered Daniel grasping her hand, pulling her toward the open car door, the townspeople standing still, bewitched. No one moving, save Jotham, kicking his last few desperate kicks before dying. She heard the voices of the men atop the tower, calling out as loudly as they could, saying nothing, their power lost forever. Her mother screaming for her to run.

Hanna scooped up little Ahmre in her arms. She grabbed Emily's hand and this time the girl came with her. Hanna in her torn dress. The bride fleeing into the back seat of the car with her sisters. The other children clinging to Charliss's protective arms. Daniel pressing on the gas. Dust billowing in their wake. The people of Clearhaven, the town growing smaller as it drifted from view, as though it was moving away from her, not the other way around. Then The Road. Darkness. Ahmre crying and refusing to let go, the young girl finally falling asleep in Emily's lap. Nothing except their car's headlights for the longest time, until a single light of a farmhouse. Then another. Civilization and buildings as tall as the sky. Morning. Waking up to the smell of bacon and eggs sizzling in the pan. Safety. Her sisters in her arms.

The vision was so real, so lifelike, it felt as though only moments had passed, not years.

Then the present roared into being and Hanna looked up to see Daniel rushing in from the other room; Daniel, her partner of seven years, reaching out to help her up off the floor; Daniel whose amber-tinted words had proven true.

Emily leaned against the table beside him, concern etched in her face.

"Did it happen again?" she said. "Did you see Clearhaven?"

Hanna nodded. She took Daniel's hand and climbed to her feet.

"What's Clearhaven?" Ahmre said.

Hanna sat down beside Ahmre, who placed a comforting hand on her arm. Hanna had never intended on becoming her sister's mother. But, before the age of four, Ahmre had started calling her Mama. Hanna corrected her a dozen times and another dozen after that, before she started answering to the name. She looked at Ahmre now, at the family she and Daniel had made their own. Hanna steadied herself. She closed her eyes and opened them again. Clearhaven couldn't take away these past seven years. It couldn't change the love they'd shared.

"Clearhaven is what we call the past," Hanna told Ahmre.

Daniel steered Emily toward the front steps. "How about you and I pick up some breakfast on the beach?" he said. Daniel kissed Hanna and Ahmre on the top of their heads and then he and Emily stepped off the porch and onto the sand.

Once more, Ahmre leaned into Hanna's shoulder to smell the scent of tea leaves from her sweater, to run her hand along Hanna's wrist. "Is Clearhaven where my birth mother lived? Is that where she lives now?"

"I thought you were born from the ocean," Hanna said.

That gleam returned to Ahmre's eyes. She sat up straight, barely able to contain her excitement.

"Tell me again," she said. "And please don't leave anything out."

Hanna smiled. Off in the sunrise, the pink, pristine color had dissolved, leaving the early-morning sky behind. Crimson and then indigo and crimson again. The beginning of blue. Hanna held Ahmre close. She ran her fingers through the girl's hair one more time and began. "Once there was a beautiful girl, a kind girl, a brave girl who wasn't born like everyone else. Instead, she swam out of the ocean . . ."

AUTHOR'S NOTE

Some books are written rather quickly, with the author typing up a manuscript over a few months, spending another year or so polishing it up and then hoping (and often praying) an agent and publisher will pick it up. The story behind *Hanna Who Fell from the Sky* is slightly more complicated.

I first came up with the title for this novel the day I returned home from a trip to Europe in 2004. I reached into my suitcase and handed my then girlfriend (now wife) a hand-painted mask. She asked where I got it and — being playful and a little mischievous — I told her it was given to me by a little old man in a small antiques shop in Florence who refused to accept payment, so long as I gave the mask to someone I loved. "This is Hanna Who Fell from the Sky," I said. "The old man told me she was an angel so beautiful that all the other angels grew jealous and cast her out of Heaven.

That look on the mask is the sorrow, anguish and astonishment on Hanna's face when she landed on Earth."

My wife looked at me, mystified. "Really?" she said.

"No," I said. "I bought it for $3 from a street vendor. But I bought it for you."

She eventually forgave me and has since become wise to my stories. (Far too wise, I think.)

The name Hanna and the idea of an angel falling to Earth stuck with me and in summer 2005, during three intense, sleepless days, I wrote the very first draft of *Hanna Who Fell from the Sky*. As it stood, the story was far too short and much too rough for publication. Instead of revising my novella-sized manuscript, I set it aside to work on getting my short stories published in literary magazines.

In 2007, when my first daughter was born, we named her Hanna after the girl in the unpublished (and still largely unfinished) manuscript. This is how I have a child (born in 2007) who was named after the main character in this book (released in 2017). And how, as amazing as it would've been, time travel was not involved in naming her.

In the following years, I wrote three quirky and (what I hope are) funny novels that were released by an awesome small press in Canada. As much as I put my heart and soul into those books, something inside me kept telling me to return to the story of Hanna in Clearhaven. To retell it. To rewrite it with the perspective additional years and fatherhood had given me.

Then fate intervened.

One evening I was playing hockey (like all good Canadian kids do) when I got hit in the head. It was bad. Really bad. I was chasing the puck, skating as fast as I could, when an opposition player rammed his shoulder into my head. The world went black. My feet left the ice and my body hung momentarily in midair. I couldn't see. I could barely think. My vision returned immediately. But an hour later, I could hardly talk. I couldn't walk a hundred feet without collapsing.

I suffered a traumatic brain injury that night, one that left me unable to read a single sentence or even watch television for weeks. One that left me stuttering for ten months and with a chronic feeling that there was a bell inside me that wouldn't stop ringing. My brain injury left me unable to hold a proper conversation, let alone write a book.

All was not lost. It took over a year, but

with the help of some heavy-duty painkillers, I returned to the manuscript I'd left behind years ago: *Hanna Who Fell from the Sky.* I reread what I'd written during that sleepless long weekend in 2005. The story — of Hanna being forced to marry Edwin and her mother's fantastical tale of her falling from the sky — was there. But the prose was not. I realized I had to rewrite it from scratch. And that's what I did. An hour a day was all my head would allow. If I tried to do more, my concussion symptoms would return tenfold and I'd be forced to go into a dark room and lie there in agony until, hours later, the sensation would pass.

Still, I kept writing one hour at a time. Then eventually, two hours at a time. I forced myself to focus and tell Hanna's story as best I could.

After many months, I had a brand-new version of the book. Only six words remained from the original manuscript. And I was thrilled with the result. Rewriting *Hanna* was one of the hardest things I've ever done. But it was also one of the most rewarding. If anything kept me sane through three years of the worst concussion symptoms you can imagine, it was telling Hanna's story in the way I always wanted to tell it. As much as I am Hanna's creator and the one who dreamed her up in the first place, she is the one who helped me get well again.

And I am well. My concussion symptoms are mostly a thing of the past. Some days I feel like I could step onto the ice and throw a body check just like old times. Although, other days I'm concerned a swift breeze might take me down. I'll never be able to play contact sports again. But I'm able to chase my kids around the park and watch their smiling faces as I throw them into the air. I'm able to write for hours and days at a time again.

I hope you enjoy Hanna's story. Publishing this book was my dream and one I never gave up on, even in the darkest of days. For the readers out there (if I'm lucky enough for you to read my book), at the risk of sounding cliché . . . never give up on your dreams. I am proof . . . Hanna is proof . . . that no matter what life throws at you, no matter the obstacles, you can do anything you set your mind to.

ACKNOWLEDGMENTS

Thank you to Wendy for being my first reader and for showing me what it's like to still live the dream. Thank you to Hanna (age nine) for being kind and imaginative and for occasionally listening to your daddy. Thank you to Claire (age seven) for your creativity and joy.

Thank you to my editor, Erika Imranyi, for taking on this novel when it still needed a great deal of work. And to Erika and Natalie Hallak for their keen insight into my manuscript and for steering this story in the way it definitely needed to go. To the rest of the team at Harlequin/MIRA Books/Park Row Books, thank you for your hard work. Writing is a solitary pursuit, but it takes a village to publish a novel and I really appreciate everyone who's had a hand in this book.

Thank you to my agent, Anne Bohner, for believing in Hanna's story and for representing me with diligence and kindness. Thank you to Jen Hale, my literary BFF, whose opinion I can always trust. Thank you to Sarah Le Huray for your boundless encouragement and for reading this book at least a dozen times. Thank you to Nicholas Komick for always having my back.

Thank you to my cousins Joanne Knox and Jim Witty, who read every word I write with enthusiasm and (surprisingly) without complaint. Thank you to my aunts Joan Witty and Anne Craig. I grew up feeling like I had three mothers, and with my mom having passed away, I am incredibly lucky to still have you two. Thank you to John Dewan, my uncle Johnny, for his honesty and his support, and for $20 in an envelope every Christmas morning throughout the entire 1980s.

Thank you to my father, Larry Meades, for reading my work and for being the best grandparent you could imagine. And to Margaret Helsdon for believing in me.

And thank you to my friends, supporters and first readers: Clare Maloney, Angela Kruger, Aaron Moyer, Brian Simmers, Nicole Harvie, Rick and Nadine Gibbs, Cara Hills, Don Meades, Traci Meades, Theresa Eriksson, Rick and Jen Pantel, Deb Carter,

Joalina Tolentino and Wayne Edward Gilchrist.

ABOUT THE AUTHOR

Christopher Meades is the author of three previous novels, including *The Last Hiccup*, which won the 2013 Canadian Authors Association Award for Fiction. In addition, Meades's work has appeared in several literary journals including *The Potomac Review* and *The Fiddlehead*. He lives in British Columbia, Canada, with his family.